SEEING

José Saramago was born in Portugal in 1922 and has been a full-time writer since 1979. His oeuvre embraces plays, poetry, short stories, non-fiction and several novels, which have been translated into more than forty languages and have established him as Portugal's most influential living writer. In 1998 he was awarded the Nobel Prize for Literature.

Margaret Jull Costa has translated works by Eça de Queiroz, Fernando Pessoa and José Régio, as well as a number of leading Spanish authors. Her translation of José Saramago's *All the Names* won the Weidenfeld Translation Prize.

JOSÉ SARAMAGO

Seeing

TRANSLATED FROM THE PORTUGUESE BY
Margaret Jull Costa

VINTAGE BOOKS
London

Published by Vintage 2007

10

First published in Great Britain in 2006 by
Harvill Secker

First published with the title *Ensaio sobre a Lucidez* by
Editorial Caminho, SA, Lisbon, 2004

Vintage
Random House, 20 Vauxhall Bridge Road, London SW1V 2SA

www.vintage-books.co.uk

Addresses for companies within The Random House Group Limited
can be found at: www.randomhouse.co.uk/offices.htm

The Random House Group Limited Reg. No. 954009

A CIP catalogue record for this book
is available from the British Library

The Portuguese Institute for Books and Libraries supported this book

INSTITUTO PORTUGUÊS DO
LIVRO E DAS BIBLIOTECAS   MINISTÉRIO DA CULTURA

ISBN 9780099483625

MIX
Paper from
responsible sources
FSC® C016897

Printed and bound in Great Britain by Clays Ltd, St Ives plc

Translator's acknowledgements

I would like to thank José Saramago, Manucha Lisboa, Ben Sherriff and Sílvia Morim for all their help and advice, and, in particular, my fellow Saramago translator Maartje de Kort.

For Pilar, every single day
For Manuel Vázquez Montalbán, who lives on

Let's howl, said the dog
The Book of Voices

TERRIBLE VOTING WEATHER, REMARKED THE PRESIDING OFFICER OF polling station fourteen as he snapped shut his soaked umbrella and took off the raincoat that had proved of little use to him during the breathless forty-metre dash from the place where he had parked his car to the door through which, heart pounding, he had just appeared. I hope I'm not the last, he said to the secretary, who was standing slightly away from the door, safe from the sheets of rain which, caught by the wind, were drenching the floor. Your deputy hasn't arrived yet, but we've still got plenty of time, said the secretary soothingly, With rain like this, it'll be a feat in itself if we all manage to get here, said the presiding officer as they went into the room where the voting would take place. He greeted, first, the poll clerks who would act as scrutineers and then the party representatives and their deputies. He was careful to address exactly the same words to all of them, not allowing his face or tone of voice to betray any political and ideological leanings of his own. A presiding officer, even of an ordinary polling station like this, should, in all circumstances, be guided by the strictest sense of independence, he should, in short, always observe decorum.

As well as the general dampness, which made an already oppressive atmosphere still muggier, for the room had only two narrow windows that looked out onto a courtyard which was gloomy even on sunny days, there was a sense of unease which, to use the vernacular expression, you could have cut with a knife. They should have postponed the elections, said the representative of the party in the middle, or the p.i.t.m., I mean, it's been raining non-stop since yesterday, there are landslips and floods everywhere, the abstention rate this time around will go sky-high. The representative from the party on the right, or the p.o.t.r., nodded in agreement, but felt that his contribution to the conversation should be couched in the form of a cautious comment, Obviously, I wouldn't want to underestimate the risk of that, but I do feel that our fellow citizens' high sense of civic duty, which they have demonstrated before on so many occasions, is deserving of our every confidence, they are aware, indeed, acutely so, of the vital importance of these municipal elections for the future of the capital. Having each said their piece, the representative of the p.i.t.m. and the representative of the p.o.t.r. turned, with a half-sceptical, half-ironic air, to the representative of the party on the left, the p.o.t.l., curious to know what opinion he would come up with. At that precise moment, however, the presiding officer's deputy burst into the room, dripping water everywhere, and, as one might expect, now that the cast of polling station officers was complete, the welcome he received was more than just cordial, it was positively enthusiastic. We therefore never heard the viewpoint of the representative of the p.o.t.l., although, on the basis of a few known antecedents, one can assume that he would, without fail, have taken a line of bright historical optimism, something like, The people who vote for my party are not the sort to let themselves be put off by a minor obstacle like this, they're not the kind to stay at home just because of a few miserable drops of rain falling from the skies. It was not, however, a matter of a few miserable drops of rain, there were bucketfuls, jugfuls, whole niles, iguaçús and yangtses of the stuff, but faith, may it be eternally blessed, as well as removing mountains from the path of those who benefit from its influence, is capable of plunging into the most torrential of waters and emerging from them bone-dry.

With the table now complete, with each officer in his or her

2

allotted place, the presiding officer signed the official edict and asked the secretary to affix it, as required by law, outside the building, but the secretary, demonstrating a degree of basic common sense, pointed out that the piece of paper would not last even one minute on the wall outside, in two ticks the ink would have run and in three the wind would have carried it off. Put it inside, then, out of the rain, the law doesn't say what to do in these circumstances, the main thing is that the edict should be pinned up where it can be seen. He asked his colleagues if they were in agreement, and they all said they were, with the proviso on the part of the representative of the p.o.t.r. that this decision should be recorded in the minutes in case they were ever challenged on the matter. When the secretary returned from his damp mission, the presiding officer asked him what it was like out there, and he replied with a wry shrug, Just the same, rain, rain, rain, Any voters out there, Not a sign. The presiding officer stood up and invited the poll clerks and the three party representatives to follow him into the voting chamber, which was found to be free of anything that might sully the purity of the political choices to be made there during the day. This formality completed, they returned to their places to examine the electoral roll, which they found to be equally free of irregularities, lacunae or anything else of a suspicious nature. The solemn moment had arrived when the presiding officer uncovers and displays the ballot box to the voters so that they can certify that it is empty, and tomorrow, if necessary, bear witness to the fact that no criminal act has introduced into it, at dead of night, the false votes that would corrupt the free and sovereign political will of the people, and so that there would be no electoral shenanigans, as they're so picturesquely known, and which, let us not forget, can be committed before, during or after the act, depending on the efficiency of the perpetrators and their accomplices and the opportunities available to them. The ballot box was empty, pure, immaculate, but there was not a single voter in the room to whom it could be shown. Perhaps one of them is lost out there, battling with the torrents, enduring the whipping winds, clutching to his bosom the document that proves he is a fully enfranchised citizen, but, judging by the look of the sky right now, he'll be a long time coming, if, that is, he doesn't end up simply going home and leaving the fate of the city to those with a black car to drop them off at the door and pick them up again once the person in the back seat has fulfilled his or her civic duty.

After the various materials have been inspected, the law of this country states that the presiding officer should immediately cast his vote, as should the poll clerks, the party representatives and their respective deputies, as long, of course, as they are registered at that particular polling station, as was the case here. Even by stretching things out, four minutes was more than enough time for the ballot box to receive its first eleven votes. And then, there was nothing else for it, the waiting began. Barely half an hour had passed when the presiding officer, who was getting anxious, suggested that one of the poll clerks should go and see if anyone was coming, voters might have turned up to find the door blown shut by the wind and gone off in a huff, grumbling that the government might at least have had the decency to inform people that the elections had been postponed, that, after all, was what the radio and television were for, to broadcast such information. The secretary said, But everyone knows that when a door blows shut it makes the devil of a noise, and we haven't heard a thing in here. The poll clerk hesitated, will I, won't I, but the presiding officer insisted. Go on, please, and be careful, don't get wet. The door was open, the wedge securely in place. The clerk stuck his head out, a moment was all it took to glance from one side to the other and then draw back, dripping, as if he had put his head under a shower. He wanted to proceed like a good poll clerk, to please the presiding officer, and, since it was

4

the first time he had been called upon to perform this function, he also wanted to be appreciated for the speed and efficiency with which he had carried out his duties, who knows, with time and experience, he might one day be the person presiding over a polling station, higher flights of ambition than this have traversed the sky of providence and no one has so much as batted an eye. When he went back into the room, the presiding officer, half-rueful, half-amused, exclaimed, There was no need to get yourself soaked, man, Oh, it doesn't matter, sir, said the clerk, drying his cheek on the sleeve of his jacket, Did you spot anyone, As far as I could see, no one, it's like a desert of water out there. The presiding officer got up, took a few uncertain steps around the table, went into the voting chamber, looked inside and came back. The representative of the p.i.t.m. spoke up to remind the others of his prediction that the abstention rate would go sky-high, the representative of the p.o.t.r. once more played the role of pacifier, the voters had all day to vote, they were probably just waiting for the rain to let up. This time the representative of the p.o.t.l. chose to remain silent, thinking what a pathetic figure he would be cutting now if he had actually said what he was going to say when the presiding officer's deputy had come into the room, It would take more than a few miserable drops of rain to put off my party's voters. The secretary, on whom all eyes were expectantly turned, opted for a practical suggestion, You know, it might not be a bad idea to phone the ministry and ask how the elections are going elsewhere in the city and in the rest of the country too, that way we would find out if this civic power cut was a general thing or if we're the only ones whom the voters have declined to illumine with their votes. The representative of the p.o.t.r. sprang indignantly to his feet, I demand that it be set down in the minutes that, as representative of the p.o.t.r., I strongly object to the disrespectful manner and the unacceptably mocking tone in which the secretary has just referred to the voters, who are the supreme defenders of democracy, and without whom tyranny, any of the many tyrannies that exist in the world, would long ago have overwhelmed the nation that bore us. The secretary shrugged and asked, Shall I make a note of the representative of the p.o.t.r.'s comments, sir, No, I don't think that will be necessary, it's just that we're all a bit tense and perplexed and puzzled, and, as we all know, in that state of mind, it's very easy to say things we don't really believe, and I'm sure the secretary didn't mean to offend anyone, why, he himself is a voter conscious of his responsibilities, the proof being that he, as did all of us, braved the elements to answer the call of duty, nevertheless, my feelings of gratitude, however sincere, do not prevent me asking the secretary to keep rigorously to the task assigned to him and to abstain from any comments that might shock the personal or political sensibilities of the other people here. The representative of the p.o.t.r. made a brusque gesture which the presiding officer chose to interpret as one of agreement, and the argument went no further, thanks, in large measure, to the representative of the p.i.t.m., who took up the secretary's proposal, It's true, he said, we're like shipwreck victims in the middle of the ocean, with no sails and no compass, no mast and no oars, and with no diesel in the tank either, Yes, you're quite right, said the presiding officer, I'll phone the ministry now. There was a telephone on another table and he walked over to it, carrying the instruction leaflet he had been given days before and on which were printed, amongst other useful things, the telephone numbers of the ministry of the interior.

The call was a brief one, It's the presiding officer of polling station number fourteen here, I'm very worried, there's something distinctly odd going on, so far, not a single voter has turned up to vote, we've been open for more than an hour, and not a soul, yes, sir, I know there's no way of stopping the storm, yes, sir, I know, rain, wind, floods, yes, sir, we'll be patient, we'll stick to our guns, after all, that's why we're here. From that point on the presiding officer contributed nothing to the dialogue apart from a few affirmative nods of the head, the occasional muted interjection and three or four phrases which he began but did not finish. When he replaced the receiver, he looked over at his colleagues, but without, in fact, seeing them, it was as if he had before him a landscape composed entirely of empty voting chambers, immaculate electoral rolls, with presiding officers and secretaries waiting, party representatives exchanging distrustful glances as they tried to work out who might gain and who might lose from this situation, and, in the distance, the occasional rain-soaked poll-clerk returning from the door to announce that no one was coming. What did the people at the ministry say, asked the representative of the p.i.t.m., They don't know what to make of it either, after all, it's only natural that the bad weather would keep a lot of people at home, but apparently pretty much the same thing is happening all over the city, that's why they can't explain it, What do you mean pretty much, asked the representative of the p.o.t.r., Well, a few voters have turned up at some polling stations, but hardly any really, no one's ever known anything like it, And what about the rest of the country, asked the representative of the p.o.t.l., after all, it's not only raining in the capital, That's what's so odd, there are places where it's raining just as heavily as it is here and yet, despite that, people are still turning out to vote, I mean, obviously there are more voters in areas where the weather is good, speaking of which, the forecasters are saying that the weather should start to improve later on this morning, It might go from bad to worse, you know what they say, rain at midday either gets much worse or clears away, warned the second clerk, who had not, until then, opened his mouth. There was a silence. Then the secretary put his hand into one of his jacket pockets, produced a mobile phone and keyed in a number. While he was waiting for someone to answer, he said, It's a bit like the mountain and Mahomet, since we can't ask the voters, whom we don't know, why they haven't come in to vote, let's ask our own families, whom we do know, hi, it's me, yes, how come you're still there, why haven't you been to vote, I know it's raining, my trouser legs are still sopping wet, oh, right, sorry, I forgot you'd told me you'd be over after lunch, sure, I only phoned because things are a bit awkward here, oh, you've no idea, if I told you that not a single voter has yet come in to vote, you probably wouldn't believe me, right, fine, I'll see you later then, take care. He turned off the phone and remarked ironically, Well, at least one vote is guaranteed, my wife will be coming this afternoon. The presiding officer and the clerks looked at each other, they were obviously supposed to follow the secretary's example, but not one of them wanted to be the first to do so, that would be tantamount to admitting that when it came to quick thinking and self-confidence the secretary won hands down. It did not take long for the clerk who had gone over to the door to see if it was raining to conclude that he would have to eat a lot of bread and salt before he could compete with the secretary we have here, capable of casually pulling a vote out of a mobile phone like a magician pulling a rabbit out of a hat. Seeing that the presiding officer, in one corner, was now calling home on his mobile, and that the others, using their own phones, were discreetly, in whispers, doing likewise, this same clerk privately applauded the honesty of his colleagues who, by not using the phone provided in principle for official use only, were nobly saving the state money. The only person who, for lack of a mobile phone, had to resign himself to waiting for news from the others was the representative of the p.o.t.l., of whom it should be said that, living as he did alone in the city, with his family in the provinces, the poor man had no one to call. The conversations gradually came to an end, one after the other, the longest being that of the presiding officer, who appears to be demanding that the person he is talking to come immediately to the polling station, we'll see if he has any luck with that, but the fact is he's the one who should have spoken first, but, then, if the secretary decided to get in ahead of him, too bad, he is, as we've already seen, a bit of a smart aleck, if he had as much respect for hierarchy as we do, he would have merely suggested the idea to his superior. The presiding officer let out the sigh that had long been trapped within his breast, put the phone away in his pocket and asked, So, what did you find out. The question, as well as being superfluous, was, how can we put it, just the teensiest bit dishonest, firstly, because, when it comes down to it, everyone would have found out something, however irrelevant, secondly, because it was obvious that the person asking the question was taking advantage of the authority inherent in his position to shirk his duty, since it was up to him, in voice and person, to initiate any exchange of information. If we bear in mind the sigh he uttered and the rather querulous tone we thought we detected at one point in the phone conversation, it would be logical to suppose that the dialogue, presumably with a member of his family, had not proved to be as placid and instructive as his perfectly justifiable interest as a citizen and as a presiding officer deserved, and that he does not feel sufficiently calm to launch into some hastily concocted extemporaneous comment, and is now sidestepping the difficulty by inviting his subordinates to have their say first, which, as we also know, is another, more modern way of being the boss. What the clerks and party representatives said, aside from the representative of the p.o.t.l, who, having no information of his own, is there in a purely listening capacity, was that their family members either didn't fancy getting a soaking and were waiting for the heavens to clear once and for all, or, like the secretary's wife, were intending to come and vote in the afternoon. Only the clerk who had gone over to the door earlier on seemed pleased with himself, his face bore the complacent expression of one who has reason to be proud of his own merits, which, translated into words, came down to this, No one answered at my house, which can only mean that they're on their way here now. The presiding officer resumed his seat and the waiting began again.

Nearly an hour later, the first voter arrived. Contrary to the general expectation, and much to the dismay of the clerk who had gone over to the door earlier on, it was a stranger. He left his dripping umbrella at the entrance to the room and, still wearing his plastic cape glistening with water and his plastic boots, went over to the table. The presiding officer looked up at him with a smile on his lips, for this voter, a man of advanced years, but still robust, signalled a return to normality, to the usual line of dutiful citizens moving slowly and patiently along, conscious, as the representative of the p.o.t.r. had put it, of the vital importance of these municipal elections. The man handed his identity card and voter's card to the presiding officer, the latter then announced in a sonorous, almost joyful voice the number on the card and its owner's name, the clerks in charge of the electoral roll leafed through it and, when they found both name and number, repeated them out loud and drew a straight line against the entry to indicate that the man had voted, then, the man, still dripping, went into a voting booth clutching his ballot paper, returned shortly afterwards with the piece of paper folded into four, handed it to the presiding officer, who slipped it solemnly into the ballot box, retrieved his documents and left, taking his umbrella with him. The second voter took another ten minutes to appear, but from then on, albeit unenthusiastically, one by one, like autumn leaves slowly detaching themselves from the boughs of a tree, the ballot papers dropped into the ballot box. However long the presiding officer and his colleagues took to scrutinise documents, a queue never formed, there were, at most, at any one time, three or four people waiting, and three or four people, try as they might, can never make a queue worthy of the name. I was quite right, commented the representative of the p.i.t.m., the abstention rate will be enormous, massive, there'll be no possible agreement on the result after this, the only solution will be to hold the elections again, The storm might pass, said the presiding officer and, looking at his watch, he murmured as if he were praying, It's nearly midday. Resolutely, the man to whom we have been referring as the clerk who had gone over to the door earlier on got up and said to the presiding officer, With your permission, sir, since there are no voters here at present, I'll just pop out and see what the weather's doing. It took only an instant, he was there and back in a twinkling, this time with a smile on his face and bearing good news, It's raining much less now, hardly at all really, and the clouds are beginning to break up too. The poll clerks and the party representatives very nearly embraced, but their happiness was not long-lived. The monotonous drip-drip of voters did not change, one came, then another, the wife, mother and aunt of the officer who had gone over to the door came, the elder brother of the representative of the p.o.t.r. came, so did the presiding officer's mother-in-law, who, showing a complete lack of respect for the electoral process, informed her crestfallen son-in-law that her daughter would only be coming later in the afternoon and added cruelly, She said she might go to the cinema, the deputy presiding officer's parents came, as well as other people who were members of none of their families, they entered looking bored and left looking bored, the atmosphere only brightened somewhat when two politicians from the p.o.t.r. arrived and, minutes later, one from the p.i.t.m., and, as if by magic, a television camera appeared out of nowhere, filmed a few images and returned into nowhere, a journalist asked if he could put a question, How's the voting going, and the presiding officer replied, It could be better, but now that the weather seems to be changing, we're sure the flow of voters will increase, The impression we've been getting from other polling stations in the

11

city is that the abstention rate is going to be very high this time, remarked the journalist, Well, I prefer to take a more optimistic line, a more positive view of the influence of meteorology on the way the electoral mechanisms work, and as long as it doesn't rain this afternoon, we'll soon make up for what this morning's storm tried to steal from us. The journalist left feeling contented, it was a nice turn of phrase, he could even use it as a subtitle to his article. And because the time had come to satisfy their stomachs, the electoral officers and the party representatives organised themselves so that, with one eye on the electoral roll and the other on their sandwiches, they could take turns to eat right there.

It had stopped raining, but nothing seemed to indicate that the civic hopes of the presiding officer would be satisfactorily fulfilled by a ballot box in which, so far, the votes barely covered the bottom. All those present were thinking the same thing, the election so far had been a terrible political failure. Time was passing. The clock on the tower had struck half past three when the secretary's wife came in to vote. Husband and wife exchanged discreet smiles, but there was also just a hint of an indefinable complicity, which provoked in the presiding officer an uncomfortable inner spasm, perhaps the pain of envy, knowing that he would never exchange such a smile with anyone. It was still hurting him in some fold of his flesh when, thirty minutes later, he glanced at the clock and wondered to himself if his wife had, in the end, gone to the cinema. She'll turn up, if she ever does, at the last possible moment, he thought. The ways of warding off fate are many and almost all are useless, and this one, forcing oneself to think the worst in the hope that the best will happen, is one of the most commonplace, and might even be worthy of further consideration, although not in this case, because we have it from an unimpeachable source that the presiding officer's wife really has gone to the cinema and, at least up until now, is still undecided as to whether to cast her vote or not. Fortunately, the oft-invoked need for balance which has kept the universe on track and the planets on course means that whenever something is taken from one side, it is replaced by something else on the other, something that more or less corresponds, something of the same quality and, if possible, the same proportions, so that there are not too many complaints about unfair treatment. How else can one explain why it was that, at four o'clock in the afternoon, an hour which is neither late nor early, neither fish nor fowl, those voters who had, until then, remained in the quiet of their homes, apparently blithely ignoring the election altogether, started to come out onto the streets, most of them under their own steam, but others thanks only to the worthy assistance of firemen and volunteers because the places where they lived were still flooded and impassable, and all of them, absolutely all of them, the healthy and the infirm, the former on foot, the latter in wheelchairs, on stretchers, in ambulances, headed straight for their respective polling stations like rivers which know no other course than that which flows to the sea. It will probably seem to the sceptical or the merely suspicious, the kind who are only prepared to believe in miracles from which they hope to gain some advantage, that the present circumstance has shown the above-mentioned need for balance to be utterly wrong, that the trumped-up question about whether the presiding officer's wife will or will not vote is, anyway, far too insignificant from the cosmic point of view to require compensation in one of Earth's many cities in the form of the unexpected mobilisation of thousands and thousands of people of all ages and social conditions who, without having come to any prior agreement as to their political and ideological differences, have decided, at last, to leave their homes in order to go and vote. Those who argue thus are forgetting that not only does the universe have its own laws, all of them indifferent to the contradictory dreams and desires of humanity, and in the formulation of which we

13

contribute not one iota, apart, that is, from the words by which we clumsily name them, but everything seems to indicate that it uses these laws for aims and objectives that transcend and always will transcend our understanding, and if, at this particular point, the scandalous disproportion between something which might, but for now only might, have seen the ballot box deprived of, in this case, the vote cast by the presiding officer's supposedly unpleasant wife and the tide of men and women now on the move, if we find this difficult to accept in the light of the most elementary distributive justice, prudence warns us to suspend for the moment any definitive judgement and to watch with unquestioning attention how events, which have only just begun to unfold, develop. Which is precisely what the newspaper, radio and television journalists, carried away by professional enthusiasm and by an unquenchable thirst for news, are doing now, racing up and down, thrusting tape-recorders and microphones into people's faces, asking What was it made you leave your house at four o'clock to go and vote, doesn't it seem extraordinary to you that everyone should have come out onto the street at the same time, and receiving in return such abrupt or aggressive replies as, It just happened to be the time I'd decided to go and vote, As free citizens, we can come and go as we please, we don't owe anyone an explanation, How much do they pay you to ask these stupid questions, Who cares what time I leave or don't leave my house, Is there some law that obliges me to answer that question, Sorry, I'm only prepared to speak with my lawyer present. There were polite people too, who replied without the reproachful acrimony of the examples given above, but they were equally unable to satisfy the journalists' devouring curiosity, merely shrugging and saying, Look, I have the greatest respect for the work you do and I'd love to help you publish a bit of good news, but, alas, all I can tell you is that I looked at my watch, saw it was four o'clock and said to the family Right, let's go, it's now or never, Why now or never, That's the funny thing, you see, that's just how it came out, Try to think, rack your brains, No, it's not worth it, ask someone else, perhaps they'll know, But I've asked fifty people already, And, No one could give me an answer, Exactly, But doesn't it strike you as a strange coincidence that thousands of people should all have left their houses at the same time to go and vote, It's certainly a coincidence, but perhaps not that strange, Why not, Ah, that I don't know. The commentators, who were following the electoral process on the various television programmes and, for lack of any firm facts on which to base their analyses, were busily making educated guesses, inferring the will of the gods from the flight and the song of birds, regretting that animal sacrifice was no longer legal and that they were thus prevented from poring over some creature's still twitching viscera to decipher the secrets of chronos and of fate, these commentators woke suddenly from the torpor into which they had been plunged by the gloomy prospects of the count and, doubt-less because it seemed unworthy of their educational mission to waste time discussing coincidences, hurled themselves like wolves upon the fine example of good citizenship that the population of the capital were, at that moment, setting the rest of the country by turning up en masse at polling stations just when the spectre of an abstention on a scale unparalleled in the history of our democracy had seemed to be posing a grave threat to the stability not just of the regime but, even more seriously, of the system itself. The statement emanating from the ministry of the interior did not go quite that far, but the government's relief was evident in every line. As for the three parties involved in the election, the parties on the right, in the middle and on the left, they, having first made rapid calculations as to the losses and gains that would result from this unexpected influx of voters, issued congratulatory statements in which, along with other stylistic niceties, they affirmed that democracy had every reason to celebrate. With the national flag draped on the wall behind them, the president in his palace and the prime minister in his mansion both expressed themselves in similar terms, give or take a comma. At the polling stations, the lines of voters, standing three deep, went right round the block and as far as the eye could see.

Like all the other presiding officers in the city, the one at polling station number fourteen was all too aware that he was living through a unique moment in history. When, late that night, after the ministry of the interior had extended the deadline for voting by two hours, a period that had to be extended by a further half an hour so that the voters crammed inside the building could exercise their right to vote, when, at last, the poll clerks and the party representatives, exhausted and hungry, stood before the mountain of ballot papers that had been emptied out of the two ballot boxes, the second one had been an emergency requisition from the ministry, the immensity of the task that lay before them made them tremble with an emotion we would not hesitate to describe as epic or heroic, as if the nation's honoured ghosts, brought back to life, had magically rematerialised in those ballot papers. One of the ballot papers belonged to the presiding officer's wife. She had been propelled out of the cinema by some strange impulse, she had then spent hours in a queue that advanced at a snail's pace, and when she finally found herself face to face with her husband, when she heard him speak her name, she felt in her heart something that was perhaps the shadow of a former happiness, only the shadow, but even so, she felt it had been worth going there just for that. It was gone midnight when the counting finished. The number of valid votes did not quite reach twenty-five per cent, with the party on the right winning thirteen per cent, the party in the middle nine per cent and the party on the left two and a half per cent. There were very few spoiled ballots and very few abstentions. All the others, more than seventy per cent of the total votes cast, were blank.

FEELINGS OF CONFUSION AND STUPEFACTION, BUT ALSO OF MOCKERY AND scorn swept the country from north to south. The provincial town councils, where the elections had taken place without incident or upset, apart from the occasional delay caused by the bad weather, and which had obtained results that differed little from the norm, the usual number of straightforward voters, the usual number of inveterate abstainers, and no very significant number of spoiled or blank votes, these councils, who had felt humiliated by the display of centralist triumphalism that had been paraded before the rest of the country as an example of the purest electoral public spirit, could now return that slap in the face and laugh at the foolish presumption of those ladies and gentlemen who thought they were the bee's knees simply because they happened to live in the country's capital. The words Those ladies and gentlemen, pronounced with a curl of the lips that oozed disdain with every syllable, if not with every letter, were directed not at the people who had remained at home until four in the afternoon and then suddenly rushed out to vote as if they had received some irresistible order, but at the government who had hung out the flags too soon, at the political parties who had pounced on the blank votes as if they were a vineyard to be harvested and they were the harvesters, at the newspapers and the other media for the ease with which they moved from applause on the capitoline hill to having people hurled from the tarpeian rock, as if they themselves did not play an active part in the genesis of such disasters.

The provincial scoffers were right to some extent, but not as right as they thought there were. Beneath the political agitation that is racing through the capital like a gunpowder trail in search of a bomb one can sense a disquiet that avoids being spoken out loud, unless in a discussion amongst peers, or between individuals and their closest friends, members of a political party and the party machinery, or the government and itself. What will happen when the election is held again, that is the question everyone is asking in a quiet, controlled whisper, so as not to wake the sleeping dragon. There are those who feel that the best plan would be to resist sticking the spear between the creature's ribs and leave things as they are, with the p.o.t.r. in government and the p.o.t.r. on the city council, to pretend that nothing has happened, to imagine, for example, that the government has declared a state of emergency in the capital and that, consequently, all constitutional guarantees are suspended, and then, after a time, when the dust has settled and the whole tragic incident has entered the list of long-forgotten past events, to prepare for new elections, starting with a carefully planned elec- toral campaign, full of solemn oaths and promises, at the same time trying to prevent, at all costs, without worrying too much about any minor or major illegalities, the possibility of the repetition of a phenomenon which a celebrated expert on such matters has already rather harshly dubbed socio-political teratology. There are also those who take an entirely different view, they protest that the laws are sacred, that what is written is there to be obeyed, regard- less of who gets hurt in the process, and that if we follow the path of subterfuges and take the short-cut of under-the-table deals we will be heading straight for chaos and an end to conscience, in short, if the law stipulates that in the event of a natural disaster, the elections should be repeated eight days later, then they must be repeated eight days later, that is, on the following Sunday, and may god's will be done, since that is what he's there for. It should be noted, however, that when expressing their opinions, the political parties prefer not to take too many risks, in the spirit of trying to please everyone all the time, they say yes, but then again no. The leaders of the party on the right, which is in government and runs the city council, start by assuming that this undoubted trump card will hand them victory on a silver platter, and so they have adopted a tactic of serenity tinged with diplomacy, trusting to the judgement of the government upon whom it is incumbent to see that the law is respected, As is only logical and natural in a long-standing democracy like ours, they conclude. The leaders of the party in the middle also want the law to be obeyed, but are asking the government for something which they know to be totally impossible, that is, the establishment and application of rigorous measures to ensure that the next election takes place absolutely normally and, presumably, produces absolutely normal results, In order, they allege, that there will be no repetition in this city of the shameful spectacle it has just presented to the country and to the world. As for the party on the left, they have gathered together all their top people and, after a long debate, drawn up and published a statement in which they express their firm and genuine hope that the approaching election will bring into being the necessary political conditions for the advent of a new era of development and social progress. They don't actually say that they're hoping to win the next election and take over the city council, but the implication is there. That night, the prime minister went on television to announce to the people that, in accordance with the current legislation, the municipal elections would be held again on the following Sunday, and a new period of electoral campaigning, of four days only, would begin at midnight and end at midnight on Friday. Putting on a grave face and speaking with great emphasis, he added that the government was sure that the capital's population, when called upon to vote again, would exercise their civic duty with the dignity and decorum they had always shown in the past, thus declaring null and void the regrettable event during which, for reasons that have yet to be clarified, but into which investigations are already fairly well advanced, the usual clear judgement of the city's electorate had become unexpectedly confused and distorted. The message from the president will be kept back until the close of the campaign on Friday night, but its concluding phrase has already been chosen, Sunday, my dear compatriots, will be a fine day.

And it really was a fine day. From early morning on, with the protecting sky in all its splendour and the golden sun blazing forth against a backdrop of crystalline blue, to use the inspired words of a television reporter, the voters started leaving their homes and heading for their respective polling stations not in a blind mass as had appeared to happen a week before, but with each person setting out alone, and so conscientiously and diligently that even before the doors were opened there were already long, long queues of citizens awaiting their turn to vote. Not everything, alas, was pure and honest at these gatherings. There was not a single queue, not one amongst the more than forty that formed at various points of the city, that did not have amongst them one or more spies whose mission was to listen and record the comments of the people present, the police authorities being convinced that, as happens, for example, in doctors' waiting rooms, a prolonged wait will always sooner or later loosen tongues, revealing, even if only by the merest slip, the secret intentions of the electorate. The great majority of the spies are professionals and belong to the secret service, but some are volunteers, patriotic amateurs of espionage who offered to help out of a desire to serve, without remuneration, as it said in the sworn declaration they signed, whilst others, quite a few, were attracted merely by the morbid pleasure of being able to denounce someone. The genetic code of what, somewhat unthinkingly, we have been content to call human nature, cannot be reduced to the organic helix of deoxyribonucleic acid, or dna, there is much more to be said about it and it has much more to tell us, but human nature is, figuratively speaking, the complementary spiral that we have not yet managed to prise out of kindergarten, despite the multitude of psychologists and analysts from the most diverse schools and with the most diverse abilities who have broken their nails trying to draw its bolts. These scientific considerations, whatever their value now or in the future, should not allow us to forget today's disquieting realities, like the one we have just seen, for not only are there spies in the queues, trying to look nonchalant as they listen and secretly record what people say, there are also cars that glide quietly past the queues, apparently looking for a place to park, but which carry inside them, invisible to our eyes, high-definition video cameras and state-of-the-art microphones capable of projecting onto a screen the emotions apparently hidden in the diverse murmurings of a group of people who believe, individually, that they are thinking of something else. The word has been recorded, as has the emotion behind it. No one is safe. Up until the moment when the doors of the polling stations were opened and the queues began to move, the recorders had captured only insignificant phrases, the most banal of comments on the beauty of the morning and the pleasant temperature or about the hurried breakfast they had eaten, brief exchanges on the important subject of what to do with the children while their mothers came to vote, Their father is looking after them at the moment, we're just going to have to take turns, first me, then him, I mean, obviously we'd rather have come to vote together, but it was just impossible, and, as the saying goes, what can't be cured must be endured, We've left our youngest with his older sister, she's not reached voting age yet, yes, this is my husband, Pleased to meet you, Nice to meet you too, It's a lovely morning, isn't it, It's almost as if it had been laid on deliberately, Well, I suppose it was bound to happen some time.

Despite the auditory acuity of the microphones passing and re-passing, white car, blue car, green car, red car, black car, with their aerials bobbing in the morning breeze, nothing overtly suspicious raised its head from beneath the skin of such innocent, ordinary expressions as these, or so, at least, it appeared. However, one did not need to have a doctorate in suspicion or a degree in distrust to notice something unusual about those last two phrases, about someone having laid on the lovely morning deliberately, and especially the second phrase, about how it was bound to happen some time, ambiguities which were perhaps unwitting, perhaps unconscious, but, for that very reason, potentially even more dangerous and therefore worth contrasting with a detailed analysis of the tone of voice in which those words had been uttered, but, above all, with the range of frequencies they generated, we are referring here to subtones, which, if recent theories are to be believed, must be taken into consideration, otherwise, the degree of comprehension of any oral discourse will inevitably be insufficient, incomplete and limited. The spy who happened to be there had been given very precise instructions on what to do in such cases, as had all his colleagues. He must not allow himself to become separated from the suspect, he must place himself in third or fourth position behind him in the queue of voters, he must, as a double guarantee, and regardless of the sensitivity of his concealed recording equipment, commit to memory the voter's name and number when the presiding officer said them out loud, he must then pretend to have forgotten something and withdraw discreetly from the queue, go out into the street and phone headquarters to tell them what had happened, and, having done that, return to the hunting ground and take up another place in the queue. This activity cannot, strictly speaking, be compared to an exercise in target shooting, what they are hoping for here is that chance, destiny, luck, or whatever you want to call it, will place the target in front of the shot.

As the hours passed, information rained down upon the centre of operations, but none of it revealed in a clear-cut and consequently irrefutable manner the intentions of the voter thus caught, all that appeared on the list were phrases of the kind described above, and even the phrase that seemed more suspicious than all the others, Well, I suppose it was bound to happen some time, would lose much of its apparent slipperiness once restored to its context, a conversation between two men about the recent divorce of one of them, not that they spoke of it explicitly, in order not to arouse the curiosity of the people nearby, but which had concluded thus, with a touch of rancour, a touch of resignation, and with a tremulous sigh that came forth from the divorced man's breast and that should have led any sensitive spy, assuming, of course, that sensitivity is a spy's best attribute, to come down clearly on the side of resignation. The fact that the spy may not have considered this worthy of note, and that the recording equipment may not have captured it, can be put down to mere human failure and to technological blips which any good judge, knowing what men are like, and not unaware either of the nature of machines, would have to take into account, even if, and, although at first sight this may appear shocking, it would, in fact, be magnificently just, even if in the documents bearing on the case there was not the slightest indication of the accused's non-culpability. Were this innocent man to be interrogated tomorrow, we tremble at the mere thought of what could happen to him, Do you admit that you said to the person you were with Well, I suppose it was bound to happen some time, Yes, I do, Now, think carefully before answering, what were you talking about when you said that, About my separation from my wife, Separation or divorce, Divorce, And what were or are your feelings about that divorce, Half-angry, half-resigned, More angry or more resigned, More resigned, I guess, Don't you think, in that case, that the natural thing would have been to utter a sigh, especially since you were

23

talking to a friend, Well, I can't be sure I didn't sigh, I really don't remember, Well, we know that you didn't, How can you know that, you weren't there, Who told you we weren't there, Maybe my friend remembers hearing me sigh, you'd have to ask him, You obviously don't care much for your friend, What do you mean, Summoning your friend and getting him into all kinds of trouble, Oh, I wouldn't want that, Good, Can I go now, Certainly not, don't be in such a hurry, you still haven't answered the question we asked you, What question, What were you really thinking about when you said those words to your friend, But I've already told you, Give us another answer, that one won't do, It's the only answer I can give because it's the true one, That's what you think, Unless you want me to make one up, Yes, do, we don't mind at all if you come up with answers which, with time and patience, could be made to fit the proper application of certain techniques, that way, you'll end up saying what we want to hear, Tell me what the answer is then, and let's be done with it, Oh, no, that wouldn't be any fun at all, who do you think we are, sir, we have our scientific dignity to consider, our professional conscience to defend, it's very important to us that we should be able to demonstrate to our superiors that we deserve the money they pay us and the bread that we eat, Sorry, you've lost me, Don't be in such a hurry.

The impressive serenity of the voters in the streets and in the polling stations was not mirrored by an identical state of mind in ministerial offices and at party headquarters. The question that most worries them all is what the abstention rate will be this time, as if therein lay the way to salvation out of the tricky social and political situation in which the country has been plunged for over a week now. A reasonably high abstention rate, or even above the maximum recorded in the previous elections, as long as it wasn't too high, would signify a return to normality, to the known routine of those voters who had never seen the point of voting and are noticeable by virtue of their persistent absence, or those others who preferred to make the most of the good weather and go and spend the day at the beach or in the country with their family, or those who, for no other reason than invincible idleness, stayed at home. If the crowds outside the polling stations, which were as large as they had been for the previous election, showed, without any room for doubt, that the percentage of abstentions was going to be extremely low, possibly non-existent, what most confused the authorities, and was nearly driving them crazy, was the fact that the voters, with very few exceptions, responded with impenetrable silence to the questions asked by the people running exit polls on how they had voted, It's just for statistical purposes, you don't have to identify yourself, you don't have to give your name, they insisted, but even that did not convince the distrustful voters. A week earlier, journalists had at least managed to get answers out of them, although it's true that these had been given in impatient or ironic or scornful tones and were really another way of saying nothing at all, but at least there had been an exchange of words, one side had asked the question and the other had pretended to give an answer, but it was nothing like this dense wall of silence, as if it were built around a mystery shared by everyone and which everyone had sworn to defend. To many people it will seem astonishing, not to say impossible, this coincidence of behaviour amongst so many thousands of people who do not know each other, who do not think the same, who belong to different social classes or strata, who, in short, despite being politically to the right or in the middle or to the left, or, indeed, nowhere at all, resolved individually to keep their mouth shut until the votes were counted, thus leaving the unveiling of the secret until later. This, with great hopes of being right, was what the interior minister wanted to tell the prime minister, this was what the prime minister hastened to pass on to the president, who, being older, more experienced and more case-hardened, who

25

had, in brief, seen more of life, merely replied sardonically, If they're not prepared to talk now, give me one good reason why they should talk later. The only reason this bucket of cold water from the nation's supreme arbiter did not cause the prime minister or the interior minister to lose all hope and to fall into the grip of despair was because they had nothing else to cling to, even if only for a short time. The interior minister had preferred not to mention that, fearing possible irregularities in the electoral process, a concern which the facts themselves, meanwhile, proved to be entirely unfounded, he had ordered the posting at all polling stations of two plain-clothes policemen, each from a different police department, both being authorised to oversee the count, and each of whom was charged also with keeping an eye on his or her colleague, just in case there should be any kind of complicity between them, be it honourably political in nature or a deal struck at the market of petty treacheries. In this way, what with spies and vigilantes, recording devices and video cameras, they appeared to have everything under control, safe from any malign interference that might sully the purity of the electoral process, and now that the game was over, all that remained for them to do was to wait, arms folded, for the final verdict of the ballot boxes. When the presiding officer of polling station number fourteen, to whose workings we had the great pleasure of devoting, in homage to those dedicated citizens, an entire chapter, even down to the personal problems of certain of its members, and when the presiding officers of all the other polling stations, from number one to number thirteen, from number fifteen to number forty-four, at last emptied out the votes onto the long rows of benches that had served them as tables, the impetuous rumble of an avalanche was heard all over the city. It was a foreshadowing of the political earthquake that would soon follow. In homes, in cafés, in pubs and in bars, in all the public places where there was a television or a radio, the capital's inhabitants, some more calmly than others, awaited the final result of the count. No one confided in their nearest and dearest as to how they had voted, the closest of friends kept silent on the matter, and even the most talkative people seemed to have forgotten their words. Finally, at ten o'clock that night, the prime minister appeared on television. His face looked drawn, he had dark circles under his eyes, the result of a whole week of sleepless nights, and beneath the healthy glow of make-up he was pale. He was holding a piece of paper in his hand, but he didn't really read from it, he just glanced at it from time to time so as not to lose the thread of his speech, Dear fellow citizens, he said, the result of the elections carried out today in our country's capital was as follows, the party on the right, eight per cent, the party in the middle, eight per cent, the party on the left, one per cent, abstentions, none, spoiled votes, none, blank votes, eighty-three per cent. He paused to take a sip from the glass of water beside him, then went on, While we realise that today's vote is both a confirmation and an exacerbation of the trend established last Sunday and while we are in unanimous agreement as to the need for a serious investigation into the first and last causes of these troubling results, the government considers, after due consultation with his excellency the president, that its legitimacy in office was not called into question, not only because the election just held was merely a local election, but also because it declares and believes that its pressing and urgent duty is to carry out an in-depth investigation into the anomalous events of the last seven days, events in which we have all been both astonished witnesses and bold participants, and it is with profound sorrow that I say this, for those blank votes which have struck a brutal blow against the democratic normality of our personal and collective lives did not fall from the skies or rise up from the bowels of the earth, they were in the pockets of eighty-three out of every one hundred voters in this city, who placed them in the ballot boxes with their own unpatriotic hands. Another sip of water, this time more necessary, for his mouth had suddenly gone dry, There is still time to rectify this mistake, not by means of another election, which, given the current state of affairs, might prove not only useless but counter-productive, but through a rigorous examination of conscience, which, from this public platform, I urge on all the inhabitants of the capital, some so that they may better protect themselves from the terrible threat hanging over their heads, others, be they guilty or innocent in their intentions, so that they can either turn from the evil into which they have been dragged by who knows who or else risk becoming the direct target of the sanctions foreseen under the state of emergency whose declaration the government will be seeking from his excellency the president, after, of course, initial consultation with parliament, which has been convened tomorrow in extraordinary session, and from whom we expect to obtain unanimous approval. A change of tone, arms slightly spread, hands raised to shoulder height, The nation's government feels sure that in coming here, like a loving father, to remind that section of the capital's population who strayed from the straight and narrow of the sublime lesson to be learned from the parable of the prodigal son and by saying to them that there is no fault that cannot be forgiven a heart that is truly contrite and wholly repentant, the goverment is merely giving expression to the fraternal will of the rest of the country, of all those citizens who, with praiseworthy civic feeling, properly fulfilled their electoral duties. The prime minister's final flourish, Honour your country, for the eyes of the country are upon you, complete with drumrolls and bugle blasts, unearthed from the attics of the mustiest of nationalistic rhetoric, was ruined by a Good night that rang entirely false, but then that is the great thing about ordinary words, they are incapable of deceit.

In towns, houses, bars, pubs, cafés, restaurants, associations or party headquarters where voters from the party on the right, the party in the middle and even the party on the left were gathered together, the prime minister's message was much discussed, although, as is only natural, in different ways and from diverse points of view. Those most satisfied with his performance, and that barbaric term is theirs not the narrator's, were those of the p.o.t.r., who, with knowing looks and winks, congratulated themselves on their leader's excellent technique, an approach that is often rather curiously described as carrot-and-stick, and which, in olden times, was mainly applied to asses and mules, but which modernity, with notable success, has turned to human use. Some, however, the blustering, braggadocio types, felt that the prime minister should have finished his speech at the point where he announced the imminent declaration of a state of emergency, that everything he said afterwards was entirely unnecessary, that the only thing the rabble understands is the big stick, start with half-measures and you'll get nowhere, never give your enemy so much as the time of day, and other outspoken expressions in the same vein. Their colleagues argued that it really wasn't like that, that their leader must have his reasons, but these pacifists, always so ingenuous, were unaware that the intemperate reaction of their intransigent colleagues was, in fact, a tactical manoeuvre, the aim of which was to keep alive the combative mood of the party members. Be prepared for everything, had been the slogan. Those in the p.i.t.m., as members of the principal opposition party, were in agreement with the main thrust of the speech, that is, the urgent need to find out who was responsible and to punish the culprits or conspirators, but they felt that the declaration of a state of emergency was entirely disproportionate, especially as they had no idea how long it would last, and besides, it was arrant nonsense to take away the rights of someone whose only crime had been to exercise one of those rights. What will happen, they wondered, if a citizen takes it into his head to go to the constitutional court, The truly intelligent and patriotic thing to do, they added, would be to form a government of national salvation consisting of representatives from all the parties, because, if this really is a collective emergency, declaring a state of siege isn't going to resolve it, the p.o.t.r. have just gone off at the deep end and will very likely drown. The members of the p.o.t.l. ridiculed any idea that they could possibly form part of a coalition government, what they were really concerned about was coming up with an interpretation of the election result that would disguise the disastrous drop in the party's percentage of the poll, for, having polled five per cent in the last election and two and a half in the first round of this one, they now found themselves with a miserable one per cent and a very bleak future. The results of their analysis culminated in the preparation of a statement which would suggest that, since there was no objective reason to think that the blank votes had constituted an attempt on the security of the state or on the stability of the system, the desire for change thus expressed could correctly be read as coinciding, quite by chance, with the progressive proposals contained in the p.o.t.l.'s manifesto. Nothing more and nothing less.

There were also people who just turned off the television as soon as the prime minister had finished speaking and, before going to bed, sat around talking about their lives, and there were others who spent the rest of the evening tearing up and burning papers. They weren't conspirators, they were simply afraid.

TO THE MINISTER OF DEFENCE, A CIVILIAN WHO HAD NEVER EVEN DONE his military service, the declaration of a state of emergency seemed pretty small beer, he had wanted a proper, full-blooded state of siege, a state of siege in the literal sense of the word, hard, implacable, like a moving wall capable of isolating the source of the sedition and then crushing it in one devastating counter-attack, Before the pestilence and the gangrene spread to the part of the country that's still healthy, he warned. The prime minister acknowledged the extreme seriousness of the situation, and that the country had been the victim of a vile assault on the very foundations of representative democracy, the minister of defence, however, begged to differ, I would compare it, rather, to a depth charge launched against the system, Quite so, but I think, and the president agrees with me on this, that, without losing sight of the dangers of the immediate situation, and in order to be able to vary the means and objectives of any action taken as and when it proves necessary, it would be preferable to begin by using methods which, while more discreet and less ostentatious, are possibly more effective than sending the army out onto the streets, closing the airport and setting up road blocks at all routes out of the city, And what methods would those be exactly, asked the minister of defence, making not the slightest attempt to disguise his annoyance, Nothing that you don't know about already, after all, the armed forces have their own espionage system, We call ours counter-espionage, Which comes to the same thing, Ah, I see what you're getting at, Good, I knew you'd understand, said the prime minister, at the same time gesturing to the interior minister, who spoke next, Without going into actual operational detail, which, as I'm sure you'll understand, is confidential, not to say top secret, the plan drawn up by my ministry is based, in general terms, on a broad and systematic infiltration of the population by specially trained agents, which may help us to uncover the reasons behind what has happened and equip us to take the necessary measures to destroy the evil ab ovo, Ab ovo, you say, as far as I can see, it's already hatched, remarked the justice minister, It was just a manner of speaking, replied the interior minister, sounding slightly irritated, then he went on, The time has come to inform this council of ministers, in complete and utter confidence, if you'll forgive the redundancy, that the espionage services under my orders, or rather, who answer to the ministry for which I am responsible, do not exclude the possibility that what happened may have its real roots abroad, and that what we are seeing may be only the tip of the iceberg of a gigantic, global destabilisation plot, doubtless anarchist in inspiration, and which, for reasons we still do not comprehend, has chosen our country as its first guinea pig, Sounds a bit odd to me, said the minister of culture, to my knowledge, anarchists have never, even in the realm of theory, proposed committing acts of this nature and of this magnitude, That, said the minister of defence sarcastically, may be because my dear colleague's knowledge dates back to the idyllic world of his grandparents, and, strange though it may seem, things have changed quite a lot since then, there was a time when nihilism took a rather lyrical and not too bloody form, but what we are facing today is terrorism, pure and unadulterated, it may wear different faces and expressions, but it is, essentially, the same thing, You should be careful about making such wild claims and such facile extrapolations, commented the justice minister, it seems risky to me, not to say, outrageous, to label as terrorism, especially pure and unadulterated terrorism, the appearance in the ballot boxes of a few blank votes, A few votes, a few votes, spluttered the minister of defence, rendered almost speechless, how, I'd like to know, can you possibly call eighty-three out of every hundred votes a few votes, what we have to grasp, what we have to take on board, is that each one of those votes was like a torpedo striking below the water line, My knowledge of anarchism may be out of date, I don't deny it, said the minister of culture, but, as far as I'm aware, although I certainly don't consider myself an expert on naval battles either, torpedoes always strike below the water line, they don't have much option, that is what they were made to do. The interior minister suddenly sprang to his feet, perhaps to defend his colleague, the defence minister, from this sneering comment, perhaps to condemn the lack of political empathy evident at the meeting, but the prime minister brought his hand down hard on the table, demanding silence, The ministers of culture and of defence can continue elsewhere the academic debate in which they appear to be so hotly engaged, but I would just like to remind you that the reason we are gathered together in this room, which, even more than parliament, represents the heart of democratic power and authority, is in order to take decisions that will save the country from the gravest crisis it has faced in centuries, that is the challenge we face, I believe, therefore, that, confronted by this enormous task, we should call a halt to any further verbal poppycock or, indeed, to squabbles over interpretation, as being unworthy of our responsibilities. There was a pause, which no one dared to interrupt, then he continued, Meanwhile, I would like to make it perfectly clear to the minister of defence that the fact that, during this first stage of dealing with the crisis, the president has favoured the application of the plan drawn up by the relevant staff at the ministry of the interior does not mean and never could mean that the possibility of declaring a state of siege has been entirely rejected, everything will depend on what direction events take, on the reactions of the population in the capital, on the response of the rest of the country, and on the not always predictable behaviour of the opposition, especially, in this case, the p.o.t.l., who now have so little to lose that they won't mind betting the little that remains to them on some high-risk move, Oh, I don't think we need worry ourselves too much about a party that could only manage one per cent of the votes, remarked the interior minister, with a scornful shrug, Did you read their statement, asked the prime minister, Of course I did, reading political statements is part of my job, one of my duties, it's true that there are those who pay assistants to chew their food for them first, but I belong to the old school, and I only trust my own head, even if I'm wrong, You're forgetting that ministers are, in the final analysis, the prime minister's advisors, And it's an honour to be one, sir, the difference, the vast difference, is that we bring you your food ready digested, That's all very fine, but let's leave gastronomy and the chemistry of the digestive processes for now and go back to the p.o.t.l.'s statement, give me your opinion, what did you think of it, It's a crude, naïve version of the old saying that if you can't beat 'em, join 'em, And when applied to the present case, Applied to the present case, sir, it's a case of if they're not your votes, then try to make it look as if they are, Even so, it's as well to remain on the alert, their little trick just might work on the more left-leaning segment of the population, Although we have no idea at the moment which segment that is, said the justice minister, it seems to me that what we are refusing to face up to, frankly and openly, is that the vast majority of that eighty-three per cent are our own voters or the p.i.t.m.'s voters, and that we should be asking ourselves why it is that they cast those blank votes, that's the crux of the matter, not whatever wise or naïve arguments the p.o.t.l. might come up with, Yes, when you think about it, replied the prime minister, our tactic is not so very different from the one the p.o.t.l. is using, that is, if

34

most of the votes aren't yours, then pretend they don't belong to your opponents either, In other words, piped up the minister of transport and communications from the corner of the table, we're all up to the same tricks, A somewhat flippant way of summing up the situation in which we find ourselves, and note that I am speaking here from a purely political viewpoint, but one not entirely lacking in sense, said the prime minister and drew the discussion to a close.

The rapid implementation of the state of emergency, like a kind of solomonic sentence dictated by providence, swiftly cut the gordian knot that the media, especially the newspapers, had, with more or less skill and with more or less delicacy, been trying to undo ever since the unhappy results of the first elections and, even more dramatically, of the second, although they always took great care not to draw too much attention to their efforts. On the one hand, it was their duty, as obvious as it was elementary, to condemn, with an energy tinged with civic indignation, in editorials and in specially commissioned opinion pieces, the unexpected and irresponsible behaviour of an electorate who, apparently rendered blind to the superior interests of the nation as a whole by some strange and dangerous perversion, had complicated public life to an unprecedented degree, corralling it into a dark alleyway from which not even the brightest spark was able to see a way out. On the other hand, they had to weigh and measure every word they wrote, to ponder susceptibilities, to take, as it were, two steps forward and one step back, lest their readers should turn against a newspaper that had started calling them traitors and lunatics after years and years of perfect harmony and assiduous readership. The declaration of the state of emergency, by allowing the government to assume the relevant powers and to suspend at the stroke of a pen all constitutional guarantees, removed that uncomfortable weight, that threatening shadow hanging over the heads of editors and administrators. With freedom of expression and communication strictly

35

regulated, with censorship always peering over the editor's shoulder, they had the very best of excuses and the most complete of justifications. We would really love, they would say, to provide our esteemed readers with the opportunity, which is also their right, to have access to news and opinions untrammelled by unreasonable interference and intolerable restrictions, especially during the extremely delicate times we are living through, but that is the way things are, and only someone who has worked in the honourable profession of journalism can know how painful it is having to work under virtual twenty-four-hour surveillance, but then, between you and me, the people who bear the greatest responsibility for what is happening are the voters in the capital, not the voters in the provinces, but, alas, to make matters worse, and despite all our pleading, the government will not allow us to produce a censored version for the capital and an uncensored one for the rest of the country, why, only yesterday, a high-up ministry official was telling us that censorship proper is like the sun, which, when it rises, rises for everyone, this is hardly news to us, we know the way the world works, and it is always the just who have to pay for the sinners. Despite all these precautions as regards both form and content, it soon became clear that the public's interest in reading newspapers had greatly declined. Driven by an understandable urge to try and please everyone, some newspapers thought they could combat the absence of readers by plastering their pages with naked bodies, whether male or female, together or alone, singly or in pairs, at rest or in action, disporting themselves in modern gardens of delight, but the readers, grown impatient with images whose minimal and not particularly arousing variations in colour and configuration had, even in remote antiquity, been considered banal commonplaces of man's exploration of the libido, continued, out of apathy, indifference and even nausea, to cause print-runs and sales to plummet. Likewise, the search for and the exhibition of rather grubby intimacies, of all kinds of scandals and outrages, the old game of public virtues masking private vices, the jolly carousel of private vices elevated to the status of public virtues, which, until recently, had never lacked for spectators or for candidates willing to strut their stuff, failed to have a favourable impact on the day-to-day balance sheet of debit and credit, which was at an irremediably low ebb. It really seemed as if the majority of the city's inhabitants were determined to change their lives, their tastes and their style. Their great mistake, as they would soon begin to see, had been casting those blank votes. They wanted a clean-up and they would get one.

This was the firm view of the government and, in particular, of the ministry of the interior. The process of selecting the agents, some from the secret service, others from public bodies, who would surreptitiously infiltrate the bosom of the masses, had been swift and efficient. Having revealed, under oath, as evidence of their exemplary character as citizens, the name of the party for whom they had voted and the nature of that vote, having signed, again under oath, a document in which they expressed their active rejection of the moral plague that had infected a large part of the population, the first action of all agents, of both sexes, it must be said, so that it cannot be alleged, as it so often is, that all evil things are the work of man, who were organised into groups of forty as if in a class and led by teachers trained in the discrimination, recognition and interpretation of electronic recordings of both sound and image, their first action, as we were saying, consisted in sifting through the enormous quantity of material gathered by spies during the second ballot, the material collected by those who had stood in the queues listening and by those who, wielding video cameras and microphones, had driven slowly past them in cars. By starting off with this operation of rummaging around in the informational intestines, the agents were given, before they launched themselves with enthusiasm and the keen nose of a gun dog into action and work in the field, an immediate taste of a behind-closed-doors investigation the tone of which we had occasion to provide a brief but elucidatory example some pages back. Simple, ordinary expressions, such as, I don't generally bother to vote, but here I am, Do you think it'll turn out to have been worth all the bother, The pitcher goes so often to the well that, in the end, it leaves its handle there, I voted last week too, but that day I could only leave home at four, This is just like the lottery, I almost always draw a blank, Still, you've got to keep trying, Hope is like salt, there's no nourishment in it, but it gives the bread its savour, for hours and hours, these and a thousand other equally innocuous, equally neutral, equally innocent phrases were picked apart syllable by syllable, reduced to mere crumbs, turned upside down, crushed in the mortar by the pestle of the question, Explain to me again that business about the pitcher, Why did the handle come off at the well and not on the way there or back, If you don't normally vote, why did you vote this time, If hope is like salt, what do you think should be done to make salt like hope, How would you resolve the difference in colour between hope, which is green, and salt, which is white, Do you really think that a ballot paper is the same as a lottery ticket, What did you mean when you used the word blank, and then, What pitcher, Did you go to the well because you were thirsty or in order to meet someone, What does the handle of the pitcher symbolise, When you sprinkle salt on your food, are you thinking that you're actually sprinkling hope, Why are you wearing a white shirt, Tell me, was the pitcher a real pitcher or a metaphorical one, And what colour was it, black, red, Was it plain or did it have a design on it, Was it inlaid with quartz, Do you know what quartz is, Have you ever won a prize in the lottery, Why is it that, during the first election, you only left home at four, when it had stopped raining two hours before, Who is that woman beside you in this photo, What are the two of you laughing about, Don't you think that an important act like voting requires all responsible voters to wear a grave, serious, earnest expression or do you consider democracy to be a laughing matter, Or perhaps you think it is a crying matter, Which do you think, a laughing matter or a crying matter, Tell me about that pitcher again, why didn't you consider gluing the handle back on, there are glues made specially for the purpose, Does that pause mean that you, too, are lacking a handle, Which one, Do you like the age in which you happen to live, or would you prefer to have lived in another, Let's go back to salt and hope again, how much would you have to add before the thing you were hoping for became inedible, Do you feel tired, Would you like to go home, I'm in no hurry, haste is a bad counsellor, if a person doesn't think through the answers he or she is going to give, the consequences can be disastrous, No, you're not lost, the very idea, you obviously haven't yet quite grasped that, here, people don't lose themselves, they find themselves, Don't worry, we're not threatening you, we just don't want you to rush, that's all. At this point, with the prey cornered and exhausted, they would ask the fateful question, Now I want you to tell me how you voted, that is, which party you gave your vote to. Since five hundred suspects picked from the queues of voters had been summoned to be interrogated, a situation in which anyone could have found himself given the patent insubstantiality of an accusation based on the kind of phrases, of which we have just given a convincing example, captured by all those directional microphones and tape-recorders, the logical thing, bearing in mind the relative breadth of the statistical universe questioned, would be that the replies would be distributed, albeit with a small and natural margin of error, in the same proportion as the votes cast, that is, forty people declaring proudly that they had voted for the party on the right, the party in government, an equal number seasoning their reply with just a pinch of defiance by affirming that they had voted for the only opposition party worthy of the name, that is, the party in the middle, and five, no more than five, pinned down, backs to the wall, I voted for the party on the left, they would say firmly, but in the tone of someone apologising for a stubborn streak which they are helpless to correct. The remainder, that enormous remainder of four hundred and fifteen replies should have said, in accordance with the modal logic of surveys, I cast a blank vote. That clear response, shorn of the ambiguities of presumption or prudence, would be the one given by a computer or a calculator and would be the only one that their inflexible, honest natures, that of the computer and the machine, would have allowed themselves, but we are dealing here with human beings, and human beings are known universally as the only animals capable of lying, and while it is true that they sometimes lie out of fear and sometimes out of self-interest, they also occasionally lie because they realise, just in time, that this is the only means available to them of defending the truth. To judge by appearances, therefore, the ministry of the interior's plan had failed, indeed, during those first few moments, the confusion amongst the advisors was both shameful and complete, there seemed no possible way round the unexpected obstacle, unless orders were given for all those people to be tortured, which, as everyone knows, is unacceptable in democratic but right-wing states skilful enough to achieve the same ends without resorting to such rudimentary, medieval methods. It was whilst embroiled in this complicated situation that the interior minister showed both political nous and a rare tactical and strategic flexibility, possibly, who knows, an indication of greater things to come. He took two decisions, both of them important. The first, which would later be denounced as perversely machiavellian, took the form of an official note from the ministry distributed to the mass media via the unofficial state agency and which, in the name of the whole government, offered heartfelt thanks to the five hundred exemplary citizens who, in recent days, had come forward of their own volition and presented themselves to the authorities, offering their loyal support and any help they could give that would advance the ongoing investigations into abnormal factors uncovered in the last two elections. As well as this elementary expression of gratitude, the ministry, anticipating questions, warned families that they should not be surprised or worried by the lack of news from their absent loved ones, because in that very silence lay the key that could guarantee their personal safety, given the maximum degree of secrecy, red/red, that had been accorded to this delicate operation. The second decision, for internal eyes and use only, was a complete inversion of the plan drawn up earlier, which, as you will recall, predicted that the mass infiltration of investigators into the bosom of the masses would be the means, par excellence, that would lead to the deciphering of the mystery, the enigma, the charade, the puzzle, or whatever you care to call it, of those blank ballot papers. From now on, the agents would work in two numerically unequal groups, the smaller group would work in the field, from which, if truth be told, they no longer expected great results, the larger group would continue with the interrogation of the five hundred people retained, not detained you notice, increasing, as and when, the physical and psychological pressure to which they were already being subjected. As the old saying has been telling us now for centuries, Five hundred birds in the hand are worth five hundred and one in the bush. Confirmation of this was not long in coming. When, after the application of great diplomatic skill, after many digressions and much testing of the water, the agent in the field, that is, in the city, managed to ask the first question, Would you mind telling me who you voted for, the reply he was given, like a message learned by heart, was, word for word, the one given in law, No one can, under any pretext, be forced to reveal his or her vote or be questioned about this by any authority. And when, in the nonchalant tone of someone who

41

did not consider the subject to be of much importance, he asked the second question, Forgive my curiosity, but did you by any chance cast a blank vote, the reply he was given skilfully reduced the scope of the question to a simple academic matter, No, sir, I didn't, but if I had I would be just as much within the law as if I had voted for one of the parties listed or had made my vote void by drawing a caricature of the prime minister, casting a blank vote, mister questioner, is an unrestricted right, which the law had no option but to allow the electorate, it is clearly stated that no one can be persecuted for having cast a blank vote, but just to set your mind at rest, I repeat that I was not one of those who did so, I was just talking for talking's sake, it was merely an academic hypothesis, that's all. Normally speaking, hearing such a response twice or three times would be of no particular significance, all it would show was that there are a few people in the world who know the law of the land and make a point of telling you, but being forced to listen to it, unruffled, without so much as raising an eyebrow, a hundred times, a thousand times, like a litany learned by heart, was more than patience could bear for someone who, having been painstakingly prepared for this delicate task, found himself unable to carry it out. It is not, therefore, surprising that the electorate's systematically obstructive behaviour caused some of the agents to lose control and to resort to insult and aggression, encounters from which, indeed, they did not always emerge unscathed, given that they were acting alone in order not to frighten off their prey and that it was not unusual, especially in so-called dodgy areas, for other voters to pitch in and help the aggrieved party, with easily imagined consequences. The reports that the agents sent back to the centre of operations were discouragingly thin on content, not a single person, not one, had admitted to having cast a blank vote, some pretended not to understand, others said they'd talk another day when they had more time, but they had to rush off now, before the shops shut, but the worst of all were the old, devil take 'em, for it seemed that an epidemic of deafness had sealed them all inside a soundproof capsule, and when the agent, with disconcerting ingenuity, wrote the question down on a piece of paper, the cheeky so-and-sos would either say that their glasses were broken or that they couldn't make out the writing or, quite simply, that they didn't know how to read at all. There were other, wilier agents, however, who, taking the idea of infiltration seriously, in its literal sense, frequented bars, bought people drinks, lent money to penniless poker players, went to sports events, especially football and basketball, where people mingle more in the stands, and got chatting to their fellow spectators, and, in the case of football, if there was a goal-less draw, they would, with sublime cunning, refer to it knowingly as a blank result, just to see what happened. Pretty much nothing happened. Sooner or later, the moment would come to ask the questions, Would you mind telling me what party you voted for, Forgive my curiosity, but did you by any chance cast a blank vote, and then the familiar answers would be repeated, either solo or in chorus, Me, the very idea, Us, don't be daft, and they would immediately adduce the legal reasons, with all their articles and clauses, and so fluently that it was as if all the city's inhabitants of voting age had been through an intensive course in electoral law, both domestic and foreign.

As the days passed, it became noticeable, in a way that was, at first, imperceptible, that the word blank, as if it had suddenly become obscene or rude, was falling into disuse, that people would employ all kinds of evasions and periphrases to replace it. A blank piece of paper, for example, would be described instead as virgin, a blank on a form that had all its life been a blank became the space provided, blank looks all became vacant instead, students stopped saying that their minds had gone blank, and owned up to the fact that they simply knew nothing about the subject, but the most interesting case of all was the sudden disappearance of the riddle with

43

which, for generations and generations, parents, grandparents, aunts, uncles and neighbours had sought to stimulate the intelligence and deductive powers of children, You can fill me in, draw me and fire me, what am I, and people, reluctant to elicit the word blank from innocent children, justified this by saying that the riddle was far too difficult for those with limited experience of the world. It seemed, therefore, that the high political office promised to the interior minister had been cut short at birth, that he was fated, after having come so close to touching the sun, to be drowned ignominiously in the hellespont, but another idea, as sudden as a lightning flash illuminating the night, made him rise again. All was not lost. He ordered back to base the agents confined to fieldwork, blithely dismissed those on short-term contracts, gave the secret police a thorough dressing-down and set to work.

It was clear that the city was a termites' nest of liars and that the five hundred he had in his power were also lying through all the teeth they had in their head, but there was one difference between these two groups, the former were free to enter and leave their homes, and, elusive and slippery as eels, could appear as easily as they could disappear, only to reappear later on and again vanish, whereas dealing with the latter was the easiest thing in the world, it was enough just to go down into the ministry cellars, all five hundred were not there, of course, there wasn't room, most were distributed around other investigatory units, but the fifty or so kept under permanent observation should be more than enough for an initial attempt. The reliability of the machine may have been called into question by certain sceptical experts and some courts may even have refused to admit as evidence the results obtained from the tests, but the interior minister was nonetheless hopeful that the use of the machine might at least give off a small spark that would help him find his way out of the dark tunnel into which the investigation had stuck its head. His plan, as you will no doubt have guessed, was to bring back into the fray the famous polygraph, also known as the lie detector, or, in more scientific terms, a machine that is used to record, simultaneously, various psychological and physiological functions, or, in more descriptive detail, an instrument for registering physiological phenomena of which an electrical recording is made on a sheet of damp paper impregnated with potassium iodide and starch. Connected to the machine by a tangle of wires, armbands and suction pads, the patient does not suffer, he simply has to tell the truth, the whole truth and nothing but the truth, and to cease to believe in the universal assertion, the old, old story, which, since the beginning of time, has been drummed into us, that the will can do anything, for you need look no further than the following example, which denies it outright, because that wonderful will of yours, however much you may trust it, however tenacious it may have been up until now, cannot control twitching muscles, cannot staunch unwanted sweat or stop eyelids blinking or regulate breathing. In the end, they'll say you lied, you'll deny it, you'll swear you told the truth, the whole truth and nothing but the truth, and that might be true, you didn't lie, you just happen to be a very nervous person, with a strong will, it's true, but you are nevertheless a tremulous reed that shivers in the slightest breeze, so they'll connect you up to the machine again and it will be even worse, they'll ask if you're alive and you'll say, of course I am, but your body will protest, will contradict you, the tremor in your chin will say no, you're dead, and it might be right, perhaps your body knows before you do that they are going to kill you. It would be unlikely that this could happen in the cellars of the ministry of the interior, the only crime these people have committed is to cast a blank vote, and that would have been of no importance if they had merely been the usual suspects, but there were a lot of them, too many, almost everyone, who cares if it's your inalienable right when they tell you it's to be used only in homeopathic doses, drop by

45

drop, you can't come here with a pitcher filled to overflowing with blank votes, that's why the handle dropped off, we always thought there was something suspicious about that handle, if something that could always carry a lot was satisfied with carrying little, that shows a most praiseworthy modesty, what got you into trouble was ambition, you thought you could fly up to the sun and, instead, you fell headfirst into the dardanelles, you will recall that we said the same about the interior minister, but he belongs to a different race of men, the macho, the virile, the bristly-chinned, those who will not bow their head, let's see now how you escape the hunter of lies, let's see what revealing lines your large and small transgressions will leave on that strip of paper impregnated with potassium iodide and starch, and you thought you were something special, this is what the much-vaunted supreme dignity of the human being can be reduced to, a piece of damp paper.

Now the polygraph is not a machine equipped with a disc that goes backwards and forwards and tells us, depending on the case, He lied, He didn't lie, if that were the case, being a judge with the ability to condemn and absolve would be the easiest thing in the world, police stations would be replaced by departments of applied mechanical psychology, lawyers, for lack of clientele, would pull down the shutters, the courts would be abandoned to the flies until some other use had been found for them. A polygraph, as we were saying, cannot go anywhere without help, it needs to have by its side a trained technician who can interpret the lines on the paper, but this doesn't mean that the technician must be a connoisseur of the truth, all he has to know is what is there before his eyes, that the question asked of the patient under observation has produced what we might innovatively call an allergographic reaction, or in more literary but no less imaginative terms, the outline of a lie. Something, nevertheless, would have been gained. At least it would be possible to proceed to an initial selection, wheat on the one side, tares on the other, and restore to liberty and family life, thereby freeing up the detention centres, those people, finally vindicated, who, without being contradicted by the machine, responded No to the question Did you cast a blank vote. As for the rest, those who had the guilt of electoral transgressions weighing on their conscience, any mental reserves of the jesuitical kind or spiritual introspection of the zen variety would prove useless to them, for the polygraph, implacable, unfeeling, would immediately sniff out a falsehood, whether they denied casting a blank vote or claimed to have voted for such and such a party. One can, if the circumstances are favourable, survive one lie, but not two. Just in case, the interior minister had given orders that whatever the result of the tests, for now, no one would be released, Leave them be, one never knows how far human malice will go, he said. And he was right, the wretched man. After many dozens of metres of squiggled-on, scribbled-on paper, on which had been recorded the tremors of the souls of everyone observed, after questions and answers repeated hundreds of times, always the same, always identical, one secret service agent, still a young lad, with little experience of temptation, fell with the innocence of a newborn lamb for the challenge thrown out to him by a pretty young woman who had just been submitted to the polygraph test and been declared to be deceitful and false. This mata-hari said, That machine is useless, Useless, why, asked the agent, forgetting that dialogue did not form part of the task with which he had been entrusted, Because in a situation like this, when everyone is under suspicion, all you would have to do is to say the word Blank, nothing more, without even bothering to find out if the person had voted, to provoke negative reactions, turmoil, anxiety, even if the person being examined was the purest, most perfect personification of innocence, Oh, come off it, I don't believe that, retorted the agent confidently, anyone at peace with his conscience would simply tell the truth and pass the polygraph test

47

easily, We're not robots or talking stones, mister agent, said the woman, and within every human truth there is always an element of anxiety or conflict, we are, and I am not referring simply to the fragility of life, we are a small, tremulous flame which threatens at any moment to go out, and we are afraid, above all, we are afraid, You're wrong there, I'm not afraid, I've been trained to overcome fear in all circumstances and, besides, I am not by nature a scaredy-cat, I wasn't even as a child, responded the agent, In that case, why don't we try a little experiment, suggested the woman, you let your-self be connected up to the machine and I'll ask the questions, You're mad, I'm the one with the authority here and, besides, you're the suspect, not me, So you are afraid, No, I'm not, Then connect yourself up to that machine and show me what it means to be a truthful man. The agent looked at the woman, who was smiling, he looked at the technician, who was struggling to conceal a smile, and said, All right, then, once won't hurt, I agree to submit to the experiment. The technician attached the wires, tightened the arm-bands, adjusted the suction pads, I'm ready when you are. The woman took a deep breath, held the breath in her lungs for three seconds and then, in a rush, uttered one word, Blank. It wasn't a question, more of an exclamation, but the needles moved, leaving a mark on the paper. In the pause that followed, the needles did not stop completely, they continued moving, making tiny traces, like the ripples made by a stone thrown into the water. The woman was looking at the needles, not at the bound man, but when she did turn and look him in the eye, she asked in a gentle, almost tender voice, Tell me, please, did you cast a blank vote, No, I didn't, I never did and never will cast a blank vote, replied the man vehemently. The needles moved rapidly, precipitately, violently. Another pause. Well, asked the agent. The technician took a while to respond, the agent repeated, Well, what does the machine say. The machine says that you lied, sir, said the embarrassed technician, That's impossible, cried the agent, I told the truth, I didn't cast a blank vote, I'm a professional secret service agent, a patriot trying to defend the interests of the nation, there must be something wrong with the machine, Don't waste your energy, don't try to justify yourself, said the woman, I believe you told the truth, that you didn't cast a blank vote and never will, but that, I must remind you, is not the point, I was just trying to demonstrate to you, successfully as it turns out, that we cannot entirely trust our bodies, It's all your fault, you made me nervous, Of course it was my fault, it was the temptress eve's fault, but no one came to ask us if we were feeling nervous when they hooked us up to that contraption, It's guilt that makes you feel nervous, Possibly, but go and ask your boss why it is that you, who are innocent of all our evils, behaved like a guilty man, There's nothing more to be said, replied the agent, it's as if what happened just now never happened at all. Then, addressing the technician, Give me that strip of paper, and remember, say nothing, if you do, you'll regret you were ever born, Yes, sir, don't worry, I'll keep my mouth shut, So will I, said the woman, but at least tell the minister that no amount of cunning will do any good, we will all continue to lie when we tell the truth, and to tell the truth when we lie, just like him, just like you, now just imagine if I had asked if you wanted to go to bed with me, what would you have said then, what would the machine have said.

THE DEFENCE MINISTER'S FAVOURITE EXPRESSION, A DEPTH CHARGE launched against the system, partially inspired by the unforgettable experience of an historic trip he had made aboard a submarine, a trip that had lasted all of half an hour and had taken place in flat calm seas, began to gain in strength and to attract attention when the interior minister's plans, despite one or two minor successes of no appreciable significance to the situation as a whole, revealed themselves to be impotent when it came to achieving the main aim, namely, persuading the inhabitants of the city, or, more precisely, the degenerates, delinquents and subversives who had cast the blank votes, to acknowledge the error of their ways and to beg for the mercy and the penance of a new election to which, at the chosen moment, they would rush en masse to purge themselves of the sins of a folly which they would swear never to repeat. It had become clear to the whole government, with the exception of the ministers of justice and culture, who both had their doubts, that there was an urgent need to tighten the screw still further, especially given that the declaration of a state of emergency, for which they had both had such high hopes, had produced no perceptible shift in the desired direction, for, since the citizens of this country were not in the healthy habit of demanding the proper enforcement of the rights bestowed on them by the constitution, it was only logical, even natural, that they had failed even to notice that those rights had been suspended. As a consequence, a state of siege proper was declared, one not purely for show, but complete with a curfew, the

closure of theatres and cinemas, constant army street patrols, a prohibition on gatherings of more than five people, and an absolute
ban on anyone entering or leaving the city, along with a simultaneous
lifting of the restrictive, although far less rigorous, measures still in
force in the rest of the country, a clear difference in treatment that
would make the humiliation of the capital all the more explicit and
damning. What we are trying to tell them, said the minister of
defence, and let's hope they finally get the message, is that, having
shown themselves to be unworthy of trust, they will be treated
accordingly. The interior minister, forced somehow to disguise the
failure of his secret agents, thoroughly approved of the immediate
declaration of a state of siege, and, to show that he still had a few
cards in his hand and had not withdrawn from the game entirely,
he informed the council of ministers that, after an exhaustive investigation, and in close collaboration with interpol, he had reached
the conclusion that the international anarchist movement, If it exists
to do anything more than to write a few jokes on walls, and he
paused briefly for the knowing laughter of his colleagues, then,
feeling equally pleased himself and with them, completed the
sentence, Had absolutely nothing to do with the election boycott
of which we have been the victims, and that this is, therefore, merely
an internal matter, Forgive me saying so, said the minister of foreign
affairs, merely does not seem to me the most appropriate of adverbs,
and I must remind this council that a number of other states have
expressed their concern to me that what is happening here could
cross the border and spread like a modern-day black death, You
mean blank death, don't you, said the prime minister with a placa-
tory smile, In that case, the minister of foreign affairs went on
unperturbed, we can, quite correctly, speak of depth charges
launched against the stability of the democratic system, not simply,
not merely, of one country, this country, but of the entire planet.
The interior minister sensed that the role of major national figure

to which recent events had elevated him was slipping from his grasp, and in order not entirely to lose his grip, having first thanked the minister of foreign affairs and, with great magnanimity, acknowledged the truth of what had been said, he was now keen to show that he, too, was capable of the most subtle of semiological interpretations, It is interesting to observe, he said, how the meanings of words change without our noticing, how we often use them to mean precisely the opposite of what they used to mean and which, in a way, like a fading echo, they still continue to mean, That's just a normal consequence of the semantic process, muttered the minister of culture, And what has that got to do with blank ballot papers, asked the minister for foreign affairs, Oh, it has nothing to do with blank ballot papers, but it has everything to do with the state of siege, declared the interior minister triumphantly, You've lost me, said the minister of defence, It's quite simple, It may be simple for you, but I don't understand, For example, what does the word siege mean, it's all right, that's a purely rhetorical question, I don't expect an answer, we all know that siege means blockade or encirclement, isn't that right, As sure as two and two are four, Therefore, declaring a state of siege is tantamount to saying that the country's capital is besieged, blockaded or encircled by an enemy, when the truth is that the enemy, if I may call it that, is not outside but inside. The other ministers looked at each other, the prime minister pretended not to be listening and started shuffling through some papers. But the minister of defence was about to triumph in this semiological battle, There's another way of looking at it too, What's that, That in unleashing this rebellion, and I don't think I'm exaggerating when I call what is happening a rebellion, the capital's inhabitants were, and quite right too, besieged or blockaded or encircled, the choice of term is, to be frank, a matter of complete indifference to me, May I remind our dear colleague and the council as a whole, said the minister for justice, that, when they decided to cast their blank votes, the citizens were only doing what the law explicitly allows them to do, therefore, to speak of rebellion in such a case is, as well as being, I imagine, a grave semantic error, and you will forgive me, I hope, for venturing into an area of which I know nothing, is also, from the legal point of view, a complete nonsense, Rights are not abstractions, retorted the minister of defence, people either deserve rights or they don't, and these people certainly don't, anything else is just so much empty talk, You're quite right, said the minister of culture, rights aren't abstractions, they continue to exist even when they're not respected, Now you're getting philosophical, Has the minister of defence got anything against philosophy, The only philosophy I'm interested in is military philosophy, and then only if it leads us to victory, I am, gentlemen, a barrack-room pragmatist, and my approach, whether you like it or not, is to call a spade a spade, but now, just so that you don't start looking down on me as someone of inferior intelligence, I would appreciate it if you could explain to me, as long as it's not a question of demonstrating that a circle can be transformed into a square of an equal area, how a right, if it isn't respected, can still continue to exist, Very simple, that right exists potentially in the duty of others to respect and comply with it, No offence, but civic sermons and demagoguery will get us nowhere, slap a state of siege on them and see how they like it, Unless it backfires on us, of course, said the minister of justice, How exactly, That I don't know yet, we'll just have to wait, no one had even dared to imagine that what is happening in our country could ever happen anywhere, but there it is, like a tight knot we can't undo, here we are gathered round this table to make decisions which, despite all the proposals put forward as sure solutions to the crisis, have, until now, achieved nothing, let's just wait, we'll find out soon enough how people will react to the state of siege, Sorry, but I can't just let that comment pass unchallenged, spluttered the interior minister, the measures we took were unanimously approved by this council and, as far as I recall, no one present at that meeting brought to the debate any different or better proposals, the burden of the catastrophe, yes, I'll call it a catastrophe and I'll call it a burden, even though some of my fellow ministers may think I'm exaggerating, as that smug, ironic air of theirs so clearly demonstrates, the burden of the catastrophe, I say again, has fallen, firstly, as is only right, on his excellency the president and on the prime minister, and secondly, given the responsibilities inherent in the posts we occupy, on the minister of defence and on myself, as for the others, and I refer in particular to the minister of justice and the minister of culture, who have been so kind as to shine the light of their intellects upon us, I have yet to hear a single idea that was worth considering for longer than it took us to listen to it, The light with which, according to you, I was kind enough to illuminate this council, was not my own, but the light of the law and nothing but the law, replied the minister of justice, And as regards my own humble person and my part in this wholesale ticking-off, said the minister of culture, given the miserable budget I'm allotted, you can hardly expect more, Ah, now I understand those anarchist leanings of yours, said the interior minister tartly, sooner or later, you always come out with the same old gibes.

The prime minister had run out of papers to shuffle. He tapped his pen lightly on his glass of water, calling for attention and silence, I hate to interrupt this interesting debate of yours, from which, although I may well have seemed somewhat distracted, I feel I have learned a great deal, because, as experience should teach us, there is nothing like a good argument to release accumulated tension, especially in a situation like this, which is constantly reminding us that we have to do something, although quite what we don't know. He paused very deliberately, pretended to consult some notes, then went on, So, now that we are all calm and relaxed, with our spirits less inflamed, we can, at last, approve the proposal put forward by the minister of defence, namely, the declaration of a state of siege for an indeterminate period and with immediate effect from the moment it is made public. There was a more or less general murmur of assent, albeit with variations of tone whose origins were impossible to identify, despite the minister of defence taking his eyes on a rapid panoramic excursion to catch any note of disagreement or muted enthusiasm. The prime minister went on, Experience, alas, has also taught us that when the time comes for them to be acted upon even the most perfect and polished of ideas can fail, whether because of some last-minute hiccup, or because of a gap between expectation and reality, or because, at some critical point, the situation got out of control, or because of a thousand other possible reasons that it is not worth our while going into right now and for which we would not have time, it is therefore vital always to have at the ready a replacement or complementary idea, which would prevent, as might well happen in this case, the emergence of a power vacuum, or to use another more alarming expression, of street power, either of which would have disastrous consequences. Accustomed to the prime minister's rhetoric, which took the form of three steps forward and two steps back, or, put another way, sitting firmly on the fence, his ministers were patiently awaiting his final, concluding, definitive word, the one that would explain everything. It did not come. The prime minister took a sip of water, dabbed at his lips with a white handkerchief which he took from his inside jacket pocket, made as if to consult his notes, but instead, at the last moment, pushed them to one side and said, If the results of the state of siege fall below expectations, that is, if they prove incapable of restoring the citizens to democratic normality, to the balanced, sensible use of an electoral law which, due to an imprudent lack of attention by the legislators, left the door open to something which, without fear of paradox, it would be reasonable to classify as a legal abuse, then I would like to inform this council now that I, as prime minister, foresee the application of another measure which, as well as providing psychological reinforcement of the measure we have just taken, I am referring, of course, to the declaration of a state of siege, could, I feel sure, by itself reset the troubled needle of our country's political scales and put an end once and for all to the nightmare situation into which we have been plunged. Another pause, another sip of water, another dab with the handkerchief, then he went on, You might well ask why, in that case, we do not simply implement that measure now instead of wasting our time setting up a state of siege which, as we well know, will make every aspect of life very difficult for the capital's population, both the guilty and the innocent, and that question is not without relevance, there are, however, important factors that cannot be ignored, some purely logistical in nature, others not, the main one being the effect, which it would be no exaggeration to describe as traumatic, of the sudden introduction of this extreme measure, which is why I feel we should opt for a gradual sequence of actions, of which the state of siege will be the first. The prime minister again shuffled his papers, but did not, this time, touch his glass of water, I understand your curiosity on the subject, he said, but I will say nothing further about the matter now, except to inform you that I was received in audience this morning by his excellency the president of the republic, to whom I presented my idea, which received his entire and unconditional support. You will learn more later, now, before closing this productive meeting, I ask all of you, in particular the ministers of defence and of the interior, who will, together, shoulder responsibility for the complex actions required to impose and carry out the declaration of the state of siege, to work diligently and energetically towards the same desired end. The armed forces and the police, whether acting within the ambit of their specific areas of competence or in joint operations, always observing the most rigorous mutual respect and avoiding any arguments over precedence that would prove prejudicial to our aims, are charged with the patriotic task of leading the lost sheep back to the fold, if you will allow me to use an expression so beloved of our forefathers and so deeply rooted in our pastoral traditions. And remember, you must do everything possible to ensure that those who are, for the moment, only our opponents do not instead become the enemies of the nation. May god go with you and guide you on your sacred mission so that the sun of concord may once more light the consciences of our fellow citizens and so that peace may restore to their daily lives the harmony that has been lost.

While the prime minister was appearing on television to announce the establishment of a state of siege, invoking reasons of national security resulting from the current political and social instability, a consequence, in turn, of the action taken by organised subversive groups who had repeatedly obstructed the people's right to vote, units of infantry and military police, supported by tanks and other combat vehicles, were, at the same time, occupying train stations and setting up posts at all the roads leading out of the capital. The main airport, about twenty-five kilometres to the north of the city, was outside the army's specific area of control and would, therefore, continue to function without any restrictions other than those foreseen at times of amber alert, which meant that planes carrying tourists would still be able to land and take off, although journeys made by those native to the country, while not, strictly speaking, prohibited, would be strongly discouraged, except in special circumstances to be examined on a case-by-case basis. Images of these military operations invaded the houses of the capital's bewildered inhabitants with, as the reporter put it, the unstoppable force of a straight punch. Images of officers giving orders, of sergeants yelling at their men to carry out these orders, of sappers erecting barriers, of ambulances and transmitters, of spotlights lighting up the highway as far as the first bend, of waves of soldiers, armed to the teeth, jumping out of trucks and taking up positions, as well equipped for an immediate hard-fought battle as for a long war of attrition. Families whose members worked or studied in the capital merely shook their heads at this war-like display and murmured, They must be mad, but others, who, every morning, despatched a father or a son to a factory on one of the industrial estates that surround the city and who waited every evening to welcome them back, now asked themselves how and on what they were going to live if they were not allowed to leave or enter the city. Perhaps they'll issue safe-conduct passes to those with jobs outside, said an old man, who had retired so many years ago that he still used terminology from the days of the franco-prussian wars or other ancient conflicts. Yet the wise old man was not so very wrong, the proof being that, the following day, business associations were quick to bring their well-founded anxieties to the government's notice, While we unreservedly and with an unwavering sense of patriotism support the energetic measures taken by the government, they said, as being a necessary campaign of national salvation to oppose the harmful effects of thinly disguised subversive acts, allow us, nonetheless, and with the greatest respect, to ask the competent authorities for the urgent issue of passes to our employees and workers, at the risk, if such a provision is not made at once, of causing grave and irreversible damage to our industrial and commercial activities, with the subsequent, inevitable harm this would cause to the national economy as a whole. On the afternoon of that same day, a joint communiqué from the ministries of defence, the interior and finance, expressed the national government's understanding and sympathy for the employers' legitimate concerns, but explained that any such distribution of passes could never be carried out on the scale desired by businesses, moreover, such liberality on the part of the government would inevitably imperil the security and efficacy of the military units charged with guarding the new frontier around the capital. However, as a demonstration of their openness and readiness to avoid the very worst problems, the government was prepared to give such documents to any managers and technical teams who were judged to be vital to the regular running of the companies, who would then have to take full responsibility for the actions, criminal or otherwise, inside and outside the city, of the people chosen to benefit from this privilege. Assuming the plan was approved, these people would have to gather each workday morning at designated places in order to be transported in buses under police escort to the city's various exit points, where more buses would take them to the factories or other premises where they worked and whence they would have to return at the end of the day. The cost of these operations, from the hiring of buses to the remuneration paid to the police for providing the escorts, would have to be covered by the companies themselves, an outlay that might well be made tax-deductible, although a firm decision on this could only be taken after a feasibility study had been carried out by the ministry of finance. As you can imagine, the complaints did not stop there. It is a basic fact of life that people cannot live without food and drink, now, bearing in mind that the meat came from outside, that the fish came from outside, that the vegetables came from outside, that, everything, in short, came from outside, and that what this city could, on its own, produce or store away would not provide enough even for one week, it would be necessary to lay on supply systems very like those that would provide businesses with technicians and managers, only far more complex, given the perishable nature of certain products. Not to mention the hospitals and the pharmacies, the kilometres of ligatures, the mountains of cotton wool, the tons of pills, the hectolitres of injectable fluids, the many gross of condoms. And then there's the petrol and the diesel to think about, how to transport them to the service stations, unless someone in the government has had the machiavellian idea of punishing the inhabitants of the capital twice over by making them walk. It took only a few days for the government to realise that there is more to a state of siege than meets the eye, especially if there is no real intention of starving the besieged population to death as was the usual practice in the distant past, that a state of siege is not something that can be cobbled together in a moment, that you need to know exactly what your objectives are and how to achieve them, to weigh the consequences, to evaluate reactions, ponder the problems, calculate the gains and the losses, if only to avoid the vast mountain of work that suddenly faces the ministries, overwhelmed by an unstoppable flood of protests, complaints and requests for clarification, for almost none of which they can provide answers, because the instructions from on high had looked only at the general principles of the state of siege and had shown a complete disregard for the bureaucratic minutiae of its implementation, which is where chaos invariably finds a way in. One interesting aspect of the situation, which the satirical vein and sardonic eye of the capital's wits could not help but notice, was the fact that the government, the de facto and de jure besieger, was, at the same time, one of the besieged, not just because its chambers and ante-chambers, its offices and corridors, its departments and archives, its filing cabinets and stamps, were all in the very heart of the city, and, indeed, formed an organic part of it, but also because some of its members, at least three ministers, a few secretaries of state and under-secretaries, as well as a couple of directors-general, lived on the outskirts, not to mention the civil servants who, morning and evening, in one way or another, had to use the train, metro or bus if they did not have their own transport or did not want to submit themselves to the complexities of urban traffic. The stories that were told, not always sotto voce, explored the well-known theme of the hunter hunted or the biter bit, but did not restrict them-selves to such childishly innocent comments, to the humour of a belle époque kindergarten, there was a whole kaleidoscope of variations, some of them utterly obscene and, from the point of view of the most elementary good taste, reprehensibly scatological. Unfortunately, and here we have further proof of the limited range and structural weakness of all sarcastic remarks, lampoons, burlesques, parodies, satires and other such jokes with which people hope to wound a government, the state of siege was not lifted and the problems of supply remained unresolved.

The days passed, and the difficulties continued to increase, they grew worse and multiplied, they sprang up underfoot like mushrooms after rain, but the moral strength of the population did not seem inclined to humble itself or to renounce what it had considered to be a just stance and to which it had given expression through the ballot box, the simple right not to follow any consensually established opinion. Some observers, usually foreign correspondents hurriedly despatched to cover the events, as they say in the jargon of the profession, and therefore unfamiliar with local idiosyncrasies, commented with bemusement on the complete lack of conflict amongst the city's inhabitants, even though they had observed what later proved to be agents provocateurs at work, trying to create the kind of unstable situations which might justify, in the eyes of the so-called international community, the leap that had not yet been taken, that is, the move from a state of siege to a state of war. One of these commentators, in his desire to be original, went so far as to describe this as a unique, never-before-seen example of ideological unanimity, which, if it were true, would make the capital's population a fascinating case, a political phenomenon worthy of study. Whichever way you looked at it, the idea was complete nonsense, and had nothing to do with the reality of the situation, for here, as anywhere else on the planet, people differ, they think differently, they are not all poor or all rich, and, even amongst the reasonably well-off, some are more so and some are less. The one subject on which they were all in agreement, with no need for any prior discussion, is one with which we are already familiar, and so there is no point going over old ground. Nevertheless, it is only natural that one would want to know, and the question was often asked, both by foreign journalists and by local ones, what singular reason lay behind the fact that there had, until now, been no incidents, no fights, no shouting matches or fisticuffs or worse amongst those who had cast blank votes and those who had not. The question amply demonstrates how important a knowledge of the elements of arithmetic is for the proper exercise of the profession of journalist, for they need only have recalled that the people casting blank votes represented eighty-three per cent of the capital's population and that the remainder, all told, accounted for no more than seventeen per cent, and one must not forget the debatable thesis put forward by the party on the left, according to which a blank vote and a vote for them were, metaphorically speaking, one bone and one flesh, and that if the supporters of the party on the left, and this is our own conclusion, did not all cast blank votes, although it is clear that many did in the second poll, it was simply because they had not been ordered to do so. No one would believe us if we were to say that seventeen people had decided to take on eighty-three, the days when battles were won with the help of god are long since gone. Natural curiosity would also lead one to ask two questions, what happened to the five hundred people plucked from the queues of voters by the ministry of the interior's spies and who subsequently underwent the torment of interrogation and the agony of seeing their most intimate secrets revealed by the lie detector and, the second question, what exactly are those specialist secret service agents and their less qualified assistants up to. On the first point, we have only doubts and no way of resolving them. There are those who say that the five hundred prisoners are, in accordance with that popular police euphemism, still helping the authorities

62

with their enquiries in the hope of clarifying the facts, others say that they are gradually being freed, although only a few at a time so as not to attract too much attention, however, the more sceptical observers believe a third version, that they have all been removed from the city and are now in some unknown location and that, despite the dearth of results obtained hitherto, the interrogations continue. Who knows who is right. As for the second point, about what the secret service agents are up to, that we do know. Like all honest, worthy workers, they leave home every morning, tramp the city from end to end, and when they think the fish is about to bite, they try a new tactic, which consists of dropping all the circumlocutions and saying point-blank to the person they're with, Let's talk frankly now, like friends, I cast a blank vote, did you. At first, those questioned merely gave the answers described above, that no one was obliged to reveal how they voted, that no one can be questioned about it by any authority, and if one of them had the excellent idea of demanding that the impertinent questioner should identify himself and declare there and then on whose power and authority he was asking the question, then we would be treated to the pleasurable spectacle of seeing a secret service agent all in a fluster and scampering off with his tail between his legs, because, of course, it wouldn't occur to anyone that he would actually open his wallet and show them the card that would prove who he was, complete with photograph, official stamp and edged with the national colours. But, as we said, that was at the beginning. After a while, the general consensus deemed that, in such situations, the best attitude to take was to ignore the person asking the question and simply turn your back on them, or, if they proved extremely insistent, to say loudly and clearly Leave me alone, or, if preferred, and with more chance of success, to tell them, even more simply, to go to hell. Naturally, the reports sent by the secret service agents to their superiors camouflaged these rebuffs and disguised these setbacks, instead restating the stubborn and systematic absence of any collaborative spirit amongst the suspect sector of the population. You might think that things had reached a point very like that of two wrestlers endowed with equal strength, one pushing this way, the other pushing that, and while it was true that they had not moved from the spot where they had started, neither had they managed to advance even an inch, and, consequently, only the final exhaustion of one of them would give victory to the other. In the opinion of the person in charge of the secret services, this stalemate would be rapidly resolved if one of the wrestlers were to receive help from another wrestler, which, in this particular situation, would mean abandoning, as futile, the persuasive techniques employed up until then and adopting, without reserve, dissuasive methods that did not exclude the use of brute force. If the capital, for its own many faults, finds itself under a state of siege, if it is up to the armed forces to impose discipline and proceed accordingly in the case of any grave disruption of the social order, if the high command take responsibility, on their word of honour, not to hesitate when it comes to making decisions, then the secret services will take it upon themselves to create suitable focal points of unrest that would justify a priori the harsh crackdown which the government, very generously, has tried, by all peaceful and, let us repeat the word, persuasive means, to avoid. The insurrectionists would not be able to come to them later with complaints, assuming they wanted to and assuming they had any. When the interior minister took this idea to the inner council, or emergency council, which had been formed meanwhile, the prime minister reminded him that he still had one weapon as yet undeployed in the resolution of the conflict and only in the unlikely event of that weapon failing would he consider this new plan or any others that happened to arise. Whilst the interior minister expressed his disagreement laconically, in four words, We are wasting time, the defence minister needed far more to guarantee that the armed forces would do their duty, As they always have throughout our long history, giving no thought to the sacrifice entailed. And that was how the delicate matter was left, the fruit, it seemed, was not yet ripe. Then it was that the other wrestler, grown tired of waiting, decided to risk taking a step. One morning, the streets of the capital were filled by people wearing stickers on their chest bearing the words, in red letters on a black background, I cast a blank vote, huge placards hung from windows declaring, in black letters on a red background, We cast blank votes, but the most astonishing sight, waving above the heads of the advancing demonstrators, was the endless stream of blank, white flags, which would lead one unthinking correspondent to run to the telephone and inform his newspaper that the city had surrendered. The police loudspeakers bellowed and screamed that gatherings of more than five people were not allowed, but there were fifty, five hundred, five thousand, fifty thousand, and who, in such a situation, is going to bother counting in fives. The police commissioner wanted to know if he could use tear-gas and water-cannon, the general in charge of the northern division if he was authorised to order the tanks to advance, the general of the southern airborne division if the conditions were right to send in paratroopers, or if, on the contrary, the risk of them landing on rooftops made this inadvisable. War was, however, about to break out.

Then it was that the prime minister revealed his plan to the government, who had been brought together in plenary session and with the president in the chair, The time has come to break the back of the resistance, he said, let's call a halt to all the psychological game-playing, to the espionage, the lie detectors and the other technological contraptions, since, despite the interior minister's worthy efforts, these methods have all proved incapable of solving the problem, I must add, by the way, that I also consider inappropriate any direct intervention by the armed forces, given the more than likely inconvenience of a mass slaughter which it is our duty to avoid at all costs, what I have to offer you instead is neither more nor less than a proposed multiple withdrawal, a series of actions which some may perhaps feel to be absurd, but which I am sure will lead us to total victory and a return to democratic normality, these actions are, namely, the immediate removal of the government to another city, which will become the country's new capital, the withdrawal of all the armed forces still in place, and the withdrawal of all police forces, this radical action will mean that the rebel city will be left entirely to its own devices and will have all the time it needs to understand the price of being cut off from the sacrosanct unity of the nation, and when it can no longer stand the isolation, the indignity, the contempt, when life within the city becomes a chaos, then its guilty inhabitants will come to us hanging their heads and begging our forgiveness. The prime minister looked about him, That is my plan, he said, I submit it to you for your examination and discussion, but, needless to say, I am counting on your unanimous approval, desperate diseases must have desperate remedies, and if the remedy I am prescribing is painful to you, the disease afflicting us is, quite simply, fatal.

IN WORDS THAT CAN BE GRASPED BY THE INTELLIGENCE OF THOSE CLASSES, who, though less educated, are nonetheless not entirely ignorant of the gravity and diversity of the many and various ailments that threaten the already precarious survival of the human race, what the prime minister had proposed was neither more nor less than a flight from the virus that had attacked the majority of the capital's inhabitants and which, given that the worst is always waiting just behind the door, might well end up infecting all the remaining inhabitants and even, who knows, the whole country. Not that he and his government were themselves afraid of being contaminated by the bite of this subversive insect, for apart from a few clashes between certain individuals and a few very minor differences of opinion, which were, anyway, more to do with means than ends, we have had ample proof of the unshakeable institutional cohesion of the politicians responsible for the running of a country which, without a word of warning, had been plunged into a disaster never before seen in the long and always troubled history of the known world. Contrary to what certain ill-intentioned people doubtless thought or suggested, this was not the coward's way out, but rather a strategic move of the first order, unparalleled in its audacity, one whose future results can almost be touched with the hand, like ripe fruit on a tree. Now all that was needed for the task to be crowned with success was that the energy put into carrying out the plan should be up to the resolve of its aims. First, they will have to decide who will leave the city and who will stay. Obviously, his excellency the president and the whole of the government down to under-secretary level will leave, along with their closest advisors, the members of the national parliament will also leave so that the legislative process suffers no interruption, the army and the police will leave, including the traffic police, but all the members of the municipal council will remain, along with their leader, the fire fighters' organisations will stay too, so that the city does not burn down because of some act of carelessness or sabotage, just as the staff of the city cleansing department will stay in case of epidemic and, needless to say, the authorities will ensure continued supplies of water and electricity, those utilities so essential to life. As for food, a group of dieticians, or nutritionists, have already been charged with drawing up a list of basic dishes which, while not bringing the population to the brink of starvation, would make them aware that a state of siege taken to its ultimate consequences would certainly be no holiday. Not that the government believed things would go that far. It would not be many days before the usual delegations appeared at a military post on one of the roads out of the city, bearing the white flag, the flag of unconditional surrender not the flag of insurgency, the fact that both are the same colour is a remarkable coincidence upon which we will not now pause to reflect, but there will be plenty of reasons to return to the matter later on.

After the plenary meeting of the government, to which we assume sufficient reference was made on the last page of the previous chapter, the inner ministerial cabinet or emergency council discussed and took a handful of decisions which will, in the full-ness of time, be revealed, always assuming, as we believe we have warned on a previous occasion, that events do not develop in a way that renders those decisions null and void or requires them to be replaced by others, for, as it is always wise to remember, while it is true that man proposes, it is god who disposes, and there have been very few occasions, almost all of them tragic, when both man and god were in agreement and did all the disposing together. One of the most hotly disputed matters was the government's withdrawal from the city, when and how it should be done, with or without discretion, with or without television coverage, with or without military bands, with or without garlands on the cars, with or without the national flag draped over the bonnet, and an endless series of details which required repeated discussions about state protocol which had never, not since the founding of the nation itself, known such difficulties. The final plan for the withdrawal was a masterpiece of tactics, consisting basically of a meticulous distribution of different itineraries so as to make things as hard as possible for any large concentrations of demonstrators who might gather together to express the city's possible feelings of displeasure, discontent or indignation at being abandoned to its fate. There was one itinerary for the president, one for the prime minister and one for each member of the council of ministers, a total of twenty-seven different routes, all under the protection of the army and the police, with assault vehicles stationed at crossroads and with ambulances following behind the cortèges, ready for all eventualities. The map of the city, an enormous illuminated panel over which, with the help of military commanders and expert police trackers, they had laboured for forty-eight hours, showed a red star with twenty-seven arms, fourteen turned towards the northern hemisphere, thirteen towards the southern hemisphere, with an equator dividing the capital into two halves. Along these arms would file the black automobiles of the public institutions, surrounded by bodyguards and walkie-talkies, antiquated contraptions still used in this country, but for which there was now an approved budget for modernisation. All the people involved in the various phases of the operation, whatever the degree of their participation, had to be sworn to absolute secrecy, first with their right hand placed on the gospels, then on a copy of the constitution bound in blue morocco leather, and finally, completing this double commitment, by uttering a truly binding oath, drawn from popular tradition, If I break this oath may the punishment fall upon my head and upon that of my descendants unto the fourth generation. With secrecy thus sealed for any leaks, the date was set for two days hence. The hour of departure, which would be simultaneous, that is, the same for everyone, was three o'clock in the morning, a time when only the seriously insomniac are still tossing and turning in their beds and saying prayers to the god hypnos, the son of night and twin brother of thanatos, to help them in their affliction by dropping on their poor, bruised eyelids the sweet balm of the poppy. During the remaining hours, the spies, who had returned en masse to the field of operations, did nothing but pound, in more than one sense, the city's squares, avenues, streets and sidestreets, surreptitiously taking the population's pulse, probing ill-concealed intentions, connecting up words heard here and there, in order to find out if there had been any leak of the decisions taken by the council of ministers, in particular the government's imminent withdrawal, because any spy worthy of the name must take it as a sacred principle, a golden rule, the letter of the law, that oaths are never to be trusted, whoever made them, even an oath sworn by the very mother who gave them life, still less when instead of one oath there were two, and less still when instead of two there were three. In this case, however, they had no alternative but to recognise, with a certain degree of professional frustration, that the official secret had been well kept, an empirical truth that tallied with the ministry of the interior's central system of computation, which, after much squeezing, sieving and mixing, shuffling and reshuffling of the millions of fragments of recorded conversations, found not a single equivocal sign, not a single suspicious clue, not even the tiniest end of a thread which, if pulled, might have at its other end a nasty surprise. The messages despatched by the secret service to the ministry of the interior were wonderfully reassuring, as were the messages sent to the defence ministry's colonels of information and psychology by the highly efficient military intelligence, who, without the knowledge of their civilian competitors, were carrying out their own investigation, indeed, both camps could have used that expression which literature has made into a classic, All quiet on the western front, although not, of course, for the soldier who has just died. Everyone, from the president to the very least of government advisors, gave a sigh of relief. The withdrawal, thank god, would take place quietly, without any undue trauma to a population who had perhaps already, in part, repented their entirely inexplicable seditious behaviour, but who, despite this, in a praiseworthy display of civic-mindedness, which augured well for the future, seemed to have no intention of harming, either in word or deed, their legitimate leaders and representatives at this moment of painful, but necessary, separation. This was the conclusion drawn from all the reports, and so it was.

At half past two in the morning everyone was ready to cut the ropes still attaching them to the president's palace, to the prime minister's mansion and to the various ministerial buildings. The gleaming black automobiles were lined up waiting, the trucks containing all the files were surrounded by security guards armed to the teeth and who were, incredible though it may seem, capable of spitting poisoned darts, the police outriders were in position, the ambulances were ready, and inside, in the offices, the fugitive leaders, or deserters, whom we should, in more elevated language, describe as tergiversators, were still opening and closing the last cupboards and drawers, sadly gathering up a final few mementos, a group photograph, another bearing a dedication, a ring made out of human hair, a statuette of the goddess of happiness, a pencil sharpener from schooldays, a returned cheque, an anonymous letter, an embroidered handkerchief, a mysterious key, a redundant pen with a name engraved on it, a compromising piece of paper, another compromising piece of paper, but the latter is only compromising for a colleague in the next department. A few people were almost in tears, men and women barely able to control their emotions, wondering if they would ever return to the beloved places that witnessed their rise up the hierarchical ladder, others, to whom the fates had proved less helpful, were dreaming, despite previous disappointments and injustices, of different worlds and new opportunities that would place them, at last, where they deserved to be. At a quarter to three, when the army and the police were already strategically stationed along all twenty-seven routes, not forgetting the assault vehicles guarding all the major crossroads, the order was given to dim the street lights as a way of covering the retreat, however harshly that last word may grate on the ear. In the streets along which the cars and trucks would have to pass, there was not a soul, not one, not even in plain clothes. As for the continual flow of information from the rest of the city, this remained unchanged, no groups were gathering, there was no suspicious activity, and any nightbirds returning to their homes or leaving them did not seem a cause for concern, they were not carrying flags over their shoulders or concealing bottles of petrol with bits of rag protruding from the neck, they weren't whirling clubs or bicycle chains above their heads, and if the occasional one appeared to stray from the straight and narrow, there was no reason to attribute this to deviations of a political nature, but to perfectly forgivable alcoholic excesses. At three minutes to three, the engines of the cars in the convoys were started up. At three o'clock on the dot, precisely as planned, the retreat began.

Then, O surprise, O astonishment, O never-before-seen prodigy, first confusion and perplexity, then disquiet, then fear, dug their nails into the throats of the president and the prime minister, of the ministers, secretaries of state and under-secretaries, of the deputies, security men and police outriders, and even, although to a lesser degree, of the ambulance staff, who were, by their profession, accustomed to the worst. As the cars advanced along the streets, the façades of the buildings were lit up, one by one, from top to bottom, by lanterns, lamps, spotlights, torches, candelabra when available, even perhaps by old brass oil lamps, every window was wide open and aglow, letting out a great river of light like a flood, a multiplication of crystals made of white fire, marking the road, picking out the deserters' escape route so that they would not get lost, so that they would not wander off down any short-cuts. The first reaction of those in charge of convoy security was to throw caution to the wind and say put your foot down and drive like billy-o, and that is what began to happen, to the irrepressible joy of the official drivers, who, as everyone knows, hate pootling along at a snail's pace when they've got two hundred horsepower in their engine. The burst of speed did not last long. That brusque, precipitate decision, like all decisions born of fear, meant that, on nearly every route, further ahead or further back, minor collisions took place, usually it was the vehicle behind bumping into the one in front, fortunately without any very grave consequences for the passengers, a bit of a fright and that was all, a bruise on the forehead, a scratch on the face, a ricked neck, nothing which, tomorrow, would justify the awarding of a medal for injuries sustained, a croix de guerre, a purple heart or some other such monstrosity. The ambulances raced ahead, the medical and nursing staff eager to help the wounded, there was terrible confusion, deplorable in every way, the convoys ground to a halt, telephone calls were made to find out what was happening on the other routes, someone was demanding loudly to be told exactly what the situation was, and then, on top of that, there were those lines of buildings lit up like Christmas trees, all that was missing were the fireworks and the merry-go-rounds, it was just as well that no one appeared at the windows to enjoy the free entertainment down in the street, to laugh, to mock, to point a finger at the colliding cars. Short-sighted subalterns, the sort who are only interested in the present moment, which is nearly all of them, would certainly think like that, as perhaps would a few under-secretaries and advisors with little future, but never a prime minister, certainly not one as far-sighted as this one has shown himself to be. While a doctor was dabbing at the prime minister's chin with some antiseptic and wondering to himself if it would be going too far to give the injured man an anti-tetanus injection, the prime minister kept thinking about the tremor of unease that had shaken his spirit as soon as the first lights in the buildings came on. It was, without a doubt, enough to upset even the most phleg-matic of politicians, it was, without a doubt, troubling, unsettling, but worse, much worse, was the fact that there was no one at those windows, as if the official convoys were foolishly fleeing from nothing, as if the army and the police, along with the assault ve-hicles and the water cannon, had been spurned by the enemy and been left with no one to fight. Still somewhat stunned by the colli-sion, but with a plaster on his chin, and having refused with stoical impatience the anti-tetanus injection, the prime minister suddenly remembered that his first duty should have been to phone the presi-dent and ask him how he was, to enquire after the well-being of the presidential person, and that he should do this now, without more ado, lest the president, out of sheer mischief and political astuteness, should get in first, And catch me with my pants down, he muttered, not thinking about the literal meaning of the phrase. He asked his secretary to make the call, another secretary responded, the secretary at this end said that the prime minister wished to speak to the president, the secretary at the other end said one moment, please, the secretary at this end passed the phone to the prime minister and, he, as was only fitting, waited, How are things over there, asked the president, A few dents, but nothing serious, replied the prime minister, We've had no problems at all, Not even any collisions, Just a few bumps, Nothing grave, I hope, No, this armour-plating is pretty much bomb-proof, Alas, sir, no armour-plated vehicle is bomb-proof, You don't need to tell me that, for every breastplate there's a spear and for every armour-plated vehicle a bomb, Are you hurt, Not a scratch. The face of a police officer appeared at the car window, indicating that they could drive on, We're on the move again, the prime minister told the president, Oh, we've barely had to stop at all, replied the president, May I say something, sir, Of course, Well, I must confess to feeling worried, much more so than on the day of the first election, Why, These lights that came on just as we were leaving and which will, in all probability, continue to light our way along the whole route, until we're out of the city, the complete absence of people, I mean, there isn't a soul to be seen at any of the windows or in the streets, it's odd, very odd, I'm beginning to think that I may have to consider something which, up until now, I have always rejected, that there is some purpose behind all this, an idea, a planned objective, because things are happening as if the population really were obeying some plan, as if there were some central co-ordination, Oh, I don't think so, prime minister, you know better than I do that the anarchist conspiracy theory doesn't hold water at all, and that the other theory positing an evil foreign state bent on destabilising our country is equally invalid, We thought we had everything completely under control, that we were masters of the situation, and then they spring a surprise on us that no one could possibly have imagined, a real coup de théâtre, What do you think you'll do, For the moment, continue with our plan, if future circumstances require us to introduce any alterations, we will only do so after an exhaustive examination of the new data, whatever they may be, as for the fundamentals, though, I don't feel we need to make any changes, And in your opinion, the fundamentals are what, We discussed this and reached an agreement, sir, our aim is to isolate the population and then leave them to simmer, sooner or later there are bound to be fights, conflicts of interest, life will become increasingly difficult, the streets will fill up with rubbish, imagine, sir, what the place will be like when the rains come, and, as sure as I'm prime minister, there are bound to be serious problems with the supply and distribution of foodstuffs, problems which, if necessary, we will take care to create, So you don't think the city will be able to hold out for very long, No, I don't, besides, there's another important factor, possibly the most important of all, What's that, However hard people have tried and continue to try, it's impossible to get everyone to think the same way, It seems to have worked this time, It's too perfect to be real, sir, And what if there really is, as you have just admitted as a hypothesis, some secret organisation, a mafia, a camorra, a cosa nostra, a cia or a kgb, The cia isn't a secret organisation, sir, and the kgb no longer exists, Well, I shouldn't think that will make much difference, but let's just imagine something similar or, if that were possible, even worse, something more machiavellian, invented to create this near-unanimity around, well, to be perfectly honest, I don't know quite what, Around the blank ballot papers, sir, the blank ballot papers, That, prime minister, is a conclusion I could have reached on my own, what interests me is what I don't know, Of course, sir, But you were saying, Even if I were forced to accept, in theory and only in theory, the possible existence of a clandestine organisation out to destroy state security and opposed to the legitimacy of the democratic system, these things can't be done without contacts, without meetings, without secret cells, without incentives, without documents, yes, without documents, you yourself know that it is impossible to do anything in this world without documents, and we, as well as having not a scrap of information about any of the activities I have just mentioned, have also failed to find even a page from a diary saying Onwards, comrades, le jour de gloire est arrivé, Why would it be in French, Because of their revolutionary tradition, sir, What an extraordinary country we live in, a place where things happen that have never happened on any other part of the planet, But this is not the first time, as I'm sure I need not remind you, sir, That is precisely what I meant, prime minister, There is not the faintest possibility of a link between the two incidents, Of course not, one was a plague of white blindness and the other a plague of blank ballot papers, We still haven't found an explanation for the first plague, Or for this one either, We will, sir, we will, If we don't come up against a brick wall first, Let us remain confident, sir, confidence is fundamental, Confident in what, in whom, In the democratic institutions, My dear fellow, you can reserve that speech for the television, only our secretaries can hear us now, so we can speak plainly. The prime minister changed the subject, We're leaving the city now, sir, Yes, we are too over here, Would you mind just looking back for a moment, sir, Why, The lights, What about them, They're still on, no one has turned them off, And what conclusions do you think I should draw from these illuminations, Well, I don't rightly know, sir, the natural thing would be for them to go out as we progressed, but, no, there they are, why, I imagine that, seen from the air, they must look like a huge star with twenty-seven arms, It would seem I have a poet for prime minister, Oh, I'm no poet, but a star is a star is a star, and no one can deny it, sir, So what next, The government isn't just going to sit around doing nothing, we haven't run out of munitions yet, we've still got some arrows in our quiver, Let's hope your aim is true, All I need is to have the enemy in my sights, But that is precisely the problem, we don't know where the enemy is, we don't even know who they are, They'll turn up, sir, it's just a matter of time, they can't stay hidden for ever, As long as we don't run out of time, We'll find a solution, We're nearly at the frontier, we'll continue our conversation in my office, see you there later, at about six o'clock, Of course, sir, I'll be there.

The frontier was the same at all the exit points from the city, a heavy, movable barrier, a pair of tanks, one on either side of the road, a few huts, and armed soldiers in battledress and with daubed faces. Powerful spotlights lit up the scene. The president got out of his car, returned the commanding officer's impeccable salute with a polite though slightly disdainful gesture, and asked, How are things here, Nothing to report, sir, absolute calm, Has anyone tried to leave, No, sir, You are, I assume, referring to motorised vehicles, to bicycles, to carts, to skateboards, To motorised vehicles, sir, And people on foot, Not a single one, You will, of course, already have considered the possibility that any fugitives might not come by road, We have, sir, but they still wouldn't manage to get through, as well as the conventional patrols guarding the area between us and the two closest exit points on either side, we also have electronic sensors that would pick up a mouse if we had them adjusted to detect anything that small, Excellent, you're familiar, I'm sure, with what is always said on these occasions, the nation is watching you, Yes, sir, we are aware of the importance of our mission, You will, I assume, have received orders on what to do if there is any attempt at a mass exodus, Yes, sir, What are they, First, tell them to stop, That much is obvious, Yes, sir, And if they don't, If they don't, then we fire into the air, And if, despite that, they continue to advance, Then the squad of riot police assigned to us would take action, And what would they do, Well, sir, that depends, they would either use tear-gas or attack with water cannon, the army doesn't do that kind of thing, Do I note a hint of criticism in your words, It's just that I don't think that is any way to carry on a war, sir, An interesting observation, and if the people do not withdraw, They must withdraw, sir, no one can withstand tear-gas attacks and water cannon, Just imagine that they do withstand it, what are your orders in that situation, To shoot at their legs, Why their legs, We don't want to kill our compatriots, But that could well happen, Yes, sir, it could,

Do you have family in the city, Yes, sir, What if you saw your wife and children at the head of the advancing multitude, A soldier's family knows how to behave in all situations, Yes, I'm sure, but just try to imagine, Orders must be obeyed, sir, All orders, Up until today, it has been my honour to have obeyed all the orders given to me, And tomorrow, Tomorrow, I very much hope not to have to come and tell you, sir, So do I. The president took two steps in the direction of his car, then asked suddenly, Are you sure your wife did not cast a blank vote, Yes, sir, I would put my hand in the fire, sir, Really, It's a manner of speaking, sir, I just meant that I'm sure she would have fulfilled her duty as a voter, By voting, Yes, But that doesn't answer my question, No, sir, Then answer it, No, sir, I can't, Why not, Because the law does not allow me to, Ah. The president stood looking at the officer for a long time, then said, Goodbye, captain, it is captain, isn't it, Yes, sir, Good night, captain, perhaps we'll see each other again sometime, Good night, sir, Did you notice that I didn't ask if you had cast a blank vote, Yes, sir, I did. The car sped away. The captain put his hands to his face. His forehead was dripping with sweat.

THE LIGHTS STARTED TO GO OUT AS THE LAST ARMY TRUCK AND THE last police van left the city. One after the other, like someone saying goodbye, the twenty-seven arms of the star gradually disappeared, leaving the vague route map of deserted streets marked only by the dim street lamps that no one had thought to restore to their normal level of brightness. We will find out how alive the city is when the intense black of the sky begins to dissolve into the slow tide of deep blue which anyone with good eyesight would already be able to make out rising up from the horizon, then we will see if the men and women who inhabit the different floors of these buildings do, indeed, set off to work, if the first buses pick up the first passengers, if the metro trains race, thundering, through the tunnels, if the shops open their doors and remove the shutters, if newspapers are delivered to kiosks. At this early morning hour, while they wash, get dressed and drink their usual breakfast cup of coffee, people are listening to the radio which is announcing, in excited tones, that the president, the government and the parliament left the city in the early hours, that there are no police left in the city, and that the army has withdrawn too, then they turn on the television, which, in identical tones, gives them the same news, and both radio and television, with only the briefest of intervals, continue to report that, at seven o'clock precisely, an important message from the president will be broadcast to the whole country, and, in particular, of course, to the capital's obstinate inhabitants. Meanwhile, the kiosks have not yet opened, so there is no point in going out into the street to buy a newspaper, just as it is not worth searching the web, the worldwide web, although some more up-to-date citizens have already tried, for the president's predictable stream of invective. Official secrecy, while it may occasionally be plagued by leaks and disclosures, as demonstrated a few hours earlier by the synchronised switching on of lights in buildings, exercises extreme rigour when it comes to any higher authorities, who, as everyone knows, will, for the most frivolous of motives, not only demand swift and detailed explanations from those found wanting, they will, from time to time, also chop off their heads. It is ten minutes to seven, many of those people still lazing about should, by rights, be out in the street on their way to work, but not all days are alike, and it seems that public servants have been given permission to arrive late, and, as for private businesses, most of them will probably remain closed all day, just to see where all this leads. Caution and chicken soup never hurt anyone, in good health or bad. The world history of crowds shows us that, whether it's a specific breach of public order, or merely the threat of one, the best examples of prudence are generally given by those businesses and industries with premises on the streets, a nervous attitude which we have a duty to respect, given that they are the areas of professional activity who have most to lose, and who inevitably do lose, in terms of shattered shop windows, robberies, lootings and acts of sabotage. At two minutes to seven, with the lugubrious face and voice required by the circumstances, the television and radio presenters finally announce that the president is about to address the nation. The image that follows, as a way of setting the scene, shows the national flag flapping lazily, languidly, as if it were, at any moment, about to slip helplessly down the pole. There obviously wasn't much wind on the day they took its picture, remarked one inhabitant. The symbolic insignia seemed to revive with the opening chords of the national anthem, the gentle breeze had suddenly given way to a brisk wind that must have blown in from the vast ocean or from some triumphant scene of battle, if it blows any harder, even just a little bit harder, we're sure to see valkyries on horseback with heroes riding pillion. Then, as it faded into the distance, the anthem took the flag with it, or the flag took the anthem with it, the order doesn't matter, and then the president appeared to the people, seated behind a desk, his stern eyes fixed on the teleprompter. To his right, standing to attention, the flag, not the one just mentioned, but an indoor flag, arranged in discreet folds. The president interlaced his fingers, perhaps to disguise some involuntary tic, He's nervous, said the man who had remarked upon the lack of wind, I want to see his expression when he explains the low trick they've just played on us. The people awaiting the president's imminent oratorical display could not, for one moment, imagine the efforts expended on preparing the speech by the president of the republic's literary advisors, not so much as regards any actual statements made, which would merely involve plucking a few strings on the stylistic lute, but the form of address with which, according to the norm, the speech should begin, the standard words that usually introduce tirades of this type. Indeed, given the delicate nature of his message, it would be little short of insulting to say My dear compatriots, or Esteemed fellow citizens, or even, were it the moment for playing, with just the right amount of vibrato, the bass string of patriotism, that simplest and noblest mode of address, Men and women of Portugal, that last word, we hasten to add, only appears due to the entirely gratuitous supposition, with no foundation in objective fact, that the scene of the dire events it has fallen to us to describe in such meticulous detail, could be, or perhaps could have been, the land of the aforesaid Portuguese men and women. It was merely an illustrative example, nothing more, for which, despite all our good intentions, we apologise in advance, especially given that they are a people with a reputation around the world for having always exercised their electoral duties with praiseworthy civic discipline and religious devotion.

Now, returning to the home that we have made into our observation post, we should say that, contrary to one's natural expectations, not a single listener or viewer noticed that none of these usual forms of address issued from the president's mouth, neither this, that or the other, perhaps because the plangent drama of the first words tossed into the ether, I speak to you with my heart in my hands, had made the president's literary advisors realise that the introduction of any of the aforementioned refrains would have been superfluous and inopportune. It would, indeed, have been quite incongruous to begin by saying affectionately, Esteemed fellow citizens or My dear compatriots, as if he were about to announce that tomorrow the price of petrol will go down by fifty per cent, only to proceed to present to the eyes of a horror-struck audience a bleeding, slippery, still pulsating internal organ. What the president was about to say, goodbye, goodbye, see you another day, was common knowledge, but, understandably enough, people were curious to see just how he was going to extricate himself. Here then is the whole speech, without, of course, given the impossibility of transcribing them into words, the tremor in the voice, the grief-stricken face, the occasional glimmer of a barely repressed tear, I speak to you with my heart in my hands, I speak to you as one torn asunder by the pain of an incomprehensible rift, like a father abandoned by his beloved children, all of us equally confused and perplexed by the extraordinary chain of events that has destroyed our sublime family harmony. And do not say that it was us, that it was me, that it was the government of the nation, along with its elected deputies, who were the ones to break away from the people. It is true that this morning we withdrew to another city which, from henceforth, will be the country's capital, it is true that we imposed on the city that was but no longer is the capital a rigorous state of siege, which will, inevitably, seriously hamper the smooth functioning of an urban area of such importance and of such large physical and social dimensions, it is true that you are currently besieged, surrounded, confined inside the perimeter of the city, that you cannot leave it, and that if you try, you will suffer the consequences of an immediate armed response, but what you will never be able to say is that it is the fault of those to whom the popular will, freely expressed in successive, peaceful, honest, democratic contests, entrusted the fate of the nation so that we could defend it from all dangers, internal and external. You are to blame, yes, you are the ones who have ignominiously rejected national concord in favour of the tortuous road of subversion and indiscipline and in favour of the most perverse and diabolical challenge to the legitimate power of the state ever known in the history of nations. Do not find fault with us, find fault rather with yourselves, not with those who spoke in my name, I am referring, of course, to the government, who again and again asked you, nay, begged and implored you to abandon your wicked obstinacy, whose ultimate meaning, despite the enormous investigatory efforts set in train by the state authorities, remains to this day impenetrable. For centuries and centuries, you were the head of the country and the pride of the nation, for centuries and centuries, in times of national crisis and collective anxiety, our people were accustomed to turn their eyes to this city, to these hills, knowing that thence would come the remedy, the consoling word, the correct path to the future. You have betrayed the memory of your ancestors, that is the harsh truth that will for ever torment your consciences, yes, stone upon stone, they built the altar of the nation, and, shame on you, you chose to tear it down. With all my soul, I want to believe that your madness will prove a transitory one, that it will not last, I want to think that tomorrow, a tomorrow which I pray to heaven will not be long in coming, that tomorrow remorse will seep gently into your hearts and you will become reconciled with legality and with that root of roots, the national community, returning, like the prodigal son, to the paternal home. You are now a lawless city. You will not have a government to tell you what you should and should not do, how you should and should not behave, the streets will be yours, they belong to you, use them as you wish, there will be no authority to stop you in your tracks and offer you sound advice, but equally, and listen carefully to my words, there will be no authority to protect you from thieves, rapists and murderers, that will be your freedom, and may you enjoy it. You may mistakenly imagine that, guided by your free will and by your every whim, you will be able to organise and defend your lives better than we did using the old methods and the old laws. A very grave mistake on your part. Sooner or later, you will be obliged to find leaders to govern you, if they do not irrupt like beasts out of the inevitable chaos into which you will fall and impose their own laws upon you. Then you will realise the tragic nature of your self-deception. Perhaps you will rebel as you did in the days of authoritarian rule, as you did in the grim days of dictatorship, but do not delude yourselves, you will be put down with equal violence, and you will not be called upon to vote because there will be no elections, or if there are, they will not be free, open and honest like the elections you scorned, and so it will be until the day when the armed forces who, along with myself and the national government, today decided to abandon you to your chosen fate, are obliged to return to liberate you from the monsters you yourselves have engendered. All your suffering will have been futile, all your stubbornness in vain, and then you will understand, too late, that rights only exist fully in the words in which they are expressed and on the piece of paper on which they are recorded, whether in the form of a constitution, a law or a regulation, you will understand and, one hopes, be convinced, that their wrong or unthinking application will convulse the most firmly established society, you will understand, at last, that simple common sense tells us to take them as a mere symbol of what could be, but never as a possible, concrete reality. Casting a blank vote is your irrevocable right, and no one will ever deny you that right, but, just as we tell children not to play with matches, so we warn whole peoples of the dangers of playing with dynamite. I will close now. Take the severity of my warnings not as a threat, but as a cautery for the foul political suppuration that you have generated in your own breast and in which you are steeped. You will only see and hear from me again when you deserve the forgiveness which, despite all, we still wish to bestow on you, I, your president, the government which, in happier times, you elected, and those of our people who remain healthy and pure and of whom you are not at present worthy. Until that day, goodbye, and may the lord protect you. The grave, sad face of the president disappeared and in his place stood the raised flag. The wind shook it furiously about as if it were shaking a lunatic, while the anthem repeated the bellicose chords and the martial accents that had been composed in times of unstoppable patriotic pride, but which now sounded somewhat cracked. The man certainly talks well, said the oldest member of the family, and of course he's quite right when he says children shouldn't play with matches, because, as everyone knows, they'll only pee their beds afterwards.

The streets, which, up until then, had been almost deserted, with most of the shops and businesses closed, filled up with people within a matter of minutes. Those who had stayed at home leaned out of the windows to watch the concourse, which is not to say that everyone was heading in the same direction, they resembled, rather, two rivers, one flowing up and one flowing down, and they waved to each other from river to river, as if the city were celebrating, as if it were a local holiday, and, contrary to the fugitive president's ill-intentioned prognostications, there were no thieves or rapists or murderers. Here and there, on some floors of some buildings, the windows remained closed, and, where there were blinds, these were kept grimly drawn, as if the families who lived there were the victims of a painful bereavement. On those floors, no bright lights had been lit in the early hours, at most, the inhabitants would have peered out from behind their curtains, hearts tight with fear, for the people who lived there had very firm political views, they were the people who had voted, both in the first election and the second, for the parties they had always voted for, the party on the right and the party in the middle, they had no reason now to celebrate, on the contrary, they feared attack by the ignorant masses who were singing and shouting in the streets, feared that the sacrosanct doors of their homes would be kicked in, their family memories besmirched, their silver stolen, Let them sing, they'll be crying soon enough, they said to each other to give themselves courage. As for those who voted for the party on the left, the only reason they are not standing at their windows applauding is because they have already joined the crowds, as evidenced in this very street by the occasional flag which, now and then, as if testing the waters, rises above the fast-flowing river of heads. No one went to work. The newspapers in the kiosks sold out, all of them carried the president's speech on the front page, along with a photograph taken while he was giving it, probably, to judge by the pained expression on his face, at the moment when he said he was speaking with his heart in his hands. Very few wasted time reading about something they knew already, most people were more interested in the views of the newspaper editors, the editorialists, the commentators, or some last-minute interview. The main headlines drew the attention of the curious, they were huge, enormous, others, on the inside pages, were normal size, but they all seemed to have sprung from the brain of the same genius of headline synthesis, allowing one blithely to dispense with reading the news item that followed. The headlines were by turns sentimental, Capital City Orphaned Overnight, ironic, Electoral Bombshell Blows Up In Voters' Faces or Blank Voters Blanked By Government, pedagogical, State Teaches Lesson To Insurrectionist Capital, vengeful, Time For A Settling of Accounts, prophetic, Everything Will Be Different From Now On or Nothing Will Ever Be The Same Again, alarmist, Anarchy Just Around The Corner or Suspicious Manoeuvres On Frontier, rhetorical, An Historic Speech For An Historic Moment, fawning, Dignified President Defies Irresponsible Capital, war-like, Army Surrounds City, objective, Withdrawal Of Government Agencies Takes Place Without Incident, radical, City Council Should Assume Total Control, and tactical, Solution Lies In Municipalist Tradition. There were only a few references to the marvellous star, the one with the twenty-seven arms of light, and these were stuck in willy-nilly amongst all the other news, not even graced with a headline, not even an ironic one, not even a sarcastic one, along the lines of And They Complain About The Price Of Electricity. Some of the editorials, while approving of the government's attitude, All Power To Them, urged one of them, dared to express certain doubts about the alleged fairness of the prohibition on leaving the city that had been imposed on the inhabitants, Once again, as always, the just are going to have to pay for the sinners, the honest for the criminals, the worthy men and women of this city who, having scrupulously fulfilled their duty as voters by voting for one of the legally constituted parties that make up the framework of political and ideological options recognised and endorsed by society, now find their freedom of movement restricted because of a freak majority of troublemakers whose one characteristic, some say, is that they don't know what they want, but who, in fact, as we understand it, know perfectly well what they want and are now preparing for a final assault on power. Other editorials went further, calling for the abolition, pure and simple, of the secret ballot and proposing that in future, when the situation returned to normal, as, somehow or other, it was bound to do, every voter should have a record card on which the presiding officer, having first ascertained before the ballot paper was put in the box how the person had voted, would note down, for all legal intents and purposes, both official and personal, that the bearer had voted for this or that party, And which I, the undersigned, hereby declare and confirm to be true. Had such a record card existed, had a legislator, aware of the possibility of the dissolute use of the vote, dared to take that step, bringing together form and content of a totally transparent democratic system, all the people who had voted for the party on the right or the party in the middle would now be packing their bags in order to emigrate to their true homeland, the one that always has its arms wide open to receive those it can most easily clasp to its bosom. Convoys of cars and buses, of minibuses and removal vans, bearing the flags of the different parties and honking rhythmically, p.o.t.r., p.i.t.m., would soon be following the government's example and heading towards the military posts on the frontier, with girls and boys sticking their bottoms out of the windows or yelling at the foot soldiers of the insurrection, You'd better watch your backs, you miserable traitors, You'll get the beating of your life when we come back, you frigging bandits, You rotten sons-of-bitches, or yelling the worst possible insult in the vocabulary of democratic jargon, Illegals, illegals, illegals, which would not, of course, be true, because the people they were abusing would have at home or in their pocket their very own voter's record card, where, ignominiously, as if branded with irons, would be written or stamped I cast a blank vote. Only desperate remedies can cure desperate diseases, concluded the editorialist seraphically.

The celebrations did not last long. It's true that no one actually got around to going to work, but an awareness of the gravity of the situation soon muted the demonstrations of joy, someone even asked, What have we got to be happy about, when they've just put

89

us in isolation as if we were plague victims in quarantine, with an army out there with their rifles cocked, ready to fire at anyone who tries to leave the city, what possible reason have we got to be happy. And others said, We must organise ourselves, but they didn't know how or with whom or why. Some suggested that a group should go and talk to the leader of the city council to offer him their loyal support, to explain that the people who cast the blank votes had not done so in order to bring down the system and to take power, they wouldn't know what to do with it anyway, that they had voted the way they voted because they were disillusioned and could find no other way of making it clear just how disillusioned they were, that they could have staged a revolution, but then many people would undoubtedly have died, something they would never have wanted, that all their lives they had patiently placed their vote in the ballot box, and the results were there for all to see, This isn't democracy, sir, far from it. Others were of the opinion that they should consider the facts more carefully, that it would be best to let the council have the first word, if we go to them with all these explanations and ideas, they'll think there's some political organisation behind it, pulling the strings, and we're the only ones who know that isn't true, they're in a tricky situation too, mind, the government has left them holding a real hot potato, and we don't want to make it any hotter, one newspaper proposed that the council should assume full authority, but what authority, and how, the police have left, there isn't even anyone to direct the traffic, we certainly can't expect the councillors to go out into the streets and do the work of the very people they used to give orders to, there's already talk of the refuse collectors going on strike, if that's true, and we shouldn't be surprised if it is, it can only be seen as a provocation, either on the part of the council itself or, more likely, under orders from the government, they're going to do everything possible to make our lives more difficult, we have to be prepared for anything, including or, perhaps, especially, those things that now seem impossible to us, after all, they're holding the whole deck of cards, not to mention the cards up their sleeves. Others, of a pessimistic and fearful bent, felt that there was no way out of the situation, that they were doomed to failure, it'll all pan out the way it always does, with every man for himself and to hell with the others, the moral imperfection of the human race, as we have often said before, is hardly a novelty, it's historical fact, as old as the hills, it might seem now that we're all very supportive of each other, but tomorrow the bickering will start, and the next stage will be open war, discord, confrontation, while they sit back and enjoy it from their ringside seats, laying bets on how long we'll hold out, it'll be fine while it lasts, my friend, but defeat is certain and guaranteed, I mean, let's be reasonable, who could possibly have thought that something like this would get us what we wanted, people en masse casting blank votes and completely unprompted, it's madness, the government hasn't quite got over its surprise yet and is still trying to catch its breath, but the first victory has gone to them, they've turned their backs on us and told us we're nothing but a pile of shit, which, in their opinion, is what we are, and then there's the pressure from abroad to consider too, I bet you anything you like that right now governments and political parties all around the world are thinking of nothing else, they're not stupid, they can see how easily this could become a fuse, light it here and wait for the explosion over there, but then, if all we are to them is a pile of shit, then let's be shit all the way, shoulder to shoulder, because they're bound to get splattered with some of the shit that we supposedly are.

The next day, the rumour was confirmed, the refuse trucks did not go out onto the streets, the refuse collectors had announced an all-out strike and had made public a demand for more pay which a council spokesperson had immediately pronounced completely unacceptable, still less at a time like this, he said, when our city is grappling with an entirely unprecedented crisis from which it is difficult to see a way out. In the same alarmist vein, a newspaper which, from its inception, had specialised in acting as an amplifier of all governmental strategies and tactics, regardless of the government's party colours, whether from the middle, the right or any shade in between, published an editorial signed by the editor himself in which he stated that it was highly likely that the rebellion by the capital's inhabitants would end in a bloodbath if, as everything seemed to indicate, they refused to abandon their stubborn stance. No one, he said, could deny that the government's patience had been stretched to unthinkable limits, no one could expect them to do more, if they did, we would lose, possibly for ever, that harmonious binomial authority-obedience in whose light the happiest of human societies had always bloomed and without which, as history has amply shown, none of them would have been feasible. The editorial was read, extracts were broadcast on the radio, the editor was interviewed on television, and then, at midday exactly, while all this was going on, from every house in the city there emerged women armed with brooms, buckets and dustpans, and, without a word, they started sweeping their own patch of pavement and street, from the front door as far as the middle of the road, where they encountered other women who had emerged from the houses opposite with exactly the same objective and armed with the same weapons. Now, the dictionaries state that someone's patch is an area under their jurisdiction or control, in this case, the area outside somebody's house, and this is quite true, but they also say, or at least some of them do, that to sweep your own patch means to look after your own interests. A great mistake on your part, O absentminded philologists and lexicographers, to sweep your own patch started out meaning precisely what these women in the capital are doing now, just as their mothers and grandmothers before them used to do in their villages, and they, like these women, were not just looking after their own interests, but after the interests of the community as well. It was possibly for this same reason that, on the third day, the refuse collectors also came out onto the street. They were not in uniform, they were wearing their own clothes. It was the uniforms that were on strike, they said, not them.

THE INTERIOR MINISTER, WHOSE IDEA THE STRIKE HAD BEEN, WAS NOT at all pleased to learn of the refuse collectors' spontaneous return to work, a stance which, in his ministerial understanding of the matter, was not a demonstration of solidarity with the admirable women who had made cleaning their streets a question of honour, a fact unhesitatingly recognised by any impartial observer, but bordered, rather, on criminal complicity. As soon as he received the bad news, he phoned the leader of the city council and commanded him to bring to book those responsible for disregarding orders and to force them to obey, which, in plain language, meant going back on strike, under penalty, if their insubordination continued, of all the punitive consequences foreseen by the laws and regulations, from suspension without pay to outright dismissal. The council leader replied that problems always seem much easier to resolve when seen from a distance, but the person on the ground, the person who actually has to deal with the workers, must listen to them closely before making any decisions, For example, minister, just imagine that I was to give that order to the men, I'm not going to imagine anything, I'm telling you to do it, Yes, minister, of course, but at least allow me to imagine it, for example, I can imagine giving them the order to go back on strike and them telling me to go and take a running jump, what would you do in that case, if you were in my position, how would you force them to do their duty, In the first place, no one would tell me to take a running jump, in the second place, I am not and never will be in your position, I am a minister, not a council leader, and while I'm on the subject, I would just like to say that I would expect from a council leader not only the official and institutional collaboration to which he is, by law, committed and which is my natural due, but also an esprit de corps which, it seems to me, is currently conspicuous by its absence, You can always count on my official and institutional collaboration, minister, I know my obligations, but as for esprit de corps, perhaps we'd better not talk about that just now, let's see how much of it is left when this crisis is over, You're running away from the problem, council leader, No, I'm not, minister, I simply need you to tell me how I am supposed to force the workers to go back on strike, That's your problem, not mine, Now it's my esteemed party colleague who is trying to run away from the problem, Never in my entire political career have I run away from a problem, Well, you're running away from this one, you're trying to run away from the obvious fact that I have no means at my disposal by which to carry out your order, unless you want me to call in the police, but, in that case, I would remind you that the police are not here, they left the city along with the army, both of them carried off by the government, besides, I'm sure we would agree that it would be a gross abnormality to use the police to persuade workers to go on strike, when, in the past, they have always been deployed to break strikes up, by infiltration or other less subtle means, Well, I'm astonished to hear a member of the party on the right talking like that, Minister, in a few hours' time it will be dark, and I will have to say that it is night, I would have to be either stupid or blind to say then that it is day, What has that got to do with the strike, Whether you like it or not, minister, it is night now, pitch-black night, we know that something is happening that goes far beyond our understanding, that exceeds our meagre experience, but we are behaving as if it were the same old bread, made with the usual flour and cooked in the usual oven, but it's simply not true, You know, I will

95

seriously have to consider asking you to tender your resignation, If you do, it will be a weight off my shoulders, and you can count on my profound gratitude. The interior minister did not reply at once, he allowed a few seconds to pass in order to recover his composure, then he asked, So what do you think we should do, Nothing, My dear fellow, in a situation like this, you cannot ask a government to do nothing, Allow me to say that in a situation like this, a government doesn't govern, it just looks as if it were governing, There I must disagree, we've managed to do a few things since this whole thing began, Yes, we're like a fish on a hook, we thrash about, we shake the line, we tug at it, but we cannot understand how a little piece of bent wire could be capable of catching us and keeping us trapped, we might yet escape, I'm not saying we won't, but we risk ending up with the hook stuck in our gut, Frankly, I'm confused, There is only one thing to do, What's that, didn't you just say there was no point in our doing anything, Just pray that the prime minister's strategy works, What strategy, Leave them to simmer, he said, but I'm afraid even that could rebound against us, Why, Because they are the ones doing the cooking, So we do nothing, Let's be serious, minister, would the government be prepared to put an end to this farcical state of siege by ordering the army and the air force in to attack the city, to wound and kill ten or twenty thousand people just to set an example, and then put three or four thousand more in prison, accused of no one quite knows what because no real crime has been committed, This isn't a civil war, all we want is to make people see reason, to show them the error into which they have fallen or were made to fall, that's what we need to do, to make them realise that the unfettered use of the blank ballot paper would make the democratic system unworkable, The results so far haven't, it would seem, been exactly brilliant, It will take time, but people will, in the end, see the light, Why, minister, I had no idea you had mystical tendencies, My dear fellow, when situations become as complicated and as desperate as this, we tend to grab hold of anything, I'm even convinced that some of my colleagues in government, if they thought it would do any good, wouldn't be averse to going on a pilgrimage to a shrine, candle in hand, to make a vow, While we're on the subject, I would appreciate you and your candle visiting a few shrines here of a rather different nature, Meaning, Can you please tell the newspapers and the television and radio people not to pour more petrol on the bonfire, if we don't act sensibly and intelligently, this whole thing could explode, you must have heard that the editor of the government newspaper was stupid enough to admit the possibility that this could all end in a bloodbath, It's not a government newspaper, If you'll allow me to say so, minister, I would have preferred to hear some other comment from you, The little man went too far, he overstepped the mark, it's what always happens when someone tries to do more than he was asked to do, Minister, Yes, What shall I do about the council refuse collectors, Let them work, that way the city council will look good in the eyes of the populace and that could prove useful to us in the future, besides, the strike was, of course, only one element in the strategy, and certainly not the most important, It wouldn't be good for the city, now or in the future, if the city council were to be used as a weapon of war against its citizens, In a situation like this, the council can't afford to remain on the sidelines, the council is, after all, part of this country and no other, But I'm not asking you to let us remain on the sidelines, all I ask is that the government doesn't put any obstacles in my way when it comes to exercising my responsibilities, that it should, at no point, give the public the impression that the city council is merely a tool, if you'll forgive the expression, of its repressive policies, firstly, because it isn't true, and secondly, because it never will be, Um, I'm afraid I don't quite understand or perhaps I understand all too well, One day, minister, although when I don't know, this city will once again be the country's capital, That's possible, but by no means certain, it depends how far they want to take their rebellion, Be that as it may, it is vital that this council, whether with me as leader or with someone else, should never be seen, however indirectly, to be an accomplice in or a co-author of a bloody repression, the government that orders such a repression will have no alternative but to take the consequences, but the council, this council, belongs to the city, the city does not belong to the council, I hope I have made myself clear, minister, You've made yourself so clear that I'm going to ask you a question, Feel free, minister, Did you cast a blank vote, Could you repeat the question, please, I didn't quite hear, I asked if you cast a blank vote, I asked if the ballot paper you put in the box was blank, Who can say, minister, who can say, When all this is over, I hope we can meet and have a long conversation, As you wish, minister, Goodbye, Goodbye, What I'd really like to do is come over there and give you a clip round the ear, Alas, I'm too old for that, minister, If you ever become interior minister, you will learn that clips round the ear and other such correctives have no age limit, Don't let the devil hear you, minister, The devil has such good hearing he doesn't need things to be spoken out loud, Well, god help us then, There's no point asking him for help either, he was born stone-deaf.

Thus ended this illuminating and prickly conversation between the interior minister and the council leader, with each having bandied about points of view, arguments and opinions which will, in all probability, have disoriented the reader, who must now doubt that the two interlocutors do in fact belong, as he or she thought, to the party on the right, the very party which, as the administrative power, is carrying out a vile policy of repression, both on a collective level, with the capital city submitted to the humiliation of a state of siege ordered by the country's own government, and on an individual level, with harsh interrogations, lie detectors, threats and, who knows, the very worst kinds of torture, although the truth impels us to say that if any such tortures were carried out, we could not bear witness to them, we were not there, not, however, that this means very much, for we were not present either at the parting of the red sea, and yet everyone swears that it happened. As for the interior minister, you must already have noticed that in the armour of the indomitable fighter, which he tries so hard to appear to be when locked in combat with the defence minister, there is a subtle fault, or to put it more colloquially, a crack big enough to poke your finger through. Were that not so, we would not have been witness to the successive failures of his plans, and the speed and facility with which the blade of his sword grows blunt, as this dialogue has just confirmed, for while he came in like lion, he went out like a lamb, if not something worse, one has only to look, for example, at the lack of respect evident in his categorical statement that god was born stone-deaf. As regards the council leader, we are, to use the words of the interior minister, pleased to note that he has seen the light, not the one the minister would like the capital's voters to see, but the light that those casters of blank votes hope that someone will begin to see. The most common occurrence in this world of ours, in these days of stumbling blindly forwards, is to come across men and women mature in years and ripe in prosperity, who, at eighteen, were not just beaming beacons of style, but also, and perhaps above all, bold revolutionaries determined to bring down the system supported by their parents and to replace it, at last, with a fraternal paradise, but who are now equally firmly attached to convictions and practices which, having warmed up and flexed their muscles on any of the many available versions of moderate conservatism, become, in time, pure egotism of the most obscene and reactionary kind. Put less respectfully, these men and these women, standing before the mirror of their life, spit every day in the face of what they were with the sputum of what they are. The fact that a politician belonging to the party on the right, a man in his forties, who has spent his whole life under the parasol of a tradition cooled by the air-conditioning of the stock exchange and lulled by the steamy zephyr of the markets, should have been open to the revelation, or, indeed, manifest certainty, that there was some deeper meaning behind the gentle rebellion in the city he had been appointed to administer, is something that is both worthy of record and deserving of our gratitude, so unaccustomed have we become to such singular phenomena.

It will not have gone unnoticed, by particularly exacting readers and listeners, that the narrator of this fable has paid scant, not to say non-existent, attention to the place in which the action described, albeit in rather leisurely fashion, is taking place. Apart from the first chapter, in which there were a few careful brush-strokes applied to the area of the polling station, although, even then, these were applied only to doors, windows and tables, and with the exception of the polygraph, that machine for catching liars, everything else, which is quite a lot, has passed as if the characters in the story inhabited an entirely insubstantial world, were indifferent to the comfort or discomfort of the places in which they found themselves, and did nothing but talk. In the room in which the government of the country has, more than once, and occasionally with the presence and participation of the president, gathered to debate the situation and take the necessary measures to pacify minds and restore peace to the streets, there would doubt-less be a large table around which the ministers would sit on comfortable, upholstered chairs, and on which there were bound to be bottles of mineral water and glasses to match, pencils and pens in different colours, markers, reports, books on legislation, notebooks, microphones, telephones, and all the usual parapher-nalia one finds in places of this calibre. There would be ceiling lights and wall lights, there would be padded doors and curtained windows, there would be rugs on the floor, there would be paintings on the walls and perhaps an antique or modern tapestry, there would, inevitably, be a portrait of the president, a bust representing the republic and the national flag. None of this has been mentioned, nor will it be mentioned in future. Even here, in the more modest, but nonetheless spacious office of the leader of the city council, with a balcony overlooking the square and a large aerial photograph of the city hanging on the main wall, there would be ample opportunity to fill a page or two with detailed descriptions, and to make the most of that generous pause in order to take a deep breath before confronting the disasters to come. It seems to us far more important to observe the anxious lines furrowing the brow of the council leader, perhaps he is thinking that he said too much, that he gave the interior minister the impression, if not the stark certainty, that he had joined the ranks of the enemy, and that, by his imprudence, he would, perhaps irremediably, have compromised his political career inside and outside the party. The other possibility, as remote as it is unimaginable, would be that his reasoning might have given the interior minister a push in the right direction and caused him to rethink entirely the strategies and tactics with which the government hopes to put an end to the sedition. We see him shake his head, a sure sign that, having swiftly examined the possibility, he has discarded it as being foolishly ingenuous and dangerously unrealistic. He got up from the chair where he had remained seated throughout his conversation with the minister and went over to the window. He did not open it, he merely drew back the curtain a little and gazed out. The square looked as it always did, various passers-by, three people sitting on a bench in the shade of a tree, the café terraces and their customers, the flower-sellers, a woman and a dog, the newspaper kiosks, buses, cars, the usual scene. I need to go out, he thought. He went back to his desk and phoned his chief administrative officer, I'm going out for a while, he said, tell any councillors who are in the building, but only if they ask for me, as for the rest, I leave you in charge, Certainly, sir, I'll tell your driver to bring the car round to the front door, Yes, if you would, but tell him that I won't be needing him, I'll drive myself, Will you be coming back to the town hall today, Yes, I hope so, but I'll let you know if I decide otherwise, Very well, How are things in the city, Oh, nothing very grave to report, the news we've received has been no more serious than usual, a few traffic accidents, the occasional bottleneck, a minor fire in which no one was hurt, a failed bank robbery, How did they manage, now that there are no police, The robber was an amateur, and the gun, although it was a real one, wasn't loaded, Where have they taken him, The people who disarmed him took him to a fire station, Whatever for, they haven't any facilities for detaining prisoners, Well, they had to put him somewhere, So what happened next, Apparently, the firemen spent an hour giving him a good talking-to and then let him go, There wasn't much else they could do, I suppose, No, sir, there wasn't, Tell my secretary to let me know when the car arrives, Yes, sir. The council leader leaned back in his chair, waiting, and his brow was again deeply furrowed. Contrary to the predictions of the gloommongers, there had been no more robberies, rapes or murders than before. It seemed that the police were, after all, not essential for the city's security, that the population itself, spontaneously and in a more or less organised manner, had taken over their work as vigilantes. The robbery at the bank was a case in point. No, the robbery at the bank, he thought, was irrelevant, the man had obviously been very nervous and unsure of himself, a mere novice, and the bank employees had seen that they were in no danger, but tomorrow it might be different, what am I saying, tomorrow, today, right now, over the last few days crimes will have been committed in the city that will obviously go unpunished, if we have no police, if the criminals aren't arrested, if there's no investigation and no trial, if the judges go home and the courts don't work, criminality will inevitably increase, it's as if everyone were expecting the council to take over the policing of the city, they're asking for it, demanding it, protesting that without some form of security, there can be no peace of mind, and I keep wondering how, by issuing a call for volunteers, for example, by creating urban militias, surely we're not going to go out into the street dressed like gendarmes straight out of a comic opera, with uniforms rented from the theatre's costume department, and what about guns, where are we going to get those, and what about using them, not just knowing how to use them, but being capable of using them, taking out a gun and firing it, can anyone imagine me, the councillors, the town hall civil servants, engaged in a rooftop pursuit of the midnight murderer, the Tuesday rapist or the white-gloved cat burglar of high-society salons. The phone rang, it was his secretary, Sir, your car is here, Thank you, he said, I'm going out now and I'm not sure yet whether I'll be back today or not, but if there are any problems, just call me on my mobile, Take care, sir, Why do you say that, Given the way things are, sir, that's the least we can wish each other, May I ask you a question, Of course, as long as I have an answer for it, If you don't want to, don't answer, What's the question, Who did you vote for, No one, sir, Do you mean you abstained, No, I mean that I cast a blank vote, Blank, Yes, sir, blank, And you're telling me just like that, You asked me the question just like that, And that gave you the confidence to reply, Just about, sir, but only just, If I understand you rightly, you also thought it could be a risk, Well, I hoped that it wouldn't be, As you see, your confidence was rewarded, Does that mean that I won't be asked to hand in my notice, No, you can sleep easy on that score, It would be far better if we didn't need to sleep in order to feel at ease, sir, Well put, Anyone could have said the same, sir, it certainly wouldn't win any literary prizes, You will have to be satisfied with my applause, then, That's reward enough, sir, So let's leave it that if you need me, you can call me on my mobile, Yes, sir, Right, then, I'll see you tomorrow, if not later on today, Yes, see you later, or tomorrow, replied the secretary.

The council leader quickly tidied up the papers scattered about his desk, most of them might have been written about another country and another century, not about this capital now, under a state of siege, abandoned by its own government, surrounded by its own army. If he tore them up, if he burned them, if he threw them in the wastepaper basket, no one would come to him demanding an explanation for what he had done, people had far more important things to think about now, the city, after all, is no longer part of the known world, it's a pot full of putrefying food and maggots, an island set adrift in a sea not its own, a dangerous source of infection, a place which, as a precautionary measure, has been quarantined until the plague becomes less virulent or until it runs out of people to kill and ends up devouring itself. He asked his secretary to bring him his raincoat, picked up his briefcase containing papers to be studied at home and went downstairs. The driver, who was waiting for him, opened the car door, They said you won't be needing me, sir, No, I won't, you can go home, See you tomorrow, then, sir, See you tomorrow. It's odd how we spend every day of our life saying goodbye, saying and hearing others say see you tomorrow when, inevitably, on one of those days, which will be someone's last, either the person we said it to will no longer be here, or we who said it will not. We will see if on today's tomorrow, what we normally refer to as the following day, when the council leader and his chauffeur meet again, they will be capable of grasping what an extraordinary, near-miraculous thing it is to have said see you tomorrow and to find that what had been no more than a problematic possibility has come to pass as if it had been a certainty. The council leader got into his car. He was going for a drive around the city, to have a look at the people on the way, not in any hurry, but stopping now and then to get out and walk for a while, listening to what was being said, in short, taking the pulse of the city, assessing the strength of the incubating fever. From his childhood reading he remembered a king in some far eastern country, he wasn't sure now whether he had been a king or an emperor, he was, more than likely, the caliph of the time, who was in the habit of disguising himself and leaving his palace to go and mingle with the ordinary people, the lower orders, and to eavesdrop on what was said about him during frank exchanges in the squares and streets. The truth is that such exchanges would not have been as frank as all that, because in those days, as ever, there would have been no shortage of spies to take note of opinions, complaints and criticisms and of any embryonic conspiracies. It is an unvarying rule for those in power that, when it comes to heads, it is best to cut them off before they start to think, afterwards, it might be too late. The council leader is not the king of this besieged city, and as for the vizier of the interior, he has exiled himself to the other side of the frontier and he will, at this moment, doubtless be in some meeting with his collaborators, we will find out who and why in a while. For this reason the council leader does not need to disguise himself with a false beard and moustache, the face he is wearing is the one he usually wears, except that it looks a little more preoccupied than normal, as we have noticed before from the lines on his forehead. A few people recognise him, but few say hello. Do not assume, however, that the indifferent or the hostile are to be found only amongst those who originally cast blank votes, and who would, therefore, see him as an adversary, quite a few voters from his own party and from the party in the middle also look at him with ill-disguised suspicion, not to say with clear antipathy, What's he doing around here, they will think, what's he doing mixing with this rabble of blankers, he should be at work earning his salary, perhaps now that the majority has changed hands, he's come looking for votes, well, if he has, he hasn't got a hope in hell, there won't be any elections round here for a while, if I was the government, I know what I would do, I'd get rid of this whole council and instead appoint a decent administrative committee, who could be trusted politically. Before continuing this story, it would be as well to explain that the use of the word blanker a few lines earlier was neither accidental nor fortuitous, nor was it a slip of the fingers on the computer keyboard, and it certainly isn't a neologism that the narrator has hastily invented in order to fill a gap. The term exists, it really does, you can find it in any up-to-date dictionary, the problem, if it is a problem, lies in the fact that people are convinced that they know the meaning of the word blank and of all its derivatives, and therefore won't waste their time going back to the source to check, or else they suffer from chronic intellectual lazyitis and stay right where they are, refusing to take even one step towards making a possibly beautiful discovery. No one knows who in the city first came up with it, which inquisitive researcher or chance discoverer, but one thing is certain, the word spread rapidly and immediately took on the pejorative meaning that its very appearance seems to provoke. Although we may not previously have mentioned the fact, which is in every way deplorable, even the media, especially the state television channels, are already using the word as if it were one of the very worst of obscenities. When you see it written down, you don't notice it so much, but as soon as you hear it spoken with that angry curl of the lips and in that snide tone of voice, you would have to have the moral armour of a knight of the round table not to put a noose around your neck, don a penitent's tunic and walk along beating your chest and renouncing all your old principles and precepts, A blanker I was, a blanker no more, forgive me, my country, forgive me, my lord. The council leader, who will have nothing to forgive, since he is no one's lord and never will be, who will not even be a candidate at the next elections, has stopped watching the passers-by, he is looking now for signs of shabbiness, neglect, decline, and, at least at a first glance, he can find none. The shops and department stores are all open, although they don't appear to be doing much business, the traffic is flowing, impeded only by the occasional minor jam, there are no queues of anxious customers at the doors of the banks, the kind of queue that always forms in time of crisis, everything seems to be normal, there are no violent muggings, no shoot-outs or knife-fights, there is nothing but this luminous afternoon, neither too cold nor too hot, an afternoon that seems to have come into the world to satisfy all desires and to calm all anxieties. But not the council leader's unease or, to be more literary, his inner disquiet. What he feels, and he may be the only person amongst those passing by to feel this, is a kind of menace floating in the air, the kind that sensitive temperaments feel when the thick clouds covering the sky grow tense with waiting for the thunderbolt to fall, or as we might feel when a door creaked open in the darkness and a current of icy air brushed our cheek, when an awful feeling of foreboding opened the gates of despair to us, when a diabolical laugh sundered the delicate veil of the soul. Nothing concrete, nothing we could describe with any authority or objectivity, but the fact is that the council leader has to make a real effort not to stop the first person who passes and say to him, Be careful, don't ask me why or about what, just be careful, I've got a feeling that something bad is going to happen, If you, the council leader, with all your responsibilities, don't know, how do you expect me to, they would ask him, It doesn't matter, what matters is that you should be very careful, Is it some epidemic, No, I don't think so, An earthquake, This isn't an area prone to earthquakes, there's never been one here, A flood, then, a deluge, It's been years since the river broke its banks, What then, Look, I don't know, Forgive me for asking, You're forgiven before you've even asked, No offence, sir, but have you perhaps had one drink too many, you know what they say, the last one is always the worst, No, I only drink at mealtimes, and then only in moderation, I'm certainly not an alcoholic, Well, in that case, I don't understand, When it's happened, you will, When what has happened, The thing that is going to happen. Bewildered, his interlocutor glanced around him, If you're looking for a policeman to arrest me, said the council leader, don't bother, they've all gone, No, I wasn't looking for a policeman, lied the other man, I'd arranged to meet a friend here, oh, there he is, see you again, then, sir, and take care, you know, to be perfectly frank, if I were you, I'd go straight home to bed, when you sleep you forget everything, But I never go to sleep at this hour, As my cat would say, all hours are good for sleeping, May I ask you a question too, Of course, sir, feel free, Did you cast a blank vote, Are you doing a survey, No, I'm just curious, but if you'd rather not answer, don't. The man hesitated for a second, then, very gravely, he replied, Yes, I did, it's not, as far as I know, forbidden to do so, No, it's not forbidden, but look at the result. The man seemed to have forgotten about his imaginary friend, Look, sir, I have nothing against you personally, I'm even prepared to acknowledge that you've done a good job on the city council, but I'm not to blame for what you call the result, I voted as I wanted to vote, within the law, now it's up to you, the council, to respond, if the potato's too hot, blow on it, Don't get upset, I just wanted to warn you, You still haven't told me about what, Even if I wanted to, I couldn't, Then I've been wasting my time here, Forgive me, your friend's waiting for you, There isn't any friend waiting, I was just using that as an excuse to get away, Then thank you for having stayed a little longer, Sir, Please don't stand on ceremony, From what I know about what goes on in people's minds, I would say that it's your conscience that's troubling you, For something I didn't do, Some people say that's the worst kind of remorse, for something you allowed to happen, Maybe you're right, I'll think about that, but, anyway, be careful, I will, sir, and thank you for the warning, Even though you still don't know what I'm warning you against, Some people deserve our trust, You're the second person who's said that to me today, Then you can safely say that you've had a very good day indeed, Thank you, See you again, sir, Yes, see you again.

The council leader walked back to where he had parked his car, he was pleased, at least he had managed to warn one person, if the man passed the word on, then in a matter of hours, the whole city would be on the alert, ready for whatever might happen, I'm clearly not in my right mind, he thought, the man won't say anything to anyone, he's not a fool like me, well, it's not foolishness exactly, the fact that I felt a threat I'm incapable of defining is my problem, not his, I should just take his advice and go home, any day during which we've been offered a piece of good advice can never be considered to have been wasted. He got into his car and phoned his office to say that he wouldn't be going back to the town hall. He lived in a street in the centre, not far from the overground metro station that served a large part of the eastern sector of the city. His wife, who is a surgeon, will not be at home, she's on night duty at the hospital, and as for their two children, the boy is in the army, he might even be one of the men defending the frontier with a heavy machine-gun at the ready and a gas mask hanging round his neck, and the girl works abroad as a secretary-cum-interpreter for an international organisation, of the sort that always build their vast, luxurious headquarters in the most important cities, important politically speaking, of course. She, at least, will have benefited from having a father well placed in the official system of favours received and paid back, made and returned. Since even the very best advice is, at best, only ever half-obeyed, the council leader did not go to bed. He looked through the papers he'd brought home with him, made decisions about some of them and put others aside for further examination. When supper time approached, he went into the kitchen, opened the fridge, but found nothing that he fancied eating. His wife had prepared something for him, she wouldn't let him go hungry, but the effort of laying the table, heating up the food and then washing the dishes seemed to him tonight a superhuman one. He left the house and went to a restaurant. When he had sat down at a table and while he was waiting for his food to come, he phoned his wife. How's work, he asked her, Oh, not too bad, how about you, Oh, I'm fine, just a bit anxious, Well, in the current situation, I hardly need ask you why, No, it's more than that, a kind of inner shudder, a shadow, a bad omen, Hm, I had no idea you were superstitious, There's a time for everything, Where are you, I can hear voices, In a restaurant, I'll go home afterwards, or perhaps I'll drop in and see you first, being council leader opens many doors, But I might be in the operating theatre and I'm not sure how long I'll be, All right, I'll think about it, lots of love, And to you too, Loads, Tons. The waiter brought him his first course, Here you are, sir, enjoy your meal. He was just raising his fork to his mouth when an explosion shook the whole building, the glass in the windows inside and out shattered, tables and chairs were overturned, people were screaming and groaning, some were injured, others were stunned by the blast, others were trembling with fright. The council leader was bleeding from a cut to his face caused by a piece of glass. The restaurant had obviously been hit by the shock wave from an explosion. It must have been in the metro station, sobbed a woman struggling to get to her feet. Pressing a napkin to his wound, the council leader ran out into the street. Broken glass crunched beneath his feet, up ahead rose a thick column of black smoke, he thought he could even see the glow of flames, It happened, it's at the station, he thought. He had discarded the napkin when he realised that holding his hand to his head was slowing him down, now the blood was running freely down his face and neck and soaking into his shirt collar. Wondering if the service would still be working, he stopped for a moment to dial the emergency number on his mobile phone, but the nervous-sounding voice that answered told him that the incident had already been reported, It's the council leader here, a bomb has exploded in the main overground station in the eastern part of the city, send all the help you can, firemen, civil defence people, scouts, if there are any, nurses, ambulances, first-aid equipment, whatever you have to hand, oh, and another thing, if there is some way of finding out where any retired police officers live, call them too and ask them to come and help, The firemen are already on their way, sir, we're doing everything we can do. He rang off and started running again. Other people were running alongside him, some overtook him, his legs felt like lead and it was as if his lungs were refusing to breathe the thick, malodorous air, and a pain, a pain that rapidly fixed itself in his trachea, kept getting worse and worse. The station was about fifty metres away now, the grey, grubby smoke, illuminated by the fire, rose up in furious tangled skeins. How many dead will there be inside, who planted the bomb, the council leader was asking himself. The sirens of the fire engines could be heard getting closer now, the mournful wailing, more like someone asking for help than bringing it, grew shriller and shriller, at any moment now they will come hurtling round one of these corners. The first vehicle appeared as the council leader was pushing his way through the crowd of people who had rushed to see the disaster, I'm the council leader, he said, I'm the leader of the city council, let me through, please, and he felt painfully foolish having to repeat this over and over, aware that the fact of being council leader would not open all doors to him, indeed, inside, there were people for whom the doors of life had closed once and for all. Within minutes, great jets of water were being projected through openings that had once been doorways and windows, or were aimed up into the air to soak the upper part of the buildings in order to reduce the risk of the fire spreading. The council leader went over to the chief fire officer, What do you make of it, he asked, It's the worst fire I've ever seen, in fact, it has a distinct whiff of arson about it, Don't say that, it's not possible, It may just be an impression, let's hope I'm wrong. At that moment, a television recording van arrived, followed by others from the press and the radio, now, surrounded by lights and microphones, the council leader is answering questions, How many lives do you think will have been lost, What information do you have so far, How many people have been injured, How many people have suffered burns, When do you think the station will be back to normal, Have you any idea who might have been behind the attack, Was any warning received before the explosion, If so, who received it and what measures were taken to evacuate the station in time, Do you think it was a terrorist attack carried out by a group with links to the subversive movement active in the city, Do you think there will be more such attacks, As council leader and sole authority left in the city, what means do you have to carry out the necessary investigations. When the rain of questions had stopped, the council leader gave the only possible reply in the circumstances, Some of these questions are outside my competence, and so I can't really answer them, I assume, however, that the government will be making an official statement soon, as for the other questions, all I can say is that we are doing everything humanly possible to help the victims, let's just hope we get there in time, at least for some of them, But how many dead are there, insisted a journalist, We'll only know that when we go into that inferno, so, until then, please, spare me any more stupid questions. The journalists protested that this was no way to treat the media, who were, after all, only fulfilling their duty to inform and therefore deserved to be treated with respect, but the council leader cut short this corporate speech, One of the newspapers today went so far as to call for a bloodbath, that didn't happen this time, the burned don't bleed, they just get fried to a crisp, now, please, let me through, I have nothing more to add, we'll let you know when we have any concrete information. There was a general murmur of disapproval, and further back a sneering voice said, Who does he think he is, but the council leader made no attempt to find out who the dissenter was, during the last few hours, he, too, had done nothing but ask, Who do I think I am.

Two hours later, the fire was declared to be under control, the intense heat from the charred ruins took another two hours to abate, but it was still impossible to know how many people had died. About thirty or forty people were taken to hospital, suffering from injuries of varying degrees of severity, having escaped the worst of the blast because they had been in a part of the ticket hall farthest from the place where the bomb had exploded. The council leader remained there until the fire had died down completely, and he only left when the fire chief told him, Go and rest, sir, leave us to deal with things, and do something about that cut on your face, I can't understand why no one here noticed it, It's all right, they had more serious things on their minds. Then he asked, And now, Now we have to locate and remove the bodies, some will have been blown to pieces, most will have been burned, Yes, I don't know if I could bear that, In your present state, I don't think you could either, I'm a coward, It's not cowardice, sir, even I passed out the first time, Thank you, do what you can, All I can do is put out the last burning ember, which is nothing, At least you'll be here. Covered in soot, his cheek black with dried blood, he started walking grimly back home. His whole body ached, from running, from nervous tension, from being on his feet for hours. There was no point trying to phone his wife, the person who answered would doubtless tell him, I'm sorry, sir, your wife is in the operating theatre, she can't come to the phone. On either side of the road, people were looking out of their windows, but no one recognised him. A real council leader travels in his official car, has a secretary with him to carry his briefcase, three bodyguards to clear a path for him, but the man walking along the street is a filthy, stinking tramp, a sad man on the verge of tears, a ghost to whom no one would even lend a bucket of water in which to wash his sheet. The mirror in the lift revealed to him the blackened face he would have had now if he had been in the ticket hall when the bomb exploded, Horror, horror, he murmured. He opened the door with tremulous hands and went straight to the bathroom. He took the first-aid box out of the cabinet, the packet of cotton wool, the hydrogen peroxide, some liquid disinfectant containing iodine, some large sticking plasters. He said to himself, It probably needs a few stitches. His shirt was stained with blood all the way down to the waistband of his trousers, I bled more than I thought. He took off his jacket, painfully undid the sticky knot of his tie and took off his shirt. His vest was stained with blood too, I should have a wash, get in the shower, no, don't be ridiculous, that would just wash away the dried blood covering the wound and start it bleeding again, he said softly, I should, yes, I should, I should what. The word was like a dead body he had stumbled upon, he had to find out what the word wanted, he had to remove the body. The firemen and the civil defence people are going into the station. They are carrying stretchers and wearing protective gloves, most of them have never before touched a burned body, now they will know what it is like. I should. He went out of the bathroom and into his study, where he sat down at his desk. He picked up the phone and dialled a confidential number. It is almost three o'clock in the morning. A voice answers, The interior minister's office, who's calling, It's the leader of the city council in the capital, I'd like to speak to the minister, it's extremely urgent, if he's in, can you please put me straight through to him, One moment, please. The moment lasted two minutes, Hello, A few hours ago, minister, a bomb exploded in the overground train station in the eastern sector of the city, we don't yet know how many people have died, but everything indicates that the death toll will be high, there are already about forty or fifty wounded, Yes, I know, The reason I'm phoning you now is that I've been at the scene of the explosion all this time, Very commendable. The council leader took a deep breath, then asked, Haven't you anything to say to me, minister, What do you mean, About who could have planted the bomb, Well, it seems fairly obvious, your friends who cast the blank votes have clearly decided to go in for a bit of direct action, Sorry, but I don't believe that, Whether you believe it or not, that is the truth, Is or will be, You can make up your own mind about that, What happened here, minister, was a heinous crime, Yes, I suppose you're right, that's what people usually call it, Who planted the bomb, minister, You seem upset, why don't you get some rest and call me when it gets light, but not before ten o'clock, Who planted the bomb, minister, What are you trying to insinuate, A question is not an insinuation, it would be an insinuation if I were to tell you what we are both thinking at this moment, There's no reason on earth why my thoughts should coincide with those of the leader of a municipal council. Well, they do this time, Careful now, you're going too far, Oh, I'm not just going too far, I've arrived, What do you mean, That I am speaking to the person directly responsible for the blast, You're mad, If only I was, How dare you cast aspersions on a member of the government, it's unheard of, From now on, minister, I am no longer the council leader of this besieged city, We'll talk tomorrow, but bear in mind that I have no intention of accepting your resignation, You'll have to accept it, just pretend that I died, In that case, I warn you, in the name of the government, that you will bitterly regret doing so, in fact, you won't even have time to regret it if you don't keep quiet about this whole affair, but that shouldn't prove too difficult, given that you say you're dead,

Yes, I never imagined anyone could be so dead. The communication was cut at the other end. The man who had been the council leader got up and went into the bathroom. He took off his clothes and stood under the shower. The hot water quickly washed away the dried blood that had formed over the wound and the blood began to flow again. The firemen have just found the first charred body.

TWENTY-THREE DEATHS SO FAR, AND WE'VE NO IDEA HOW MANY MORE they'll find under the rubble, that's at least twenty-three deaths, interior minister, said the prime minister, bringing the flat of his hand down on the newspapers that lay open on his desk, The media are almost unanimous in attributing the attack to some terrorist group with links to the insurrection by the blankers, sir, Firstly, purely as a matter of good taste, please do me the great favour of not using the word blanker in my presence, secondly, please explain what you mean by the expression almost unanimous, It means that there are only two exceptions, two newspapers who do not accept the version that is doing the rounds and who are demanding a proper investigation, Interesting, Read what this one says, sir. The prime minister read out loud, We Demand To Know Who Gave The Order, And this one, sir, less direct, but along the same lines, We Want The Truth Whoever It May Hurt. The interior minister went on, It's nothing to get alarmed about, I don't think we need worry, in fact, it's rather a good thing that there should be a few doubts, that way people can't say they're all speaking with their master's voice, Do you mean that twenty-three or more deaths don't worry you, It was a calculated risk, sir, In the light of what happened, a very badly calculated one, Yes, I suppose you could see it like that, We assumed it would be a less powerful bomb, just something to give people a bit of a fright, There was clearly an unfortunate failure in the chain of command, If only I could be sure that was the only reason, The order was, I can assure you, correctly given, you have my word, sir, Your word, interior minister, For what it's worth, sir, Yes, for what it's worth, In either case, we knew there would be deaths, But not twenty-three, Even if there had been only three, they would have been no less dead than these twenty-three, it isn't a question of numbers, No, but it is also a question of numbers, May I remind you that he who wills the ends, wills the means, Oh, I've heard that refrain many times before, And this won't be the last time, even if, next time, you hear it from someone else's lips, Appoint a commission of enquiry at once, minister, To reach what conclusions, prime minister, Just set it to work, we'll sort that out later, Very good, sir, Give all necessary help to the families of the victims, both those who died and those who are currently in hospital, tell the council to take charge of the funerals, In the midst of all this confusion, I forgot to inform you that the council leader has resigned, Resigned, why, Well, to be more precise, he walked out, At this precise moment, I don't really care whether he resigned or walked out, my question is why, He arrived at the station immediately after the explosion took place and his nerve went, he couldn't cope with what he saw, No one could, I know I couldn't, indeed, I imagine even you couldn't, minister, so there must be some other reason for his abrupt departure, He thinks the government is responsible, and he didn't just hint at his suspicions either, he was quite explicit about it, Do you think he was the one who passed the idea on to those two newspapers, Frankly, prime minister, I don't, and, believe you me, I would love to be able to lay the blame at his door, What will the man do now, His wife is a doctor, Yes, I know her, They'll have to get by until he finds a new job, And meanwhile, Meanwhile, prime minister, I will keep him under the strictest possible surveillance, if that's what you mean, Whatever was the man thinking of, he seemed so trustworthy, a loyal party member, with an excellent political career, a future, The minds of human beings are not always entirely at one with the world in which they

118

live, some people have trouble adjusting to reality, basically they're just weak, confused spirits who use words, sometimes very skilfully, to justify their cowardice, You're obviously something of an expert on the subject, did you glean all this from your own experiences, If I had, would I be in the post of interior minister, No, I suppose not, but everything is possible in this world, no doubt our finest torture specialists kiss their children when they get home, and some may even cry at the cinema, And I sir, am no exception, in fact, I'm just an old sentimentalist really, Glad to hear it. The prime minister leafed slowly through the newspapers, he looked at the photographs one by one with a mixture of repugnance and apprehension, and said, You probably want to know why I don't sack you, Yes, sir, I'm curious to know your reasons, Because if I did, people would think one of two things, either that, independent of the nature and degree of guilt, I considered you directly responsible for what had happened, or that I was quite simply punishing you for your supposed incompetence for not having foreseen the possibility of such an act of violence in abandoning the capital to its fate, Yes, knowing as I do the rules of the game, I thought those would be your reasons, Obviously, there's a third reason, possible, as all things are, but improbable, and therefore out of the question, What's that, That you might make public the truth behind the attack, You know better than anyone that no interior minister, in any age or in any country in the world, has ever opened his mouth to speak of the mean, dishonourable, treacherous, criminal deeds committed in the course of his work, so you can rest easy on that score because I will prove no exception, If it becomes known that we ordered the bomb to be planted, we will give the people who cast the blank votes the final reason they needed, If you'll forgive me, prime minister, that way of thinking offends against logic, Why, And, if you'll allow me to say so, it does an injustice to the usual rigour of your thinking, Get to the point, Whether they find out or not, if they are then shown to be right, it's because they were right already. The prime minister pushed the newspapers away and said, This whole business reminds me of the story of the sorcerer's apprentice, the one who couldn't control the magical forces he had unleashed, Who, in your view, prime minister, is the sorcerer's apprentice in this case, them or us, Well, I very much fear that both of us are, they set off down a dead-end road with no thought for the consequences, And we followed them, Exactly, and now it's just a matter of waiting to see what the next step will be, As far as the government is concerned, we simply have to keep up the pressure, although after what has just happened, we obviously don't want to take any further action right now, And what about them, If the information I received before coming here is true, then they are preparing to hold a demonstration, What on earth do they hope to achieve by that, demonstrations never achieve anything, if they did, we wouldn't allow them, Presumably they want to protest against the attack, and as for getting authorisation from the ministry of the interior, on this occasion, they won't even have to waste their time asking for it, Will we ever get out of this mess, That is not a matter for sorcerers, prime minister, the fully qualified or the apprentices, but, in the end, as always, the strongest side will win, The one who is strongest at the last moment will win, and we haven't yet reached that moment, the strength we have now may not be sufficient by then, Oh, I have every confidence, prime minister, an organised state cannot possibly lose a battle like this, it would be the end of the world, Or the beginning of another, Now I'm not quite sure what I should make of those words, prime minister, Well, don't go spreading it around that the prime minister is entertaining defeatist ideas, Such a thought would never even enter my head, Just as well, You were clearly speaking hypothetically, Of course, If you don't need me for anything else, I'll get back to work, The president tells me he's had a brilliant idea, What's that, He didn't want to go into detail, he is awaiting events, To some purpose one hopes, He is the president, That's what I meant, Keep me informed, Yes, prime minister, Goodbye, Goodbye, prime minister.

The information received by the ministry of the interior was correct, the city was preparing for a demonstration. The final death toll had risen to thirty-four. No one knows where or how the idea came about, but it was immediately taken up by everyone, the bodies were not to be buried in cemeteries like the ordinary dead, their graves were to remain per omnia sæcula sæculorum in the land-scaped area opposite the station. However, a few families known for their right-wing allegiances and who were utterly convinced that the attack had been the work of a terrorist group with, as all the media affirmed, direct links to the conspiracy against the present government, refused to hand over their innocent dead to the community. Yes, they clamoured, they truly were innocent of all guilt, because they had all their lives respected their own rights and those of others, because they had voted as their parents and their grandparents had, because they were orderly people and had now become the victims and martyrs of this murderous act of violence. They also alleged, in another tone entirely, perhaps so as not to scandalise anyone with such a lack of civic solidarity, that they had their own historical family vaults and it was a deep-rooted family tradition that those who had always been united in life should remain so after death, again per omnia sæcula sæculorum. The collective burial would not, therefore, be of thirty-four bodies, but twenty-seven. This was still a large number of people. Sent by who knows who, but certainly not by the council, which, as we know, will be without a leader until the interior minister approves the necessary appointment of a replacement, anyway, as we were saying, sent by who knows who, there appeared in the garden a vast machine with many arms, one of those so-called multipurpose machines, like a gigantic quick-change artist, which can uproot a tree in the time it takes to utter a sigh and which would have been capable of digging twenty-seven graves in less time that it takes to say amen, if the gravediggers from the cemeteries, who were equally attached to tradition, had not turned up to carry out the work by hand, that is, using spade and shovel. What the machine had, in fact, come to do was to uproot half a dozen trees that were in the way, so that the area, once trodden down and levelled, looked as if it had been born to be a cemetery and a place of eternal rest, and then it, the machine that is, went off and planted the trees and the shade that they cast elsewhere.

Three days after the attack, in the early morning, people started to flood out into the streets. They were silent and grave-faced, many carried white flags, and all wore a white armband on their left arm, and don't let any experts in the etiquette of funeral rites go telling you that white cannot be a sign of mourning, when we are reliably informed that it used to be so in this very country, and we know that it has always been so for the Chinese, not to mention the Japanese, who, if it was left up to them, would all be wearing blue. By eleven o'clock, the square was already full, but all that could be heard was the great breathing of the crowd, the dull whisper of air entering and leaving lungs, in and out, feeding with oxygen the blood of these living beings, in, out, in, out, until suddenly, we will not finish the phrase, that moment, for those who have come here, the survivors, has not yet come. There were innumerable white flowers, quantities of chrysanthemums, roses, lilies, especially arum lilies, the occasional translucent white cactus flower, and thousands of marguerites who were forgiven their black hearts. Lined up twenty paces apart, the coffins were lifted onto the shoulders of the relatives and friends of the deceased, those who had them, and carried in procession to the graves, where, under the skilled guidance of the professional gravediggers, they were slowly lowered down on ropes until, with a hollow thud, they touched bottom. The ruins of the station still seemed to give off a smell of burned flesh. It will seem incomprehensible to some that such a moving ceremony, such a poignant display of collective grief, was not graced by the consolatory influence that would doubtless have come from the ritual practices of the country's sundry religious institutions, thus depriving the souls of the dead of their most certain viaticum and depriving the community of the living of a practical demonstration of ecumenicalism that might have contributed to leading the straying population back to the fold. The reason for this deplorable absence can only be explained by the various churches' fear that they might become the focus of suspicions, possibly tactical, or at worst strategic, of conniving with the blank-voting insurgency. This absence might also have to do with a number of phone calls, with minimal variations on the same theme, made by the prime minister himself, The nation's government would find it deeply regrettable if the chance presence of your church at the funeral service, while, of course, spiritually justified, should come to be considered, and subsequently exploited, as evidence of your political, and even ideological, support for the stubborn and systematic disrespect with which a large part of the capital's population continues to treat the legitimate and constitutional democratic authority. The burials were, therefore, purely secular, which is not to say that, here and there, a few private, silent prayers did not rise up to the various heavens to be welcomed there with benevolent sympathy. The graves were still open, when someone, doubtless with the best of intentions, stepped forward to give a speech, but this was immediately repudiated by the other people present, No speeches, we each have our own grief and we all feel the same sorrow. And the person who came up with this clear formulation of feelings was quite right. Besides, if that were the intention of the frustrated orator, it would be impossible to make a funeral oration for twenty-seven people, both male and female, not to mention some small child with no history at all. Unknown soldiers do not need the names that they used in life in order to be showered with the right and proper honours, and that's fine, if that's what we agree to do, but if these dead, most of them unrecognisable, and two or three of them still unidentified, want anything, it is to be left in peace. To those punctilious readers, showing a praiseworthy concern for the good ordering of the story, who want to know why the usual, indispensable dna tests were not carried out, the only honest answer we can give is our own total ignorance, allow us, however, to imagine that the famous and much-abused expression, Our dead, so commonplace, so much part of the routine patter of patriotic harangues, were to be taken literally in these circumstances, that is, if these dead, all of them, belong to us, we should not consider any of them exclusively ours, which would mean that any DNA analysis which took into account all the factors, including, in particular, the non-biological ones, and however hard it rummaged around inside the double helix, would only succeed in confirming a collective ownership which required no proof anyway. That man, or perhaps woman, had more than enough reason to say, as we noted above, Here, we each have our own grief and we all feel the same sorrow. Meanwhile, the earth was shovelled back into the graves, the flowers were shared out equally, those who had reasons to weep were embraced and consoled by the others, if such a thing is possible with such a recent grief. The loved one of each person, of each family, is here, although one does not know quite where, perhaps in this grave, perhaps in that, it would be best if we wept over all of them, as a shepherd once so rightly said, although heaven knows where he learned it, One can show no greater respect than to weep for a stranger.

The trouble with these narrative digressions, taken up as we have been with bothersome detours, is that one can find, too late, of course, almost without noticing, that events have moved on, have gone on ahead, and instead of us announcing what is about to happen, which is, after all, the elementary duty of any teller of tales worth his salt, all we can do is to confess contritely that it already has. Contrary to what we had supposed, the crowd has not dispersed, the demonstration continues and is now advancing en masse, filling the streets, in the direction, as the shouts are telling us, of the presidential palace. And on the way lies neither more nor less than the prime minister's official residence. The journalists from press, radio and television, who are at the head of the demonstration, take nervous notes, describe the events over the phone to the offices where they work, and excitedly unburden themselves of their professional and citizenly disquiets, No one seems to know quite what is going to happen, but we have reason to fear that the crowd is preparing to storm the presidential palace, which does not exclude, indeed we would say it remains highly likely, the possibility that they will also sack the prime minister's official residence and any ministerial buildings they pass on the way, this is not some apocalyptic vision, the mere fruit of our own fears, you have only to see the people's distraught faces, it would be no exaggeration to say that each of those faces is calling for blood and destruction, and thus, although it pains us to have to say this out loud and to the whole country, we reach the dreadful conclusion that the government, which has shown itself to be so efficient in other ways and was, for that very reason, applauded by all honest citizens, acted with a reprehensible lack of caution when it decided to abandon the city to the instincts of the angry mob, without the fatherly, dissuasive presence of the police on the streets, with no riot squads, with no tear-gas, no water-cannon, no dogs, in a word, unchecked. This speech warning of certain disaster reached a peak of media hysteria when they came in sight of the prime minister's residence, a bourgeois mansion, late-eighteenth-century in style, where the journalists' shouts became screams, Now, now, anything could happen, may the holy virgin protect us all, may the glorious and revered spirits of our nation, up there in the empyrean into which they ascended, quell the wrathful hearts of these people. Anything could have happened, it's true, but, in the end, nothing did, apart from the demonstration, the small section of it that we can see, coming to a halt at the crossroads where the mansion, with its small surrounding park, occupies one corner, the rest of the crowd spilled over onto the pavements, into the adjoining squares and streets, if the police arithmeticians were here, they would say that, all in all, there were only about fifty thousand people, when the exact number, the real number, because we counted them all, one by one, was ten times higher.

It was here, where the demonstration had come to a halt and was standing in absolute silence, that a sharp-eyed television reporter discovered amidst that sea of heads a man whose face, despite half of it being covered by a dressing, he nonetheless recognised, especially since he had been lucky enough to catch a fleeting glimpse of his normal, healthy face, which, as is perfectly understandable, both confirms and is confirmed by the wounded half. Dragging his cameraman along behind him, the reporter began pushing his way through the crowd, saying to the people on either side of him, Excuse me, excuse me, may I come through, out of the way, please, this is very important, and then, when he was getting close, Sir, sir, excuse me, although what he was thinking was less polite, What the hell is this guy doing here. Reporters usually have good memories and this particular reporter had not forgotten the public attack delivered by the council leader on the night of the bomb blast and of which the news networks had been the entirely undeserving targets. Now the council leader would find out just how wounded they had been. The reporter stuck the microphone in his face and made a kind of secret sign to the cameraman which could as easily have meant Start recording as Beat him to a pulp, and which, in the present situation, probably meant both, Sir, may I say how astonished I am to see you here, Astonished, why, For the reason I've just given, to see you taking part in this demonstration, Well, I'm a citizen like any other, I can demonstrate when and how I want to, especially now that there's no need to ask for authorisation, But you're not just any citizen, you're the council leader, No, I'm not, I stopped being council leader three days ago, I'd have thought that was common knowledge by now, It's the first I've heard of it, we haven't received any official statement about it as yet, from the council or from the government, You're surely not expecting me to call a press conference, You resigned, No, I walked out, Why, The only answer I have is a closed mouth, mine, The city's population will want to know why their council leader, As I said, I'm no longer council leader, Why their council leader has joined an anti-government demonstration, This is not an anti-government demonstration, it's a demonstration of grief, the people here came to bury their dead, The dead have been buried and yet the demonstration is continuing, how do you explain that, Ask these other people, At the moment, it's your opinion I'm interested in, Well, I'm just going where they're going, Do you sympathise with the electors who cast blank votes, with the blankers, They voted as they wanted to vote, and whether I sympathise or not is irrelevant, And what about your party, what will they say when they find out you joined the demonstration, Ask them, You're not afraid they'll impose sanctions on you, No, What makes you so sure, For the simple reason that I no longer belong to the party, Did they expel you, No, I left, just as I left the post of council leader, What was the interior minister's reaction, Ask him, Who has taken over from you or will take over, Find out for yourself, Will we see you on more demonstrations, Turn up and you'll find out, So you've left the party on the right, in which you've spent your entire political career, and have gone over to the left, One day, I hope to understand just where it is I have gone, Sir, Don't call me that, Sorry, force of habit, and I have to confess to feeling confused, Careful, now, moral confusion, because I'm assuming your confusion is moral, is the first step along the path to disquiet and after that, as you yourselves are so fond of saying, anything can happen, No, I really am baffled, sir, I don't know what to think, Turn off the recording equipment, your bosses might not like what you just said, and, please, don't call me sir, The camera is already off, Just as well, that way you won't get yourself into any trouble, They say that the demonstration is heading for the presidential palace, Ask the organisers, Where are they, who are they, Everyone and no one, I suppose, There must be a leader, movements like this don't organise themselves, spontaneous generation doesn't exist, still less in the case of mass actions on this scale, Not until now, no, Do you mean that you don't believe the blank vote movement was spontaneous, It's outrageous of you to make such an inference, My impression is that you know much more about this business than you're letting on, The time always comes when we discover that we knew much more than we thought we did, now, leave me alone and get on with your job, find someone else to question, look, the sea of heads has started to move, What amazes me is that there isn't a single shout, a single long live or down with, not a single slogan saying what it is the people want, just this threatening silence that sends shivers down your spine, Forget the horror movie language, perhaps people are just tired of words, If people get tired of words, then I'll be out of a job, You won't say a truer word all day, Goodbye, sir, Once and for all, I'm not sir any more. The leading front quarter of the demonstration had turned back on itself, now it was going up a steep slope towards a long, broad avenue at the end of which it would turn to the right and receive on its face the cool caress of the breeze from the river. The presidential palace was about two kilometres away, on the flat. The reporters had received orders to leave the demonstration and to run on to take up positions outside the palace, but the general idea, amongst both the professionals working on the ground and those back at the editorial desks, was that, from the point of view of news interest, the coverage had been a pure waste of time and money, or to put it more crudely, a real kick in the balls for the media, or, in more delicate and refined terms, an undeserved slight. These guys aren't even any good at demonstrations, they said, they might at least throw the odd stone, burn the president in effigy, break a few windows, sing one of the old revolutionary songs, anything to show the world that they're not as dead as the people they've just buried. The demonstration did not live up to their expectations. The people arrived and filled the square, they stood for half an hour staring in silence at the closed-up palace, then they dispersed, and, some walking, others in buses, still others cadging lifts from supportive strangers, they all went home.

This peaceful demonstration did what the bomb had failed to do. Troubled and frightened, the loyal voters of the party on the right and the party in the middle, or the p.o.t.r. and the p.i.t.m., gathered together in their respective family councils and decided, each according to their own lights, but unanimous as regards their final decision, to leave the city. They felt that the current situation, another bomb that might tomorrow be aimed at them, the rabble taking over the streets with absolute impunity, should convince the government of the need to revise the rigorous parameters they had established when imposing the state of siege, especially the scandalous injustice of having the same harsh punishment fall, without distinction, on the steadfast defenders of peace and on the declared fomenters of disorder. So as not to embark on this venture blindly, some of them, with friends in high places, set about sounding out by telephone the government's likely position on giving authorisation, explicitly or tacitly, that would allow those who, quite rightly, were already beginning to describe themselves as prisoners in their own country, to enter free territory. The answers received, generally vague and in some cases contradictory, while not allowing them to draw hard and fast conclusions regarding the government's thinking on the matter, were, nevertheless, sufficient for them to admit as a valid hypothesis that, if certain conditions were observed and certain material compensations stipulated, the success of the escape, even though it was relative, even though not all their requests could be met, was, at least, conceivable, which meant that they could at least hold out some hope. For a week, in absolute secrecy, the committee responsible for organising future convoys of cars, made up in equal numbers of militants of different categories from both parties and with the presence of consultants drawn from the capital's various moral and religious institutions, debated and finally approved an audacious plan of action which, in memory of the famous retreat of the ten thousand, received, on the suggestion of a learned hellenist from the party in the middle, the name of xenophon. The families who were candidates for emigration were given three days and no more to decide, with pencil in hand and a tear in the eye, what they could take with them and what they would have to leave behind. Human nature being what we know it to be, there were, inevitably, examples of selfish fancies, feigned distractions, treacherous appeals to an all-too-easy sentimentality, deceptively seductive manoeuvrings, but there were also cases of admirable selflessness, of the kind that still allow us to believe that if we persevere in these and other such gestures of worthy abnegation, we will, in the end, more than fulfil our small part in the monumental project of creation. The withdrawal was set for the early hours of the fourth day, which would, as it turned out, be a night of wild rain, but that would not be a problem, on the contrary, it would give this collective migration a touch of heroism to be remembered and inscribed in the family annals as a clear demonstration that not all the virtues of the race had been lost. Now, having to transport one person in a car quietly and with the weather in repose is not the same as having to keep the windscreen wipers flailing back and forth like mad things just to keep at bay the sheets of water falling from the sky. One grave problem, which would be minutely debated by the committee, was the question placed on the table as to how the casters of blank votes, commonly known as blankers, would react to this mass flight. It is important to bear in mind that many of these anxious families live in buildings that are also inhabited by tenants who come from the other political shore and who might take a deplorably vengeful attitude and, to put it mildly, obstruct their departure or, more brutally, stop it altogether. They'll puncture our tyres, said one, They'll erect barricades on the landings, said another, They'll jam the lifts, offered a third, They'll put silicon in the locks of the cars, added the first, They'll smash the windscreens, suggested the second, They'll attack us as soon as we step out of the front door, They'll hold grandpa hostage, sighed another in such a way that made one think that this was, unconsciously, precisely what he wanted. The discussion went on, becoming more and more impassioned, until someone reminded them that the behaviour of all those thousands of people during the demonstration had, however you looked at it, been impeccable, I'd even say exemplary, and consequently there seemed little reason to fear that things would now be any different, In fact, I think they'll be relieved to be rid of us, That's all very well, intervened a sceptic, they may be lovely people, wonderfully gentle and responsible, but there is something we have, alas, forgotten, What's that, The bomb. As we said on a previous page, this committee, of public salvation, as it occurred to someone to call it, a name that was immediately rejected for more than justified ideological reasons, was broadly representative, which means that on this occasion there were over two dozen people sitting round the table. You should have seen the reaction. Everyone else present bowed their head, then an admonitory look reduced to silence, for the rest of the meeting, the rash person who appeared to be ignorant of a basic tenet of social behaviour which teaches that in the house of the hanged man, one should never mention the word rope. The embarrassing incident had one virtue, it brought everyone together in agreement on the optimistic thesis they had formulated. What happened next would prove them right. At precisely three o'clock on the morning of the appointed day, just as the government had done, the families started leaving home with their suitcases large and small, their bags and their bundles, their cats and their dogs, the occasional tortoise roused from its sleep, the occasional Japanese fish in a bowl, the occasional cage of para-keets, the occasional macaw on a perch. But the doors of the other tenants did not open, no one came out onto the landing to make fun of the spectacle, no one made jokes, no one insulted them, and it was not just because it was raining that no one went and leaned out of the windows to watch the convoys driving off in their different directions. Naturally, with all the noise, just imagine, going down the stairs dragging all that junk, the lifts buzzing up and down, the suggestions, the sudden alarms, Careful with the piano, careful with the tea service, careful with the silver platter, careful with the painting, careful with grandpa, naturally, we were saying, the tenants in the other apartments woke up, but none of them got out of bed to go and peer through the spyhole in the front door, they merely said to each other as they snuggled down beneath the blankets, They're leaving.

THEY ALMOST ALL CAME BACK. TO ECHO THE WORDS USED BY THE interior minister some days before when obliged by the prime minister to explain the discrepancy between the size of the bomb he had been ordered to plant and the bomb that had actually exploded, there was, in the case of this exodus, another grave failure in the chain of command. As experience has never tired of showing us, after long examination of many cases and their respective circumstances, victims not infrequently bear some responsibility for the misfortunes that befall them. Preoccupied as they were with political negotiations, none of which, as will soon become apparent, had been carried out at a high enough level to ensure the perfect execution of operation xenophon, the busy leaders of the committee had forgotten, or perhaps such a thing had simply never entered their heads, to check that the military would also be informed of their escape and, equally important, of the agreements they had reached. Some families, a half dozen at most, did manage to cross the line at one of the frontier posts, but this was because the young officer in charge had allowed himself to be convinced not just by the fugitives' repeated protestations of ideological purity and loyalty to the regime, but by their insistent declarations that the government knew about their retreat and had approved it. Meanwhile, in order to free himself from the doubts that soon assailed him, he phoned two other posts nearby, and his colleagues there were kind enough to remind him that their orders, since the beginning of the blockade, had been not to let through a living soul, not even someone on their way to save their father from the gallows or to give birth to a new baby in their house in the country. Terrified that he had made the wrong decision, which would doubtless be perceived as flagrant and possibly premeditated disobedience of orders received, with the consequent court-martial and more than likely loss of rank, the officer gave orders for the barrier to be lowered at once, thus blocking the kilometre-long caravan of cars and vans, all packed to the gills, that stretched back along the road. The rain continued to fall. Needless to say, brought face to face with their responsibilities, the committee members did not stand by waiting for the red sea to part. Mobile phone in hand, they started waking up all the influential people whom they felt they could safely be wrenched from sleep without provoking too angry a reaction, and it is quite possible that the whole complicated affair could have been resolved in the best possible way for the anxious fugitives had it not been for the fierce intransigence of the minister of defence, who decided to dig his heels in, No one gets through without my say-so, he said. As you will no doubt have guessed, the committee had forgotten to consult him. You might say that a minister of defence is not that important, that above a minister of defence there is a prime minister to whom the former owes obedience and respect, that higher still, is a president who is owed the same, if not greater, obedience and respect, although, if truth be told, as far as this particular president is concerned, this is mostly a matter of show. And indeed, after a hard dialectical battle between the prime minister and the minister of defence, in which the reasons put up by both sides flashed and flickered like an exchange of tracer bullets, the minister finally surrendered. He was greatly put out, it's true, and in the blackest of moods, but he nevertheless gave in. You will naturally want to know what decisive, unanswerable argument the prime minister used to force his recalcitrant interlocutor into submission. It was simple and direct, My dear minister, he said, put that brain of yours to work and imagine the consequences tomorrow were we to shut the doors today on the very people who voted for us, As I recall, the order from the cabinet was to let no one pass, May I congratulate you on your excellent memory, but when it comes to orders, one has, from time to time, to be prepared to bend them, especially when it suits one to do so, which is precisely the case now, Sorry, I don't understand, Allow me to explain, tomorrow, once this problem has been resolved, with subversion crushed and spirits calmed, we will call new elections, isn't that right, It is, Do you think we could expect those we had turned away to vote for us again, No, they probably wouldn't, And we need those votes, remember, the party in the middle is hot on our heels, Yes, I understand, In that case, please give the order to allow the people to pass, Yes, sir. The prime minister put down the phone, looked at his watch and said to his wife, At this rate, I might be able to get another hour and a half or two hours' sleep, and added, I have a feeling that fellow will be sent packing at the next cabinet reshuffle, You shouldn't let people be so rude to you, said his other half, No one is ever rude to me, my love, they merely take advantage of my good nature, that's all, It comes to the same thing, she retorted, turning out the light. Before five minutes had passed, the telephone rang once more. It was the minister of defence again, Forgive me, prime minister, I'm sorry to interrupt your well-deserved rest, but unfortunately I have no option, What is it now, A detail we failed to notice, What detail, asked the prime minister, not bothering to disguise the touch of irritation he felt at the other man's use of we, It's quite simple, but very important, Get on with it and don't waste my time, Well, I was just wondering how we can be sure that all the people trying to leave the capital belong to our party, should we just take their word for it that they voted in the elections, couldn't some of the hundreds of vehicles queuing up along the roads be carrying subversive agents ready to infect with the blank plague the parts of the country that are as yet uncontaminated. The prime minister felt his heart contract when he realised he had been caught out, It's certainly a possibility to bear in mind, he murmured, That's precisely why I phoned you again, said the minister of defence, giving the screw another turn. The silence that followed these words demonstrated once more that time has nothing to do with the time told by clocks, those small machines made of wheels that do not think and springs that do not feel, devoid of a spirit that would allow them to imagine that five insignificant seconds counted off, one, two, three, four, five, could be an agonising torment for the person at one end of the phone and a pool of sublime pleasure for the other. The prime minister drew one striped pyjama sleeve across his forehead, which was now beaded with sweat, then, choosing his words carefully, he said, The matter clearly requires a different approach, a careful evaluation that looks at the problem in the round, cutting corners is always a mistake, My view precisely, How is the situation at the moment, asked the prime minister, Very tense on both sides, at some posts, they've even had to fire shots in the air, Do you have any suggestion to make as minister of defence, In more manoeuvrable conditions, I would order them to charge, but with all those cars blocking the roads, it's impossible, What do you mean charge, Well, I would get the tanks out, And when the snouts of the tanks came into contact with the first car, and I know tanks don't have snouts, it's just a manner of speaking, what, in your opinion, would happen then, People normally take fright when they see a tank advancing on them, But, as I have just heard from your own lips, the roads are blocked, Yes, sir, So it wouldn't be easy for the car at the front to turn round, No, sir, it would be very difficult indeed, but then, one way or another, if we don't let them in, they're going to have to do that, But not in the state of panic that would inevitably be provoked by the sight of a phalanx of tanks with their guns pointing straight at them, No, sir, In short, you have no idea how to resolve the problem, said the prime minister, ramming the point home, sure now that he had taken back both control and the initiative, I'm afraid not, prime minister, Nevertheless, I am grateful to you for having drawn my attention to an aspect of the matter that had escaped me, It could have happened to anyone, Yes, to anyone, but it shouldn't have happened to me, You have so many things to think about, And now I have another, solving a problem for which the minister of defence has failed to find a solution, If that is how you feel, then I offer my resignation, Now I don't think I heard that and I don't think I want to, Yes, prime minister. There was another silence, shorter this time, barely three seconds, during which it was clear that the sublime pleasure and the agonising torment had changed places. Another phone rang in the room. His wife answered it, she asked who was calling, then whispered to her husband, at the same time covering the mouthpiece of the phone, It's the interior minister. The prime minister gestured to her to wait, then issued his orders to the minister of defence, I want no more shots fired in the air and I want the situation stabilised until we can take the necessary measures, make it known to the people in the first few cars that the government is currently studying the situation and hopes to come up with proposals and directives shortly, and emphasise that everything will be resolved for the good of the country and of national security, May I remind you, prime minister, that there are hundreds of cars, So, We can't get the message to all of them, Don't worry, as long as the first cars at each post know, they'll make sure the information passes, like a powder trail, to the back of the queue, Yes, sir, Keep me informed, Yes, sir. The following conversation, with the interior minister, would be different, Don't waste any time telling me what's happened, I know already, They may not have told you that shots have been fired, It won't happen again, Ah, Now what we need to do is to get those people to turn round and go back, But if the army hasn't managed to do so, They haven't and they couldn't, you surely don't want the minister of defence to send in the tanks, Of course not, prime minister, From now on, the responsibility is yours, The police are no use in these situations and I have no authority over the army, Ah, but I wasn't thinking of the police, neither was I considering appointing you army chief of staff, Forgive me, prime minister, but I don't understand, Get your best speechwriter out of bed and put him straight to work, and meanwhile tell the media that the interior minister will speak on the radio at six o'clock, the television and the press can wait, it's the radio that matters now, It's almost five o'clock, prime minister, You don't have to tell me that, I have a watch, Sorry, I merely wanted to point out that there isn't much time, If your speechwriter can't come up with thirty lines in fifteen minutes, with or without syntax, then you'd better put him out in the street, And what should he write, Oh, any old line of argument that will convince these people to go home, that will inflame their patriotic feelings, tell them they're committing the crime of lèse-patrie by abandoning the capital to the subversive hordes, tell them that all those who voted for the parties who built the current political system, including, inevitably, the party in the middle, our direct competitor, constitute the first line of defence of all democratic institutions, tell them that the homes they have left behind them unprotected will be burgled and looted by insurrectionist gangs, but don't tell them that we will, if necessary, burgle them ourselves, We could add that any citizen who decides to return home, regardless of age or social class, will be considered by the government to be a loyal promoter of legality, Promoter doesn't seem to me quite the right word, it's too vulgar, too commercial, besides, legality is getting more than enough promotion, we spend all our time talking about it, All right, then, defenders, heralds or legionnaires, Legionnaires is better, it sounds strong, martial, defenders is a term that lacks pride, it would give a negative impression of passivity, and heralds has a whiff of the middle ages about it, whereas the word legionnaire immediately suggests combative action, an aggressive mindset, and is also, as we know, a word with solid traditions, Let's just hope that the people on the road hear the message, It would seem, my dear fellow, that waking up too early clouds your perceptive faculties, I would bet my post as prime minister that at this very moment every one of those car radios is turned on, what matters is that news of the broadcast to the nation is announced at once and the announcement repeated every minute, What I fear, prime minister, is that these people may not be in a frame of mind to be convinced, if we tell them there's going to be a statement from the government, they will more than likely think that we're going to authorise them to cross the frontier, and their subsequent disappointment could have very grave consequences, It's very simple, your speechwriter is going to have to justify both the bread that he eats and his salary, he's got the lexical and rhetorical skills, let him sort it out, If I may just give voice to an idea that has only this minute occurred to me, Feel free to give voice to anything you like, but may I just point out that we are wasting time, it's already five past five, The statement would carry much more force if you, as prime minister, were to make it, Oh, I don't doubt it for a moment, In that case, why don't, Because I am reserving myself for another occasion, one more suited to my station, Ah, I think I understand, It is, after all, merely a matter of common sense or, shall we say, hierarchical gradation, just as it would offend against the dignity of the nation's supreme court for the president to go on the radio to ask a few drivers to get off the roads, so must this prime minister be protected from everything that might trivialise his status as leader of the government, Hm, I see the idea, Good, it's a sign that you've finally managed to wake up, Yes, prime minister, And now to work, by eight o'clock at the latest, I want those roads cleared, and make sure the television companies get out there with all the terrestrial and aerial means at their disposal, I want the whole country to see the reports, Yes, sir, I'll do what I can, You won't do what you can, you will do what is necessary to obtain the results I have just demanded of you. The interior minister did not have time to respond, the prime minister had put the phone down. That's how I like to hear you talk, said his wife, Well, when someone gets my dander up, And what will he do if he can't solve the problem, He'll be given his marching orders and sent packing, Like the minister of defence, Exactly, You can't just dismiss ministers as if they were servants, They are servants, Yes, but you'll only have to find new ones, That is a subject that requires calm consideration, What do you mean, consideration, Look, I'd rather not talk about it at the moment, But I'm your wife, no one can hear us, your secrets are my secrets, All I mean is that, bearing in mind the gravity of the situation, it would come as no surprise to anyone if I myself were to take on the portfolios of defence and the interior, that way the state of national emergency would be reflected in the structures and workings of the government, that is, total co-ordination and total centralisation, that could be our watchword, It would be a huge risk, you could win everything or lose everything, Yes, but if I could triumph over a subversive action unparalleled anywhere, at any time, an action that attacked the system's most sensitive organ, that of parliamentary representation, then I would be assured of a lasting place in history, a unique place, as the saviour of democracy, And I would be the proudest of wives, whispered his wife, slithering closer to him, as if touched by the magic wand of a rare brand of lust, a mixture of carnal desire and political enthusiasm, but her husband, conscious of the gravity of the hour and making his the harsh words of the poet, Why do you grovel before my rough boots? / Why do you loosen your perfumed hair / and treacherously open your soft arms? / I am nothing but a man with coarse hands / and a cold heart / and if, in order to pass, / I had to trample you underfoot / then, as you well know, I would trample you underfoot, abruptly threw off the bedclothes and said, I'm going to my study to keep an eye on developments, you go back to sleep, rest. The thought flashed through his wife's mind that, in a critical situation like this, when moral support would be worth its weight in gold, always supposing moral support had a weight, the widely accepted code of basic marital obligations, in the chapter on mutual help, determined that she should, without summoning the maid, immediately get up and prepare with her own hands a comforting cup of tea with the appropriate alimentary accompaniment of a few plain biscuits, instead, annoyed, frustrated, with her nascent lust quite evaporated, she turned over in bed and firmly closed her eyes, in the faint hope that sleep might still be able to make use of the remnants of that lust to put on a brief, private, erotic fantasy for her. Oblivious to the disappointments he had left behind him, and wearing over his striped pyjamas one of those silk dressing-gowns adorned with exotic motifs, with Chinese pavilions and golden elephants, the prime minister went into his study, turned on all the lights, and switched on first the radio and then the television. The television screen still showed only the test card, it was too early for broadcasting to begin, but all the radio stations were already talking animatedly about the monstrous traffic jams on the roads, and opinions were bandied about on what was clearly an attempt at a mass escape from the unhappy prison into which the capital, through its own stupid fault, had been transformed, although there were also comments to the effect that such an unusually large circulatory blockage would mean that the vast trucks that brought food into the city every day would be unable to get through. These commentators did not yet know that these same trucks were being held, on strict orders from the army, three kilometres from the frontier. Radio reporters, travelling on motorbikes, questioned people all along the lines of cars and vans and were able to confirm that this was, indeed, a properly organised collective action, bringing together whole families, in order to escape the tyranny and the suffocating atmosphere which the forces of subversion had imposed on the city. Some household heads complained about the delay, We've been here for nearly three hours and the queue hasn't moved a millimetre, while others protested that they had been betrayed, They promised us we'd be able to get through with no problem, and here you have the brilliant result, the government scarpered, went on holiday and threw us to the lions, and now, when we had our chance to get out too, they have the nerve to slam the door in our face. There were hysterical outbursts, children crying, old people white-faced with fatigue, angry men who had run out of cigarettes, exhausted women trying to impose some order on the desperate family chaos. The occupants of one car tried to turn round and drive back into the city, but were forced to give up under the hail of insults and abuse that fell on them, Cowards, black sheep, blankers, bastards, spies, traitors, sons-of-bitches, now we know why you came, to demoralise us decent folk, but if you think we're going to let you go, you've got another think coming, if necessary, we'll let your tyres down and see if that teaches you some respect for other people's sufferings. The phone rang in the prime minister's study, it could be the minister of defence, or the interior minister, or the president. It was the president, What's going on, why wasn't I informed immediately about the general pandemonium along all the routes out of the capital, he asked, Sir, the government has the situation under control, the problem will soon be resolved, Yes, but I should have been informed, you owe me that courtesy at least, Well, I felt, and I take personal responsibility for the decision, that there was no reason to interrupt your sleep, but I was going to phone you in about twenty minutes or half an hour, but, as I say, I take full responsibility, president, Good, good, that was kind of you, but if my wife were not in the healthy habit of getting up early,

I, the president, would still be sleeping while the country burns, It's not burning, president, all the appropriate measures have been taken, Don't tell me you're going to bomb the lines of vehicles, As you should know by now, president, that is not my style, It was, of course, just a manner of speaking, obviously I never thought you would commit such a barbaric act, The radio should soon announce that the interior minister will address the nation at six o'clock, there it is, they're giving the first announcement now, and there will, of course, be others, it's all organised, president, Well, at least, that's something, It's the beginning of success, president, I have complete confidence that we will be able to persuade these people to return to their homes in peace and good order, And if they don't, If they don't, the government will resign, Oh, don't play that old trick on me, you know as well as I do that, in the situation in which the country finds itself, I couldn't accept your resignation even if I wanted to, Yes, I know, but I had to say it, Fine, anyway, now that I'm awake, be sure to keep me up to date on what's happening. The radios kept insisting, We interrupt the programme once again to inform our listeners that the interior minister will, at six o'clock, be making a statement to the nation, we repeat, at six o'clock the interior minister will make a statement to the nation, we repeat, a statement will be made to the nation by the interior minister at six o'clock, we repeat, at six o'clock the nation will be made a statement by the interior minister, the ambiguity of this last reformulation did not go unnoticed by the prime minister, who remained for a few seconds smiling at his own thoughts, amusing himself by wondering how the devil an interior minister could make the nation into a statement. He might have reached some conclusion that could have proved of future use had the test card on the television screen not vanished to give way to the usual image of the flag flapping lazily on the flagpole, as if it, too, had just woken up, while the national anthem blasted out with its trombones and drums, with the odd clarinet trill in the middle and a few persuasive belches from the bass tuba. The presenter who then appeared had the knot in his tie all awry and a sour look on his face, as if he had just been the victim of some insult that he would not readily forgive or forget, Considering the gravity of the political and social situation, he said, and in accordance with the population's sacred right to have access to a free and diverse news media, we are starting our broadcast early today. Like many of those listening, we have just learned that the interior minister will be speaking on the radio at six o'clock, presumably to express the government's attitude to the attempted exodus from the city by many of its inhabitants. This television company does not believe that it has been the object of any deliberate and intentional discrimination, but, rather, that through some inexplicable misunderstanding, unexpected in highly experienced politicians such as those who form the present national government, this particular company was somehow forgotten. At least, apparently. There will be those who will point out the relatively early hour at which the statement is to be made, but the employees of this network, throughout its long history, have given more than sufficient proof of their self-sacrifice, their dedication to the public cause and their unalloyed patriotism, not to be relegated now to the humiliating condition of bearers of second-hand news. We are confident that, before the hour fixed for the promised statement, it may still be possible to reach a basis for agreement which, without wishing to take away what has been given to our colleagues in public radio, will restore to us that which, by merit, belongs to us, that is, our position and our responsibility as the country's prime news medium. While we await this agreement, and we hope to receive news of it at any moment, we wish to report that a television helicopter is lifting off even as I speak, in order to offer our viewers the first images of the vast queues of vehicles, whose planned withdrawal was, we have learned, given the evocative and historic name of xenophon, and which now stand immobilised all along the city's exit routes. Fortunately, the rain that has been beating down on the selfless convoys all night stopped over an hour ago. The sun will soon rise above the horizon and break through the dark clouds. Let us hope that its appearance will also remove the barriers which, for reasons we fail to understand, still prevent these our courageous compatriots from reaching freedom. May they, for the good of the nation, prove successful. The following images showed the helicopter in the air, then, looking down, the tiny heliport from which it had taken off, and, afterwards, the first view of the nearby roofs and streets. The prime minister put his right hand on the phone. He did not have to wait long, Prime minister, began the interior minister, Yes, I know, no need to say anything, we made a mistake, We made a mistake, you say, Yes, we did, because if one of us was wrong and the other failed to correct him, then the mistake belongs to both, But I don't have your authority or your responsibility, prime minister, Ah, but you had my trust, So what do you want me to do then, You will speak live on television and there will be a simultaneous radio broadcast, problem solved, And we don't bother to reply to the impertinent terms and tone in which the gentlemen of the television station chose to refer to the government, In time, we will, but not now, I'll deal with them later, Good, You've got the statement with you, Yes, of course, do you want me to read it to you, No, don't bother, I'll wait to hear it live, It's nearly time, I must go, Are they expecting you, then, asked the prime minister, puzzled, Yes, I told my secretary of state to negotiate with them, Without my knowledge, You know as well as I do that we had no alternative, Without my approval, insisted the prime minister, Let me remind you that I had your trust, those are your words, besides, if one makes a mistake and the other corrects it, then both are right, If this whole business isn't sorted out by eight o'clock, I'll expect your immediate resignation, Yes, prime minister. The helicopter was flying low over one of the lines of cars, people were waving at it from the road, they must have been saying to each other, It's the television people, it's the television people, and the fact that the great gyratory bird had, indeed, been sent by the television people seemed to everyone a clear guarantee that the impasse was about to be resolved. If the television cameras are here, they said, that's a good sign. It wasn't. At six o'clock prompt, when the horizon was already becoming tinged with pink, the interior minister's voice boomed out from all the car radios, Dear fellow countrymen and women, in the last few weeks, our nation has been through what is, without doubt, the most serious crisis recorded in the history of our people since the very dawn of nationhood, never before has there been a more urgent need to defend national cohesion to the hilt, the behaviour of certain people, a tiny, ill-advised minority of the country's population as a whole, under the influence of ideas entirely at odds with the correct functioning of our current democratic institutions and with the respect that is due to them, has made them the mortal enemies of that cohesion, which is why, today, a terrible threat hovers over our normally peaceable society, the threat of a civil conflict with unforeseeable consequences for the future of the nation, the government was, needless to say, the first to understand the thirst for freedom that lay behind the attempted exodus from the capital carried out by those whom we have always known to be patriots of the first water, people who, in the most adverse of circumstances, have shown themselves, either by voting or by the simple example of their day-to-day lives, to be genuinely incorruptible defenders of legality, restoring and renewing the very best of the old legionnaire spirit and honouring its traditions by placing themselves at the service of the public good, the government was also the first to see that, by firmly turning their backs on the capital, the sodom and gomorrah of our day, these patriots were demonstrating a most praiseworthy combative spirit

146

which the government does, of course, recognise, however, taking into consideration the national interest as a whole, it is the government's belief, and, to this end, we appeal to the minds of those men and women who have spent so many anxious hours waiting for a clear message from those responsible for the country's fate, it is, I repeat, the government's belief, that the most appropriate militant action to be taken in the present circumstances is for those thousands of people to reintegrate themselves back into the life of the capital city, to return to their homes, those bastions of legality, those centres of resistance, those bulwarks where the unsullied memory of their ancestors watches over the works of their descendants, it is, I say again, the government's belief that these sincere and objective reasons, brought to you heart in hands, should be weighed by those people in their cars listening to this official statement, and although the material aspects of the situation should, of course, count for little in a calculation in which spiritual values are paramount, the government would like to take this opportunity to reveal that it has received information concerning the existence of a plan to burgle and plunder your abandoned homes, a plan which, according to our latest information, has already been set in motion, as I must conclude from the note I have just been handed, for, according to our sources, a total of seventeen apartments have so far been burgled and plundered, as you see, dear countrymen and women, your enemies are wasting no time, only a few hours have passed since your departure, and yet already the vandals are breaking down the doors of your homes, already the barbarians and savages are stealing your possessions, it lies, therefore, in your hands to avoid a still greater disaster, consult your consciences, know that the nation's government is on your side, it is up to you now to decide whether you are for us or against us. Before disappearing from the screen, the interior minister just had time to shoot a look at the camera, and in his face there was self-confidence, but also something that looked very like a challenge, although you would have to be privy to the secrets of the gods to interpret that rapid glance with total accuracy, the prime minister, however, was not fooled, for him it was just as if the interior minister had thrown in his face the words, You who pride yourself on your tactics and your strategies, could not have done better. And he had to agree that he could not, although they would have to wait and see just what the results would be. The helicopter reappeared, and there, once again, was the city, there again were the endless lines of cars. For a good ten minutes, nothing moved. The reporter was struggling to fill in time, he imagined the family councils that would be taking place inside the cars, he praised the minister's statement, he railed against the burglars, demanded that they be treated with all the rigour of the law, but it was obvious that unease was gradually seeping into him, it was plain as plain that the government's words had fallen on stony ground, not that he, still waiting for some last-minute miracle, dared to say so, but any viewer with a reasonable degree of experience in deciphering audiovisuals would have noticed the poor journalist's distress. Then the much-desired, much-longed-for marvel occurred, just when the helicopter was flying over the tail-end of one of the queues, the last car in the line turned round, followed by the car ahead, and then by another and another and another. The reporter gave an excited yelp, We are, dear viewers, witnessing a truly historic moment, for, responding with exemplary discipline to the government's appeal, in a display of civic duty that will be inscribed in letters of gold in the annals of the capital, the people are beginning their return home, thus bringing to a peaceful close what could have been a catastrophe with, as the interior minister so rightly said, unforeseeable consequences for the future of our nation. From this point on, for some minutes more, the report took on a decidedly epic tone, transforming the retreat of these ten thousand defeated people into a victorious ride of the valkyries, replacing xenophon with wagner, transmuting into odoriferous sacrifices wafting up to the gods of olympus and valhalla the foul-smelling fumes belching forth from the car exhausts. There were now brigades of reporters on the streets, from the radio and the press, and all were trying to hold the cars back for a moment so as to glean from the passengers, live and from the source itself, some description of the emotions filling them as they set off on their forced return home. As was to be expected, they encountered all sorts, frustration, disappointment, anger, a desire for revenge, we may not have got out this time, but we will the next, edifying affirmations of patriotism, exalted declarations of party loyalty, long live the party of the centre, long live the party in the middle, unpleasant odours, annoyance at not having slept a wink all night, take that camera away, will you, we don't want any photographs, agreement or disagreement as to the reasons given by the government, some scepticism about what would happen tomorrow, fear of reprisals, criticism of the authorities' shameful apathy, But there are no authorities, the reporter remarked, That's precisely the problem, there are no authorities, but mainly there was a great concern for the fate of the possessions left behind in the homes to which the occupants of the cars had only expected to return once the revolt of the blankers had been finally crushed, the number of burgled houses will doubtless now be more than seventeen, who knows how many will have been stripped of even their last rug, their last vase. The helicopter was now showing an aerial shot of how the lines of cars and vans, in which those who had been last were now first, branched off as they entered the areas near the centre and how, from a certain point onwards, it was no longer possible to distinguish amongst the confusion of traffic those who were returning from those who were already there. The prime minister phoned the president, a very brief conversation, an exchange of congratulations, These people must have lukewarm water running in their veins, the president said scornfully, if it had been me in one of those cars, I promise you I would have driven through however many barriers they put in front of me, It's lucky you're the president then, it's lucky you weren't there, said the prime minister, smiling, Yes, but if things start to get difficult again, that will be the moment to implement my idea, About which I still know nothing, One of these days, I'll tell you about it, And you will have my undivided attention, by the way, I'm calling a cabinet meeting for today in order to discuss the situation, it would be very useful if you could be there too, if, that is, you have no more pressing duties to perform, Don't worry, it's just a matter of re-arranging things, all I have to do today is go and cut a ribbon somewhere or other, Very good, sir, I will inform the cabinet. The prime minister decided that it was high time he said a kind word to the interior minister and congratulated him on the effectiveness of his state-ment, why not, after all, just because he didn't like the man didn't mean he couldn't recognise that this time he had coped very well with the problem to be resolved. His hand was just reaching for the phone when a sudden change in the voice of the television reporter made him look at the screen. The helicopter was flying so low now that it was almost touching the rooftops, you could see quite clearly various people coming out of the buildings, men and women standing on the pavement, as if they were waiting for someone, We have just been informed, said the reporter in great alarm, that the images our viewers are seeing of people leaving the buildings and waiting on the pavement are being repeated at this moment all over the city, we don't want to think the worst, but everything indicates that the inhabitants of these buildings, who are clearly insurrec-tionists, are preparing to prevent the people, who yesterday were their neighbours and whose homes they have doubtless just plun-dered, from entering the building, if that is so, then, much as it pains us to say so, the government who ordered the withdrawal of the police force from the capital must be brought to book, it is with a heavy heart that we ask ourselves how, or indeed if, the bloody physical confrontation which is clearly about to take place can possibly be avoided, president, prime minister, where are the police who should be defending innocent people from the barbarous treatment these others are preparing to mete out to them, oh, dear god, dear god, whatever is going to happen next, said the reporter, almost sobbing now. The helicopter hung motionless in the air, and there was a clear view of everything that was happening in the street. Two cars stopped outside the building. The doors opened and the occupants got out. Then the people on the pavement went over to them, This is it, this is it, we must prepare ourselves for the worst, screamed the reporter, hoarse with excitement, then the people exchanged a few inaudible words and, without more ado, began unloading the cars and carrying into the buildings in broad daylight what had been carried out under cover of a dark and rainy night. Shit, exclaimed the prime minister, and thumped the table.

THIS BRIEF SCATOLOGICAL INTERJECTION, WITH THE EXPRESSIVE POTENTIAL of an entire speech on the state of the nation, summed up and distilled the depth of disappointment that had gradually been gnawing away at the government's mental energies, in particular the energies of those ministers who, given the nature of their respective posts, had been most closely linked to the different phases of the political and repressive processes brought into play against the forces of sedition, in short, the ministers responsible for defence and the interior, who, from one moment to the next, each in his own field, had lost all the prestige gained from the good services they had rendered to the country during the crisis. Throughout the day, until it was time for the cabinet meeting to start, and, indeed, during it too, that grubby word was frequently muttered in the silence of thought, and, if there were no witnesses close by, even uttered out loud or murmured like some irrepressible unburdening of the soul, shit, shit, shit. It had occurred to neither of those ministers, of defence or the interior, or, which is truly unforgivable, to the prime minister either, to ponder briefly, even in a strict, disinterested academic sense, what might happen to the frustrated fugitives when they returned to their homes, however, if they had bothered to do so, they would probably have got no further than the horrific prophecy of the reporter in the helicopter which we failed to record earlier, Poor things, he was saying, almost in tears, they're going to be massacred, I'm sure of it. In the end, and it was not in that street alone that the marvel occurred, rivalling the most noble historical examples, both religious and profane, of love for one's neighbour, the slandered and insulted blankers went to the aid of the vanquished members of the opposing faction, and each person made this decision entirely on his or her own and in consultation with his or her own conscience, there was no evidence of any order issued from above or of a password to be learned by heart, the fact is that they all came to offer whatever help their strength permitted, and then they were the ones to say, careful with the piano, careful with the tea service, careful with the silver platter, careful with grandpa. It is understandable, therefore, that there should be so many frowning faces around the great cabinet table, so many beetling brows, so many eyes red with anger or from lack of sleep, probably nearly all of these men would have preferred some blood to have been spilt, they would not have wanted the massacre announced by the television reporter, but some incident that would have shocked the sensibilities of the population outside the capital, something that would set the whole country talking for the next few weeks, an argument, a pretext, another reason to demonise these wretched rebels. Which is why one can also understand why the minister of defence has just whispered, out of the corner of his mouth, to his colleague the interior minister, What the hell are we going to do now. If anyone else overheard the question, they were intelligent enough to pretend otherwise, because that was precisely why they were gathered there, to find out what the hell they were going to do now, and they would doubtless not leave the room empty-handed.

The first person to speak was the president of the republic, Gentlemen, he said, in my opinion, and as I think we would all agree, we are living through the most difficult and complex moment since the first election revealed the existence of a vast subversive movement hitherto undetected by the security services, not that we were the ones to make the discovery, for it chose, instead, to reveal itself, the interior minister, whose actions have otherwise always had my personal and institutional support, will, I am sure, agree with me when I say that the worst thing is that we have not, up until now, taken a single effective step towards solving the problem, and, perhaps graver still, we have been forced to watch, powerless, the rebels' brilliant tactic of helping our voters to move all their useless junk back into their apartments, that, gentlemen, could only be the brainchild of some machiavellian mastermind, someone who remains hidden behind the curtain and makes the puppets do exactly as he wants, we all know that we sent those people back out of sheer painful necessity, but now we must prepare ourselves for a more than likely chain reaction that will lead to new escape attempts, not this time of whole families, nor of spectacular convoys of cars, but of isolated individuals or small groups, and not by road, but across country, the minister of defence will assure me that these areas are regularly patrolled, that there are electronic sensors installed all along the frontier, and I could not bring myself to doubt the efficacy of such measures, however, in my view, complete containment can only be achieved by the construction of a wall around the capital, an impassable wall made out of concrete slabs, and, I would say, about eight metres high, using, of course, the system of electronic sensors already in existence and backed up by as many barbed-wire fences as are judged to be necessary, I am firmly convinced that no one would manage to get past that, not even, I would say, a fly, if you'll allow me my little joke, but not so much because flies couldn't get through it, as because, as far as one can judge from their normal behaviour, they have no reason to fly that high. The president of the republic paused to clear his throat and ended by saying, The prime minister already knows about this proposal of mine and, shortly, he will doubtless submit it for discussion by the government, who will then, as is their duty, decide upon the appropriateness and practicability of carrying it out, as for me,

I am content in the knowledge that you will bring all your experience to bear on the matter. A diplomatic murmur went round the table, which the president of the republic interpreted as one of tacit approval, an idea he would have had to correct had he heard the minister of finance's muttered remark, And where would we find the money for a crazy scheme like that.

Having shuffled the documents in front of him from one side to the other, as was his custom, the prime minister was the next to speak, The president of the republic, with the brilliance and rigour we have come to expect, has just given us a clear picture of the difficult and complex situation in which we find ourselves, and there is, therefore, no point in my adding to his exposition any details of my own, which would, after all, serve only to lend further shading to his original sketch, however, having said that, and in view of recent events, I believe that what we need is a radical change of strategy, which would pay special attention, along with all the other factors, to the possibility of the birth and growth in the capital of an atmosphere of social harmony purely as a consequence of this gesture of unequivocal solidarity, doubtless machiavellian, doubtless politically motivated, to which the whole country has borne witness in the last few hours, you have only to read the unanimously complimentary comments in the special editions brought out by the newspapers, consequently, we have no option but to recognise that all our attempts to make the rebels listen to reason have, each and every one, been a resounding failure, and that the cause of that failure, at least in my opinion, could well have been the severity of the repressive measures we chose to use, and secondly, if we continue with the strategy we have followed up until now, if we continue with the escalation of coercive methods, and if the response of the rebels also continues to be what it has been up until now, which is to say no response at all, we will be forced to resort to drastic measures of a dictatorial nature, such as the indefinite withdrawal of civil rights from the city's population, which, to avoid ideological favouritism, would have to include our own voters too, or, with the aim of preventing the spread of the epidemic, the passing of an emergency electoral law that would apply to the whole country and would make blank votes void, and so on. The prime minister paused to take a sip of water, then went on, I spoke of the need for a change of strategy, however, I did not say that I had such a strategy drawn up and prepared for immediate implementation, we need to bide our time, to allow the fruit to ripen and for brave resolutions to rot, I must confess that I myself would actually prefer a period of slight relaxation during which we could work to gain as much advantage as possible from the few signs of concord that seem to be emerging. He paused again and seemed to be about to continue speaking, but then said only, Now let me hear your opinions.

The interior minister raised his hand, I notice that you are confident of the persuasive influence our voters may have on the minds of those to whom I must confess I was somewhat astonished to hear you refer merely as rebels, but you did not, I believe, speak of the contrary possibility, that the subversives might use their harmful theories to confuse those citizens who are still respecters of the law, You're quite right, I don't think I did mention that possibility, said the prime minister in response, because I imagined that were that to happen, it would not bring about any fundamental change, the worst possible consequence would be that the current eighty per cent of people who cast blank votes would become one hundred per cent, and the quantitative change introduced into the problem would have no qualitative impact, apart, obviously, from creating unanimity. What shall we do then, asked the minister of defence, That is precisely why we are here, to analyse, consider and decide, Including, I assume, the proposal made by the president of the republic, which, of course, has my wholehearted support, The president's proposal, given the scale of the work involved and its many implications, requires an in-depth study to be undertaken by an ad hoc commission that will have to be set up for that purpose, on the other hand, it is, I think, fairly obvious that the building of a wall of partition would not immediately resolve any of our difficulties and would inevitably create others, the president knows my views on the subject, and the personal and institutional loyalty I owe him would not allow me to remain silent about it here at this cabinet meeting, but this does not, I repeat, mean that the commission's work should not begin as early as possible, as soon as it has been appointed, within the next few days. The president of the republic was visibly put out, I am the president, of course, and not the pope, and I do not, therefore, presume to any kind of infallibility, but I would like my proposal to be discussed with some urgency, As I said before, sir, came the prime minister's prompt reply, I give you my word that you will receive news of the commission's findings sooner than you might imagine, Meanwhile, I suppose we'll just have to continue groping our way blindly forwards, said the president. The silence that fell was thick enough to blunt the blade of even the sharpest of knives. Yes, blindly, he repeated, unaware of the general embarrassment. From the back of the room came the minister of culture's calm voice, Just as we did four years ago. The minister of defence rose, red-faced, to his feet, as if he had been the object of a brutal, unforgivable obscenity, and, pointing an accusing finger, he said, You have just shamefully broken a national pact of silence to which we all agreed, As far as I know, there was no pact, far less a national one, I was a grown man four years ago, and I have no recollection of the population being summoned to sign a piece of parchment promising never to utter one word about the fact that for several weeks we were all of us blind, You're right, there was no formal pact, said the prime minister, intervening, but we all thought, without any need for any agreement on paper, that the dreadful test we had been through would, for the sake of our mental health, be best thought of as a terrible nightmare, something that existed as a dream rather than as a reality, In public maybe, but you are surely not telling me that you have never spoken about what happened in the privacy of your own home, Whether we have or not is of no importance, a lot of things happen in the privacy of one's home that never go beyond its four walls, and, if I may say so, your allusion to the as yet unexplained tragedy that occurred amongst us four years ago shows a degree of bad taste that I would not have expected in a minister of culture, The study of bad taste, prime minister, must be one of the longest and juiciest chapters in the history of culture, Oh, I didn't mean that kind of bad taste, but the other sort, otherwise known as a lack of tact, It would seem, prime minister, that you share the belief that death exists only because it has a name, that things have no real existence if we have no name to give them, There are endless things for which I don't know the name, animals, vegetables, tools and machines of every shape and size and for all conceivable purposes, But you know that they have names, and that puts your mind at rest, We're getting off the subject, Yes, prime minister, we are getting off the subject, all I said was that four years ago we were blind and what I'm saying now is that we probably still are. The indignation was general, or almost so, cries of protest leapt up and jostled for position, everyone wanted to speak, even the transport minister, who, being possessed of a strident voice, usually spoke very little, but was now setting his vocal cords to work, May I speak, may I speak. The prime minister looked at the president of the republic as if asking his advice, but this was pure theatre, the president's diffident attempt at a gesture, whatever it was intended to mean, was quashed by the raised hand of his prime minister, Bearing in mind the emotive and passionate tone of the interpolations, it is clear that a debate would get us nowhere, which is why I will let none of you speak, especially since, possibly without realising it, the minister of culture was spot on when he compared the plague currently afflicting us to a new form of blindness, That is not a comparison of my making, prime minister, I merely remarked that we were blind and that we very probably continue to be blind, any extrapolation not logically contained in my initial proposition is not allowable, Changing the position of words often changes their meaning, but they, the words, when weighed one by one, continue physically, if I may put it like that, to be exactly what they were and, therefore, In that case, allow me to interrupt you, prime minister, I want to make it quite clear that responsibility for any changes in the position or meaning of my words lies entirely with you and that I had nothing whatsoever to do with it, Let's say that you provided the nothing and I contributed the whatsoever and that the nothing and the whatsoever together authorise me to state that the blank vote is as destructive a form of blindness as the first one, Either that or a form of clear-sightedness, said the minister of justice, What, asked the interior minister, who thought he must have misheard, I said that the blank vote could be seen as a sign of clear-sightedness on the part of those who used it, How dare you, in the middle of a cabinet meeting, utter such antidemocratic garbage, you ought to be ashamed of yourself, no one would think you were the minister of justice, cried the minister of defence, Actually, I wonder if I've ever been more of a minister of justice or for justice than I am at this moment, Soon you'll have me believing that you, too, cast a blank vote, said the interior minister drily, No, I didn't cast a blank vote, but I'll certainly consider doing so next time. When the scandalised clamour of voices resulting from this last statement had begun to die away, a question from the prime minister brought it to a complete halt, Do you realise what you have just said, Yes, so much so that I place in your hands the post with which you entrusted me, I am tendering my resignation, replied the man who was now no longer either minister or minister of justice. The president of the republic turned pale, he looked like an old rag that someone had distractedly left behind on the back of the chair, I never thought I would live to see the face of treachery, he said, and felt that history was sure to record the phrase, and should there be any risk of history forgetting, he would make a point of reminding it. The man who had up until now been the minister of justice got to his feet, bowed in the direction of the president and the prime minister and left the room. The silence was interrupted by the sudden scraping of a chair, the minister of culture had got up and, from the bottom of the table, in a strong, clear voice, was announcing, I wish to resign too, Oh, come on, don't tell me that, as your friend promised us just now in a moment of commendable frankness, you're considering casting a blank vote next time as well, the prime minister said, trying to be ironic, I doubt that will be necessary, I did so last time, Meaning, Exactly what you heard, nothing more, Kindly leave the room, Yes, prime minister, I was about to, the only reason I turned back was to say goodbye. The door opened, then closed, leaving two empty chairs at the table. Well, exclaimed the president of the republic, we hardly had time to get over the first shock when we got another slap in the face, That was no slap in the face, president, ministers come and ministers go, it's the most common thing in the world, said the prime minister, anyway, the government entered this room with a full complement of ministers and will leave with a full complement, I'll take over the post of justice minister and the minister for public works will take care of cultural affairs, But I don't have the necessary qualifications, remarked the latter, Yes, you do, culture, as certain people in the know are always telling me, is also a public work, it will, therefore, be perfectly safe in your hands. He rang the bell and ordered the clerk who appeared at the door, Take those chairs away, then, addressing the meeting, Let's have a short break of fifteen or twenty minutes, the president and I will be in the next room.

Half an hour later, the ministers resumed their places round the table. The absences went unnoticed. The president of the republic came in looking utterly perplexed, as if he had just been given a piece of news whose meaning was completely beyond his comprehension. The prime minister, on the other hand, seemed very pleased with himself. The reason would soon become clear. When, earlier on, I brought to your attention the urgent need for a change of strategy, given the failure of all the actions drawn up and executed since the beginning of this crisis, he began, I never for one moment expected that an idea capable of carrying us forward to victory would come precisely from a minister who is no longer with us, I refer, as you will doubtless have surmised, to the ex-minister of culture, who has shown once again how important it is to examine the ideas of your adversary in order to discover which aspects of those ideas can be used to your advantage. The ministers of defence and of the interior exchanged indignant glances, that was all they needed, to hear the intelligence of a despised traitor being praised to the skies. The interior minister scribbled a few rapid words on a piece of paper and passed it to his colleague, My instinct was right, I distrusted those guys right from the start, to which the minister of defence replied by the same means and with the same emotion, There we were trying to infiltrate them, and it turns out they had infiltrated us. The prime minister was continuing to discuss the conclusions he had reached based on the ex-minister of culture's sibylline statement about how we had all been blind yesterday and continued to be blind today, Our mistake, our great mistake, for which we are paying right now, lay in that attempt at obliteration, not of our memories, since we would all of us be capable of recalling what happened four years ago, but of the word, the name, as if, as our ex-colleague remarked, in order for death to cease to exist, we would simply have to stop saying the word we use to describe it, Aren't we getting away from the main problem, asked the president of the republic, we need concrete proposals, objectives, the cabinet is going to have to take some important decisions, On the contrary, president, this is the main problem, and if I'm right, this is the idea that will give us, on a plate, the possibility of resolving once and for all a problem which we have, at most, managed only to patch up here and there, but those patches quickly come unstitched and leave everything exactly as it was, What are you getting at, explain yourself, please, President, gentlemen, let us dare to take a step forwards, let us replace silence with words, let us put an end to this stupid, pointless pretence that nothing happened four years ago, let us talk openly about what life, if it can be called a life, was like during the time that we were blind, let the newspapers report it, let writers write about it, let the television show us images of the city taken immediately after we recovered our sight, let's encourage people to talk about the many and various evils we had to endure, let them talk about the dead, the disappeared, the ruins, the fires, the rubbish, the putrefaction, and then, when we have torn off the rags of false normality with which we have tried to bind up the wound, we will say that the blindness of those days has returned in a new guise, we will draw people's attention to the parallel between the blankness of that blindness of four years ago and the blind casting of blank ballot papers now, the comparison is crude and fallacious, as I would be the first to recognise, and there will be those who will reject it at once as an offence to intelligence, to logic and to common sense, but it is just possible that many people, and I hope they will soon become the overwhelming majority, will be convinced, will stand before the mirror and ask themselves if they are, again, blind, if this blindness, more shameful than the other blindness, is not leading them from the straight and narrow, propelling them towards the ultimate disaster which would be the possibly definitive collapse of a political system which, without our even noticing the threat, carried within it, right from the start, in its vital nucleus, in the voting process itself, the seeds of its own destruction or, a no less disquieting hypothesis, of a transition to something entirely new and unknown, so different that we would probably have no place in it, raised as we were in the shelter of an electoral routine which, for generations and generations, managed to conceal what we now realise was one of its great trump cards. I firmly believe, the prime minister continued, that the strategic change we needed is in sight, yes, the restoration of the system to the status quo ante is within our grasp, however, I am the prime minister of this country and not some vulgar snake-oil salesman promising miracles, but I will say that, while we may not get results in twenty-four hours, I am sure we will begin to see them within twenty-four days, the struggle, though, will be long and hard, because sapping the energy of this new blank plague will take time and much effort, not forgetting, ah, not forgetting the dreaded head of the tapeworm, which can hide itself away anywhere, for until we can locate it in the foul innards of the conspiracy, until we can drag it out into the light of day to be given the punishment it deserves, that fatal parasite will continue to produce its rings and to undermine the strength of the nation, but we will win the final battle, my word and your word, now and until the final victory, will be the guarantee of that promise. Pushing back their chairs, the ministers rose as one man and stood applauding enthusiastically. Purged of its troublesome members, the cabinet was, at last, a cohesive whole, one leader, one will, one plan, one path. Seated in his armchair, as befitted the dignity of his office, the president of the republic was clapping too, but only with the tips of his fingers, thus letting it be known, as well as by the stern look on his face, how piqued he was not to have been the object of some reference, however minimal, in the prime minister's speech. He should have known better who he was dealing with. When the clamorous crackle of applause was beginning to subside, the prime minister raised his right hand to call for silence and said, Every voyage needs a captain, and during the dangerous voyage on which the country is now embarked, that captain is and must be your prime minister, but woe betide the ship that does not carry a compass to guide it over the vast ocean and through the storms, well, gentlemen, the compass that guides me and the ship, the compass, in short, that guides us all, is here, by our side, always keeping us on course with his vast experience, always encouraging us with his wise advice, always instructing us with his peerless example, a thousand rounds of applause, then, and a thousand thanks to his excellency the president of the republic. The ovation was even warmer than the first and seemed as if it would never end, nor would it end as long as the prime minister continued to clap his hands or until the clock in his head said, Enough, stop there, he's won. Just two minutes more to confirm that victory and, at the end of those two minutes, the president of the republic, with tears in his eyes, was embracing the prime minister. Perfect, nay, even sublime moments can occur in the life of a politician, he said afterwards, his voice choked with emotion, but whatever tomorrow may hold for me, I assure you that this moment will never be erased from my memory, it will be my crowning glory in happy times, my consolation in sad ones, I thank you with all my heart, with all my heart, I embrace you. More applause.

Perfect moments, especially when they verge on the sublime, have the grave disadvantage of being very short-lived, which fact, being obvious, we would not need to mention were it not that they have a still greater disadvantage, which is that we do not know what to do once they are over. This awkward pause, however, reduces down to almost nothing when there is an interior minister present. As soon as the cabinet had resumed their usual places, with the minister of public works and culture still wiping away a furtive tear, the interior minister raised his hand to ask permission to speak,

Carry on, said the prime minister, As the president of the republic so touchingly pointed out, there are perfect, truly sublime moments in life, and we have had the great privilege of experiencing two such moments here, with the president's speech of thanks and the prime minister's new strategy, which has, of course, received our unanimous approval and to which I will refer in this intervention, not in order to withdraw my applause, nothing could be further from my mind, but, if I may be so immodest, to amplify and facilitate the effects of that strategy, I am referring to what the prime minister said about not being able to guarantee results in twenty-four hours, but being sure of getting them before twenty-four days were up, now, with respect, I do not believe that we can afford to wait twenty-four days, or twenty or fifteen or even ten, cracks are beginning to appear in the social edifice, the walls are shaking, the foundations are trembling, it could all come crashing down at any moment, Do you have you any real proposal to make, asked the prime minister, apart from describing the imminent collapse of a building, Oh, yes, replied the interior minister, unperturbed, as if he had not noticed the prime minister's sarcastic tone, Be so kind as to enlighten us, then, First of all, prime minister, I must make it clear that my proposal is merely intended to complement the proposal you presented to us and which we approved, it does not seek to amend, correct or perfect, it is simply another suggestion which is, I hope, deserving of everyone's attention, Oh, get on with it and stop beating about the bush, get to the point, What I propose, prime minister, is a rapid action, a shock offensive, with helicopters, You're surely not thinking of bombarding the city, Yes, sir, I am, but with paper, With paper, Exactly, prime minister, with paper, first, in order of importance, we would have a proclamation signed by the president of the republic and addressed to the population of the capital, second, a series of brief, punchy messages intended to pave the way and prepare people's minds for the doubtless slower actions advocated by the prime minister, that is, newspaper articles, television programmes, memories of the time when we were blind, stories by writers, etc., by the way, I would just mention that my ministry has its own team of writers, people highly trained in the art of persuasion, which, as I understand it, writers normally achieve only briefly and after much effort, It seems an excellent idea to me, said the president of the republic, but obviously the text would have to be submitted to me for my approval so that I could make any changes I deem appropriate, but, on the whole, I like it, it's a splendid idea, which, above all, has the enormous political advantage of placing the figure of the president of the republic in the front line of battle, oh, yes, a fine idea. The murmur of approval in the room indicated to the prime minister that this last move had been won by the interior minister, So be it, then, take all the necessary steps, he said, and on the appropriate page in the government's school progress report he mentally added another black mark against the minister's name.

THE REASSURING IDEA THAT, LATER OR SOONER, AND, MORE LIKELY, sooner than later, fate will always strike down pride, was roundly confirmed by the humiliating opprobrium suffered by the interior minister, who, believing that he had, in extremis, won the latest round in the pugilistic battle in which he and the prime minister had been engaged, saw his plans fizzle out after an unexpected intervention from the skies, which, at the last moment, decided to change sides and join the enemy. However, in the final analysis and, indeed, in the first, the blame for this, in the view of the most attentive and competent of observers, lay entirely with the president of the republic for having delayed his approval of the manifesto which, bearing his signature and intended for the moral edification of the city's inhabitants, should have been distributed by the helicopters. During the three days that followed the cabinet meeting the celestial vault revealed itself to the world in its magnificent suit of seamless blue, perfect weather, smooth and faultless, and above all with no wind, ideal for hurling papers out into the air and watching them float down, dancing the dance of the elves, to be picked up by anyone who happened to be passing or who had come out into the street curious to learn what news or orders were drifting down from above. During those three days, the much-thumbed text traipsed back and forth between the presidential palace and the ministry of the interior, sometimes more profuse in arguments, sometimes more concise in ideas, with words crossed out and replaced by others that would immediately suffer the same fate, with phrases which, shorn of what went before, no longer fitted what came after, so much wasted ink, so much torn-up paper, this, we will have you know, is what is meant by the torment of writing, the torture of creation. On the fourth day, the sky, grown tired of waiting, and seeing that things down below still kept chopping and changing, decided to start off the morning covered by a layer of low, dark clouds, of the sort that usually bring the rain they promise. By late morning, a few sparse droplets had begun to fall, stopping now and then and starting up again, an irritating drizzle which, despite threatening more, seemed unlikely to get much worse. This on-off state of affairs continued until mid-afternoon, and then, suddenly, without warning, like someone who has grown weary of hiding his true feelings, the heavens opened to give way to a continuous, steady, monotonous rain, intense but not violent, the kind of rain that can continue falling for a whole week and for which farmers are generally grateful. Not so the ministry of the interior. Even assuming that the air force's supreme command would authorise the helicopters to take off, which, would, in itself, be highly problematic, hurling papers down from above in weather like this would be utterly ridiculous, and not just because there would be hardly any people in the streets, and the main concern of the few who were would be to remain as dry as possible, even worse was the thought that the presidential manifesto might land in the mud, be swallowed up by the devouring drains, might crumble and dissolve in the puddles that the wheels of cars splash rudely through, throwing up fountains of grubby water as they go, in truth, in truth I say to you, only a fanatical believer in legality and the respect one owes to one's superiors would bother to stoop down and rescue from the ignominious slime an explanation about the relationship between the general blindness of four years ago and this majority blindness now. To the interior minister's vexation, he had to stand by and watch, powerless, as, on the pretext of the on-going and unpostponable national emergency, the prime minister, with, more-over, the reluctant agreement of the president of the republic, set in motion the media machinery, encompassing press, radio, tele-vision and all the other written, aural and visual submedia avail-able, both current and concurrent, whose task it would be to persuade the capital's population that it was, alas, once more blind. When, days later, the rain stopped and the upper air had once more clothed itself in azure, only the stubborn and ultimately angry insis-tence of the president of the republic managed to get the postponed first part of the plan put into action, My dear prime minister, said the president, do not think for a moment that I have reneged on or am even considering reneging on the decision taken by the cabinet, I continue to believe that it is my duty to address the nation personally, But, sir, it really isn't worth it, the clarification process is already underway and I'm sure we'll soon be getting results, Those results could be about to appear around the corner the day after tomorrow, but I want my manifesto to be launched first, The day after tomorrow is, of course, just a manner of speaking, All the better, get that manifesto distributed now, Believe me, sir, A word of warning, if you don't do it, I'll blame you for the inevitable loss of personal and political trust between us, Allow me to remind you, sir, that I still have an absolute majority in parliament, any threat-ened loss of trust would be merely personal in nature and would have no political repercussions, It would if I made a statement to parliament declaring that the word of the president of the republic had been hijacked by the prime minister, Please, sir, that isn't true, It's true enough for me to say so, in parliament or out of it, Distributing the manifesto now, The manifesto and the other papers, Distributing the manifesto now would be pointless, That's your opinion, not mine, But president, The fact that you call me president means that you recognise me as such, so do as I say, Well, if you put it like that, Oh, I do, and another thing, I'm tired of watching your battles with the interior minister, if you think he's no good, then sack him, but if you don't want to sack him or can't, then put up with it, if you yourself had come up with the idea of a manifesto signed by the president, you would probably have issued orders for it to be delivered door to door, Now that's unfair, sir, Maybe it is, I don't deny it, but people get upset and lose their temper and end up saying things they didn't intend to or hadn't even thought, Let's consider the matter closed, All right, the matter is closed, but tomorrow morning I want those helicopters in the air, Yes, president.

If this acerbic exchange had not taken place, if the presidential manifesto and the other leaflets had, because unnecessary, ended their brief life in the rubbish, the story we are telling would have developed quite differently from this point on. We can't imagine exactly how or in what way, we just know it would have been different. Obviously, any reader who has been paying close attention to the meanderings of the plot, one of those analytical readers who expects a proper explanation for everything, would be sure to ask whether the conversation between the prime minister and the president of the republic was simply added at the last moment to justify such a change of direction, or if it simply had to happen because that was its destiny, from which would spring soon-to-be-revealed consequences, forcing the narrator to set aside the story he was intending to write and to follow the new course that had suddenly appeared on his navigation chart. It is difficult to give such an either-or question an answer likely to satisfy such a reader totally. Unless, of course, the narrator were to be unusually frank and confess that he had never been quite sure how to bring to a successful conclusion this extraordinary tale of a city which, en masse, decided to return blank ballot papers, in which case this violent exchange of words between the prime minister and the president of the republic, which ended so happily, would have been as welcome to him as flowers in May. What other explanation is there for his abrupt abandonment of the complex narrative thread he had been developing merely in order to set off on gratuitous digressions not about what-did-not-happen-but-might-have, but about what-did-happen-but-might-not-have. We are referring, to put it plainly, to the letter which the president of the republic received three days after the helicopters had showered the capital's streets, squares, parks and avenues with the coloured leaflets in which the ministry of the interior's writers set out their conclusions about the likely connection between the tragic collective blindness of four years ago and the present-day electoral madness. The signatory was fortunate in that his letter fell into the hands of a particularly scrupulous clerk, the sort who looks at the small print before he starts reading the large, the sort who is capable of discerning amongst the untidy scrawl of words the tiny seed that requires immediate watering, if only to find out what it might grow into. This is what the letter said, Your excellency, Having read, with due and deserved attention, the manifesto addressed by you to the people and, in particular, to the inhabitants of the capital, and being keenly aware both of my duty as a citizen of this country and of the need, during the crisis into which the nation is currently plunged, for every one of us to maintain a close, constant, zealous watch for anything strange that we might see now or might have seen in the past, I wish to bring to the attention of your excellency's renowned powers of judgement a few unknown facts which may help towards a better understanding of the nature of the plague that befell us. I say this because, although I am just an ordinary man, I believe, as you do, that there must be some link between the recent blindness of casting blank ballot papers and that other blindness which, for weeks that none of us will ever forget, made us all outcasts from the world. What I am suggesting, your excellency, is that the first blindness might perhaps help to explain this blindness now, and that both might be explained by the existence, and possibly by the actions, of one person. Before going on, however, impelled as I am by a sense of civic duty upon which I would challenge anyone to cast doubt, I wish to make it clear that I am not an informer or a sneak or a grass, I am simply trying to be of service to my country in the distressing situation in which it currently finds itself, without so much as a lantern with which to illumine the path to salvation. I do not know, how could I, if the letter I am writing will be enough to light that lantern, but I repeat, duty is duty, and at this moment, I see myself as a soldier taking a step forward and presenting myself as a volunteer for a mission, and this mission, your excellency, consists in revealing, and I use the word reveal because this is the first time I have spoken of this matter to anyone, that four years ago, together with my wife, I fell in with a group of people who, like so many others, were struggling desperately to survive. It will seem that I am not telling you anything that you, through your own experiences, do not know already, but what no one knows is that one of the people in our group, the wife of an ophthalmologist, did not go blind, her husband went blind like the rest of us, but she did not. At the time, we made a solemn vow never to speak about the matter, she said that she did not want to be seen afterwards as a rare phenomenon, to be subjected to questions and submitted to examinations once we had all recovered our sight, that it would be best just to forget and pretend it had never happened. I have respected that vow until today, but can no longer remain silent. Your excellency, allow me to say that I would feel deeply offended if this letter were seen as a denunciation, although, on the other hand, perhaps it should be seen as such, because, and this is something else you do not know, during that time, a murder was committed by the person I am telling you about, but that is a matter for the courts, I content myself with the thought that I have done my duty as a patriot by drawing your lofty attention to a fact which has, until now, remained a secret and which, once examined, might perhaps produce an explanation for the merciless attack of which the present political system has been the target, this new blindness which, if I may humbly reproduce your excellency's own words, strikes at the very foundations of democracy in a way in which no totalitarian system ever succeeded in doing. Needless to say, sir, I am at your disposal, or at the disposal of whichever institution is charged with carrying out what is clearly a necessary investigation, to amplify, develop and elaborate on the information contained in this letter. I assure you that I feel no animosity towards the person in question, however, what counts above all else is this our nation, which has found in you the most worthy of representatives, that is my one law, the only one I hold to with the serenity of a man who has done his duty. Yours faithfully. There followed the signature and below that, on the left, the signatory's full name, address and telephone number, as well as his identity card number and e-mail address.

The president of the republic slowly placed the piece of paper on his desk and, after a brief silence, asked his cabinet secretary, How many people know about this, No one apart from the clerk who opened it and recorded the letter in the register, Can he be trusted, Yes, I suppose so, president, he's a party member, but it might be a good idea to let him know that the slightest hint of disloyalty on his part could cost him very dear, and, if I may make a suggestion, that warning should be delivered directly, By me, No, sir, by the police, it's more effective that way, the man is summoned to the main police station where the toughest policeman they have takes him into an interrogation room and puts the fear of god into him, Oh, I don't doubt the results would be excellent, but I see one grave difficulty, What's that, sir, It will be a few days before the case reaches the police and, meanwhile, the fellow's tongue will start to wag, he'll tell his wife, his friends, he might even talk to a journalist, in short, he'll drop us in the soup, You're quite right, sir, the solution would be to have an urgent word with the chief of police, if you like, sir, I'll happily do that myself, Short-circuit the hierarchical chain of government, go over the prime minister's head, is that your idea, Obviously I wouldn't dare to do so if the case were not so serious, sir, My friend, in this world, and, as far as we know, there is no other, everything gets out in the end, now while I believe you when you say that the clerk is to be trusted, I couldn't say the same of the chief of police, what if, as is more than likely, he's in cahoots with the interior minister, imagine the fuss there would be, the interior minister demanding an explanation from the prime minister because he can't demand one from me, the prime minister wanting to know if I'm trying to by-pass his authority and his responsibilities, in a matter of hours, the thing we are trying so hard to keep secret will be out in the open, Once again, sir, you are right, Well, I wouldn't go so far as to say, as a certain fellow politician once did, that I'm always right and rarely have any doubts, but I'm not far off, So what shall we do, sir, Send the man in, The clerk, Yes, the one who read the letter, Now, In another hour it might be too late. The cabinet secretary used the internal phone to summon the clerk, Come to the president's office immediately and be quick about it. Walking down the various corridors and through the various rooms usually took at least five minutes, but the clerk appeared at the door after only three. He was breathing hard and his legs were shaking. There was no need to run, said the president, smiling kindly, The cabinet secretary said I should be quick, sir, said the clerk, panting, Good, now the reason I wanted to see you was this letter, Yes, sir, You read it, of course, Yes, sir, Do you remember what was in it, More or less, sir, Don't use such expressions with me, answer my question, Yes, sir, I remember it as if I had read it this minute, Do you think you could try to forget its contents, Yes, sir, Think carefully now, you know, of course, that trying to forget and actually forgetting are not the same thing, No, sir, they're not, So mere effort won't be enough, you'll need to do something more, You have my word of honour, sir, You know, I was almost tempted to tell you again not to use such expressions, but I'd prefer you to explain precisely what you so romantically call your word of honour means to you in the present situation, It means, sir, a solemn declaration that, whatever happens, I will in no way divulge the contents of the letter, Are you married, Yes, sir, Right, I'm going to ask you a question, And I will answer it, sir, Supposing you were to reveal the nature of the letter to your wife and only to your wife, do you think you would, in the strict sense of the term, be divulging anything, I refer, of course, to the letter, not to your wife, No, sir, because divulge, strictly speaking, means to broadcast, to make public, Correct, I am pleased to see that you know your etymologies, But I wouldn't even tell my wife, Do you mean that you will tell her nothing, Nor anyone else, sir, Give me your word of honour, Forgive me, sir, but I already have, Imagine that, I had forgotten already, if the fact escapes me again, the cabinet secretary here will remind me, Yes, sir, said the two voices in unison. The president fell silent for a few seconds, then asked, What if I were to look in the letter register and see what you had written, can you save me the bother of getting out of my chair and tell me what I would find there, Just one word, sir, You must have a remarkable capacity for synthesis if you can sum up such a long letter in one word, Petition, sir, What, Petition, that's the word in the register, Nothing more, Nothing more, But that way no one will know what the letter is about, That was exactly my thinking, sir, that it would be best if no one knew, the word petition covers everything. The president leaned contentedly back and gave the prudent clerk a broad, toothy smile, then he said, Well, if you had said that in the first place you wouldn't have had to give away something as serious as your word of honour, One precaution guarantees the other, sir,

Not bad, not bad at all, but have a look at the register from time to time, just in case someone should think to add something else to the word petition, I've already blocked the line, sir, so that nothing can be added, You can go now, As you wish, sir. When the door had closed, the cabinet secretary said, I must confess I hadn't thought him capable of showing such initiative, I believe we have just satisfactorily proved to ourselves that he deserves our trust, He might deserve yours, said the president, but not mine, But I thought, You thought rightly, my friend, but, at the same time, wrongly, the safest way of categorising people is not by dividing them up into the stupid and the clever, but into the clever and the too clever, with the stupid, we can do what we like, with the clever, the trick is to get them on our side, whereas the too clever, even when they're on our side, are still intrinsically dangerous, they can't help it, the oddest thing is that in everything they do, they are constantly warning us to be wary of them, but, generally speaking, we pay no attention to the warnings and then have to face the consequences, Do you mean to say, sir, Yes, I mean that our prudent clerk, that prestidigitator of the letter register, capable of transforming a troubling letter like that into a mere petition, will soon be getting a call from the police so that they can give him the fright that you and I, between ourselves, had promised him, he himself said as much, though without quite realising it, one precaution guarantees the other, You're right as usual, sir, you're always so far-sighted, Yes, but the biggest mistake I made in my political life was letting them sit me down in this chair, I didn't realise at the time that the arms of this chair had handcuffs on them, That's because it's not a presidentialist regime, Exactly, and that's why all they allow me to do is cut ribbons and kiss babies, Now, though, you're holding a trump card, As soon as I hand it to the prime minister, it will be his trump card, and I will simply have acted as postman, And the moment he hands it to the interior minister, it will belong to the police, since the police are at the end of the assembly line, You've learned a lot, I'm at a good school, sir, Do you know something, I'm all ears, sir, Let's leave the poor devil alone, who knows, tonight, when I get home, or later on, in bed, I might tell my own wife what the letter said, and you, my dear cabinet secretary, will probably do the same, your wife will look at you as if you were a hero, her own sweet husband privy to all the secrets and webs that the state weaves, who's in the know, who inhales, without benefit of a mask, the putrid stench of the gutters of power, Please, sir, Oh, take no notice, I don't think I'm as bad as the worst, but sometimes I'm suddenly very conscious that that isn't enough, and my soul aches more than I can say, Sir, my mouth is and will remain closed, As will mine, as will mine, but there are times when I imagine what the world would be like if we all opened our mouths and didn't stop talking until, Until what, sir, Oh, nothing, nothing, leave me alone now.

Less than an hour had passed when the prime minister, summoned urgently to the palace, entered the office. The president gestured to him to sit down and, as he handed him the letter, said, Read this and tell me what you think. The prime minister sat down in the chair and started to read. He must have been about halfway through the letter when he looked up with an interrogative expression on his face, like someone who has not quite grasped what someone has just said to him, then he went on and, without further interruptions or other gestural manifestations, read to the end. A patriot full of good intentions, he said, and, at the same time, a complete swine, Why a swine, asked the president, If what he says here is true, if this woman, always assuming she did exist, really didn't go blind and helped these six other people to survive that terrible time, it is not beyond the bounds of possibility that the writer of this letter owes her the good fortune of being alive today, my parents might be alive too if they had had the good fortune to meet her, He says that she murdered someone, No one knows for certain how many people were killed during that period, president, it was decided that all the bodies found had died accidentally or from natural causes and the matter was laid to rest, Even things laid to rest can be woken, That's true, president, but, in this case, I don't feel it would be for the best, it's highly unlikely there were any witnesses to the crime and, even if there were, they were just the blind amongst the blind, it would be absurd, a complete nonsense, to bring that woman to trial for a murder no one saw her commit and where the corpus delicti does not exist, The writer of the letter states that she killed someone, Yes, but he doesn't say that he was a witness to the murder, besides, sir, as I said before, the person who wrote this letter is a complete swine, Moral judgements are beside the point, As I well know, sir, but it does one good sometimes to say what one feels. The president took the letter back, looked at it as if it wasn't there and asked, What do you think you'll do, Me, nothing, replied the prime minister, there isn't a thread of evidence to go on, You noticed, of course, that the writer of the letter suggests the possibility of a link between the fact that this woman didn't go blind and the massive casting of blank votes that got us into this mess in the first place, Sir, we haven't always agreed with each other, That's only natural, Yes it is, as natural as it is for me not to have the slightest doubt that your intelligence and your common sense, which I greatly respect, will reject out of hand the idea that a woman, simply because she did not go blind four years ago, should today be deemed responsible for the fact that a few hundred thousand people, who had never even heard of her, chose to cast blank ballot papers when summoned to vote in an election, Well, put like that, There is no other way to put it, sir, my advice is to file the letter under correspondence from nutters and let the matter drop, while we continue the search for a solution to our problems, real solutions, not the fantasies or grudges of an imbecile, You're quite right, I was taking a lot of inconsequential twaddle far too seriously and I've wasted your time by asking you to come over here to see me, Oh, that doesn't matter, sir, my wasted time, if you want to call it that, has been more than made up for by our having reached agreement, Thank you, I'm glad you see it like that, Right, then, I'll leave you to get on with your work and I'll return to mine. The president of the republic was about to hold out his hand to say goodbye when the phone rang. He picked up the receiver and heard his secretary say, The interior minister would like to speak to you, sir, Put him through. The conversation was a long one, the president listened and, as the seconds passed, the expression on his face altered, sometimes he murmured Yes, on one occasion he said It's certainly worth looking into, and he ended with the words Speak to the prime minister about it. He put the receiver down, That was the interior minister, And what did that delightful man want, He's received a letter along the same lines and he's decided to begin an investigation, Bad news, But I told him to talk to you first, So I heard, but it's still bad news, Why, If I know the interior minister, and I'm sure few can know him as well as I do, he will have already spoken to the chief of police by now, Stop him, Oh, I'll try, but I'm afraid it might be useless, Use your authority, What, and be accused of blocking an investigation into facts that affect the nation's security, at a moment when everyone knows that the nation is in grave danger, asked the prime minister, adding, You would be the first to withdraw your support from me, the agreement we've just reached would be a mere illusion, it already is, since it serves no purpose. The president nodded, then said, A little while ago, in connection with this letter, my cabinet secretary came out with a very illuminating phrase, What was that, He said that the police were at the end of the assembly line, Let me congratulate you, sir, on having such an excellent cabinet secretary, meanwhile, you had better warn him that there are some truths that should not be spoken out loud, This room is soundproof, That doesn't mean there aren't a few microphones hidden about the place, Perhaps I'd better have the room searched, Please believe me when I say that, if you do find any microphones, I was not the one who ordered them to be placed here, Very funny, Very sad, May I say how sorry I am, my friend, that circumstances have left you in this blind alley, Oh, there'll be some way out, although, I confess, I can't see one at the moment, and going back is impossible. The president accompanied the prime minister to the door, It's odd, he said, that the man who wrote the letter didn't write to you as well, He probably did, but your secretariat and that of the interior minister are clearly more diligent than mine, Very funny, No, sir, very sad.

THE LETTER ADDRESSED TO THE PRIME MINISTER, BECAUSE THERE WAS A letter, took two days to reach his hands. He realised at once that the clerk in charge of recording the letter had been less discreet than the president's clerk, how else explain the rumours that had been flying around for the last two days, rumours which, in turn, were either the result of a leak by mid-level civil servants eager to demonstrate that they were au courant or in the know, or else had been deliberately started by the ministry of the interior as a way of stopping in its tracks any attempt by the prime minister to oppose the police investigation or, however symbolically, obstruct it. There remained the possibility, which we will describe as the conspiracy theory, that the supposedly secret conversation between the prime minister and his interior minister that took place after the former had been summoned to the presidential palace, had been far less private than one might have thought, given the padded walls, which, who knows, may have concealed a few latest-generation microphones, of the kind that only an electronic gun-dog with the finest pedigree could sniff out and find. Whatever the truth of the matter, there was nothing to be done about it, it is a sad moment for state secrets, which have no one to defend them. The prime minister is so conscious of this deplorable certainty, so convinced of the pointlessness of secrets, especially when they have ceased to be so, that, with the look of someone observing the world from a very high vantage point, as if he were saying Don't say a word, I know everything, he slowly folded the letter up and put it in one of his inside jacket pockets, It came straight from the blindness of four years ago, I'll keep it with me, he said. The air of shocked surprise on his cabinet secretary's face made him smile, Don't worry, my friend, there are at least two other letters identical to this, not to mention the many photocopies that are doubtless already doing the rounds. His cabinet secretary's face suddenly assumed a look of feigned innocence or abstraction, as if he had not quite understood what he had heard, or as if his conscience had suddenly leapt out at him along the road, accusing him of some ancient, or else very recent, misdeed. You can go now, I'll call you if I need you, said the prime minister, getting up from his chair and going over to one of the windows. The noise he made in opening it concealed the sound of the door closing. From there, he could see little more than a succession of low roofs. He felt a nostalgia for the capital city, for the happy times when votes did as they were told, for the monotonous passing of the hours and days spent either at his petit-bourgeois official residence or at the national parliament, for the agitated and not infrequently jolly and amusing political crises, which were like sudden eruptions of foreseeable duration and controlled intensity, almost always put on, and through which one learned not only not to tell the truth, but, when necessary, to make it correspond, point by point, with the lie, just as the wrong side and the right side of things are, quite naturally, always found together. He wondered if the investigation would already have begun, he paused to speculate upon whether the agents taking part in the police action would be those who had fruitlessly remained behind in the capital charged with obtaining information and submitting reports, or if the interior minister would have preferred, for this new mission, people whom he knew and trusted, who were to hand and within easy reach, and, who knows, were seduced by the glamorous movie adventure element of a clandestine breaking of the blockade, crawling, with a knife tucked in their belt, underneath barbed-wire fences, outwitting the dreaded electronic sensors with magnetic desensitisers, and emerging on the other side in enemy territory, heading for their objective, like moles endowed with the agility of a cat and with night-vision glasses. Knowing the interior minister as he did, only slightly less bloodthirsty than dracula, and even more theatrical than rambo, this was sure to be the mode of action he would order them to adopt. He was absolutely right. Hidden in the small area of forest that almost borders the perimeter of the besieged city, three men are waiting for night to become early dawn. However, not everything that the prime minister imagined from his office window corresponds to the reality we see before us. For example, these men are dressed in plain clothes, there are no knives tucked into belts, and the weapon they have in their holster is the gun which is always so reassuringly described as regulation. As for the dreaded magnetic desensitisers, there is, amongst the various bits of apparatus the men are carrying, nothing that looks as if it fulfilled that function, which, when one thinks about it, could mean merely that magnetic desensitisers are quite simply and deliberately made not to look like magnetic desensitisers. We will soon learn, however, that, at a pre-arranged time, the electronic sensors in this section of the border will be turned off for five minutes, which was considered more than enough time for three men, one by one, without undue haste or hurry, to cross the barbed-wire barrier, part of which was cut today precisely for the purpose of avoiding torn trousers and lacerated skin. The army's sappers will be back to repair it before the rosy fingers of dawn return to reveal the threatening barbs rendered harmless only very briefly, as well as the enormous rolls of wire stretching out along both sides of the frontier. The three men are already through, in front goes the leader, who is the tallest, and they cross, in indian file, a field whose wet grass oozes and creaks beneath their shoes. On a minor road on the outskirts of the city, about five hundred metres from there, a car is waiting to carry them through the silence of the night to their destination in the capital, a bogus insurance and reinsurance company which a complete dearth of clients, whether local or foreign, had not as yet managed to bankrupt. The orders that these men received directly from the lips of the interior minister are clear and categorical, Bring me results and I won't ask by what means you obtained them. They have no written instructions with them, no safe-conduct pass to cover them or which they could show as a defence or as a justification if things should turn out worse than they expect, and there is, of course, always the possibility that the ministry would simply abandon them to their fate if they committed some action that might prejudice the state's reputation and the immaculate purity of its objectives and processes. These three men are like a commando group entering enemy territory, there seems no reason to think that they will risk their lives there, but they are all aware of the delicate nature of a mission that demands a talent for interrogation, flexibility in drawing up strategy and swiftness in carrying it out. All to the maximum degree. I don't think you'll need to kill anyone, the interior minister had said, but if, in an extreme situation, you consider that there's no other option, then don't hesitate, I'll sort things out with the minister for justice, Whose post has just been taken over by the prime minister, remarked the leader of the group. The interior minister pretended not to hear, he merely glared at the importunate speaker, who had no alternative but to look away. The car drove into the city, stopped in a square so that they could change drivers, and finally, after going round various blocks thirty or so times in order to throw off any unlikely pursuer, deposited them at the door of the building where the insurance and reinsurance office has its base. The porter did not come out to see who was arriving at what was a most unusual hour for an office building, one assumes he had received a visit from someone the previous afternoon who had persuaded him

gently to' go to bed early and advised him not to slip out from
between the sheets, even if insomnia kept him from closing his
eyes. The three men took the lift up to the fourteenth floor, went
down a corridor to the left, another to the right, a third to the
left, and finally reached the office of providential ltd, insurance and
reinsurance, as anyone can read on the notice on the door, in black
letters on a tarnished, rectangular brass plate, affixed with nails that
have brass heads in the shape of truncated pyramids. They went
in, one of the subordinates turned on the light, the other closed the
door and put the security chain on. Meanwhile the leader of the
group walked through the various rooms, checked phone lines,
plugged in machines, went into the kitchen, into the bedrooms and
bathrooms, opened the door to what was intended to be the filing
room and had a quick look at the various armaments stored in
there, at the same time breathing in the familiar smell of metal and
lubricant, he will inspect it all properly tomorrow, piece by piece,
weapon by weapon. He summoned his assistants, sat down and told
them to sit down too, Later this morning, at seven o'clock, he said,
we will begin the work of following the suspect, notice that I call
him the suspect, even though, as far as we know he has committed
no crime, I do so not only to simplify communication between
ourselves, but also because, for security reasons, it is best that his
name is not mentioned, at least not during these first few days, I
would add that with this operation, which I hope will last no longer
than a week, our first objective is to get an idea of the suspect's
movements around the city, where he works, where he goes, who
he meets, the usual routine for a basic investigation, reconnoitring
the terrain before making a direct approach, Should he be aware
that he's being followed, asked the first assistant, Not for the first
four days, but after that, yes, I want him to feel worried, uneasy,
Having written that letter, he must surely be expecting someone to
come looking for him, We'll do that when the moment comes, what

185

I want, and it's up to you to achieve this effect, is to frighten him into thinking that he's being followed by the people he denounced, By the doctor's wife, No, not by her, but by her accomplices, the people who cast the blank votes, Aren't we taking things a bit fast, asked the second assistant, we haven't even started work yet, and here we are talking about accomplices, All we're doing is making a preliminary sketch, a simple sketch, that's all, I want to put myself in the shoes of the guy who wrote that letter and, from there, try to see what he sees, Well, a week spent tailing the guy seems far too long to me, said the first assistant, it should take us three days at most to bring him to boiling point. The leader frowned, he was going to say, Look, I said one week and it will be one week, but then he remembered the interior minister, he didn't recall him having expressly asked for rapid results, but since that is the demand most often heard from the lips of those in charge, and since there was no reason to think that the present case would be any exception, quite the contrary, he showed no more reluctance in agreeing to the period of three days than that considered normal between a superior and a subordinate, on the rare occasions when the person issuing the orders is forced to give in to the reasoning of the person receiving them. We have photographs of all the adults who live in the building, I mean, of course, those of the male sex, said the leader, adding unnecessarily, One of them is that of the man we are looking for, We can't start following him until we've identified him, said the first assistant, True, replied the leader, but nevertheless, at seven o'clock, I want you to be strategically positioned in the street where he lives and to follow the two men you think most closely resemble the kind of person who would have written that letter, that's where we'll start, intuition and a good police nose must have their uses, Can I say something, asked the second assistant, Of course, To judge by the tone of the letter, the guy must be a total bastard, Does that mean, asked the first assistant, that we should only follow the ones who look like bastards, then he added, Although in my experience, the worst bastards are precisely the ones who don't look like they're bastards, It would have made much more sense to have gone straight to the identity card people and asked for a copy of the guy's photograph, it would have saved time and work. Their leader decided to cut this discussion short, I presume you're not intending to teach the priest to say the our father or the mother superior the hail mary, if they didn't tell us to do that it must be because they didn't want to arouse any curiosity that could have caused the operation to be aborted, With respect, sir, I disagree, said the first assistant, everything indicates that the guy is dying to spill the beans, in fact, I think if he knew we were here, he'd be banging on our door right now, You may be right, said the group leader, struggling to control the irritation he felt at what had every appearance of being a devastating critique of his plan of action, but we want to know as much as we can about him before we make direct contact, How's this for an idea, piped up the second assistant, Not another one, said his chief sourly, This is a good one, I guarantee it, one of us disguises himself as an encyclopaedia salesman, that way we'll be able to see who opens the door, That encyclopaedia salesman trick went out with the ark, said the first assistant, besides, it's usually the wives who come to open the door, I mean, it would be a great idea if our man lived on his own, but, as I recall from what he says in the letter, he's married, Oh, rats, exclaimed the second assistant. They sat in silence, looking at each other, the two assistants knowing that the best thing now would be to wait for their superior to have an idea of his own. They would, in principle, be prepared to applaud it even if it was as leaky as an old boat. The leader of the group was weighing up everything that had been said, trying to fit the various suggestions together in the hope that two pieces of the puzzle might just slot into place and that something would emerge, something so holmesian, so poirotesque, that it would make these two men under orders from him open their mouths wide in amazement. And suddenly, as if the scales had fallen from his eyes, he saw the way forward, Most people, he said, unless, of course, they're physically incapacitated, don't spend all their time stuck at home, they go out to work, go shopping or for a walk, so my idea is that we should wait until there's no one in the apartment and then break in, the guy's address is on the letter, we've got plenty of skeleton keys, and there are bound to be photos around, it wouldn't be hard to identify him from the various photographs and that way we'd have no problem following him, and if we want to find out when the place is empty, we'll use the phone, we'll get his number tomorrow from directory enquiries, or we could look it up in the telephone book, one or the other, it doesn't really matter. As he uttered this rather lame conclusion, he realised that the pieces of the puzzle really didn't fit. Although, as explained before, the two assistants' attitude towards the results of their leader's cogitations was one of total benevolence, the first assistant, trying to find a tone of voice that would not wound his chief's susceptibilities, felt obliged to observe, Correct me if I'm wrong, but wouldn't it be best, since we know the guy's address, just to go and knock on his door and ask whoever answers Does So-and-so live here, if it's him, he'll say Yes, that's me, if it's his wife, she'll probably say I'll just go and call my husband, that way we would have the bird in our hand without having to beat about the bush. The leader raised his clenched fist like someone about to give the desk an almighty thump, but, at the last moment, he checked the violence of that gesture, slowly lowered his arm and said in a voice that seemed to fade with every syllable, We'll examine that possibility tomorrow, I'm going to bed now, good night. He was just going over to the door of the bedroom he would occupy during the time the investigation lasted when he heard the second assistant ask, So do we still start the operation at seven o'clock as planned. Without turning round, the group leader replied, That plan of action is suspended until further orders, you will receive your instructions tomorrow, once I have read through any messages from the ministry, and, if necessary, so as to speed up the work, I will make any changes I see fit. He said good night again, Good night, sir, replied his two subordinates, and then he went into his room. As soon as the door had closed, the second assistant prepared to continue the conversation, but the other man quickly put a fore-finger to his lips and shook his head, indicating to him not to speak. He was the first one to push back his chair and say, Right, I'm off to bed, if you're staying up, be careful not to wake me when you come in. Unlike their leader, these two men, as the subordinates they are, do not have the right to a room of their own, they are both going to sleep in a large room with three beds, a kind of small dormitory which is rarely fully occupied. The bed in the middle is always the one least used. When, as in this case, there were two agents, they invariably used the beds on either side, and if only one policeman was sleeping there, he was also sure to prefer to sleep in one of those, never in the middle bed, perhaps because sleeping there would make him feel as if he were under siege or a prisoner under arrest. Even the hardest, most thick-skinned of policemen, and these two have not yet had the opportunity to prove that they are, need to feel protected by the proximity of a wall. The second assistant, who had understood the message, got to his feet and said, No, no, I'm not sitting up, I'm going to bed too. According to rank, first one, then the other, made use of the bathroom which was, as it should be, equipped with everything necessary for their ablu-tions, for we have not at any point in this report mentioned that the three policemen each brought with them only a small suitcase or a simple rucksack with a change of clothing, a toothbrush and a razor. It would be surprising if an enterprise christened with the fortunate name of providential did not take care to provide those to whom it gave temporary shelter with the various articles and products essential for their comfort and for the successful fulfilment of the mission with which they had been charged. Half an hour later, the two assistants were in their respective beds, wearing their official pyjamas, with the police emblem over their heart. So the plan from the ministry of the interior's planning department was useless, said the second assistant, It's always the same when they don't take the elementary precaution of consulting the people who've got the experience, replied the first assistant, Our leader's got plenty of experience, said the second assistant, if he hadn't, he wouldn't be where he is today, Sometimes, being too close to the centres of decision-making brings on myopia, makes you short-sighted, replied the first assistant sagely, Do you mean to say that if we ever get to a position of real power, like the chief, the same thing will happen to us, asked the second assistant, There's no reason why, in this particular case, the future should be any different from the present, replied the first assistant wisely. Fifteen minutes later, both were asleep. One was snoring, the other wasn't.

It was not yet eight o'clock in the morning, when the group leader, already washed, shaved and dressed, came into the room where the ministry's plan of action, or, to be more precise, the interior minister's plan of action that had been so rudely loaded onto the patient shoulders of the police authorities, had been torn to shreds by his two assistants, albeit with praiseworthy discretion and considerable respect, and even a slight touch of dialectical elegance. He had no problem in acknowledging this and bore them no rancour, on the contrary, he was clearly very relieved. With the same energetic strength of will with which he had overcome the incipient insomnia that had caused him to toss and turn for a while in bed, he took total control of operations, generously rendering unto caesar what could not be denied to caesar, but making it quite clear that, in the end, all benefits will sooner or later revert to god and to authority, god's other name. It was, therefore, a serene, confident man whom the two sleepy assistants found when, minutes later, they, in turn, shuffled into the living-room, still in their dressing-gowns, which were also adorned with the police emblem, and in their pyjamas and bedroom slippers. Their chief had calculated as much, he had foreseen that the first point of the day would go to him, and he had already noted it on the blackboard. Good morning, lads, he said in a cordial tone, I hope you slept well. Yes, sir, said one. Yes, sir, said the other, Let's have breakfast, then get yourselves washed and dressed, who knows, we might catch him still in his bed, that would be fun, by the way, what day is it today, Saturday, today is Saturday, no one gets up early on Saturday, you wait, he'll open the door looking just the way you do now, in dressing-gown and pyjamas, shuffling down the corridor in his slippers, and consequently with his defences down, psychologically at a low ebb, come on, come on, who's the brave man who's going to volunteer to make breakfast, Me, said the second assistant, knowing full well that there was no third assistant to do the job. In a different situation, that is, if, instead of being thrown out, the ministry's plan had been accepted without further discussion, the first assistant would have stayed behind with his chief to agree and fine-tune, however unnecessarily, some detail of the investigation they were about to embark upon, but, in the circumstances, especially now that he, too, had been reduced to the inferiority of bedroom slippers, he decided to make a great gesture of camaraderie and say, I'll help you. Their leader agreed, it seemed a good idea, and he sat down to go over some notes he had made before going to sleep. Barely fifteen minutes had passed when the two assistants reappeared carrying a tray each, bearing the coffee pot, the milk jug, a packet of plain biscuits, orange juice, yoghurt and jam, no doubt about it, the catering corps of the political police had once again done honour to their hard-won reputation. Resigned to drinking their coffee with cold milk or having to reheat it, the assistants said that they were going to get washed and dressed and would be back in a moment, We'll be as quick as we can. In fact, it seemed to them a grave lack of respect, with their superior there in suit and tie, to join him in their dishevelled state, unshaven, eyes blinking, and emanating the thick, nocturnal smell of unwashed bodies. There was no need for them to explain, what was left unspoken was, for once, more than eloquent. Naturally, given this new atmosphere of peace, and with his assistants put firmly back in their places, it cost their chief nothing to urge them to sit down and share bread and salt with him, We're colleagues, we're in the same boat, a fine boss I'd be if I had to keep flaunting my stripes in order to get people to obey me, anyone who knows me knows I'm not like that, sit down, sit down. Slightly embarrassed, the assistants sat down, conscious that, whatever anyone said, there was something improper about the situation, two down-and-outs having breakfast with a person who, in comparison, looked like a dandy, they were the ones who should have got their arses out of bed early, more than that, they should have had the table laid and ready for when their chief came out of his room, in dressing-gown and pyjamas if he so wished, but us, no, we should have been properly dressed and with our hair combed, it is these small cracks in the varnish of behaviour, rather than noisy revolutions, which, slowly, through repetition and persistence, finally bring down the most solid of social edifices. It is a wise dictum that says, If you want to be respected, don't encourage familiarity, let us hope, for the good of the job, that this particular chief does not have reason to regret this moment. In the meantime, he seems confident of his authority, we have only to hear him, This operation has two objectives, a main one and a secondary one, the secondary objective, which I'll deal with now so as not to waste time, is to find out as much as possible, but without, in theory, too much outlay of energy, about the supposed murder committed by the woman who led the group of six blind people mentioned in the letter, the main objective, to which we will apply all our efforts and abilities and for which we will use all reasonable means, whatever they may be, is to establish whether or not there is any connection between this woman, who is said to have retained her sight while the rest of us were all staggering around blind, and this new epidemic of blank ballot papers, It won't be easy to find her, said the first assistant, That's why we're here, all attempts to unearth the roots of the boycott have failed up until now and it might well be that this guy's letter won't get us very far either, but it at least opens a new line of enquiry, It seems pretty unbelievable to me that this woman could be behind a movement that involves some hundreds of thousands of people and that, tomorrow, if we don't stamp the whole business out now, she might gather together millions and millions more, said the second assistant, Both things are equally impossible, but if one of them happened, so could the other one, replied the chief, and concluded, with the look of someone who knows more than he is authorised to say, never imagining how true his words will prove to be, Impossibilities never come singly. With this happy concluding phrase, the perfect close to a sonnet, breakfast also came to an end. The assistants cleared the table and carried the crockery and what remained of the food into the kitchen, We'll go and get washed and dressed now, we won't be a moment, they said, Wait, said the chief, then, addressing himself to the first assistant, You'd better use my bathroom, otherwise we'll never get out of here. The lucky assistant blushed with contentment, his career had just taken a great leap forward, he was going to pee in his chief's toilet.

In the underground garage a car was waiting for them, the keys of which had been deposited the day before on the chief's bedside table, along with a brief explanatory note indicating its make, colour, registration number and the parking place where the vehicle had been left. Avoiding the foyer, they took the lift straight down to the garage and had no difficulty in finding the car. It was nearly ten o'clock. The chief said to the second assistant as the latter was opening the back door for him, You drive. The first assistant sat in the front, next to the driver. It was a pleasant, very sunny morning, which shows yet again that the punishments of which the sky was such a prodigal source in the past, have, with the passing of the centuries, lost their force, those were good and just times, when any failure to obey the divine diktat was enough for several biblical cities to be annihilated and razed to the ground with all their inhabitants inside. Yet here is a city that cast blank votes against the lord and not a single bolt of lightning has fallen upon it, reducing it to ashes, as happened, in response to far less exemplary vices, to sodom and gomorrah, as well as to admah and to zeboyim, burned down to their very foundations, although the last two cities are mentioned less often than the first, whose names, perhaps because of their irresistible musicality, have remained forever in people's ears. Nowadays, having abandoned their blind obedience to the lord's orders, lightning bolts fall only where they want to, and, as has become manifest, one can clearly not count on them to lead this sinful city and caster of blank votes back to the path of righteousness. In their place, the ministry of the interior has sent three of its archangels, these three policemen, chief and subalterns, who, from now on, we will designate by their corresponding ranks, which are, following the hierarchical scale, superintendent, inspector and sergeant. The first two sit watching the people walking along, none of them innocent, all of them guilty of something, and they wonder if that venerable-looking old gentleman, for example, is not perhaps the grand master of outer darkness, if that girl with her arms about her boyfriend is not the incarnation of the undying serpent of evil, if that man walking along, head down, is not going to some unknown cave where the potions that poisoned the spirit of the city are distilled. The sergeant, whose lowly condition means that

194

he is under no obligation to think elevated thoughts or to harbour suspicions about what lies beneath the surface of things, has rather homelier concerns, like this one with which he is about to dare to interrupt his superiors' meditations, With weather like this, the man might have gone to spend the day in the country, What country, asked the inspector in an ironic tone, What do you mean what country, The real country is on the other side of the frontier, on this side, it's all city. It was true. The sergeant had missed a golden opportunity to remain silent, but he had learned a lesson, asking such questions would get him nowhere. He concentrated on his driving and swore to himself that he would only open his mouth if asked to. That was when the superintendent spoke, We will be hard and implacable, we won't resort to any of the classic tricks, like that old, outmoded hard cop, soft cop routine, we are a commando of operatives, feelings don't count here, we will imagine that we are machines made to perform a specific task and we will simply carry out that task without so much as a backward glance, Yes, sir, said the inspector, Yes, sir, said the sergeant, breaking his own oath. The car turned into the street where the man who wrote the letter lives, over in that building, on the third floor. They parked the car a little further on, the sergeant opened the door for the superintendent, the inspector got out the other side, the commando is complete, on the firing line, fists clenched, action.

Now we see them on the landing. The superintendent gestures to the sergeant, who rings the doorbell. Total silence inside. The sergeant thinks, You see, I was right, he has gone to spend the day in the country. Another gesture, another ring on the doorbell. A few seconds later, they hear someone, a man, ask from behind the door, Who is it. The superintendent looks at his immediate subordinate, who says in a loud voice, Police, One moment, please, said the man, I have to get dressed. Four minutes passed. The superintendent made the same gesture, the sergeant again rang the doorbell, this time keeping his finger pressed down. One moment, one moment, please, I'm coming, I've only just got up, these last words were spoken with the door open by a man wearing shirt and trousers and still in his slippers, Today is the day of the slipper, thought the sergeant. The man did not seem alarmed, he wore the look of someone finally seeing the arrival of the visitors he has been waiting for, any hint of surprise was probably due only to the fact that there were so many of them. The inspector asked him his name and he told them, adding, Do come in, and I apologise for the state the place is in, I never imagined you would come so early, besides, I thought you would call me in to make a statement, but you've come to me instead, it's about the letter, I assume, Yes, it's about the letter, said the inspector bluntly, Come in, come in. The sergeant went in first, sometimes the hierarchy works in reverse, followed by the inspector, with the superintendent bringing up the rear. The man shuffled down the corridor, Follow me, this way, he opened a door that gave onto a small sitting-room and said, Sit down, please, and if you don't mind, I'll just go and put some shoes on, this is no way to receive visitors, We're not exactly what you would call visitors, remarked the inspector, No, of course not, it was just a manner of speaking, Go and put some shoes on, then, and be quick about it, we're in a hurry, No, we're not, we're not in any hurry at all, said the superintendent, who had not until then said a word. The man looked at him, and this time he did so with an air of slight alarm, as if the tone in which the superintendent had spoken was not what had been agreed, and all he could think of to say was, You can, I assure you, count on my entire cooperation, sir, Superintendent, said the sergeant, Superintendent, repeated the man, and you, sir, Don't worry, I'm just a sergeant. The man turned to the third member of the group, replacing his question with an interrogative lift of the eyebrows, but the answer came from the superintendent, This gentleman is an inspector and my chief officer, then he added,

Now go and put some shoes on, we'll wait for you. The man left the room. I can't hear anyone else in the apartment, it looks as if he lives alone, whispered the sergeant, His wife's probably gone to spend the day in the country, said the inspector with a smile. The superintendent signalled to them to be quiet, I'll ask the first questions, he said, lowering his voice. The man came back in and, as he sat down, said May I, as if he were not in his own house, and then, Here I am, now how can I help you. The superintendent nodded kindly, then began, Your letter, or, rather, your three letters, because there were three of them, Yes, I thought it was safer that way, because you never know, one of them might have got lost, the man began, Don't interrupt, just answer any questions I ask you, Yes, superintendent, Your letters, I repeat, were read with great interest by their recipients, especially as regards what you say about a certain unidentified woman who committed a murder four years ago. There was no question in these words, it was a simple reiteration of facts, and so the man said nothing. There was an expression of confusion and perplexity on his face, he could not understand why the superintendent did not get straight to the heart of the matter instead of wasting time on an episode which he had only mentioned in order to cast a still darker light on an already disquieting portrait. The superintendent pretended not to notice, Tell us what you know about that murder, he asked. The man suppressed an urge to remind the superintendent that this had not been the most important part of the letter, that, compared with the country's current situation, the murder was the least of it, but no, he wouldn't do that, prudence told him to follow the music they were asking him to dance to, later on, they were sure to change the record, I know that she killed a man, Did you see her do it, were you there, asked the superintendent, No, superintendent, but she herself confessed, To you, To me and to other people, You do know, I assume, the technical meaning of the word confession, More or less, superintendent, More or less isn't

197

enough, either you do or you don't, In the sense that you mean, no, I don't, Confession means a declaration of one's own mistakes or faults, it can also mean an acknowledgement of guilt or of the truth of an accusation by the accused to someone in authority or in a court of law, now, can these definitions be applied rigorously to this case, No, not rigorously, superintendent, Fine, continue, My wife was there, my wife witnessed the man's death, What do you mean by there, There, in the old insane asylum where we were quarantined, Your wife, I assume, was also blind, As I said the only person who didn't go blind was her, Who's her, The woman who committed the murder, Ah, We were in a dormitory, And the murder was committed there, No, superintendent, in another dormitory, So none of the people from your dormitory were present when the murder was committed, Only the women, Why only the women, It's difficult to explain, superintendent, Don't worry, we've got plenty of time, There were some blind men who took over and started terrorising us, Terrorising, Yes, superintendent, terrorising, How, They got hold of all the food and if we wanted to eat, we had to pay, And they demanded women as payment, Yes, superintendent, And that woman killed a man, Yes, superintendent, Killed him how, With a pair of scissors, Who was this man, The one who was in charge of the other blind men, She's obviously a brave woman, Yes, superintendent, Now tell us why you reported her, But I didn't, I only mentioned it because it seemed relevant, Sorry, I don't understand, What I meant to say in the letter was that someone who was capable of doing that was capable of doing the other thing. The superintendent did not ask what other thing this was, he merely looked at the person whom he had, using navy language, called his chief officer, inviting him to continue the interrogation. The inspector paused for a few seconds, Would you mind asking your wife to join us, he asked, we'd like to talk to her, My wife isn't here, When will she be back, She won't, we're divorced, When did that happen, Three years ago, Would you object to telling us why you got divorced, For personal reasons, Naturally they would be personal, For private reasons then, As with all divorces. The man looked at the inscrutable faces before him and realised that they would not leave him in peace until he had told them what they wanted to know. He cleared his throat, crossed and uncrossed his legs, I'm a man of principle, he began, Oh, we know that, said the sergeant, unable to contain himself, I mean, I know that, I had the privilege of reading your letter. The superintendent and the inspector smiled, it was a justifiable blow. The man looked at the sergeant, bewildered, as if he had not expected an attack from that quarter, and, lowering his eyes, he went on, It was to do with those blind men, I couldn't bear the fact that my wife had done it with those vile men, for a whole year I put up with the shame of it, but, in the end, it became unbearable, and so I left her, got a divorce, How odd, I thought you said that these other blind men gave you food in exchange for your women, said the inspector, That's right, And your principles, I assume, did not allow you to touch the food that your wife brought to you after she had, to use your expression, done it with those vile men. The man hung his head and did not reply. I understand your discretion, said the inspector, it really is too private a matter to be bandied about amongst strangers, oh, sorry, I didn't mean to wound your sensibilities. The man looked at the superintendent as if pleading for help, or at least asking him to replace the pincers with a spell on the rack. The superintendent obliged and applied the garrotte, In your letter, you referred to a group of seven people, Yes, superintendent, Who were they, Apart from the woman and her husband, Which woman, The one who didn't go blind, The one who acted as your guide, Yes, superintendent, The one who, in order to avenge her fellow women, stabbed the leader of the bandits with a pair of scissors, Yes, superintendent, Go on, Her husband was an ophthalmologist, We know that, There was a prostitute too, Did she tell you she was a prostitute, Not that I remember, no, superintendent, So how did you know she was a prostitute, By her manner, it was clear from her manner, And, of course, manners never deceive, go on, And there was an old man who was blind in one eye and wore a black eye-patch, and he and she lived together afterwards, Who's she, The prostitute, Were they happy, I've no idea, You must have some idea, During the year that we still saw each other, yes, they seemed happy. The superintendent counted on his fingers, There's still one missing, he said, Yes, there was a boy with a squint who had lost his parents in all the confusion, Do you mean that you all met in the dormitory, No, superintendent, we had all met before, Where, At the ophthalmologist's where my then wife took me when I went blind, in fact, I think I was the first person to go blind, And you infected the others, the whole city, including your visitors today, It wasn't my fault, superintendent, Do you know the names of these people, Yes, superintendent, Of all of them, Apart from the boy, if I knew his name then, I've forgotten it now, But you remember the others, Yes, superintendent, And their addresses, Yes, unless they've moved in the last three years, Of course, unless they've moved in the last three years. The superintendent glanced round the small room, and his gaze lingered on the television as if he were hoping for some inspiration from it, then he said, Sergeant, pass your notebook to this gentleman and lend him your pen so that he can write down the names and the addresses of the people of whom he has spoken so warmly, apart from the boy with the squint, who wouldn't be of any use to us anyway. The man's hands trembled when he took the pen and the notebook, they continued to tremble as he wrote, he was telling himself that there was no reason to feel afraid, that the police were there because he had, in some way, summoned them himself, what he didn't understand was why they didn't talk about the blank ballot papers, the insurrection, the conspiracy against the state, about the only real reason he had written his letter. His hands were trembling so much that his writing was almost illegible, May I use another sheet, he asked, Use as many as you like, replied the sergeant. His writing began to grow steadier, it was no longer a motive for embarrassment. While the sergeant retrieved the pen and handed the notebook to the superintendent, the man was wondering what gesture, what word could win him, even if only belatedly, the sympathy of these policemen, their benevolence, their complicity. Suddenly, he remembered, I've got a photograph, he exclaimed, yes, I think I've still got it, What photograph, asked the inspector, Of the group, it was taken shortly after we had recovered our sight, my wife didn't want it, she said she'd get a copy, she said I should keep it so that I wouldn't forget, Were those her words, asked the inspector, but the man did not reply, he had stood up and was about to leave the room, when the superintendent ordered, Sergeant, go with this gentleman, if he has any trouble finding the photograph, help him, don't come back without it. They were absent for only a few minutes. Here it is, said the man. The superintendent went over to the window to be able to see better. In a line, side by side, the six adults stood in pairs, couple by couple. On the right, alongside his wife, stood the man himself, plainly recognisable, to the left there stood, without a shadow of a doubt, the old man with the black eye-patch and the prostitute, and in the middle, by a process of elimination, two people who could only be the doctor's wife and her husband. In front, kneeling down like a football player, was the boy with the squint. Next to the doctor's wife was a large dog looking straight at the camera. The superintendent beckoned to the man to join him, Is that her, he asked, pointing, Yes, superintendent, that's her, And the dog, If you like, I can tell you the story, superintendent, No, don't bother, she'll tell me. The superintendent left first, followed by the inspector and then the sergeant. The man who had written the letter watched them go down the stairs. The building has no lift and there is little hope that it ever will.

THE THREE POLICEMEN DROVE AROUND THE CITY FOR A WHILE, FILLING in time until lunch, although they would not eat together. The plan was to park the car near an area where there were plenty of restaurants and then to go their separate ways, each to a different place, and meet exactly ninety minutes later in a square some way off, where the superintendent, this time at the wheel, would pick his subordinates up. Obviously, no one here knows who they are, besides, none of them has a capital P branded on his forehead, but common sense and prudence tell them not to wander around as a group through the centre of a city which is, for many reasons, hostile to them. True, there are three men over there, and another three ahead of them, but a quick glance is enough to see that they are normal people, belonging to the common species of passer-by, ordinary folk, free of all suspicion of being representatives of the law or pursued by it. During the drive, the superintendent wanted to hear his two subordinates' impressions of the man who had written the letter, making it clear, however, that he was not interested in any moral judgements, We know he's a bastard of the first order, so there's no point wasting time coming up with other descriptions. The inspector was the first to speak, saying that he had particularly admired the way in which the superintendent had directed the interrogation, skilfully omitting any reference to the malicious suggestion contained in the letter, that the doctor's wife, given her exceptional personal circumstances during the plague of blindness four years ago, could be the cause of or in some way implicated in the conspiracy that led to the capital's population casting blank votes. The guy was obviously completely thrown, he said, he was expecting that to be the main and possibly the only subject the police would be interested in, but how wrong he was. I almost felt sorry for him, he added. The sergeant agreed with what the inspector had said, noting, too, how, by alternating the role of interrogator between himself and the inspector, he had succeeded brilliantly in breaking down the interrogatee's defences. He paused and, in a low voice, said, Superintendent, it is my duty to inform you that when you told me to leave the room with him I used my pistol on him, Used it, how, asked the superintendent, I stuck it in his ribs, he's probably still got the mark, But why, Well, I thought it would take a while to find the photo and that the guy would take advantage of the interruption to come up with some trick to hinder the investigation, something that would force you, sir, to change the line of enquiry in the direction that best suited him, And now what do you want me to do, pin a medal on your chest, said the superintendent mockingly, We gained time, sir, the photo appeared in an instant, And I'm sorely tempted to make you disappear, Forgive me, sir, Oh, don't worry, I'll tell you when you're forgiven, always assuming I remember, Yes, sir, One question, Yes, sir, Was the safety catch on, Yes, sir, Why, because you'd forgotten to take it off, No, sir, I really just wanted to frighten the guy, And you managed to do that, Yes, sir, Well, it looks like I'll have to give you that medal after all, but, please, don't get too excited, and mind you don't run over that old lady or jump a red light, the last thing I want is to have to explain myself to a policeman, But there are no police in the city, sir, they were withdrawn when the state of siege was declared, said the inspector, Ah, now I understand, I was wondering why it was so quiet. They drove past a park where children were playing. The superintendent looked at them with an air that seemed distracted, absent, but the sigh that suddenly emerged from his breast showed that he must have been thinking about other times and other places. After we've had lunch, he said, I'll be going back to base, Yes, sir, said the sergeant, Do you have any orders for us, sir, asked the inspector, Go for a walk, stroll around the city, go into the cafés and shops, keep your eyes and ears open, and come back in time for supper, we won't be going out tonight, there's bound to be some canned stuff in the kitchen, Yes, sir, said the sergeant, And tomorrow we'll be working on our own, our bold driver, the policeman with the gun, will go and talk to the ex-wife of the man who wrote the letter, the inspector here, sitting in the dead man's seat, will visit the old man with the black eye-patch and his prostitute, and I'll reserve the doctor's wife and the doctor for myself, as for tactics, we'll stick strictly to those we used today, no mention of blank votes, no getting involved in political debates, restrict your questions to the circumstances surrounding the murder, to the personality of the presumed murderer, get them to talk about the group, how it was formed, if they had met before, what their relationship is like today, they're probably friends and will want to protect each other, but they're bound to make mistakes if they haven't reached some prior agreement about what they should say and what it would be best to stay quiet about, our job is to help them make those mistakes, and, to cut this rather long speech short, remember the most important fact of all, tomorrow morning, we must arrive at the houses of these people at exactly half past ten, I'm not telling you to synchronise watches, because that only happens in action movies, but we mustn't give any of the suspects the chance to pass on the message, to warn the others, but now let's go and have lunch, ah, yes, and when you come back, come in through the garage, on Monday, I'll have to find out whether or not the porter can be trusted. Rather more than the stipulated ninety minutes later, the superintendent picked up his assistants, who were waiting for him in the square, then dropped them off in turn, first the sergeant, then the inspector, in different parts of the city, where they would carry out the orders they had been given, to walk about, go into cafés and shops, keep their eyes and ears open, in short, to sniff out any crime. They will return to base for the promised canned supper and to sleep, and when the superintendent asks them if they have anything to report, they will confess that they have absolutely nothing to tell him, that while the inhabitants of this city aren't any less talkative than those in any other, they certainly don't talk about the subject of most interest. That's a good sign, he will say, the proof that there is a conspiracy lies precisely in the fact that no one talks about it, silence, in this case, does not contradict, it confirms. The phrase was not his, it had been spoken by the interior minister, with whom, when he got back to providential ltd, he'd had a brief phone conversation, which, even though the line was extremely safe, complied with all the precepts of the law of basic official secrecy. Here is a summary of their conversation, Hello, puffin speaking, Hello, puffin, replied albatross, First contact made with local bird life, friendly reception, useful interrogation with the participation of hawk and gull, good results, Substantial, puffin, Very substantial, albatross, we got an excellent photograph of the whole flock, tomorrow we'll start identifying the different species, Well done, puffin, Thank you, albatross, Listen, puffin, I'm listening, albatross, Don't be fooled by occasional silences, puffin, when birds are quiet, it doesn't necessarily mean that they're on their nests, it's the calm that conceals the storm, not the other way round, the same thing happens with human conspiracies, the fact that no one mentions them doesn't mean they don't exist, do you understand, puffin, Yes, albatross, I understand perfectly, What are you going to do tomorrow, puffin, I'm going to go for the osprey, Who is the osprey, puffin, explain yourself, It's the only one on the whole coast, albatross, indeed, as far as we know, there has never been another, Ah, now I understand, Do you have any orders for me, albatross, Just carry out rigorously those I gave you before you left, puffin, They will be rigorously carried out, albatross, Keep me posted, puffin, I will, albatross. Once he had checked that all microphones were switched off, the superintendent gave muttered vent to his feelings, Ye gods of the police and of espionage, what a farce, I'm puffin and he's albatross, the next thing you know we'll be communicating by squawks and screeches, there'd be a storm then, no fear. When his subordinates finally arrived back, tired from pounding the city streets, he asked them if they had any news, and they said no, they had strained eyes and ears watching and listening, but, alas, with no result. These people talk as if they had nothing to hide, they said. It was then that the superintendent, without giving his source, uttered the interior minister's words about conspiracies and the ways in which they disguise themselves.

The following day, after breakfast, they looked at the map and in the city guide for the streets they were interested in. The nearest one to the building where providential ltd is based is the street where the ex-wife of the man who wrote the letter, formerly known as the first blind man, has her apartment, the doctor's wife and her husband are a little further off, and furthest away are the old man with the black eye-patch and the prostitute. Let's just hope they're in. As on the previous day, they took the lift down to the garage, in fact, for those leading clandestine lives, this is not the best way of proceeding, because while it is true that, up until now, they have escaped the porter's busybodying, I wonder who those spooks are, I've never seen them around here before, he would think to himself, but they will not escape the curiosity of the garage attendant, and we will soon find out with what consequences. This time, the inspector will drive, since he has the longest journey. The sergeant asked the superintendent if he had any special instructions to give him and was told that he had no special instructions, only general ones, I just hope you don't do anything stupid and that you keep your gun firmly in its holster, But I would never threaten a woman with a gun, sir, Oh, yeah, anyway, don't forget, you are forbidden to knock on her door before half past ten, Yes, sir, Go for a walk, have a coffee if you can find somewhere, buy a newspaper, look in the shop windows, you can't have forgotten everything you were taught at police college, No, sir, Good, this is your street, out you get, Where will we meet when we've finished, asked the sergeant, we need to arrange a meeting place, that's the trouble with only having one key to the office, I mean, if I, for example, was to finish my interrogation first, I wouldn't be able to go back to base, Nor would I, said the inspector, That's what comes of them not providing us with mobile phones, insisted the sergeant, sure of his reasoning and trusting that the beauty of the morning would dispose his superior to be kind. The superintendent agreed, Meanwhile, we'll have to make do with what we've got, but if the investigation calls for it, then I'll requisition more equipment, as for keys, if the ministry authorises the expense, tomorrow, you'll each have a key of your own, And what if they refuse, Then I'll sort something out, But what are we going to do about fixing a meeting place, asked the inspector, From what we know of this story already, everything indicates that my investigation is going to take the longest, so why don't you meet me there, make a note of the address, we'll see then how the people being interrogated react to the arrival of two more police officers, An excellent idea, sir, said the inspector. The sergeant merely nodded, since he could not say out loud what he was thinking, that any praise for the idea belonged to him, even if only indirectly and by a very tortuous route. He made a note of the address in his investigator's notebook and got out of the car. The inspector drove off and, as he did so, said, To be fair, he really tries, poor lad, I can remember being just like him when I was starting out, so eager to do something right that I made nothing but blunders, in fact, I sometimes ask myself how I ever came to be promoted to inspector, Or how I came to be what I am today, You too, sir, Me too, me too, my friend, all policemen start out much the same, everything else is just a question of luck, Luck and knowledge, Knowledge on its own isn't always enough, whereas with luck and time you can achieve almost anything, but don't ask me what luck is because I wouldn't be able to tell you, all I can say is that often you can get what you want just by having friends in the right places or some favour to call in, Not everyone was born to be a superintendent, True, Besides, a police force made up entirely of superintendents wouldn't work, Nor would an army made up entirely of generals. They turned into the street where the ophthalmologist lives. Drop me here, said the superintendent, I'll walk the rest of the way, Good luck, sir, And to you, Let's hope we can resolve this matter quickly, to be perfectly honest I feel as if I was lost in the middle of a minefield, Calm down, man, there's no reason to be worried, look at these streets, see how peaceful and quiet the city is, That's exactly what worries me, sir, a city like this, with no one in charge, with no government, no security, no police, and no one seems to care, there's something very mysterious going on here which I can't quite understand, That's what we were sent here to do, to understand, we have the knowledge and I just hope the rest comes with it, Luck, you mean, Yes, luck, Well, good luck, then, sir, Good luck, inspector, and if the woman who's supposed to be a prostitute shoots you a seductive look or gives you a glimpse of thigh, just pretend you haven't noticed, concentrate on the interests of the investigation, think of the eminent dignity of the organisation that we serve, The old man with the black eye-patch is sure to be there too, and old men, I'm reliably informed, are real terrors, said the inspector. The superintendent smiled, Old age is catching up with me as well, I wonder if I'll live long enough to turn into a real terror. Then he glanced at his watch, It's a quarter past ten already, I hope you manage to get there on time, As long as you and the sergeant keep to the timetable, it doesn't really matter if I'm a bit late, said the inspector. The superintendent said goodbye, See you later, and got out of the car and, as soon as he set foot on the pavement, as if he had made an appointment to meet his own flawed reasoning right there, he realised that it made no sense to have been so rigorous about the time when they should knock on the suspects' respective doors, since, with a policeman in their home, they would have neither the sangfroid nor the opportunity to phone their friends to warn them of the imagined danger, always assuming they were that astute, astute enough for them to work out that if they were the object of police attention, then their friends would be too, Besides, thought the superintendent, irritated with himself, they obviously won't be their only friends, and in that case, how many of their friends would each of them have to ring, how many. He was not just thinking these thoughts to himself now, he was muttering accusations, abuse, insults, How did such an imbecile ever manage to become superintendent, how could the government have given an imbecile like me full responsibility for an investiga-tion on which the fate of the whole country might hang, and how did this imbecile come up with that stupid order to his subordin-ates, I just hope they're not both laughing at me at this very moment, I shouldn't think the sergeant is, but the inspector is bright, too bright really, even though, at first sight, he doesn't seem to be, or perhaps he's just good at hiding it, which, of course, makes him doubly dangerous, no, I'd better be very careful with him, treat him with caution, I wouldn't want this to get out, others have found themselves in similar situations and with catastrophic results, someone once said, I can't remember who, that a moment's folly can ruin a whole career. This implacable bout of self-flagellation did the superintendent good. Seeing him crushed and ground into the mud, it was the turn of cool reflection to speak and to show him that the order had not been foolish at all, Imagine what would have happened if you hadn't given those instructions and the inspector and the sergeant had turned up at whatever time they fancied, one of them in the morning, the other in the afternoon, then you really would have been an imbecile, an out-and-out imbecile, not to see what would inevitably happen, the people who had been interrogated in the morning would rush to warn those who were to be interrogated in the afternoon, and when, that afternoon, the investigator knocked on the door of the suspects he'd been allocated he would find himself confronted by a line of defence he might not be able to break down, that's why you're a superintendent and will continue to be, not just because you know your job, but also because you're lucky enough to have me here, cool reflection, to put things in perspective, starting with the inspector, whom you won't now have to start treating with kid gloves, as was your intention, a rather cowardly one if you don't mind my saying. The superintendent didn't mind. With all this coming and going, thinking and rethinking, he was late in carrying out his own order, and it was already a quarter to eleven when he raised his hand to press the doorbell. The lift had carried him up to the fourth floor, this is the door.

The superintendent was waiting for someone inside to ask Who is it, but the door simply opened and a woman appeared and said, Yes. The superintendent put his hand in his pocket and produced his identification, Police, he said, And what do the police want with the people who live in this apartment, asked the woman, The answers to a few questions, About what, Look, I hardly think the landing is the best place to begin an interrogation, Oh, so it's an interrogation, is it, asked the woman, Madam, even if I only had two questions to ask you, it would still be an interrogation, You appreciate precision in language I see, Especially in the answers I am given, Now that's a good answer, It wasn't difficult, you served it up to me on a plate, And I'll serve you up some others if what you're after is the truth, Looking for the truth is the fundamental aim of any policeman, Well, I'm very glad to hear you say that so emphatically, you'd better come in, my husband has just popped out to buy the newspapers, he won't be long, If you prefer, if you think it would be more proper, I can wait outside, Nonsense, come in, in what safer hands could anyone be than in those of the police, said the woman. The superintendent went in, the woman walked ahead of him and opened the door to a welcoming living-room in which one sensed a friendly, lived-in atmosphere, Please, super-intendent, sit down, she said, and asked, Would you like a cup of coffee, No, thank you, we don't accept anything when we're on duty, Naturally, that's how all the great corruptions begin, a cup of coffee today, a cup of coffee tomorrow, and by the third cup, it's too late, It's one of our rules, madam, May I ask you to satisfy one little curiosity of mine, What's that, You told me that you were from the police, you showed me an identity card that says you're a super-intendent, but, as far as I know, the police withdrew from the capital some weeks ago, leaving us to fall into the clutches of the violence and crime that is rife everywhere, am I to understand from your presence here today that our policemen have come home, No, madam, we have not, to use your expression, come home, we are still on the other side of the dividing line, You must have strong reasons, then, to cross the frontier, Yes, very strong, And the ques-tions you have come to ask are, naturally, to do with those reasons, Naturally, So I'd better wait until you ask them, Exactly. Three minutes later, they heard the front door open. The woman left the room and said to the person who had come in, Guess what, we've got a visitor, a police superintendent no less, And since when have police superintendents been interested in innocent people. These last words were spoken in the room itself, the doctor preceding his wife and addressing the superintendent, who answered, getting up out of the chair in which he had been sitting, There are no innocent people, even when not guilty of an actual crime, we are all unfailingly guilty of some fault, And what crime or fault are we being blamed for or accused of, There's no rush, doctor, let's make ourselves comfortable first, that way we can talk more easily. The doctor and his wife sat down on a sofa and waited. The superintendent remained silent for a few seconds, he was suddenly unsure which was the best tactic to adopt. It was one thing for the inspector and the sergeant, in order not to start the hare too early, to limit themselves, in accordance with the instructions they had been given, to asking questions about the murder of the blind man, but he, the superintendent, had his eyes fixed on a more ambitious goal, to find out if the woman before him, sitting beside her husband as calmly as if, owing nothing, she had nothing to fear, was, as well as being a murderer, also part of the diabolical plot that had caused the government's current state of humiliation, having forced it to bow its head and kneel. It is not known who in the official department of cryptography decided to bestow on the superintendent the grotesque code-name of puffin, doubtless some personal enemy, for a more fitting and justifiable nickname would be alekhine, the grand master of chess, who has, sadly, now left the ranks of the living. The doubt that had arisen dissipated like smoke and a solid certainty took its place. Observe with what sublime, combinatorial art he is about to develop the moves that will lead him, or so he thinks, to the final checkmate. With a sly smile, he said, Actually I wouldn't mind that cup of coffee you were kind enough to offer me, It's my duty to remind you that the police accept nothing while on duty, the doctor's wife replied, enjoying the game, Superintendents are authorised to infringe the rules whenever they think it appropriate, You mean when useful to the interests of the investigation, You could put it like that, And you're not afraid that the coffee I'm about to bring you will be a step along the road to corruption, Ah, I seem to remember you saying that that only happens with the third cup of coffee, No, what I said was that the third cup of coffee completed the corrupting process, the first opened the door, the second held it open so that the aspirant to corruption could enter without stumbling, the third slammed the door shut, Thank you for the warning, which I take as a piece of advice, and so I'll stop at the first cup, Which will be served at once, said the woman, and with that she left the room. The superintendent glanced at his watch. Are you in a hurry, asked the doctor pointedly, No, doctor, I'm not in a hurry, I was just wondering if I'm keeping you from your lunch, It's too early yet for lunch, And I was also wondering how long it will take before I can leave here with the answers I want, Does that mean that you know the answers you want or that you want answers to your questions, asked the doctor, adding, they are not the same thing, You're quite right, they're not, during the brief conversation I had alone with your wife, she had occasion to remark that I admire precision in language, and I see that is also the case with you, In my profession, it's not unusual for diagnostic errors to occur simply because of some linguistic imprecision, You know, I've been calling you doctor and you haven't yet asked me how I know you're a doctor, Because it seems to me a waste of time asking a policeman how he knows what he knows or claims to know, A good answer, just as one would not ask god how he became omniscient, omnipresent and omnipotent, You're not saying that the police are god, are you, We are merely his modest representatives on earth, doctor, Oh, I thought they were the churches and the priests, The churches and the priests are only second in the ranks.

The woman came back with the coffee, three cups on a tray and a few plain biscuits. It seems that everything in this world is doomed to repeat itself, thought the superintendent, while his palate relived the tastes of breakfast at providential ltd, Thank you very much, but I'll just have the coffee, he said. When he replaced the cup on the tray, he thanked her again and added with a knowing smile,

Excellent coffee, madam, I might even reconsider my decision not to have a second cup. The doctor and his wife had already finished theirs. None of them had touched the biscuits. The superintendent produced a notebook from his jacket pocket, prepared his pen, and allowed his voice to emerge in a neutral, expressionless tone, as if he were not really interested in the answer, What explanation would you give, madam, for the fact that during the epidemic four years ago you did not go blind. The doctor and his wife looked at each other, surprised, and she asked, How do you know that I didn't go blind four years ago, Just now, said the superintendent, your husband, with great perspicacity, remarked that he considered it a waste of time asking a policeman how he knows what he knows or claims to know, Yes, but I'm not my husband, And I do not have to reveal, either to you or to him, the secrets of my profession, it's enough that I know you did not go blind. The doctor made as if to intervene, but his wife placed her hand on his arm, All right, then, tell me, and I assume that this is not a secret, of what possible interest can it be to the police that I did or did not go blind four years ago, If you had gone blind like everyone else, if you had gone blind as I myself did, you can be quite sure that I would not be here now, Was it a crime not to go blind, she asked, No, not going blind wasn't and never could be a crime, although, now that you mention it, you were able to commit a crime precisely because you weren't blind, A crime, A murder. The woman glanced at her husband as if asking his advice, then turned rapidly back to the superintendent and said, Yes, it's true, I did kill a man. She did not go on, she kept her eyes fixed on him, waiting. The superintendent pretended to be writing something down in his notebook, but all he was doing was playing for time, trying to think what his next move would be. The woman's response had surprised him less because she had confessed to a murder than because of the way she had immediately fallen silent again afterwards, as if there were nothing more to be said on the subject. And the truth is, he thought, it isn't the crime that interests me. I assume you had a good reason, he ventured, For what, asked the woman, For committing the crime, It wasn't a crime, What was it then, An act of justice, That's what the courts are for, to administer justice, But I could hardly have gone and complained to the police, for as you yourself said, at the time, you were blind, like everyone else, Apart from you, Yes, apart from me, Who did you kill, A rapist, a vile creature, Are you telling me that you killed someone who was raping you, No, not me, a friend, Was she blind, Yes, she was, And the man was blind too, Yes, How did you kill him, With a pair of scissors, Did you stab him in the heart, No, in the throat, You don't have the face of a murderer, I'm not a murderer, You killed a man, He wasn't a man, super-intendent, he was a bedbug. The superintendent wrote something else down and turned to the doctor, And where were you, sir, while your wife was busy killing this bedbug, In the dormitory of the former lunatic asylum where they had put us when they still thought that by isolating the first people to go blind they could stop the spread of the blindness, You are, I believe, an ophthalmologist, Yes, I had the privilege, if I can call it that, of dealing with the first person to go blind, A man or a woman, A man, Did he end up in the same dormitory, Yes, along with a few other people who were in my surgery at the time, Did it seem to you a good thing that your wife had murdered the rapist, It seemed necessary, Why, You wouldn't ask that question if you had been there, Possibly, but I wasn't, and so I'll ask you again why it seemed necessary to you that your wife should have killed the bedbug, that is, the man raping her friend, Someone had to do it, and she was the only one who could see, Just because the bedbug was a rapist, It wasn't just him, all the others in the same dormitory were demanding women in exchange for food, he was the ringleader, Your wife was also raped, Yes, Before or after her friend, Before. The superintendent made another note in his book, then asked, In your view, as an ophthalmologist, what explanation could there be for the fact that your wife did not go blind, In my view as an ophthalmologist, there is no explanation, You have a remarkable wife, sir, Yes, I do, but not just because of that, What happened afterwards to the people who had been interned in that old lunatic asylum, There was a fire, most of them must have been burned alive or crushed by falling masonry, How do you know there was falling masonry, Very simple, because we could hear it once we were outside, And how did you and your wife escape, We got out in time, You were lucky, Yes, she guided us, Who do you mean by us, Myself and a few other people, the ones who had been in my surgery, Who were they, The first blind man, to whom I referred earlier, and his wife, a young woman with conjunctivitis, an older man with a cataract, and a young boy with a squint who was with his mother, And your wife helped them all escape from the fire, Yes, all of them, apart from the boy's mother, she wasn't in the asylum, she had got separated from her son, and they only found each other again weeks after we had recovered our sight, Who took care of the boy during that time, We did, Your wife and yourself, Yes, well, she did, because she could see, and the rest of us helped as best we could, Do you mean to say that you lived together as a group, with your wife as guide, As guide and provider, You were very lucky, said the superintendent again, You could call it that, Did you stay in touch with the people in the group once things had got back to normal, Yes, of course, And you still do, Apart from the first blind man, yes, Why that one exception, He wasn't a very nice person, In what sense, In all senses, That's too vague, Yes, I know, And you don't want to be more specific, Speak to him yourself and make up your own mind, Do you know where they live, Who, The first blind man and his wife, They split up, they're divorced, Do you still see her, Yes, we do, But not him, No, not him, Why, As I said, he's not a nice person. The superintendent went back to his notebook and wrote down his own name so that it would not look as if he had learned nothing from such a long interrogation. He was about to make his next move, the most problematic and risky of the whole game. He raised his head, looked at the doctor's wife, opened his mouth to speak, but she anticipated him, You're a police superintendent, you came and identified yourself as such and have been asking us all kinds of questions, but aside from the matter of the premeditated murder which I committed and to which I have confessed, but for which there were no witnesses, some because they died, and all of them because they were blind, not to mention the fact that no one wants to know now what happened four years ago when everything was in chaos and the law was a mere dead letter, we are still waiting for you to tell us what brought you here, I think it's time you put your cards on the table, stopped beating about the bush and got straight down to what really interests the person who sent you here. Up until that moment, the superintendent had had a very clear idea of the aim of the mission with which he had been charged by the interior minister, neither more nor less than finding out if there was some relationship between the phenomenon of the blank votes and the woman sitting there before him, but her interpolation, blunt and to the point, had disarmed him, and, worse than that, had made him suddenly aware of how ridiculous it would seem if he were to ask her, with his eyes cast down because he would not have the courage to look at her, You wouldn't by any chance be the organiser, the leader, the head of the subversive movement that came into being in order to place democracy in a situation which it would be no exaggeration to describe as perilous, if not fatal, What subversive movement, she would ask, The one behind the blank votes, Are you telling me that casting a blank vote is a subversive act, she would ask again, If it happens in large numbers, yes, And where does it say that, in the constitution, in the electoral law, in the ten commandments, in the highway code, on the cough medicine bottle, she would insist, Well, it's not written down exactly, but anyone can see that it's a simple matter of a hierarchy of values and of common sense, first there are the valid votes, then the blank votes, then the void votes, and, finally, the abstentions, I mean, obviously, democracy will be imperilled if one of those secondary categories overtakes the primary one, the votes are there so that we can make prudent use of them, And I'm the person to blame for what happened, That's what I'm trying to find out, And just how did I manage to get the majority of the population to cast blank votes, by slipping pamphlets under their doors, offering up midnight prayers and conjurations, adding a special chemical to the water supply, promising first prize in the lottery to everyone, or buying votes with the money my husband earns at his surgery, You kept your sight when everyone else was blind and you have been unable or unwilling to explain why, And that makes me guilty of a plot against world democracy, That's what I'm trying to find out, Well, go and find out, and when you've completed your investigation, come and tell me about it, until then you won't get another word out of me. And that, above all else, was what the superintendent did not want. He was just preparing to say that he had no further questions, but would return the following day, when the doorbell rang. The doctor got up and went to see who it was. He returned to the living-room accompanied by the inspector. This gentleman says he's a police inspector and that you gave him orders to come here, Yes, I did, said the superintendent, but I've finished my work for the day, we'll continue tomorrow at the same hour, Sir, you told me and the sergeant, the inspector broke in, but the superintendent cut him off, What I did or did not tell you is of no interest now, So, tomorrow, will all three of us come, Inspector, that question is impertinent, any decisions I make are made in the proper place and at the proper time, and you will find out what they are in due course, replied the superintendent angrily. He turned to the doctor's wife and said, Tomorrow, as you requested, I won't waste time with circumlocutions, I'll come straight to the point, and you'll find what I have to ask you no less extraordinary than I find the fact that you kept your sight during the general epidemic of blindness four years ago, I went blind, the inspector went blind, your husband went blind, but you did not, we'll find out if, in this case, the old dictum holds true, she that made the saucepan made the lid, So it's to do with saucepans, then, superintendent, asked the doctor's wife in a wry tone, No, it's to do with lids, madam, lids, replied the superintendent as he withdrew, relieved that his adversary had supplied him with a reasonably nimble exit line. He had a faint headache.

THEY DID NOT HAVE LUNCH TOGETHER. STICKING TO HIS TACTIC OF controlled dispersal, the superintendent reminded the inspector and the sergeant, when they went their separate ways, that they should not go to the same restaurants they had gone to yesterday, and, just as he would have done had he been his own subordinate, he himself scrupulously carried out the orders he had given. He did so in a spirit of self-sacrifice too, for he ended up choosing a restaurant which, despite the three stars promised on the menu, only put one on his plate. This time, there was not one meeting-point, but two, the sergeant was waiting at the first, and the inspector at the second. They both saw at once that their superior was not in the mood for conversation, the encounter with the ophthalmologist and his wife had clearly not gone well. And since they, in turn, had gleaned no useful results from their investigations, the planned exchange and study of information back at providential ltd, insurance and reinsurance, did not promise to be the smoothest of rides. This professional tension was only heightened by the unexpected and troubling question put to them by the garage attendant when they arrived in their car, Where are you gentlemen from. It is true that the superintendent, all honour to him and to his experience in the job, did not lose his cool, We're from providential ltd, he replied sharply, and then, even more sharply, We're going to park where we always park, in the company's designated space, so your question is not just impertinent, it's rude, It may well be impertinent and rude, but I really don't remember seeing you here before, That, said the superintendent, is because not only are you rude, you also have a very poor memory, my colleagues here are new to the company and this is their first visit, but I've certainly been here before, now get out of our way will you, the driver's a little nervous and he might accidentally run you over. They parked the car and got into the lift. Not even considering that it might be a rash thing to say, the sergeant was eager to explain that he wasn't in the least nervous, that in the aptitude tests he'd done before joining the police, he had been described as very calm, but the superintendent silenced him with a brusque gesture. And now, protected by the reinforced walls and soundproof floor and ceiling of providential ltd, he launched a pitiless attack, Did it not even occur to you, you idiot, that there might be microphones installed in the lift, I'm sorry, sir, really I am, I wasn't thinking, spluttered the poor man, Tomorrow, you can stay here and keep watch over the place and use the time to write out five hundred times I am an idiot, Sir, please, Oh, leave it, take no notice, I know I'm exaggerating, but that man annoyed me, we've been carefully avoiding using the front door so as not to draw attention to ourselves and then that creep shows up, Perhaps we should get our people to write him a note, the way they did with the porter before we arrived, suggested the inspector, That would be counter-productive, we don't want anyone to notice us at all, It may be too late for that, sir, perhaps if the service has another place in the city, it would be best if we moved in there, Oh, they have, they have, but as far as I know, none of them is currently in operation, We could try, No, there's no time, and, besides, the ministry wouldn't like the idea, this business has got to be sorted out quickly, urgently, May I speak frankly, sir, asked the inspector, Go ahead, Well, it seems to me we're up a blind alley or, worse still, trapped inside a poisoned wasps' nest, What makes you think that, It's hard to explain really, but the fact is that I feel as if we were sitting on a barrel of gunpowder with the fuse lit, and that it's going to blow up at any moment. The superintendent could have been listening to his own thoughts, but his position and the responsibility he bore to the mission he had been charged with allowed for no swerving from the straight road of duty, I disagree, he said, and with those two words brought the matter to a close.

Now they were sitting round the table where they had eaten breakfast that morning, with their notebooks open, ready for a brainstorming session. You start, the superintendent told the sergeant, As soon as I went into the apartment, he said, I could tell no one had tipped the woman off, Of course they hadn't, we had agreed that we would all arrive at half past ten, Yes, but I was a bit late, it was actually ten thirty-seven when I knocked on the door, confessed the sergeant, That doesn't matter now, carry on, let's not waste any more time, She told me to come in and asked if I would like a coffee, and I said I would, well, I didn't see why not, I felt almost like a visitor, then I told her that I was investigating what happened four years ago in the insane asylum, but then I thought it would be best not to broach the subject of the blind murder victim immediately, which is why I decided to ask instead about the cause of the fire, she found it odd that after four years we should want to revisit the very thing that everyone had been trying to forget, and I said that the idea now was to record as many facts as possible because the weeks when those events took place could no longer remain a blank in the nation's history, but she was no fool, she immediately pointed out the incongruity, that was the word she used, of us being in the situation in which we now find ourselves, with the city isolated and under a state of siege because of the blank votes, and someone having the idea of investigating what had happened during the plague of blindness, I have to admit, sir, that, at first, I was completely thrown and didn't know what to say in response, but I managed to come up with an explanation, which was that the investigation had been decided upon before the blank votes business, but that it had got delayed by bureaucratic red tape and that it had only been possible to implement it now, then she said that she had no idea what had caused the fire, it must have been mere coincidence, something that could easily have happened at any time, then I asked her how she had managed to get out, and she started telling me about the doctor's wife and praising her to the skies, saying what a remarkable person she was, completely unlike anyone she had met in her entire life, utterly remarkable, I'm sure, she said, that if it hadn't been for her, I wouldn't be here talking to you today, she saved us all, and it isn't just that she saved us, she did more than that, she protected us, fed us, looked after us, then I asked her who she meant when she used the personal pronoun us, and she listed, one by one, the people we already know about, and finally, she said that her then husband had also been part of the group, but that she didn't want to talk about him because they'd been divorced for three years, and that was all I learned from the conversation, sir, the impression I came away with was that the doctor's wife must be some kind of heroine, a truly noble soul. The superintendent pretended not to have heard those last few words. By doing so, he would not have to reprehend the sergeant for describing as a heroine and a truly noble soul a woman who was currently under suspicion of being involved in the worst crime that could, in the present circumstances, be committed against the nation. He felt tired. And in a quiet, flat voice, he asked the inspector to report on what he had learned at the house of the prostitute and the old man with the black eye-patch, Well, if she was a prostitute, I don't think she is any more, Why, asked the superintendent, Because she doesn't have the manners or gestures or words or style of a prostitute, You seem to know a lot about prostitutes, Not really sir, only the usual things, plus a bit of personal experience, but mainly preconceived ideas, Go on, They received me politely enough, but they didn't offer me any coffee, Are they married, Well, they were both wearing wedding rings, And what did you make of the old man, He's old, and that's about all there is to be said about him, There you're wrong, there is everything to be said about the old, it's just that no one asks them anything, and so they keep quiet, Well, he didn't, Good for him, carry on, Anyway, I started talking about the fire, as my colleague here did, but then realised that I wouldn't get anywhere doing that, and so I decided to make a head-on attack, I mentioned a letter that the police had received and which described certain criminal acts committed in the asylum before the fire, amongst them a murder, and I asked them if they knew anything about it, and she said that she did, that no one could possibly know more, since she herself was the murderer, And did she say what the murder weapon was, asked the superintendent, Yes, a pair of scissors, And did she stab the man in the heart, No, sir, in the throat, And what else, To be honest, I was completely taken aback, Yes, I can imagine, Suddenly we had two perpetrators for the same crime, Go on, What comes next is pure horror, The fire, you mean, No, sir, she started describing in shocking, almost brutal detail what happened to the women who were raped in the dormitory occupied by the blind men, And what did he do while his wife was describing all this, He just looked straight at me, with his one eye, as if he could see inside me, That's just your imagination, No, sir, I learned then that one eye can see better than two, because, not having the other eye to help it, it has to do all the work itself, Perhaps that's why they say that in the country of the blind, the one-eyed man is king, Perhaps it is, sir, Go on, continue, When she had stopped talking, he began by saying that he didn't believe that the motive for my visit, that was the expression he used, had anything to do with ascertaining the causes of a fire of which nothing now remained or of clearing up the circumstances surrounding a murder that could never be proved, and that, if I had nothing more of any value to add, would I please leave, And what did you say, I invoked my authority as a policeman, said that I'd gone there with a mission to carry out and that I'd take whatever steps were necessary to do so, And what did he say, He replied that, in that case, I must be the only policeman on duty in the entire capital, since the police force had disappeared weeks ago, and that he therefore thanked me for my concern for their safety and, he hoped, my concern for the safety of a few other people too, since he couldn't quite believe that a policeman had been sent solely for the benefit of the two people in that room, And then, The situation had become difficult and I couldn't really do much more, the only way I could find of covering my retreat was by saying that they should prepare themselves for a confrontation in court because, according to the information we had, which was absolutely reliable, it was not she who had killed the leader of the blind criminals, but another person, a woman who had already been identified, And how did they react, At first, I thought I had frightened them, but the old man recovered at once and said that, there in their home, or wherever it might be, they would be accompanied by a lawyer who knew more about the law than the police, Do you think you really did frighten them, asked the superintendent, Yes, I think so, but obviously I can't be sure, They might have been afraid, but certainly not for themselves, Who for, then, sir, For the real murderer, the doctor's wife, But the prostitute, Look, I don't know that we have the right to continue calling her that, inspector, All right, the wife of the man with the black eye-patch said that she was the killer, even though it's true that the man doesn't accuse her in his letter, but the doctor's wife, Who was, in fact, the real perpetrator of the crime, she herself confessed and confirmed as much to me. At this point, it was logical for the inspector and the sergeant to assume that their superior, now that he had touched on the subject of his own investigations, would give them a more or less complete report of what he had found out from his visit, but the superintendent merely said that he would be going back to the suspects' apartment the next day to interrogate them further and only then would he decide what to do next, And what about us, what should we do tomorrow, asked the inspector, Surveillance operations, nothing more, you take care of the ex-wife of the man who wrote the letter, she doesn't know you, so you shouldn't have any problem, Which means, automatically and by a process of elimination, said the sergeant, that I'll be taking care of the old man and the prostitute, Unless you can prove that she really is a prostitute, or continues to be one if she ever was, the use of the word prostitute is henceforth banned from our conversations, Yes, sir, And even if she is, find some other way of referring to her, Yes, sir, I'll use her name, The names were all transcribed into my notebook, they are no longer in yours, If you'd just tell me what her name is, sir, then there'd be no more of this prostitute business, Sorry, I can't, I consider that information to be, for the moment, confidential, Her name, or all the names, asked the sergeant, All of them, Well, then, I don't know what to call her, You can call her, for example, the girl with the dark glasses, But she wasn't wearing dark glasses, I can swear to that, Everyone has worn dark glasses at least once in their life, replied the superintendent, getting up. Shoulders hunched, he made his way over to the part of the office where he had his bedroom and closed the door behind him. I bet you he's going to get in touch with the ministry, said the inspector, What's up with him, asked the sergeant, He feels as bewildered as we do, It's as if he doesn't believe in what he's doing, Do you, No, but I'm just following orders, he's in charge, he shouldn't be giving off these confusing signals, because we'll be the ones to suffer the consequences, when the wave hits the rock, it's always the mussels that pay, Hm, I'm not sure how accurate a comparison that is, Why, Because it's always seems to me that the mussels are really glad when the water rushes over them, Search me, but I've certainly never heard mussels laugh, Oh, they not only laugh, they positively chuckle, it's just that the sound of the waves drowns them out, and you have to put your ear really close, That's not true, you're having fun now at the expense of a lowly sergeant, Don't get annoyed with me, it's simply a harmless way of passing the time, There's a better way than that, What, Sleep, I'm tired, I'm going to bed, The superintendent might need you, What, to go and bang my head against a brick wall again, I don't think so, You're probably right, said the inspector, I'll follow your example and go and have a lie-down too, but I'll leave a note here to tell him to call us if he needs us, Good idea.

The superintendent had taken off his shoes and lain down on the bed. He was lying on his back, with his hands clasped behind his head, looking up at the ceiling, as if hoping for some advice from there or, if not that, at least what we usually call a disinterested opinion. Perhaps because it was soundproof, and therefore deaf, the ceiling had nothing to say to him, and, since it spent most of its time alone, it had practically lost the power of speech. The superintendent was going over in his mind the conversation he'd had with the doctor's wife and her husband, her face and his face, the dog that had got to its feet, growling, when he came in, only to lie down again at a word from his mistress, the old brass oil lamp which reminded him of an identical one that had been in his parents' house, but which had disappeared no one knew how, he was mixing these memories with what he had just heard from the mouths of the inspector and the sergeant and he was wondering what the hell he was doing there. He had crossed the frontier in pure movie detective style, he had convinced himself that he had come to rescue his country from mortal danger, and, in the name of that conviction, had given his subordinates ridiculous orders for which they had been kind enough to forgive him, he had tried to hold together a precarious framework of suspicions that was gradually falling apart with each minute that passed, and now he was wondering, surprised by a vague anxiety that made his diaphragm tighten, what reasonably credible information could he, the puffin, invent to transmit to an albatross who would, at this moment, be asking impatiently why he was so late in sending him news. What am I going to say to him, he wondered, that our suspicions about the osprey have been confirmed, that the husband and the others are part of the conspiracy, then he'll ask who these others are, and I'll say there's an old man with a black eye-patch who would really suit the code-name wolf-fish, and a girl with dark glasses whom we could call catfish, and the ex-wife of the guy who wrote the letter, and she could be called needle-fish, always assuming you agree with these designations, albatross. The superintendent had already got up from the bed and was talking now on the red phone, he was saying, Yes, albatross, the people I've just mentioned are not really big fish, they were just lucky enough to meet the osprey, who protected them, And what did you make of the osprey, puffin, She seemed a decent woman, normal, intelligent, and, if everything the others said about her is true, albatross, and I'm inclined to think it is, then she is clearly a quite extraordinary person, So out of the ordinary, puffin, that she was capable of killing a man with a pair of scissors, According to the witnesses, albatross, the man was a vile rapist, a totally repellent creature, Let's not delude ourselves, puffin, it's clear to me that these people have cooked up a single version of events just in case anyone should ever come and interrogate them, they've had four years to do so, and the way I see it, from the information you've given me and from my own deductions and intuitions, I would bet anything you like that these five people constitute an organised cell, probably, even, the head of that tapeworm we talked about a while ago, Neither I nor my colleagues had that impression, albatross, Well, puffin, you're going to have no option but to change your mind, We would need proof, without proof, we can do nothing, albatross, Find it, then, puffin, make a rigorous search of all their homes, But we can't make house searches without the authorisation of a judge, albatross, I would remind you, puffin, that the city is under a state of siege and that all the inhabitants' rights and guarantees have been suspended, And what if we can't find any proof, albatross, I refuse to admit that possibility, puffin, you strike me as rather too ingenuous for a superintendent, as long as I've been interior minister, any proofs that weren't there always turned up in the end, What you're asking me to do is neither easy nor pleasant, albatross, I'm not asking, puffin, I'm ordering you, Yes, albatross, but I would just like to point out that we have found no evidence of any crime, there's no proof that the person whom it was decided to consider as a suspect is, in fact, a suspect, indeed, all the contacts we have made, all the interrogations we have carried out, point to the innocence of that person, The photograph taken of a detainee, puffin, is always that of someone presumed to be innocent, only afterwards does one learn that the criminal was there all the time, May I ask a question, albatross, Ask and I will answer, puffin, I've always been good at giving answers, What will happen if no proof of guilt is found, The same as would happen if no proof of innocence were found, How should I understand that, albatross, That there are cases when the sentence has been handed down before the crime has even been committed, In that case, if I understand you rightly, albatross, I ask to be withdrawn from this mission, You will be withdrawn, puffin, I promise you, but not now, nor at your request, you will be withdrawn when this case is closed, and this case will only be closed thanks to the praiseworthy efforts of you and your assistants, now listen carefully, I'll give you five days, is that clear, five days, not a day longer, to hand over the whole cell to me, bound hand and foot, your osprey and her husband, to whom, poor thing, we didn't ever get round to giving a name, and the three little fishes who have just surfaced, the wolf, the cat and the needle,

I want them crushed beneath a weight of evidence impossible to deny, slide out of, contradict or refute, that is what I want, puffin, All right, albatross, I'll do what I can, You will do exactly what I have just said, meanwhile, so that you don't think badly of me, and being, as I am, a reasonable person, I realise that you will need some help to bring your work to a successful conclusion, Are you going to send me another inspector, albatross, No, puffin, my help will be of a different nature, but just as effective, or possibly more so, than if I were to despatch all the police at my command, I don't understand, albatross, You will be the first to understand when the bell sounds, The bell, The bell for the last round, puffin. The line went dead.

The superintendent left the room when it was twenty minutes past six by the clock. He read the message that the inspector had left on the table and wrote underneath it, I have something to sort out, wait for me. He went down to the garage, got into the car, started it and headed for the exit ramp. There he stopped and beckoned to the attendant. Still smarting from the angry exchange of words and the ill-treatment he had received from the tenant of providential ltd, the man came reluctantly over to the car window and uttered the customary phrase, Can I help you, A while ago, I was rather rough with you, Oh, that's all right, we're used to it here, Yes, but I didn't mean to offend you, No, I'm sure you didn't, sir, Superintendent, I'm a police superintendent, here's my identification, Forgive me, superintendent, I would never have imagined, and the other gentlemen, The youngest is a sergeant and the other one is an inspector, I understand, superintendent, and I promise I won't bother you again, but I had the very best of intentions, We've been carrying out an investigation here, but that's finished now, and so we're just like anyone else, it's as if we were on holiday, although, for your own sake, I nevertheless recommend great discretion, remember that, even when he's on holiday, a policeman is still a policeman, it is, if you like, in his blood, Oh, I understand perfectly, superintendent, but, in that case, if you don't mind me speaking frankly, it would have been better not to have told me anything, what the eye doesn't see, the heart doesn't grieve over, he that knows nothing sees nothing, Yes, but I needed to tell someone, and you were the person nearest to hand. The car was already going up the ramp, but the superintendent had one further piece of advice, Keep your mouth shut, I wouldn't want to have to regret what I told you. He certainly would have regretted it if he had turned round, for he would have found the man muttering secretively into the phone, perhaps telling his wife that he had just met a police superintendent, perhaps informing the porter of the identity of the three men in dark suits who always go straight up from the garage to providential ltd, insurance and reinsurance, perhaps this, perhaps that, we will probably never know the truth about this phone call. A few metres further on, the superintendent drew up by the kerb, took his note-book out of his jacket pocket, leafed through it until he reached the page where he had transcribed the names and addresses of the treacherous letter-writer's former companions, then consulted the map and the city guide to check again where the traitor's ex-wife lived, since she was closest. He also made a note of the route he would have to follow to the house of the man with the black eye-patch and the girl with the dark glasses. He smiled to remember the sergeant's confusion when he told him that this would be the perfect name for the wife of the old man with the black eye-patch, But she wasn't wearing dark glasses, the poor sergeant had replied, bewildered. That was unfair of me, thought the superintendent, I should have shown him the group photo, in which the girl is standing with her arms by her side and in her right hand is holding a pair of dark glasses, elementary, my dear watson, but one had to have a superintendent's eyes to notice such things. He started the car. An impulse had made him leave providential ltd, an impulse had made him tell the garage attendant who he was, an impulse is taking him now to the home of the divorcee, an impulse will take him to the home of the old man with the black eye-patch, and the same impulse would have driven him afterwards to the home of the doctor's wife had he not told them, both wife and husband, that he would be back tomorrow, at the same time, to continue the interrogation. What interrogation, he thought, would he say to her, for example, you are suspected of being the organiser, the leader, the king-pin of the subversive movement that has placed democracy in such grave danger, I am referring to the blank vote movement, and don't play the innocent with me, don't waste my time asking me if I have proof of what I'm saying, you, madam, are the one who will have to prove her innocence, because you can be quite sure, madam, that the proof will appear when it's needed, it's just a matter of inventing one or two irrefutable ones, and even if they're not completely irrefutable, the circumstantial evidence, however remote in time, will be enough for us, as will the incomprehensible fact that you did not go blind four years ago when everyone else in the city was stumbling around and bumping into lampposts, and before you say that one thing has nothing to do with the other, let me just say, she that made the saucepan made the lid, that, at least, albeit expressed in different words, is the opinion of my minister, whom I have to obey even if it makes my heart ache, now you will say, a superintendent's heart can't ache, well, that's what you think, you may know a lot about superintendents, but I can guarantee you know nothing about this one, it's true I didn't come here with the honest aim of finding out the truth, it's true that you will have been condemned before even being judged, but the heart of this puffin, which is what my minister calls me, is aching and I don't know how to make it stop, take my advice, confess, confess even if you're not guilty, the government will tell the people that they have been the victims of an unparalleled case of mass hypnosis, that you are a genius in the art, people might even be amused and life will get back on track, you'll spend a few years in prison, your friends will end up there too if we so choose, and meanwhile, of course, there'll be a reform of the electoral law and an end to blank votes, or else they'll be distributed equally amongst all the parties as valid votes, so that the percentages will not be affected, after all, dear lady, it's the percentages that count, as for the voters who abstain and fail to produce a medical certificate, why not publish their names in the newspapers just as, in the olden days, criminals were pilloried in the public square, the reason I'm speaking to you in this way is because I like you, and just so that you can see how much I like you, I will tell you that the greatest happiness life could have given me four years ago, apart from not having lost part of my family in that tragedy, which, alas, I did, would have been to be a member of the group that you protected, I wasn't a superintendent then, I was a blind inspector, just a blind inspector who, after recovering his sight, would be there in the photo along with the others whom you saved from the fire, and your dog would not have growled when he saw me, and if all that and more had happened, I would be able to declare on my word of honour to the interior minister that he is wrong, that an experience like that and four years of friendship are enough for anyone to say that they know a person well, and to think that I entered your house as an enemy and now don't know how to leave it, whether alone, in order to confess to the minister that I have failed in my mission, or accompanied by you, taking you to prison. These last thoughts did not come from the superintendent, he was now more concerned with finding somewhere to park than with anticipating decisions on the fate of a suspect and on his own fate. He once more consulted his notebook and rang the bell of the apartment block where the ex-wife of the man who wrote the letter lives. He rang again and again, but the door did not open. He was reaching out his hand to make a fresh attempt,

when he saw a ground-floor window open and an elderly woman
in rollers and a housecoat poke her head out, Who are you looking
for, she asked, The lady who lives in the first-floor apartment on
the right, replied the superintendent, She's not in, in fact, I saw her
go out, Do you know when she'll be back, No idea, but I'll be glad
to give her a message, said the woman, Thank you, but it doesn't
really matter, I'll come back another day. It didn't even occur to
him that the woman with the rollers might be thinking that the
divorcee on the first floor on the right had apparently taken to
receiving male visitors, the one who came this morning and this
one now, who was old enough to be her father. The superintendent
glanced at the map open on the seat beside him, started the car and
set off for his second objective. This time, no neighbours appeared
at the windows. The street door was open and so he could go straight
up to the second floor, this is where the old man with the black
eye-patch and the girl with the dark glasses live, what a strange
couple, it's understandable that their helplessness when blind would
have brought them together, but four years had passed, and while,
for a young woman, four years are nothing, for an old man, it's
more like eight. And yet they're still together, thought the superintendent. He rang the bell and waited. No one answered. He pressed
his ear to the door and listened. Silence from the other side. He
rang again out of habit, not because he expected anyone to come.
He went down the stairs, got into the car and murmured, I know
where they are. If he had had a direct line in his car and could have
phoned the minister to tell him where he was going, he was sure
the minister would reply in more or less these words, Bravo, puffin,
that's the way to do it, catch those guys red-handed, but be careful,
you should take reinforcements with you really, a man alone against
five desperate villains, that's the kind of thing you only see in movies,
besides, you don't know karate, that's after your time, Don't worry,
albatross, I may not know karate, but I know what I'm doing, Go

in there with your gun in your hand, terrify them, scare the shit out of them, Yes, albatross, Good, I'll start sorting out your medal now, There's no hurry, albatross, we don't yet know if I'll get out of this enterprise alive, It's a dead cert, puffin, I have every confidence in you, oh, I certainly knew what I was doing when I appointed you to this mission, Yes, albatross.

The streetlights come on, the evening is creeping up the ramp of the sky, soon night will begin. The superintendent rang the bell, no reason for surprise, policemen mostly do ring the bell, they don't always kick the door down. The doctor's wife appeared, I was expecting you tomorrow, superintendent, I'm afraid I can't talk to you right now, she said, we have visitors, Yes, I know them, that is, I don't know them personally, but I know who they are, That doesn't seem reason enough for me to let you in, Please, My friends have nothing to do with what brought you here, Not even you know what brought me here, and it's high time you did, Come in.

THERE IS AN IDEA ABROAD THAT, GENERALLY SPEAKING, THE CONSCIENCE of a police superintendent tends, on professional grounds and on principle, to be fairly accommodating, not to say resigned to the incontrovertible fact, theoretically and practically proven, that what must be must be and that there's nothing to be done about it. The truth is, however, that, although it may not be the most common of spectacles, it has been known for one of these valuable public servants, by chance and when least expected, to find himself caught between the devil and the deep blue sea, that is, between what he should be and what he would prefer not to be. For the super-intendent of providential ltd, insurance and reinsurance, that day has come. He had spent at most half an hour at the home of the doctor's wife, but that short time was enough to reveal to the aston-ished group gathered there the murky depths of his mission. He said he would do everything possible to divert from that place and those people the more than disquieting attentions of his superiors, but that he could not guarantee success, he told them he had been given the extremely tight deadline of five days to conclude the inves-tigation and knew that the only acceptable verdict would be one of guilty, and, addressing the doctor's wife, he said The person they want to make the scapegoat, if you'll forgive the obvious impropriety of the expression, is you, madam, and, possibly indirectly, your husband, as for the others, I don't think you're in any real danger, your crime, madam, wasn't murdering that man, your great crime was not going blind when the rest of us did, the incomprehensible can be merely an object of scorn, but not if there is always a way of using it as a pretext. It is three o'clock in the morning, and the superintendent is tossing and turning in bed, unable to get to sleep. He is mentally making plans for the next day, he repeats them obsessively and then starts all over again, telling the inspector and the sergeant that, as arranged, he will go to the doctor's house to continue the interrogation of the wife, reminding them of the task he had charged them with, following the other members of the group, but, given the present situation, none of this makes sense any more, now what he needs to do is to impede, to hinder events, to invent for the investigation advances and delays that will, without making it too obvious, simultaneously feed and hamper the minister's plans, in short, he needs to wait and see what the minister's promised help involves. It was nearly half past three when the red telephone rang. The superintendent leapt out of bed, put on the slippers bearing the police insignia and, half-ran, half-stumbled over to the desk on which the phone stood. Even before he had sat down, he was putting the receiver to his ear and saying, Hello, It's albatross here, said the voice at the other end, Hello, albatross, puffin here, Now pay attention, puffin, I have some instructions for you, Yes, albatross, Today, at nine o'clock, this morning, not tonight, a person will be waiting for you at post six-north on the frontier, the army has been warned, so there'll be no problem, Am I to understand that this person is coming to replace me, albatross, There's no reason for you to think that, puffin, you have done well so far and will, I hope, continue to do so until this affair is closed, Thank you, albatross, and what are your orders, As I said, a person will be waiting for you at nine o'clock this morning at post six-north on the frontier, Yes, albatross, I've already made a note of that, You will give this person the photograph you mentioned, the one of the group in which the main suspect appears, you will also give him the list of names and addresses you obtained and which you have in your possession. The superintendent felt a shiver run down his spine, But that photograph is necessary for my on-going investigations, he said, Well, I don't think it's as necessary as you say it is, puffin, indeed, I would go so far as to say that you don't need it at all, given that, either personally or through your subordinates, you have already made contact with all the members of the gang, You mean group, don't you, albatross, A gang is a group, Yes, albatross, but not all groups are gangs, Why, puffin, I had no idea you were so concerned about correct definitions, you obviously make good use of dictionaries, Forgive me for correcting you, albatross, my mind's still a bit fuzzy, Were you asleep, No, albatross, I was thinking about what I have to do tomorrow, Well, now you know, the person who will be waiting for you at post six-north is a man about your age and he will be wearing a blue tie with white spots, I shouldn't think there will be many other ties like that at military posts on the frontier, Do I know him, albatross, No, you don't, he's not from our department, Ah, He will respond to your password with the phrase No, there's never enough, And what's mine, There's always plenty of time, Very good, albatross, your orders will be carried out, I'll be there on the frontier at nine o'clock to meet him, Now go back to bed and sleep well for the rest of the night, puffin, I myself have been working up until now, so I'm going to do the same, May I ask you a question, albatross, Of course, but keep it short, Does the photograph have anything to do with the help you promised me, Very sharp of you, puffin, nothing gets past you, does it, So it does have something to do with it, Yes, it has everything to do with it, but don't expect me to tell you how, if I told you that, it would ruin the element of surprise, Even though I'm the person directly responsible for the investigations, Exactly, Does that mean you don't trust me, albatross, Draw a square on the ground, puffin, and put yourself inside it, within the space delineated by the lines of that square I trust you, but outside of it, I trust only myself, your investigation is that square, be content with the square and with your investigation, Yes, albatross, Sleep well, puffin, you'll hear from me before the week is out, I'll be here waiting, albatross, Good night, puffin, Good night, albatross. Despite the minister's conventional wishes for a good night's sleep, what little remained of the night did not prove of much use to the superintendent. Sleep refused to come, the doors and passageways of the brain were all closed, and inside ruled insomnia, queen and absolute mistress. Why does he want the photo, he asked himself over and over again, what did he mean by that threat that I would hear from him before the week was out, there was no threat contained in the individual words, but the tone, yes, the tone was threatening, if the superintendent, after a lifetime of interrogating all kinds of people, has learned to distinguish in amongst the tangled labyrinth of syllables the path he must follow to get out, he is also perfectly capable of noticing the shadowy zones that each word produces and trails behind it whenever it is pronounced. Say out loud the words You'll hear from me before the week is out, and you will see how easy it is to introduce into them a drop of insidious dread, the putrid stench of fear, the authoritarian timbre of a paternal ghost. The superintendent would prefer to think such soothing thoughts as these, But I have no reason to feel afraid, I do my work, I carry out the orders I'm given, and yet, in the depths of his conscience, he knew this was not true, he wasn't carrying out those orders for the simple reason that he did not believe that because the doctor's wife had not gone blind four years she was therefore to blame for eighty-three per cent of the capital's voting population having cast blank votes, as if the first odd fact were automatically responsible for the second. Even he doesn't believe it, he thought, he just wants a target to aim at, if this one fails, he'll find another, and another, and another, as many as it takes until he finally gets it right, or until, by dint of sheer repetition, the people he is trying to persuade of his merits grow indifferent to the methods and processes he adopts. In either case, the party will have won. Thanks to the skeleton key of digression, sleep had managed to open a door, escape down one of the corridors and immediately set the superintendent dreaming that the interior minister had asked him for the photograph so that he could stick a pin through the eyes of the doctor's wife, all the while singing a wizard's spell, Blind you were not, blind you will be, white you wore, black you will see, with this pin I prick you, from behind and before. Terrified, drenched in sweat, his heart pounding, the superintendent woke to the screams of the doctor's wife and the loud laughter of the minister, What an awful dream, he muttered as he turned on the light, what monstrous things the brain can generate. According to the clock, it was half past seven. He calculated how much time he would need to reach post six-north and was almost tempted to thank the nightmare for having been so kind as to wake him. He dragged himself out of bed, his head weighed heavy as lead, his legs weighed even more than his head, and he staggered uncertainly to the bathroom. He emerged twenty minutes later, slightly reinvigorated by the shower, newly shaved and ready for work. He put on a clean shirt and finished dressing, He'll be wearing a blue tie with white spots, he thought, and went into the kitchen to heat up a cup of coffee left over from the previous evening. The inspector and the sergeant must still have been sleeping, at least, they gave no sign of life. He munched his way unenthusiastically through a biscuit, and even bit into another one, then returned to the bathroom to clean his teeth. He went into the bedroom, placed in a medium-sized envelope the photograph and the list of names and addresses, having first copied the latter onto another piece of paper, and when he went back into the sitting-room, he heard noises coming from the room in the apartment where his subordinates were sleeping. He didn't wait for them, nor did he knock on their door. He scribbled a note, I had to go out early, I'm taking the car, do as I told you yesterday and concentrate on following the women, the wife of the man with the black eye-patch and the ex-wife of the man who wrote the letter, have lunch out if you can manage it, I'll be back here later this afternoon, I expect results. Clear orders, precise instructions, if only everything could be like that in this superintendent's difficult life. He left providential ltd and took the lift down to the garage. The attendant was already there, the superintendent said good morning, received a greeting in return, and wondered, in passing, if the man actually slept in the garage too, There don't seem to be any specific hours of work in this place. It was nearly half past eight, I've got time, he thought, I'll be there in less than half an hour, besides, I shouldn't be the first to arrive, albatross was quite explicit, quite clear about that, the man will be waiting for me at nine o'clock, so I can arrive a minute later, or two or three, at midday if I want. He knew this wasn't true, that he must simply not arrive before the man he was going to meet, Perhaps it's because the soldiers on guard at post six-north would get nervous seeing someone parked on this side of the dividing line, he thought, as he put his foot down on the accelerator to go up the ramp. Monday morning, but there wasn't much traffic, the superintendent would take twenty minutes at most to reach post six-north. But where the devil is post six-north, he suddenly asked out loud. In the north, of course, but six, where the hell was that. The minister had said six-north as if it were the most natural thing in the world, as if it were one of the capital's most famous monuments or else the metro station that had been destroyed by a bomb, the kind of place that everyone was sure to know, and, foolishly, it had not occurred to him to ask, Just where exactly is that, albatross. In a matter of a moment the amount of sand in the upper part of the hour-glass had dwindled dramatically, the tiny grains were rushing through the opening, each grain more eager to leave than the last, time is just like people, sometimes it's all it can do to drag itself along, but at others, it runs like a deer and leaps like a young goat, which, when you think about it, is not saying much, since the cheetah is the fastest of all the animals, and yet it has never occurred to anyone to say of another person He runs and jumps like a cheetah, perhaps because that first comparison comes from the magical late middle ages, when gentlemen went deer-hunting and no one had ever seen a cheetah running or even heard of its existence. Languages are conservative, they always carry their archives with them and hate having to be updated. The superintendent, having managed to park the car somewhere, had unfolded the map of the city and was now resting it on the steering-wheel, anxiously searching for post six-north on the northern periphery of the capital. It would be relatively easy to locate if the city were shaped like a rhombus or a lozenge or formed a parallelogram, a space whose four lines circumscribed, as albatross had so coolly put it, the amount of trust he deserved, but the city's outline is irregular and, on the fringes, on either side, it is impossible to tell where the north ends and where the east or the west begins. The superintendent looks at his watch and feels as afraid as a sergeant expecting a reprimand from his superior. He won't arrive on time, it's simply impossible. He tries to reason calmly, Logic would say, but since when has logic ruled human decisions, that the various military posts would have been numbered in a clockwise direction from the westernmost point of the northern sector, hour-glasses are clearly of no use in this instance. Perhaps this reasoning is wrong, but then since when has reason ruled human decisions, not an easy question to answer, but it's always better to have one oar than none, and, besides, it is written that a moored boat goes nowhere, and so the superintendent put a cross where it seemed to him post number six should be and set off. Since the traffic was light and there wasn't so much as the shadow of a policeman on the streets, he was sorely tempted to jump every red light he came to, a temptation he did not resist. He was not speeding, he was flying, he barely took his foot off the accelerator, and when he had to brake, he performed a controlled skid, as those acrobats of the steering-wheel do in car chases in the movies, making the more nervous spectators jump in their seats. The superintendent had never driven like this in his life and he never would again. It was already gone nine o'clock when he finally reached post six-north, and the soldier who came to find out what this agitated driver wanted told him that this was, in fact, five-north. The superintendent swore out loud and was about to turn round, but stopped this precipitate gesture just in time and asked in which direction he would find six-north. The soldier pointed east and, just in case there was any doubt, uttered two brief words, That way. Fortunately, there was a road running more or less parallel to the frontier, it was only a matter of three kilometres, the way is clear, there aren't even any traffic lights, the car started, accelerated, braked, took a bend at breathtaking speed and screeched to a halt, almost touching the yellow line painted across the street, there it is, post six-north. Next to the barrier, about thirty metres away, a middle-aged man was waiting, So he's quite a bit younger than me, thought the superintendent. He picked up the envelope and got out of the car. He couldn't see a single soldier, they must have had orders to keep out of sight or to look the other way while this ceremony of meeting and handing-over took place. The superintendent walked towards the man. He was holding the envelope in his hand and thinking, I mustn't make any excuses about being late, if I were to say Hello, good morning, sorry about the delay, I had a bit of trouble finding the place, and, do you know what, albatross forgot to tell me where post six-north was, you didn't have to be a genius to realise that this long, rambling sentence could be understood by the other man as a false password, and then one of two things would happen, the man would either summon the soldiers to arrest this liar and provocateur, or he would take out his gun and with a cry of Down with blank ballot papers, down with sedition, death to all traitors, would carry out a summary execution. The superintendent had reached the barrier. The man did not move, he just looked at him. He had his left thumb hooked in his belt, his right hand in his raincoat pocket, all far too natural to be real. He's armed, he's carrying a gun, thought the superintendent, and said, There's always plenty of time. The man did not smile or even blink, he said, No, there's never enough, and then the superintendent gave him the envelope, perhaps now they could say good morning to each other, perhaps chat for a few moments about what a pleasant Monday morning it was, but the other man merely said, Fine, you can leave now, I'll make sure this finds its way to the right person. The superintendent got into his car, reversed and drove back to the city. Feeling embittered and utterly frustrated, he tried to console himself by imagining what a good joke it would have been to hand the man an empty envelope and then wait to see what happened. The minister, ablaze with anger and incandescent with rage, would immediately phone him to demand an explanation and he, the superintendent, would then swear by all the saints in the court of heaven, including those on earth still awaiting canonisation, that the envelope had contained the photograph and the list of names and addresses, just as he had ordered, My responsibility, albatross, ended the moment that your messenger, having put down the gun he was holding, yes, I could see he was carrying a gun, took his right hand out of his raincoat pocket to receive the envelope, But the envelope was empty, I opened it myself, the minister would scream, That's nothing to do with me, albatross, he would reply with the serenity of someone at perfect peace with his conscience, Oh, I know what you're up to, the minister would bawl, you don't want me to touch so much as a hair on the head of your fancy woman, She's not my fancy woman, she's a person who is entirely innocent of the crime she's been accused of, albatross, Don't call me albatross, your father was an albatross, your mother was an albatross, but I'm the interior minister, If the interior minister has ceased to be an albatross, then the police superintendent will cease to be a puffin, At this precise moment, the puffin is very likely to cease being a superintendent, Well, anything's possible, Anyway, send me another copy of the photo today, do you hear, But I haven't got one, Oh, but you will have, more than one if necessary, How, Very easy, by going to where you'll find one, in your fancy woman's apartment or in the other two apartments, you don't expect me to believe that the photo that disappeared was the only copy, do you. The superintendent shook his head, The minister's no fool, there would be no point handing him an empty envelope. He was almost in the centre of the city now, where things were, of course, livelier, although not in any exaggerated or noisy way. He could see that the people he passed had their worries, but, at the same time, they seemed quite calm. The superintendent ignored the obvious contradiction, the fact that he could not explain in words what he saw did not mean that he couldn't feel it, that he could not sense it with his feelings. The man and woman over there, for example, you can see that they like each other, that they're fond of each other, that they love each other, you can see that they're happy, look, they just smiled, and yet, not only are they worried, they are, if I may put it like this, calmly and clearly aware of that. You can see that the superintendent is worried too, perhaps, well, what does one more contradiction matter, perhaps that is why he has gone into this café to have a proper breakfast that will distract him and make him forget the warmed-up coffee and the stale biscuits of providential ltd, insurance and reinsurance, he has just ordered some freshly squeezed orange juice, some toast and a cup of real coffee with milk. God bless whoever invented you, he murmured piously to the toast when the waiter set it down before him, wrapped in a napkin in the old-fashioned way, so that it would not get cold. He asked for a newspaper, the front page carried only foreign news, there was nothing of local interest, apart from a statement from the minister of foreign affairs announcing that the government was preparing to consult various international bodies about the former capital's anomalous situation, starting with the united nations and ending with the court in The Hague, passing through the European union, the organisation for economic cooperation and development, the organisation of petroleum-exporting countries, the north atlantic treaty organisation, the world bank, the international monetary fund, the world trade organisation, the world organisation for atomic energy, the world organisation for labour, the world meteorological organisation, and a few other bodies, which were only secondary or still under discussion, and therefore not mentioned. Albatross will be most put out, it seems they're trying to steal his sweets, thought the superintendent. He looked up from the newspaper like someone who feels a sudden need to gaze into the distance and said to himself that perhaps this news was the reason behind that unexpected and urgent demand for the photograph, He never was one to allow people to get one over on him, he's obviously preparing his next trick, and it'll probably be a dirty trick, the dirtiest of the dirty, he murmured. Then it occurred to him that he had the whole day to himself, that he could do whatever he wanted. He had set the inspector and the sergeant their task, and a useless task it was, they would, at this moment, be lurking in some doorway or behind a tree, they would already be waiting to see who left the house first, the inspector doubtless hoping it would be the girl with dark glasses, while the sergeant, because there was no one else, would have to content himself with the ex-wife of the man who wrote the letter. The worst thing that could happen to the inspector would be for the old man with the black eye-patch to appear, not so much for the reason you are thinking, that following a pretty, young woman is obviously a more attractive prospect than trailing after an old man, but because people with only one eye see twice as much, they don't have their other eye to distract them or to insist on looking at something else, we've said as much before, but truths need to be repeated many times so that they don't, poor things, lapse into oblivion. And what shall I do, wondered the superintendent. He summoned the waiter, returned the newspaper, paid the bill and left. As he was sitting down behind the wheel again, he glanced at his watch, Half past ten, he thought, a good time, precisely the hour I set for the second interrogation. A good time, he had thought, but he would not have been able to say why or for what. He could, if he chose, go back to providential ltd and rest until lunchtime, perhaps even sleep a little and make up for the sleep he had lost during the wretched night he had had to endure, the painful conversation with the minister, the nightmare, the screams of the doctor's wife when the albatross stuck the pin through her eyes, but the idea of shutting himself up between those gloomy walls seemed repulsive to him, he had nothing to do there, he certainly didn't want to spend his time reviewing the store of arms and munitions, as he had thought he would do when he first arrived, and as was his duty as superintendent, as surely as if it had been set down in writing. The morning still retained some of the luminous quality of dawn, the air was cool, the ideal weather for a walk. He got out of the car and started walking. He went to the end of the street, turned left and found himself in a square, he crossed it, set off down another street and reached another square, he had a memory of having been here four years ago, one blind man amongst other blind men, listening to speakers who were also blind, the last echoes, if one could but hear them, would be from the most recent political meetings to have been held in those places, the p.o.t.r. in the first square, the p.i.t.m. in the second, and as for the p.o.t.l., as if this were its historical fate, it had had to make do with a bit of waste ground right on the edge of the city. The superintendent walked and walked, and suddenly, how he didn't know, found himself in the street where the doctor and his wife lived, he did not, however, think, This is the street where the doctor lives. He slackened his pace, continuing along on the other side, and he was perhaps twenty metres away when the door of the building opened and the doctor's wife appeared with the dog. The superintendent immediately swung round, went over to a shop window and stood there looking in and waiting, if she crossed over, she would see him reflected in the glass. She didn't. The superintendent stared studiously in the opposite direction, the doctor's wife was moving away from him, the dog, with no lead, was walking along beside her. Then it occurred to the superintendent that he should follow her, that it wouldn't go amiss if he were to do what the sergeant and the inspector were doing at that very moment, if they were trudging the streets behind the other suspects, then he had a duty to do the same even if he was a superintendent, now where's that woman going, the dog is probably just a cover, or perhaps she uses the dog's collar for transporting secret messages, ah, what happy times they were when St Bernard dogs used to carry little barrels of brandy around their neck and with that small amount how many lives feared lost in the snowy alps were saved. His pursuit of the suspect, if we want to continue calling her that, did not last long. In a secluded spot, rather like a village forgotten in the middle of the city, there was a slightly neglected park, with large shady trees, sandy walks and flower beds, rustic, green-painted benches, and, in the middle, a lake in which a statue, representing a female figure, bent over the water with her empty water jar. The doctor's wife sat down, opened the bag she had brought with her and took out a book. Until she had opened the book and started reading, the dog would not move from there. She looked up from the page and said, Off you go, and he ran off to do, as people used to say in more euphemistic days, what no one else could do for him. The superintendent watched from a distance and remembered his question to himself after breakfast, And what shall I do. For about five minutes he lurked behind the bushes, it was lucky the dog hadn't come this way, he might have recognised him and this time done more than just growl at him. The doctor's wife wasn't waiting for anyone, she had, as so many other people do, simply taken her dog for a walk. The superintendent went straight over to her, making the sand crunch underfoot, and stopped a few feet away. Slowly, as if she found it hard to tear herself away from her reading, the doctor's wife raised her head and looked at him. She did not appear to recognise him at first, probably because she wasn't expecting to see him there, then she said, We were waiting for you, but when you didn't come and the dog was getting impatient for his walk, I decided to bring him here, but my husband's at home, he'll look after you until I get back, unless, of course, you're in a hurry, No, I'm not in a hurry, You go ahead, then, I'll be right there, once the dog has had a bit of a run, after all, it's not his fault people decided to cast blank ballot papers, If you don't mind, and since chance seems to have arranged it this way, I'd prefer to talk to you here, without witnesses, And I assumed that this interrogation, to continue calling it by that name, would take place with my husband present, like the first one, It wouldn't be an interrogation, my note-book won't leave my pocket, and I haven't got a tape-recorder concealed about my person either, besides, I have to say that my memory isn't what it was, it forgets easily, especially when I don't tell it to record what it hears, Oh, I had no idea the memory could hear, It's our second set of ears, those on the outside only serve to carry the sound inside, What do you want then, Like I said, I want to talk to you, About what, About what's happening in this city, Superintendent, I'm very grateful to you for coming to my house yesterday evening and for telling us, and my friends too, that there are people in the government interested in the strange phenomenon of the doctor's wife who failed to go blind four years ago and who now, it seems, is the organiser of a conspiracy against the state, but, to be perfectly frank, unless you have something more to say to me on the subject, I really don't think there's much point in our talking about anything else, The interior minister made me hand over the group photograph of you, your husband and your friends, this very morning I went to a military post on the frontier to do so, So you did have something to tell me, but there really wasn't any need for you to follow me, you could have gone straight to my house, you know the way, But I didn't follow you, I wasn't hiding behind a tree or pretending to read a newspaper while I waited for you to leave your house so that I could follow you, as the inspector and the sergeant engaged with me on this investigation will be doing with your friends right now, although the only reason I ordered them to do so was to keep them occupied, that's all, Do you mean to tell me you're here by chance, Yes, I happened to be walking down the street and I saw you leaving your house, It's hard to believe that it was pure chance that brought you to the street where I live, Call it what you like, But it was, at any rate, a happy coincidence, if you prefer to call it that, without it I wouldn't have found out that the photograph is now in the hands of your minister, Oh, that I would have told you on another occasion, And what, may I ask, does he want with it, I've no idea, he didn't tell me, but I'm sure it won't be for any good purpose, So you didn't come to submit me to a second interrogation, said the doctor's wife, No, not today, not tomorrow, never, as far as I'm concerned, I know all I need to know about this story, You'll have to explain yourself better, sit down, don't just stand there like that woman with the empty water jar. The dog suddenly appeared and came bounding out from behind some bushes heading straight for the superintendent, who instinctively drew back, Don't be frightened, said the doctor's wife, grabbing the dog by the collar, he won't bite you, How did you know I was afraid of dogs, Oh, I'm no witch, I just observed you when you were in our apartment, Is it that obvious, It is rather, steady, this last word was addressed to the dog, who had stopped barking and was instead producing a low, continuous noise in its throat, far more intimidating than a growl, the sound of an organ the bass notes of which have been badly tuned. You'd better sit down, that way he'll know you mean me no harm. The superintendent gingerly sat down, keeping his distance, Is his name Steady, No, it's Constant, but for us and for my friends he's the dog of tears, we called him Constant for short, Why the dog of tears, Because four years ago I was crying and this creature came and licked my face, During the time of the white blindness, Yes, during the time of the white blindness, this dog is the second marvel from those wretched days, first the woman who did not go blind when it seems it was her duty to do so, then this compassionate dog who came and drank her tears, Did that really happen, or was I dreaming, What we dream also happens, superintendent, Hopefully not everything, Do you have some reason for saying that, No, not really, I was just talking for the sake of it. The superintendent was lying, the sentence he had refused to allow his mouth to utter would have been quite different, Hopefully the albatross will not come and poke out your eyes. The dog had come closer and was almost touching the superintendent's knees with its nose. It was looking at him and its eyes were saying, I won't hurt you, don't be afraid, she wasn't when I found her on that other day. Then the superintendent slowly reached out his hand and touched the dog's head. He felt like crying and letting the tears course down his face, perhaps the marvel would be repeated. The doctor's wife put her book away in her bag and said, Let's go, Where, asked the superintendent, You'll have lunch with us, won't you, if you've nothing more important to do, Are you sure, About what, That you want to have me sitting at your table, Yes, I'm sure, And you're not afraid I might be tricking you, Not with those tears in your eyes, no.

WHEN THE SUPERINTENDENT ARRIVED BACK AT PROVIDENTIAL LTD, IT WAS gone seven o'clock in the evening, and he found his subordinates waiting for him. They were clearly not happy. How was your day, any news to report, he asked them in a bright, almost jovial tone, pretending an interest which, as we know better than anyone, he did not feel, As for the day, awful, as for news to report, even worse, replied the inspector, We would have been better off staying in bed and sleeping, said the sergeant, What do you mean, In my entire life, I cannot remember ever having been involved in such a stupid, pointless investigation, began the inspector. The superintendent would gladly have chimed in with You don't know the half of it, but he chose to remain silent. The inspector went on, It was ten o'clock by the time I reached the street where the guy who wrote the letter's ex lives, Sorry, said the sergeant, but you can't say ex, Why not, Because that could mean she was just his ex-girlfriend, Does it matter, asked the inspector, Yes, she wasn't his girlfriend, she was his spouse, All right, what I should have said was that at ten o'clock I reached the street where the guy who wrote the letter's ex-spouse lives, That's better, But spouse sounds ridiculous and pretentious, when you introduce your wife to someone, I bet you don't say and this is my spouse. The superintendent cut short the discussion, Keep that for another time, let's get to what's impor-tant, What's important, went on the inspector, is that I was there until nearly midday, and she still hadn't left her apartment, not that this really surprised me, the city's all topsy-turvy, some companies

252

have closed and others are only working half-time, people don't necessarily have to get up early, Lucky them, said the sergeant, So did she go out or didn't she, asked the superintendent, who was beginning to get impatient, She went out at precisely a quarter past twelve, Is there some reason why you say precisely, No, sir, I naturally looked at my watch and there it was, a quarter past twelve, Go on, Well, keeping an eye on any taxis that passed, in case she should get into one of them and leave me stranded in the middle of the street looking like a complete fool, I followed her, but it didn't take me long to realise that wherever it was she was going, she would be going there on foot, And where did she go, You're going to laugh, sir, I doubt it, She walked for more than half an hour, so fast I could hardly keep up, just as if she was doing it for the exercise, and suddenly, unexpectedly, I found myself in the street where the old man with the black eye-patch and the girl with the dark glasses, you know, the prostitute, live, She's not a prostitute, inspector, She may not be one now, but she was once, it's all the same, It's all the same in your mind, but not in mine, and since it's me you're talking to and I'm your superior, kindly use words in a way that I can understand, In that case, I'll say ex-prostitute, Say the man with the black eye-patch's spouse just as, a few minutes ago, you said the guy who wrote the letter's ex-spouse, as you see, I'm using your terms, Hm, Anyway, you found yourself in their street and then what happened, She went into the building where they live and stayed there, And what did you do, the superintendent asked the sergeant, I was hiding, but when she went inside, I joined the inspector to work out a strategy, And then, We decided to work together while we could, said the inspector, and agreed on how we would proceed if we had to split up again, And then, Since it was lunchtime, we took advantage of the break, So you went and had lunch, No, sir, he'd bought two sandwiches and he gave me one, and that was our lunch. The superintendent finally smiled, You deserve a medal, he said to the sergeant, who, emboldened, responded, People have won one for less, sir, You don't know how right you are, Put my name down on the list, then. The three of them smiled, but only briefly, the superintendent's face soon darkened again, What happened next, he asked, It was half past two when they all came out, they must have had lunch together there, said the inspector, we were immediately on the alert because we didn't know if the old man had a car or not, but he didn't use it, perhaps he's saving petrol, anyway, we followed them and if it was an easy job for one, imagine what it was like for two, And where did all this end, In a cinema, they went to the cinema, Did you check to see if there was another door they could have left by without you realising, There was one, but it was closed, just in case, though, I told him to keep an eye on it for half an hour, No one left, the sergeant confirmed. The superintendent felt weary of this comedy, What else, just summarise the rest, he said in a tense voice. The inspector looked at him in surprise, The rest, sir, well, there isn't much else, they left together when the film ended, they took a taxi, and we took another, we gave the driver the classic order We're the police, follow that car, it was just another straightforward trip, the wife of the guy who wrote the letter was the first to get out, Where, In the street where she lives, as we said, sir, we don't have any news to report, then the taxi took the others to their house, And what did you do, Well, I stayed behind in the first street, said the sergeant, And I stayed in the second, said the inspector, And then, Then, nothing, none of them went out again, and I was there for nearly another hour, in the end, I caught a taxi, passed by the other street to pick up my colleague and we came back together, in fact, we've just got in, A pointless task then, said the superintendent, It certainly seems like it, said the inspector, the most interesting thing about this whole business is that it started out fairly well, the interrogation of the guy who wrote the letter, for example, was worthwhile, even amusing, the poor devil didn't know what to do with himself and ended up with his tail between his legs, but after that, I don't know how, we got stuck, I mean, we got ourselves stuck, you must know a bit more, sir, since you got to interrogate the real suspects twice, Who are the real suspects, asked the superintendent, Well, first, the doctor's wife and then the husband, it seems quite clear to me that if they share a bed, they must share the blame too, What blame, You know as well as I do, sir, Imagine that I don't, explain it to me, The blame for the situation we're in, What situation, The blank ballot papers, the city under a state of siege, the bomb in the metro station, Do you really believe what you're saying, asked the superintendent, That's why we came here, to investigate and capture the guilty party, You mean the doctor's wife, Yes, sir, as far as I'm concerned the interior minister's orders were pretty clear on that front, The interior minister didn't say the doctor's wife was to blame, Sir, I may only be a police inspector who may never make it as far as superintendent, but I've learned from my experience in this job that things half-spoken exist in order to say what can't be fully expressed, When the next post for superintendent comes up, I'll support your promotion, but until then, the truth requires me to inform you that, as regards the doctor's wife, the word, not half-spoken, but fully expressed, is innocence. The inspector shot the sergeant a sideways glance, a plea for help, but the sergeant had the absorbed look of someone who has just been hypnotised, so he could expect no help from him. Cautiously, the inspector asked, Are you saying that we're going to leave here empty-handed, Or we could, if you prefer, leave here with our hands in our pockets, And that's how we should present ourselves to the minister, If there's no guilty party, we can't invent one, Are those your words or the minister's, Oh, I doubt they're the minister's words, at least, I don't remember having heard him say them, Well, sir, I've never heard them all the time I've been in the police, but I'll say no more, I won't open my mouth again. The superintendent got up, looked at his watch and said, Go and have supper in a restaurant somewhere, you hardly had any lunch at all, you must be hungry, but don't forget to bring me the bill so that I can stamp it, And what about you, sir, asked the sergeant, No, I had a good lunch, and if I do feel peckish, there's always tea and biscuits to keep hunger at bay. The inspector said, The respect I feel for you, sir, obliges me to say how concerned I am about you, Why, We're just subordinates, the worst thing that can happen to us is a reprimand, but you're responsible for the success of this mission and you seem determined to declare it a failure, Does declaring an accused person innocent mean that a mission has failed, It does if the mission was designed to put the blame on an innocent party, A short while ago, you stated categorically that the doctor's wife was to blame, now you're almost on the point of swearing on the holy gospel that she's innocent, Sir, I might well swear it on the gospel, but not in the presence of the interior minister, Of course, I understand, you have your family, your career, your life, That's right, sir, you might also add, my lack of courage, We're both human beings, and I would never go that far, my only advice to you is that, from now on, you take our sergeant here under your wing, I've a feeling you're going to need each other. The inspector and the sergeant said, See you later, sir, and the superintendent replied, Have a nice meal, and don't rush. The door closed.

The superintendent went into the kitchen for a drink of water, then he went into his room. The bed was still unmade, a pair of dirty socks lay on the floor, one here, one over there, a dirty shirt was draped untidily over a chair, not to mention the state the bathroom was in, this is a matter which providential ltd, insurance and reinsurance will have to resolve sooner or later, i.e. whether or not it is compatible with the natural discretion surrounding the work of the secret service to place at the disposal of the agents who stay here a woman who would act as housekeeper, cook and chambermaid.

The superintendent gave the sheet and bedspread a quick tug, punched the pillow a couple of times, rolled up the shirt and the socks and stuffed them in a drawer, and the desolate appearance of the room improved a little, although, naturally, any female hand would have done it better. He looked at the clock, it was a good time, although he would soon find out whether the result would be equally good. He sat down, switched on the desk lamp and dialled the number. On the fourth ring, a voice answered, Hello, It's puffin here, Albatross speaking, Just calling in to report on the day's operations, albatross, Well, I hope you have some satisfactory results to give me, puffin, That depends on what you call satisfactory, albatross, Look, I have neither the time nor the patience for the finer shades of meaning, puffin, get to the point, May I ask you first, albatross, if the package reached its destination, What package, The nine o'clock package, at post six-north, Oh, yes, it arrived perfectly, it's going to be very useful, you'll find out just how useful in due course, puffin, but now tell me what you and your men have been up to today, There's really not much to tell, albatross, a couple of surveillance operations and an interrogation, Let's take things one at a time, puffin, what was the result of the surveillance operations, Practically nil, albatross, Why, Throughout the time they were being followed, the people we would term the number two suspects behaved absolutely normally, albatross, And what about the inter- rogation of the number one suspects, which, I seem to recall, was your responsibility, puffin, To be perfectly honest, What did you say, To be perfectly honest, albatross, What's all this about honesty, puffin, It's just a way of beginning a sentence, albatross, Then will you please stop being perfectly honest and tell me, simply, whether or not you are in a position to confirm, without beating about the bush and without any further circumlocutions, that the doctor's wife, whose photo I have before me, is guilty, She admitted she was guilty of a murder, albatross, You know that for many reasons, amongst them the lack of a corpus delicti, this is not what interests us, Yes, albatross, So get straight to the point and tell me whether or not you can confirm that the doctor's wife is part of the movement behind the blank votes and that she may even be the head of the whole organisation, No, albatross, I can't confirm that, Why, puffin, Because no policeman in the world, albatross, and I consider myself to be the last of them, would find a scrap of evidence to support such an accusation, You appear to have forgotten, puffin, that we had agreed that you would provide the necessary proof, And what proof would that be in a case like this, albatross, if you don't mind my asking, That neither was nor is my affair, I left that to your judgement, puffin, when I was still confident that you would be capable of bringing your mission to a successful conclusion, With respect, albatross, deciding that a suspect is innocent of the crime he or she is accused of seems to me the most successful of conclusions, Let's drop this code-name comedy, you're a police superintendent and I'm the interior minister, Yes, minister, Now, in order to see if we can finally come to some understanding, I'm going to put the question I asked you just now in a different way, Yes, minister, Setting aside your personal beliefs, are you prepared to confirm that the doctor's wife is guilty, yes or no, No, minister, And you have weighed the consequences of what you have just said, Yes, minister, Very well, then, take a note of the decisions I have just taken, I'm listening, minister, You will tell the inspector and the sergeant that they have orders to return tomorrow morning, that at nine o'clock they must be at post six-north on the frontier where they will be met by the person who will bring them here, a man more or less your age and wearing a blue tie with white spots, tell them to bring the car you've been using and which will, of course, no longer be necessary, Yes, minister, And as for you, As for me, minister, You will remain in the capital until you receive further orders, which will doubtless not be long in coming, And the investigation, You yourself said that there is nothing to investigate, that the suspect is innocent, That is my sincere belief, minister, Then you certainly can't complain, your case is solved, But what shall I do while I'm here, Nothing, do nothing, go for walks, enjoy yourself, go to the cinema, the theatre, visit the museums, and, if you like, invite your new friends out to supper, charge it to the ministry, Minister, I don't understand, The five days I gave you for the investigation are still not yet up, perhaps in the time that remains a different light will go on in your head, I doubt it, minister, Nevertheless, five days are five days, and I'm a man of my word, Yes, minister, Good night, sleep well, superintendent, Good night, minister.

The superintendent put down the phone. He got up from the chair and went to the bathroom. He needed to see the face of the man who had just been summarily dismissed. The actual words had not been spoken, but could be clearly seen, letter by letter, in all the other words, even those wishing him a good night's sleep. He wasn't surprised, he knew exactly what his interior minister was like and knew that he would be made to pay for not having obeyed the instructions he had received, the explicit and, above all, the implied instructions, the latter had, after all, been as clear as the former, but he was surprised by the serenity of the face he saw in the mirror, a face from which the lines seemed to have vanished, a face in which the eyes had become limpid and luminous, the face of a man of fifty-seven, a police superintendent by profession, who had just been through the fire and had emerged from it as if from a purifying bath. Yes, a bath would be a good idea. He got undressed and stepped into the shower. He allowed the water to flow freely, after all, what did he care, the ministry would foot the bill, he slowly soaped himself and again the water washed away any remaining dirt from his body, then his memory carried him on its back to a time four years ago, when they were all blind and wandering, filthy and starving, about the city, ready to do anything for a crust of stale, mouldy bread, for anything that could be eaten, or at least chewed, as a way of staving off hunger with their own juices, he imagined the doctor's wife guiding through the streets, beneath the rain, her little flock of unfortunates, her six lost sheep, her six fledglings fallen from the nest, her six newborn blind kittens, perhaps one day, in some street or other, he had bumped into them, perhaps they, out of fear, had repelled him, perhaps, out of fear, he had repelled them, it was every man for himself at the time, steal before they steal from you, hit out before they hit you, your worst enemy, according to the law of the blind, is always the person nearest you, But it's not only when we have no eyes that we don't know where we're going, he thought. The hot water fell clamorously upon his head and shoulders, it coursed over his body and disappeared, clean and gurgling, down the drain. He got out of the shower, dried himself on the bath towel bearing the police emblem, picked up the clothes he had left hanging on the hook and went into the bedroom. He put on clean underwear, his last, and it would have to be his last, for he hadn't thought of packing any more for a mission lasting only five days. He looked at his watch, it was nearly nine o'clock. He went into the kitchen, boiled some water for tea, dunked one sad teabag in the water and waited for the recommended number of minutes. The biscuits were like sugary granite. He bit into them hard, reduced them to smaller pieces that were easier to chew, then slowly crumbled them up. He sipped his tea, he preferred the green variety, but had to content himself with this black stuff, so old it hardly tasted of anything, providential ltd, insurance and reinsurance, really should stop lavishing such luxuries on its temporary guests. The minister's words echoed sarcastically in his ears, The five days I gave you for the investigation are still not yet up, until they are, go for walks, enjoy yourself, go to the cinema, charge it to the ministry, and he wondered what would happen then, would they send him back to headquarters, alleging that he was incapable of active service, would they sit him down at a desk to shuffle papers, a superintendent demoted to the lowly condition of pen-pusher, that would be his future, unless they made him take early retirement and forgot about him and only mentioned his name again when he died and they could strike him from the staff records. He finished eating, he threw the cold, damp teabag into the rubbish bin, washed the cup and scooped the crumbs off the table with the edge of his hand. He did all this with great concentration in order to keep his thoughts at bay, in order to let them in only one at a time, having first asked them what they contained, because you can't be too careful with thoughts, some present themselves to us with a cloying air of false innocence and then, when it's too late, reveal their true wicked selves. He again looked at his watch, a quarter to ten, how time passes. He left the kitchen and went into the living-room, sat down on a sofa and waited. He woke to the sound of the key in the door. The inspector and the sergeant came in, they had clearly had plenty to eat and drink, not, however, to any reprehensible extent. They said their good evenings, then the inspector, on behalf of them both, apologised for coming in a little late. The superintendent looked at his watch, it was gone eleven, It's not that late, he said, but I'm afraid you're going to have to get up rather earlier than you perhaps expected, Another mission, asked the inspector, placing a package on the table, Yes, if you can call it that. The superintendent paused, glanced again at his watch and went on, At nine o'clock tomorrow morning you are to be at military post six-north with all your belongings, Why, asked the sergeant, You've been taken off the investigation that brought you here, Was that your decision, sir, asked the inspector, grave-faced, No, it was the minister's decision, But why, He didn't tell me, but don't worry, I'm sure he's got nothing against you personally, he'll ask you a lot of questions, but you'll know what to say, Does that mean you're not coming with us, sir, asked the sergeant, No, I'm staying here, Are you going to continue the investigation on your own, The investigation is over, With no concrete results, Neither concrete nor abstract, Then I don't understand why you're not coming with us, said the inspector, Orders from the minister, I'll stay here until the end of the five-day period he originally set, which means until Thursday, And what then, Perhaps he'll tell you when he questions you, Questions us about what, About how the investigation went, about how I ran it, But you just said that the investigation was over, Yes, but it's possible he may want to continue it in other ways, although not with me, Well, I can't make head nor tail of it, said the sergeant. The superintendent got up, went into the study and returned with a map, which he spread out on the table, pushing the package a little to one side to make room. Post six-north is here, he said, placing his finger on it, don't go to the wrong one, waiting for you will be a man whom the minister describes as more or less my age, but he's actually quite a lot younger, you'll recognise him by the tie he'll be wearing, blue with white spots, when I met him, we had to exchange passwords, but I don't think that will be necessary this time, at least the minister didn't say anything to me about it, I don't understand, said the inspector, It's seems pretty clear, said the sergeant, we just go to post six-north, No, what I don't understand is why we're leaving and the superintendent is staying, The minister must have his reasons, Ministers always do, But they never say what they are. The superintendent intervened, There's no point talking about it, your best bet is not to ask for any explanations and to distrust any explanations they offer you, in the unlikely event that they do, because they're nearly always lies. He carefully folded up the map and, as if the thought had just occurred to him, said, You take the car, You're not even keeping the car, asked the inspector, There are plenty of buses and taxis in the city, besides, walking is good for the health, This whole thing is just getting harder and harder to understand, There's nothing to understand, my friend, I was given my orders and I'm carrying them out, and you must do the same, you can analyse and ponder all you like, but it doesn't change the reality one millimetre. The inspector pushed the package towards him, We brought this, he said, What is it, Well, the stuff they left for our breakfast here is so awful, we decided to buy some different biscuits, a bit of cheese, some decent butter, ham and a sandwich loaf, Are you going to take it with you or leave it here, said the superintendent, smiling, Well, if you're in agreement, sir, tomorrow we'll have breakfast together and whatever's left stays, said the inspector, smiling too. They had all smiled, the sergeant keeping the others company, but now all three were serious again, not knowing what to say. In the end, the superintendent said, I'm off to bed, I slept badly last night and it's been a busy day, starting with that business at post six-north, What business, sir, asked the superintendent, we don't yet know why you went to post six-north, No, that's true, I didn't get a chance to tell you, well, on orders from the minister I went and handed over the group photograph to that man wearing the blue tie with white spots, the same man you're going to meet tomorrow, What would the minister want with that photo, To use his words, we'll find out in due course, It smells very fishy to me. The superintendent nodded and went on, Then, by pure coincidence, I bumped into the doctor's wife, joined them for lunch at their apartment, and then, to top it all, had the conversation with the minister I told you about, We have the greatest respect for you, sir, said the inspector, but there's one thing we'll never forgive you, and I know I'm speaking for both of us here because we've already talked about it, What's that, You never let us go to that woman's apartment, You went there, inspector, Only to be shooed straight out again, Yes, that's true, agreed the superintendent, Why, Because I was afraid, Afraid of what, we're not monsters, Afraid that the need to find a guilty party at all costs would stop you seeing the person who was there before you, Did you trust us so little, sir, It wasn't a question of trust, of whether I did or didn't trust you, it was more as if I had found a treasure and wanted to keep it all to myself, no, that's not it, it wasn't a question of feelings, that wasn't what I was thinking, I simply feared for that woman's safety, I thought that the fewer people who questioned her, the safer she would be, So put in plain and simple language, and forgive my boldness, sir, said the sergeant, you didn't trust us, No, you're right, I admit it, I didn't, Well, don't bother asking our forgiveness, said the inspector, you're forgiven already, especially since you may well have been right to be afraid, we could have ruined everything, we could have gone in there like a couple of bulls in a china shop. The superintendent opened the package, took out two slices of bread, put two slices of ham in between and gave an apologetic smile, I must confess I'm hungry, all I had was a cup of tea and I nearly broke my teeth on those bloody biscuits. The sergeant went into the kitchen and brought him a can of beer and a glass, Here you are, sir, this will help the bread slide down more easily. The superintendent sat down and munched his way through the ham sandwich, savouring every mouthful, then drank down the beer as if he were washing clean his soul, and when he had finished, he said, Right, now I will go to bed, sleep well, you two, and thanks for supper. He went over to the door that led to his bedroom, stopped and turned round, I'm going to miss you, he said. He paused and added, Don't forget what I told you earlier, What do you mean, sir, asked the inspector, That I have the feeling you're really going to need each other, don't be taken in by any sweet talk or promises of rapid promotion, I'm responsible for the conclusions reached by this investigation and no one else, you won't be betraying me as long as you tell the truth, but refuse to accept any lies in the name of a truth that is not your own, Yes, sir, promised the inspector, Help each other, said the superintendent, and then, That's all I wish for you, all I ask of you.

THE SUPERINTENDENT DID NOT WISH TO TAKE ADVANTAGE OF THE interior minister's prodigal munificence. He did not seek distraction in theatres and cinemas, he did not visit the museums, he only left providential ltd, insurance and reinsurance, to have lunch and supper, and when he paid the bill at the restaurant, instead of taking the bill with him, he left it on the table along with the tip. He did not go back to the doctor's house and had no reason to return to the garden where he had made his peace with the dog of tears or, as he was officially known, Constant, and where, eye to eye, spirit with spirit, he had spoken with the dog's mistress about guilt and innocence. Nor did he go and spy on what the girl with dark glasses and the old man with the black eye-patch might be doing, or the divorced wife of the man who had been the first to go blind. As for the latter, the author of the vile letter of denunciation and author, too, of many misfortunes, the superintendent had no doubt that, if he saw him, he would cross over to the other side of the road. The rest of the time, for hours on end, morning and evening, he spent sitting by the phone, waiting, and even when he was sleeping, his ears were listening. He was sure that the interior minister would phone in the end, he could not otherwise understand why the minister had wanted to drain to the very last minute, or more accurately, to the final dregs, the five days he had allocated for the investigation. The most natural thing would be for the minister to order him back to headquarters to settle all outstanding accounts, whether by enforced retirement or by resignation, but experience had shown him that anything natural was far too simple for the interior minister's tortuous mind. He remembered the inspector's words, banal but expressive, It smells very fishy to me, he had said when the superintendent had told him about handing over the photograph to the man wearing the blue tie with white spots at military post six-north, and it seemed to him that the heart of the matter must lie there, in the photograph, although he could not imagine how or why. It was in this slow waiting, which had an end in sight and which would not, as people say when they want to embellish a story, be interminable, and in thoughts such as these, which were often nothing but a continuous, irrepressible somnolence from which his half-watchful consciousness occasionally startled him awake, that he would spend the three remaining days, Tuesday, Wednesday, Thursday, three leaves from the calendar which resisted being torn from midnight's stitching and which then remained stuck to his fingers, transformed into a shapeless, glutinous mass of time, into a soft wall that both resisted and sucked him in. Finally, on Wednesday, at half past eleven at night, the minister phoned. He did not say hello or good evening, he did not ask the superintendent if he was well or how he was coping with being alone, he did not mention whether he had questioned the inspector and the sergeant, together or separately, in friendly conversation or by issuing harsh threats, he merely said in passing, as if apropos of nothing, I think you'll find something in tomorrow's newspapers to interest you, I read the papers every day, minister, Congratulations, you're obviously very well-informed, nevertheless I urge you most strongly not to miss tomorrow's editions, you'll find them most interesting, I'll be sure to read them, minister, And watch the television news too, don't miss it whatever you do, We have no television set at providential ltd, minister, What a shame, although, on second thoughts, I rather approve, it's better like that, it might distract you from the arduous investigatory problems we set you, besides, you could always go and visit one of your new friends and suggest you all get together and enjoy the show. The superintendent did not respond. He could have asked what his disciplinary situation would be after Thursday, but he preferred to say nothing, it was clear that his fate lay in the minister's hands, and so it was up to him to pronounce sentence, if he did ask, he was sure to receive some sharp riposte, along the lines of, Don't be in such a hurry, you'll find out tomorrow. Suddenly, the superintendent became aware that the silence had lasted longer than is considered normal in a telephone conversation, a mode of communication in which the pauses or rests between phrases are, generally speaking, either brief or even briefer. He had not reacted to the interior minister's spiteful suggestion and this had not appeared to trouble him, he had remained silent as if he were leaving time for his interlocutor to think of a response. The superintendent said cautiously, Minister. The electrical impulses carried the word down the line, but there was no sign of life at the other end. The albatross had hung up. The superintendent put the phone back on its rest and left the room. He went into the kitchen and drank a glass of water, it was not the first time he had noticed that talking to the interior minister created in him an almost desperate thirst, as if throughout the conversation he had been burning up inside and now had to hurry to put out his own fire. He went and sat down on the sofa in the sitting-room, but did not stay there long, the state of semi-lethargy in which he had lived for the past two days had disappeared, as if it had vanished at the minister's first word, for things, that vague agglomeration to which we usually give the generic and lazy label of things when it would take too much time and too much space to explain or merely define it, had begun to move very fast and they would not stop now until the end, but what end, and when, and how, and where. Of one thing he was sure, he did not need to be a maigret, a poirot or a sherlock holmes to know what the newspapers would publish the following day. The waiting was over, the interior minister would not phone him again, any order still to be issued would arrive through the intermediary of a secretary or directly from the police commissioner, a mere five days and five nights had been enough for him to go from being a superintendent in charge of a difficult investigation to a wind-up toy whose spring had gone and which was to be thrown out with the rubbish. It was then that it occurred to him that he still had one duty to perform. He looked up a name in the telephone book, mentally confirmed the address and dialled the number. The doctor's wife answered, Hello, Oh, good evening, it's me, the superintendent, forgive me for phoning you at this hour of the night, That's all right, we never go to bed early, Do you remember me telling you, when we were talking in the park, that the interior minister had ordered me to hand over that group photograph, Yes, I remember, Well, I have every reason to believe that the photograph will be published in tomorrow's newspapers and broadcast on television, Well, I won't ask you why, but I do remember you telling me that the minister wouldn't have wanted it for any good purpose, Exactly, but I never expected him to use it like this, What's he up to, We'll see tomorrow what the newspapers do apart from printing the photograph, but I imagine that they'll try to stigmatise you in the mind of the public, Because I didn't go blind four years ago, You know very well that the minister finds it highly suspicious that you didn't go blind when everyone else was losing their sight, and now that fact has become more than sufficient, from his point of view, for him to find you responsible, either wholly or in part, for what is happening now, Do you mean the blank votes, Yes, the blank votes, But that's absurd, utterly absurd, As I've learned in this job, not only are the people in government never put off by what we judge to be absurd, they make use of absurdities to dull consciences and to destroy reason, What do you think we should do, Hide, disappear, but don't go to your friends' apartments, you wouldn't be safe there, they'll be putting them under surveillance soon as well, if they haven't already, You're right, but, in any case, we would never put at risk the safety of someone who had chosen to protect us, right now, for example, I'm wondering if you haven't been foolish in phoning us, Don't worry, the line is secure, in fact, there aren't many lines much securer than this, Superintendent, Yes, There's a question I'd like to ask, but I'm not sure I dare, Ask it, please, Why are you doing this for us, why are you helping us, Because of something I read in a book, years ago now, and which I had forgotten, but which has come back to me in the last few days, What was that, We are born, and at that moment, it is as if we had signed a pact for the rest of our life, but a day may come when we will ask ourselves Who signed this on my behalf, Fine, thought-provoking words, what's the book called, You know I'm ashamed to say it, but I can't remember, Never mind, even if you can't remember anything else, not even the title, Not even the name of the author, Those words, which probably no one else, at least not in that precise form, would ever have said before, had the good fortune not to have lost each other, they had someone to bring them together, and who knows, perhaps the world would be a slightly better place if we were able to gather up a few of the words that are out there wandering around alone, Oh, I doubt the poor despised creatures would ever find each other, No, probably not, but dreaming is cheap, it doesn't cost any money, Let's see what the papers say tomorrow, Yes, let's see, I'm prepared for the worst, Whatever the immediate results, think about what I said, hide, disappear, All right, I'll talk to my husband, Let's hope he manages to persuade you, Good night, and thank you for everything, There's nothing to thank me for, Take care. After he had hung up, the superintendent wondered if he hadn't been rather stupid to declare, as if it were his property, that the line was secure, that there wouldn't be many lines in the country much more secure. He shrugged and murmured, What does it matter, nothing is secure, no one is secure.

He did not sleep well, he dreamed of a cloud of words that fled and scattered as he chased after them with a butterfly net, pleading, Stop, please, don't move, wait for me. Then, suddenly, the words stopped and gathered together in a clump, one on top of the other, like a swarm of bees waiting for a hive they could swoop down on, and he, with a cry of joy, lunged forward with his net. What he had caught was a newspaper. It had been a bad dream, but it would have been worse if the albatross had returned to prick out the eyes of the doctor's wife. He woke early. He pulled on some clothes and went downstairs. He no longer went out via the garage, through the tradesmen's entrance, now he went out through the main door, what one might call the pedestrian entrance, he greeted the porter with a nod of his head if he happened to see him in his lodge or exchanged a word or two with him if he was outside, but it wasn't necessary, he – the superintendent, not the porter – was, in a way, merely there on loan. The streetlights were still on, the shops wouldn't open for another two hours. He looked for and found a newspaper kiosk, one of the larger ones that receives all the papers, and he stood there waiting. Fortunately, it wasn't raining. The street lights went out, leaving the city plunged for a few moments in a last, brief darkness, which vanished as soon as his eyes grew accustomed to the change, and the bluish light of early morning descended upon the streets. The delivery van arrived, unloaded the bundles of papers and continued on its way. The newsagent started opening the bundles and arranging the newspapers according to the number of copies received, from left to right, from large to small. The superintendent went over to him, Good morning, he said, I'll have a copy of all of them. While the man was putting his purchases into a plastic bag, the superintendent looked at the rows of newspapers and saw that, with the exception of the last two, they all carried the photograph on the front page under banner headlines. The arrival of this keen customer with sufficient means to pay has got the newspaper kiosk off to good start this morning, indeed, we can safely say that the rest of the day will be no different, for every one of the newspapers will be snapped up, apart from those two piles on the right, of which only the usual number of copies will be sold. The superintendent was no longer there, he had run to catch a taxi he had spotted on the nearby corner, and having given the driver the address of providential ltd, and apologised for the shortness of the journey, he was now nervously taking the papers out of the bag and opening them. Alongside the group photo, with an arrow indicating the doctor's wife, was an enlargement of her face in a circle. And the headlines were, in red and in black, Revealed At Last – The Face Behind The Conspiracy, Four Years Ago This Woman Escaped Blindness, Mystery Of The Blank Ballot Papers Solved, Police Investigation Yields First Results. The still faint morning light and the swaying of the car as it bumped over the cobbled surface prevented him from reading the smaller print of the articles beneath. In less than five minutes the taxi had deposited him outside the door of the building. The superintendent paid, left the change in the driver's hand and rushed in. He raced past the porter without bothering to greet him and got into the lift, his state of excitement almost making him tap his toes with impatience, come on, come on, but the machinery, which had spent its whole life carrying people up and down, listening to conversations, unfinished monologues, tuneless fragments of songs, the occasional irrepressible sigh, the occasional troubled murmur, pretended that this was none of its business, it took a certain amount of time to go up and a certain amount of time to come down, like fate, if you're in that much of a hurry, take the stairs. The superintendent finally put the key in the door of providential ltd, insurance and reinsurance, turned on the light and made straight for the table on which he had spread out the map of the city and where he had eaten a last breakfast with his now absent assistants. His hands were shaking. Forcing himself to slow down and not to skip any lines, he read, word by word, the articles in the four newspapers that had published the photograph. With a few small changes in style, with slight differences in vocabulary, the information was the same in all of them and one could sense a kind of arithmetic mean calculated by the editorial consultants at the ministry of the interior to fit the original font. The primitive prose read more or less like this, Just when we were thinking that the government had decided to leave it to time, to that same time by which everything is worn away and transformed, the job of isolating and shrinking the malignant tumour that so unexpectedly grew in this nation's capital, taking the abstruse and aberrant form of the mass casting of blank ballot papers, which, as our readers know, vastly exceeded the number of votes cast for all the democratic political parties put together, our editorial desk has just received the most surprising and gratifying news. The investigatory genius and persistence of the police, in the persons of a superintendent, an inspector and a sergeant, whose names, for security reasons, we are not authorised to reveal, have managed to uncover the individual who is, in all probability, the head of the tapeworm whose coils have kept the civic conscience of the majority of the city's inhabitants of voting age entirely paralysed and in a state of dangerous atrophy. A certain woman, married to an ophthalmologist, and who, wonder of wonders, was, according to reliable witnesses, the only person to escape the terrible epidemic four years ago that made of our homeland a country of the blind, this woman is now considered by the police to be the person responsible for the current blindness, limited this time, fortunately, to what used to be the capital city, and which has introduced into political life and into our democratic system the dangerous germ of perversion and corruption. Only a diabolical mind, like those of the greatest criminals in the history of humankind, could have conceived what, according to reliable sources, his excellency the president of the republic has so eloquently described as a torpedo fired below the water line of the majestic ship of democracy. For that is what it is. If it is proved, beyond a shadow of a doubt, as everything indicates it will be, that this doctor's wife is guilty, then all those citizens who still respect order and the law will demand that the full rigour of justice falls upon her head. How strange life is. Given the singularity of her case four years ago, this woman could have become an invaluable subject of study for our scientific community, and, as such, would have deserved a prominent place in the clinical history of ophthalmology, but she will now be singled out for public execration as an enemy of her country and of her people. One is tempted to say that it would have been better if she had gone blind.

That last sentence, clearly threatening in tone, sounded like a judicial sentence, just as if it had said It would have been better if you had never been born. The superintendent's first impulse was to phone the doctor's wife, to ask if she had read the newspapers, to comfort her as best as he could, but he was prevented by the thought that, overnight, the probability of her phone being tapped had become one hundred per cent. As for the phones of providential ltd, the red and the grey ones, they, of course, were linked directly to the state's private network. He leafed through the other two newspapers, which had not printed a single word on the subject. What should I do now, he asked out loud. He went back to the article, re-read it, and found it strange that they had not identified the people in the photograph, in particular, the doctor's wife and the doctor. It was then that he noticed the caption, which read thus, The suspect is indicated by an arrow. It seems, although there is no solid confirmation of this fact, that the doctor's wife took this group under her wing during the epidemic of blindness. According to official sources, identification of these people is at an advanced stage and will be made public tomorrow. The superintendent murmured, They're probably trying to find out where the boy lives, as if that would help them. Then, after some thought, At first sight, the publication of the photograph, unaccompanied by any other measures, appears to make no sense, since all the people in the photo, as I myself advised, could seize the opportunity and vanish, but then the minister loves a spectacle, a successful manhunt would give him greater political weight and more influence in both the government and the party, and as for other measures, the homes of these people are almost certainly already under round-the-clock surveillance, the ministry has had more than enough time to get agents into the city and to set up such a programme. While all of this was true, none of it answered his question What should I do now. He could phone the ministry of the interior on the pretext that, since it was now Thursday, he wanted to know what decision had been taken about his disciplinary situation, but there was no point, he was sure the minister would not speak to him, some secretary would merely come on the line, telling him to get in touch with the police commissioner, the days of conversations between albatross and puffin are over, superintendent. What shall I do now, he asked again, just sit here rotting away until someone finally remembers me and sends orders for the corpse to be removed, try to leave the city when it's more than likely that strict orders have been given at the frontier posts not to let me pass, what shall I do. He looked at the photograph again, the doctor and his wife in the middle, the girl with the dark glasses and the old man with the black eye-patch to the left, the guy who wrote the letter and his wife to the right, the boy with the squint kneeling down in front like a football player, the dog sitting at its mistress's feet. He re-read the caption, Full identification will be made public tomorrow, will be made public, tomorrow, tomorrow, tomorrow. At that moment, he was suddenly gripped by an idea for a plan of action, but the following moment, caution was immediately protesting that it would be utter madness, The sensible thing, it said, would be not to wake the sleeping dragon, the stupid thing would be to approach while it's awake. The superintendent got out of his chair, paced twice around the room, returned to the table on which the newspapers lay, and looked again at the head of the doctor's wife surrounded by a white ring that looked already like a hangman's noose, at this hour, half the city is reading the newspapers and the other half is sitting in front of the television to hear what the newsreader on the first news bulletin is going to say or listening to the voice of the radio announcing that the woman's name will be made public tomorrow, and not only her name, but her address too, so that the whole population will know where evil has made its nest. The superintendent went to fetch the typewriter and brought it over to the table. He folded up the newspapers, pushed them to one side and sat down to work. The paper he was using bore the heading providential ltd, insurance and re-insurance, and could, if not tomorrow, certainly the day after tomorrow, be used by the state prosecution as proof of a second crime, that of using civil service stationery for his own purposes, an aggravating factor being the confidential nature of that correspondence and the conspiratorial use to which it was put. What the superintendent was typing was neither more nor less than a detailed account of the events of the last five days, from early Saturday morning when he and his two assistants had clandestinely breached the city blockade, until today, and this very moment of writing. Providential ltd does, of course, have a photocopier, but it seems to the superintendent impolite to give the original letter to one person and a mere copy to the other, however convincingly the very latest reprographic techniques may assure us that not even the eyes of a hawk could tell them apart. The superintendent belongs to the second oldest generation of those who still eat bread in this world, which is why he retains a respect for form, which means that, having

275

finished the first letter, he started carefully copying it out onto a clean sheet of paper. It is, to be sure, still a copy, but not in the same way. When he had completed this task, he folded up the letters and placed each one in an envelope bearing the company name, sealed the envelopes and wrote the respective addresses. While it is true that the letters will be delivered by hand, the addressees will understand, if only by the discreet elegance of the gesture, that these letters from providential ltd, insurance and reinsurance, deal with important matters deserving of the news media's attention.

The superintendent is about to go out again. He placed the two letters in one of his inside jacket pockets and put on his raincoat, even though the weather is as mild as one could hope for at this time of year, as, indeed, he could ascertain for himself by opening the window and looking up at the slow, sparse, white clouds passing by overhead. It is possible that there may have been another strong reason, for the raincoat, especially of the belted trench-coat variety, is a kind of identifying feature of detectives from the classic era, at least ever since raymond chandler first created the character of marlowe, so much so that seeing a man walk by, a slouch hat on his head and his raincoat collar turned up, and immediately proclaiming there goes humphrey bogart with his piercing eyes gazing out between the edge of his collar and the brim of his hat, is the kind of knowledge that is within easy grasp of any reader of detective fiction, p.o. box death. This superintendent is not wearing a hat, his head is bare, as determined by the fashion of a modern world that loathes the picturesque and, as they say, shoots to kill without even asking if you're still alive. He has got out of the lift, walked past the porter's lodge, from where the porter waved to him, and now he is in the street ready to carry out his three objectives for that morning, namely, to eat a belated breakfast, to take a walk down the street where the doctor's wife lives, and to deliver the letters to their addressees. He achieves the first in this café, a cup of milky coffee, a couple of slices of buttered toast, not as tender and succulent as those he ate the other day, but there's no surprise there, life is like that, you win some, you lose some, and there are very few cultivators of buttered toast left, both amongst those who prepare it and those who eat it. Forgive these extremely banal gastronomic thoughts in a man who is carrying a bomb in his pocket. He has eaten and paid, now he is striding towards his second objective. It took him almost twenty minutes to get there. He slowed his pace when he reached the street and adopted the air of one just out for a stroll, he knows that if there are any surveillance police about they will probably recognise him, but he doesn't care. If one of them sees him and informs his immediate boss of what he saw, and if the boss passes on the information to his immediate superior, who then tells the police commissioner, who then tells the interior minister, you can guarantee that the albatross will croak out in his harshest tones, Don't come bothering me with things I already know, tell me what I don't know, namely, what that wretched superintendent is up to. The street is more crowded than usual. There are small knots of people standing around outside the building where the doctor's wife lives, they are locals moved by a curiosity which is in some cases innocent and in other cases morbid, and who have come, newspaper in hand, to the place where the accused woman lives, a woman they know more or less by sight or from an occasional exchange of words, and there is the inevitable coincidence that the eyes of some have benefited from the expertise of her ophthalmologist husband. The superintendent has already spotted the surveillance policemen, the first has positioned himself next to one of the larger groups, the second, leaning with feigned idleness against a wall, is reading a sports magazine as if, in the world of letters, nothing more important could possibly exist. The fact that he is reading a magazine and not a newspaper can be easily explained, a magazine, while affording sufficient protection, takes up much less of the watcher's visual field and can be quickly stuffed into a pocket should it become necessary to follow someone. Policemen know these things, they learn them in kindergarten. It happens that the men here have no inkling of the stormy relations between the superintendent walking along and the ministry they all work for, which is why they assume he is just part of the operation and has come to make sure that everything is going to plan. Nothing odd about that. Although at certain levels in the organisation, there are already mutterings that the minister is dissatisfied with the superintendent's work, the proof of which is that he has ordered his two assistants to come back, leaving the superintendent to lie fallow, or, as others say, on stand-by, these mutterings have not yet reached the lower levels to which these officers belong. We should point out, however, before we forget, that the said mutterers have no very clear idea what the superintendent came to do in the capital, which just goes to show that the inspector and the sergeant, wherever they are now, have kept their mouths shut. The interesting thing, although not in the least amusing, was to see how the policemen went over to the superintendent and whispered conspiratorially out of the corner of their mouth, Nothing to report. The superintendent nodded, looked up at the windows on the fourth floor and walked away, thinking, Tomorrow, when the names and addresses are published, there will be far more people here. Further on, he saw a taxi and hailed it. He got in, said good morning and, taking the envelopes out of his pocket, read the addresses and asked the driver, Which of these is closest, The second one, Take me there, then, please. On the seat next to the driver lay a folded newspaper, the one that bore the striking headline, in letters the colour of blood, Revealed At Last – The Face Behind The Conspiracy. The superintendent was tempted to ask the driver his opinion of the sensational news published in today's newspapers, but abandoned the idea for fear that an overly inquisitive tone in his voice might betray his profession, One of the hazards of being a policeman, he thought. It was the driver who brought the subject up, I don't know about you, but I reckon this story about the woman they claim didn't go blind is just one of those whoppers they dream up to sell newspapers, I mean, I went blind, we all went blind, how was it that this one woman kept her sight, you'd have to be a fool to believe that, And what about them saying that she was behind all those people casting blank votes, That's another load of old nonsense, a woman is a woman, she wouldn't get involved in things like that, I mean, if it was a man, possibly, he could be, but a woman, pfff, Yes, it'll be interesting to see how it all turns out, Once they've squeezed the juice out of this story, they'll invent another one, it's always the same, oh, you'd be surprised the things you learn behind the wheel, and I'll tell you something else too, Go on, Contrary to what everyone thinks, the rear-view mirror isn't just for checking on the cars behind, you can use it to look into the souls of your passengers too, I bet you'd never thought of that, No, I certainly hadn't, you astonish me, Like I say, this steering-wheel teaches you a lot. After such a revelation, the superintendent thought it best to allow the conversation to lapse. Only when the driver stopped the car and said, Here we are, did he dare to ask if that business about the rear-view mirror and the soul applied to all cars and all drivers, but the driver was quite clear about it, No, only taxis, sir, only taxis.

The superintendent entered the building, went over to the reception desk and said, Good morning, I represent providential ltd, insurance and reinsurance, and I'd like to speak to the director, If you're here about insurance, perhaps it would be better to speak to the administrator, In principle, yes, you're quite right, but what brings me to your newspaper is not a mere technical matter, and it's vital, therefore, that I speak to the director himself, The director isn't here right now, and I don't imagine he'll be in until gone midday, Who do you think I should speak to then, who would be the best person, Probably the editor-in-chief, In that case, I would be grateful if you could tell him I'm here, providential ltd, insurance and reinsurance, Could you tell me your name, Providential will do fine, Oh, I see, the firm bears your name, Exactly. The receptionist made the phone call, explained the situation and, when she had hung up, said, Someone will be right down, mister providential. A few minutes later, a woman appeared, I'm the editor-in-chief's secretary, would you care to come with me. He followed her down a corridor, feeling quite calm and serene, then, suddenly, without warning, a realisation of the bold step he was about to take took his breath away as if he had been punched in the solar plexus. There was still time to go back, to make some excuse, Oh, no, what a nuisance, I've forgotten a really important document which I really must have if I'm to talk to the editor-in-chief, but it wasn't true, the document was there, in his inside jacket pocket, the wine has been poured, superintendent, you have no option now but to drink it. The secretary showed him into a small, modestly furnished room, a couple of battered sofas that had fetched up here in order to live out the rest of their long lives in reasonable peace, a table in the middle with a few newspapers on it, a jumbled bookshelf. Sit down, please, the editor-in-chief asked if you wouldn't mind waiting for a moment, he's busy right now, That's fine, I'll wait, said the superintendent. This was his second chance. If he walked out of here and retraced the path that had led him into this trap, he would be safe, like someone who, having glimpsed his own soul in a rear-view mirror, had decided it was a fool, and that souls should not go around dragging people into the most terrible of disasters, but should, on the contrary, keep them safe from such things and behave themselves, because souls, if ever they do leave the body, almost always get lost, they simply don't know where to go, and it is not just behind the wheel of a taxi that one learns such things. The superintendent did not leave, not now that the wine has been poured, etc. etc. The editor-in-chief came in, I do apologise for keeping you waiting for so long, but I was in the middle of doing something and I couldn't leave it half-finished, There's no need to apologise, it's very good of you to see me at all, So, mister providential, what can I do for you, although from what I've been told, this does seem to be more a matter for the administrative office. The superintendent raised his hand to his pocket and took out the first envelope, I'd be grateful if you would read the letter inside this envelope, Now, asked the editor-in-chief, Yes, if you wouldn't mind, but I must tell you first that my name is not Providential, So what is your name, You'll understand when you've read the letter. The editor-in-chief tore open the envelope, unfolded the piece of paper and started to read. He stopped after the first few lines and looked, perplexed, at the man before him, as if asking if it wouldn't be more prudent to stop right there. The superintendent made a gesture urging him to continue. The editor did not look up again until he had finished reading, on the contrary, it seemed as if, with each word, he were plunging deeper and deeper in, and as if he could not possibly return to the surface wearing his usual editor-in-chief's face once he had seen the fearful creatures inhabiting the lower depths. It was a deeply troubled man who finally looked up at the superintendent and said, Forgive the blunt question, but who are you, My name is there in the signature, Yes, I can see the name, but a name is just a word, it doesn't explain anything about who the person is, I'd prefer not to have to tell you, but I understand perfectly your need to know, In that case, tell me, Not unless you give me your word of honour that the letter will be published, In the absence of the director, I'm not authorised to make that commitment, They told me in reception that the director will only be in this afternoon, Yes, that's true, at around four o'clock, Right, I'll come back later then, but I just want you to know now that I have an identical letter with me and that if you're not interested in the matter, I'll deliver it to that other addressee, The letter is, I assume, addressed to another newspaper, Yes, but not to any of the papers that published the photograph, Of course, but you can't be sure that the other newspaper would be prepared to take the inevitable risks involved in publishing the facts you describe, No, I can't be sure, I'm betting on two horses and I risk losing on both, My feeling is that you risk much more if you win, Just as you do if you decide to publish. The superintendent got to his feet, I'll be here at a quarter past four, Here's your letter, since we haven't yet come to an agreement, I can't and shouldn't hold on to it, Thank you for not making me ask you for it. The editor-in-chief used the telephone in the room to call the secretary, Show this gentleman out, will you, he said, and make a note that he will be back at a quarter past four, and you'll be there to receive him and take him to the director's office, Yes, sir. The superintendent said, See you later, then, Yes, see you later, and they shook hands. The secretary opened the door for the superintendent, If you'd like to follow me, mister providential, she said, and once they were out in the corridor, If you don't mind my saying, this is the first time I've ever come across someone with that surname, it didn't even occur to me that it could exist, Well, now you know, It must be nice to be called Providential, Why, Well, because it's providential, That's the best possible answer. They had reached reception, I'll be here at the time agreed, said the secretary, Thank you, Goodbye, mister providential, Goodbye.

The superintendent looked at his watch, it wasn't yet one o'clock, too early to have lunch, besides, he wasn't hungry, the buttered toast and coffee were still there in his stomach. He hailed a taxi and asked to be taken to the park where, on Monday, he had met the doctor's wife, there's no reason why one should always do the thing one first decided to do. He had not thought of going back to the park, but here he is. He will then continue on foot, like a police superintendent quietly carrying out his patrol, he will see how crowded the street is and may even exchange professional notes with the two guards. He walked through the garden and stopped for a moment to study the statue of the woman with the empty water jar, They left me here, she seemed to be saying, and now all I'm good for is staring into this grubby water, there was a time when the stone I'm made from was white, when a fountain flowed day and night from this jar, they never told me where all that water came from, I was just here to tip up the jar, but now not a drop falls from it, and no one has come to tell me why it stopped. The superintendent murmured, It's like life, my dear, we don't know why it starts or why it ends. He dipped the fingers of his right hand into the water and raised them to his lips. It did not occur to him that the gesture could have any meaning, however, anyone watching him from afar would have sworn that he had kissed that murky water, which was green with slime and came from a muddy pond, as impure as life itself. The clock had not advanced very much, he would have had time to sit down in the shade somewhere, but he did not. He repeated the route he had taken with the doctor's wife, he went into the street, where the scene had changed completely, now he could barely push his way through, there weren't just small knots of people, but a huge crowd that blocked the traffic, it was as if everyone from the neighbouring area had left their houses to come and witness some promised apparition. The superintendent beckoned the two policemen over to the doorway of a building and asked them if anything had happened in his absence. They said that no one had left, that the windows had remained closed at all times, and they reported that two people unknown to them, a man and a woman, had gone up to the fourth floor to ask if the people in the apartment needed anything, but that the latter had replied in the negative and thanked them for their kindness. Is that all, asked the superintendent, As far as we know, replied one of the policeman, it's certainly going to be an easy report to write. He said this just in time, clipping the wings of the superintendent's imagination, which had unfurled and were already carrying him up the stairs, where he would ring the bell and announce, It's me, and then go in and tell them about the latest events, about the letters he had written, his conversation with the editor-in-chief, and then the doctor's wife would say Stay and have lunch with us, and he would, and the world would be at peace. Yes, at peace, and the policemen would write in their report, A superintendent who joined us went up to the fourth floor and only came down again an hour later, he did not say anything about what happened up there, but we both got the impression that he had had a good lunch. The superintendent went to have lunch somewhere else, but he did not eat much and showed no interest in the dish they set before him, at three o'clock, he was sitting in the park again looking at the statue of the woman with her pitcher inclined like someone still expecting the miraculous restoration of the waters. At half past three, he got up from the bench where he had sat down and walked back to the newspaper offices. He had time, he didn't need to take a taxi in which, however reluctantly, he would have been unable to keep himself from looking in the rear-view mirror, he knew quite enough about his soul already and he might see something in the mirror that he didn't like. It was not quite a quarter past four when he arrived back at the newspaper offices. The secretary was already in reception, The director is expecting you, she said. She did not add the words mister providential, perhaps she had been told that it was not his real name and perhaps she felt offended by the trap into which she had, in all good faith, fallen. They walked down the same corridor, but this time they continued to the end, where they turned the corner, on the second door on the right there is a small notice which says Director. The secretary knocked discreetly, and someone inside answered, Come in. She went in first and held the door open for the superintendent. Thank you, we won't be needing you for the moment, said the editor-in-chief to the secretary, who left immediately. I'm most grateful to you for agreeing to talk to me, sir, began the superintendent, Let me be perfectly frank with you, I foresee enormous difficulties in our publishing the material that the editor-in-chief here has described to me, although I would, of course, be delighted to read the entire document, Here it is, sir, said the superintendent, handing him the envelope, Sit down, said the director, and just give me a couple of minutes, will you. The reading of the document did not make him bow his head as it had the editor-in-chief, but he was clearly a confused and worried man when he looked up, Who are you, he asked, unaware that the editor-in-chief had asked the same question, If your newspaper agrees to make public the contents of that document, then you will find out who I am, if you don't, then I will take back my letter and leave without another word, except to thank you for letting me take up so much of your time, The director knows that you have an identical letter which you intend to give to another newspaper, said the editor-in-chief, Exactly, said the superintendent, I have it here, and if we don't reach an agreement, I will deliver it today, because it's vital that this is published tomorrow, Why, Because tomorrow there may still be time to prevent an injustice being committed, You mean to the doctor's wife, Yes, sir, they are doing all they can to make her the scapegoat for the country's current political situation, But that's ridiculous, Don't tell me that, tell the government, tell the interior minister, tell your colleagues who write what they're told to. The director exchanged a look with the editor-in-chief and said, As you can imagine, it would be impossible for us to publish your statement as it stands, with all these details, Why, Don't forget, we are still living under a state of siege, the censors have their eyes trained on the press, especially on a newspaper like ours, Publishing this would get the newspaper shut down immediately, said the editor-in-chief, So is there nothing to be done, asked the superintendent,

We can try, but we can't be sure it will succeed, How, said the super-intendent. After another brief exchange of glances with the editor-in-chief, the director said, It's time you told us, once and for all, who you are, there's a name on the letter, it's true, but we have no way of knowing that it's not a false name, you could, quite simply, be an agent provocateur sent here by the police to put us to the test and to compromise us, we're not saying that you are, of course, but I have to make it quite clear that we cannot take this conver-sation any further unless you identify yourself right now. The super-intendent reached into a pocket and pulled out his wallet, Here you are, he said, and handed the director his police identification. The expression on the director's face changed at once from mistrust to stupefaction, What, you're a police superintendent, he said, A police superintendent, repeated the editor-in-chief dully when the director passed the document to him, Yes, came the calm response, and now I think we can continue the conversation, If you'll forgive my curiosity, said the director, what made you take a step like this, Personal reasons, Tell me one of those reasons, so that I can persuade myself that I'm not dreaming, When we are born, when we enter this world, it is as if we signed a pact for the rest of our life, but a day may come when we will ask ourselves Who signed this on my behalf, well, I asked myself that question and the answer is this bit of paper, You do know what might happen to you, don't you, Yes, I've had time enough to think about that. There was a silence, which the superintendent broke, You said you could try, We've thought of a little trick, said the director, and indicated to the editor-in-chief that he should continue, The idea, the editor said, would be to publish, albeit in very different terms and without the tasteless rhet-oric, what was published elsewhere today, and then, in the final section, weave in some of the information you've given us today, it won't be easy, but it doesn't strike me as impossible, it's just a matter of skill and luck, We're relying on the boredom or even laziness of the civil servant in the censor's office, added the director, praying that he will think that since he knows this bit of news already, there's no point reading to the end, What's the probability that we'll succeed, asked the superintendent, To be perfectly frank, pretty low, admitted the editor-in-chief, we'll have to content ourselves with possibilities, And what if the ministry of the interior want to know where you got your information, To begin with we'll take refuge in insisting on the confidentiality of our sources, but that isn't going to be much use in a state of siege situation, And if they press you, if they threaten you, Then, much against our will, we will have no option but to reveal our source, we'll be punished, of course, but you will suffer the worst consequences, said the director, Fine, said the superintendent, now that we all know what to expect, let's do it, and if praying serves any purpose, I'll pray that the readers don't do as we're hoping the censor will do, that is, I'll pray that the readers do read the article through to the end, Amen, chorused the director and the editor-in-chief.

It was shortly after five o'clock when the superintendent left. He could have taken advantage of the taxi that someone else had just left at the door of the newspaper offices, but he preferred to walk. Oddly enough, he felt light and serene, as if someone had removed from some vital organ the foreign body that had been gradually gnawing away at him, a bone in the throat, a nail in the stomach, poison in the liver. Tomorrow all the cards in the deck would be on the table, the game of hide-and-seek would be over, and so he has not the slightest doubt that the minister, always assuming that the article does see the light of day, and, even if it doesn't, that news of it reaches his ears, will know immediately at whom to point the accusing finger. Imagination seemed prepared to go further, it even took a first, troubling step, but the superintendent grabbed it by the throat, Today is today, madam, and tomorrow will come soon enough, he said. He had decided to go back to providential ltd, his legs felt suddenly heavy, his nerves as lax as if they were an elastic band that had been kept fully stretched for far too long, he experienced an urgent need to close his eyes and sleep. I'll hail the first taxi that appears, he thought. He still had to walk for quite a way, all the taxis that passed were occupied, one didn't even hear him call, and finally, when he could barely drag his feet along, a small lifeboat picked up the shipwrecked man just before he drowned. The lift hoisted him charitably up to the fourteenth floor, the door opened unresistingly, the sofa received him like a dear friend, and a few minutes later, the superintendent was lying, legs outstretched, fast asleep, or sleeping the sleep of the just, as people used to say in the days when they believed that the just existed. Snuggled up in the maternal lap of providential ltd, insurance and reinsurance, whose peaceful atmosphere did full justice to the names and attributes conferred upon it, the superintendent slept for a good hour, at the end of which he awoke with renewed energy, or so at least it seemed to him. When he stretched, he felt the second envelope in his inside jacket pocket, the one he had not delivered, Perhaps I was wrong to bet everything on one horse, he thought, then quickly realised that he could not possibly have had the same conversation twice, that he could not have gone straight from one newspaper to the next and told the same story, and by repetition, worn away at its veracity, What's done is done, he thought, there's no point thinking about it any more. He went into his bedroom and saw the light on the answering machine flashing. Someone had phoned and left a message. He pressed the button, the telephonist's voice spoke first, then that of the police commissioner, Please note that tomorrow, at nine o'clock, I repeat, at nine o'clock, not at twenty-one hundred hours, your colleagues, the inspector and the sergeant, will be waiting for you at post six-north, I should tell you that, not only has your mission failed due to the technical and scientific incompetence of the person in charge, your presence in the capital has now also come to be considered inappropriate both by the interior minister and by myself, I need only add that the inspector and the sergeant are officially responsible for escorting you to my presence and have orders to arrest you if you resist. The superintendent stood staring at the answering machine, and then, slowly, like a person saying goodbye to someone setting off on a long trip, reached out his hand and pressed the erase button. Then he went into the kitchen, took the envelope out of his pocket, soaked it in alcohol and, folding it to form an inverted V in the sink, set fire to it. A gush of water carried the ashes down the drain. Having done that, he went back into the living-room, turned on all the lights, and devoted himself to a leisurely perusal of the newspapers, paying special attention to the paper to which or to whom, in some way, he had handed his fate. When it was time, he went and looked in the fridge to see if he could prepare something resembling supper from whatever was in there, but soon gave up, scarcity was not, in this case, a synonym for either freshness or quality. They should install a new fridge here, he thought, this one has given all it had to give. He went out, ate quickly in the first restaurant he came across and returned to providential ltd. He had to get up early the following day.

THE SUPERINTENDENT WAS AWAKE WHEN THE TELEPHONE RANG. HE DID not get up to answer it, he was sure that it would be someone from the police commissioner's office reminding him of the order he had received to appear at nine o'clock, note, at nine o'clock, not at twenty-one hundred hours, at military post six-north. They probably won't phone again, and one can easily understand why, for in their professional lives and, who knows, possibly in their private lives too, policemen make great use of the mental process we call deduction, also known as logical inference. If he doesn't answer, they would say, it's because he's already on his way. How wrong they were. It's true that the superintendent has now got out of bed, it's true that he has entered the bathroom to perform the appropriate actions to relieve and cleanse his body, it is true that he has got dressed and is about to leave, but not in order to hail the first taxi that appears and say to the driver, who is looking at him expectantly in the rear-view mirror, Take me to post six-north, Post six-north, I'm sorry, but I've no idea where that is, it must be a new street, No, it's a military post, I can show you where it is if you have a map. No, this dialogue will never take place, not now or ever, the superintendent is going out to buy the newspapers, that was why he went to bed early yesterday, not in order to get enough rest and arrive promptly for the meeting at post six-north. The street lamps are still on, the man at the newspaper kiosk has just raised the shutters, he is starting to set out the week's magazines, and when he finishes this work, as if it were a sign, the street lamps go out

and the distribution truck arrives. The superintendent approaches
while the man is still sorting out the newspapers into the order with
which we are already familiar, but, this time, there are almost as
many copies of one of the less popular newspapers as there are of
the papers with a larger circulation. The superintendent felt this
was a good omen, but this pleasant feeling of hope was immediately succeeded by a violent shock, the headlines on the first newspapers in the row were sinister, troubling, and all in intense red ink,
Murderess, This Woman Killed, Woman Suspect's Other Crime, A
Murder Committed Four Years Ago. At the other end of the row,
the newspaper whose offices the superintendent had visited
yesterday asked, What Haven't We Been Told. The headline was
ambiguous, it could mean this or that, or the opposite, but the
superintendent preferred to see it as a small lantern placed there to
guide his stumbling steps out of the valley of shadows. A copy of
each, he said. The newsagent smiled, thinking that he seemed to
have acquired a good customer for the future, and handed him the
plastic bag containing the newspapers. The superintendent looked
around for a taxi, he waited in vain for nearly five minutes, then
decided to walk back to providential ltd, which is not, as we know,
very far from here, but he is carrying a heavy load, a plastic bag
bursting with words, it would be easier to carry the world on one's
back. As luck would have it, though, he took a short-cut down a
narrow street and came upon a modest, old-style café, the sort that
opens early because the owner has nothing else to do and which
the customers visit in order to make sure that everything is there
in its usual place and where the taste of the breakfast muffin speaks
of eternity. He sat down at a table, ordered a white coffee, asked if
they served toast, with butter, of course, no margarine, please. The
coffee, when it arrived, was merely passable, but the toast had come
direct from the hands of an alchemist who had only failed to
discover the philosopher's stone because he had never managed

to get beyond the putrefaction stage. The superintendent had opened the newspaper that most interested him today, he did so as soon as he sat down, and a quick glance was enough for him to see that the trick had worked, the censor had allowed himself to be taken in by the confirmation of what he already knew, and the thought had clearly never even crossed his mind that one must always take great care with what one thinks one knows, because behind it one finds concealed an endless chain of unknowns, the last of which will probably prove insoluble. Nevertheless, there was no point in harbouring any great illusions, the newspaper would not be on sale at the kiosks all day, he could already imagine the enraged interior minister brandishing a copy and yelling, Get this garbage impounded at once and find out who leaked this information, the last part of the phrase had attached itself automatically, for the minister would know perfectly well that there was only one possible source for this act of treachery and betrayal. It was then that the superintendent decided that he would visit as many newspaper kiosks as his strength would allow in order to find out if the newspaper was selling in large or small numbers, to see the faces of the people who were buying it and to find out if they turned straight to the article or were distracted by frivolities. He glanced quickly at the four biggest-selling newspapers. Crudely elementary, but effective, the work of poisoning the public was continuing, two and two are four and always will be four, if that's what you did yesterday, then you must have done the same today, and anyone who has the temerity to doubt that one thing inevitably leads to another is an enemy of legality and order. Pleased, he paid the bill and left. He started with the kiosk where he himself had bought the newspapers and had the satisfaction of seeing that the relevant pile had gone down quite a bit. Interesting, isn't it, he said to the newsagent, it's selling really well, Apparently some radio station mentioned an article they published, One hand washes the other and both hands wash the face, said the superintendent mysteriously, Yes, you're right, replied the man, although he had no idea what the superintendent meant. So as not to waste time looking for other kiosks, the superintendent asked each newsagent where the next one was, and, perhaps because of his respectable appearance, they always gave him the information, but it was clear that every one of those newsagents would like to have asked him What have they got that I haven't. The hours passed, the inspector and the sergeant, over there at post six-north, had grown weary of waiting and had asked for instructions from the police commissioner's office, the commissioner had informed the minister, the minister had explained the situation to the prime minister, and the prime minister had replied, It's not my problem, it's yours, you sort it out. Then the expected happened, when he reached the tenth kiosk, the superintendent could not find the newspaper. He asked for it, pretending he was going to buy a copy, but the newsagent said, You're too late, they took them all away less than five minutes ago, They took them, why, They're collecting them from all the kiosks, Collecting them, That's another way of saying impounding them, But why, what was in the newspaper to make them do that, It was something about that woman and the conspiracy, you know, it's been in all the other papers, well, now it seems she killed a man, Couldn't you get me a copy, you'd be doing me a great favour, No, I haven't got one, and even if I had, I wouldn't sell it to you, Why not, How do I know you're not a police officer on the prowl to see if I take the bait, You're quite right, you can't be too careful, said the superintendent and walked off. He didn't want to go back to providential ltd, insurance and reinsurance, to listen to that morning's phone call and doubtless others demanding to know where he was, why he wasn't answering the phone, why he had disobeyed the order to be at post six-north at nine o'clock, but the fact is he has nowhere to go, by now, there must be a sea of people outside the house of the doctor's wife, all shouting, some in favour, some against, although they're probably all in favour, the others would be in the minority, they probably don't want to risk being insulted or worse. Nor can he go to the offices of the newspaper that published the article, if there aren't any plain-clothes policemen at the entrance, they'll be around somewhere, he can't even phone because all the lines will doubtless be tapped, and when he thought this, he understood, at last, that providential ltd, insurance and reinsurance, would be under surveillance too, that all the hotels would have been forewarned, that there is not a single soul in the city who could take him in, even if he or she wanted to. He imagines that the newspaper will have received a visit from the police, he imagines that the director will have been forced, willingly or not, to reveal the identity of the person who provided him with the subversive information they had published, he might even have been reduced to showing them the letter bearing the name providential ltd, and signed in the fugitive superintendent's own hand. He felt tired, his feet dragged, his body was bathed in sweat, although it wasn't even particularly hot. He couldn't wander these streets all day just pointlessly killing time, then, suddenly, he felt a great desire to go to the park with the statue of the woman and the water jar, to sit down by the edge of the pool, to stroke the green water with the tips of his fingers and raise them to his mouth. But then what will I do, he asked. Nothing, except plunge back into the labyrinth of streets, to get disoriented and lost and then turn back, walking and walking, eating even if he isn't hungry, just to keep his body going, spending a couple of hours in a cinema, distracting himself by watching the adventures of an expedition to mars in the days when it was still inhabited by little green men, and coming out, blinking in the bright afternoon light, considering going to another cinema to waste another two hours travelling twenty thousand leagues under the sea in captain nemo's submarine, and then entirely giving up the idea because there is clearly something strange happening in the city, men and women are handing out small sheets of paper that people stop to read and then immediately stuff into a pocket, they've just handed one to the superintendent, it's a photocopy of the article from the impounded newspaper, the one bearing the headline What Haven't We Been Told, the one which, between the lines, tells the true story of the last five days, the superintendent can control himself no longer, and right there, like a child, he bursts into convulsive sobs, a woman of about his age comes and asks if he's all right, if he needs help, and he can only shake his head, no, thank you, he's fine, don't worry, and since chance does occasionally do the right thing, someone from one of the top storeys of this building hurls out a handful of papers, and another and another, and down below the people hold up their arms to catch them, and the papers float down, they glide like doves, and one of them rests for a moment on the superintendent's shoulder before sliding to the ground. So, in the end, nothing is lost, the city has taken the matter into its own hands and set hundreds of photocopiers working, and now there are animated groups of boys and girls slipping the sheets of paper into mail boxes or delivering them to people's doors, someone asks if they're advertising something and they say, yes, sir, it's the very best of advertisements. These happy events gave the superintendent a new soul, and as if with a magic wave of the hand, white magic, not black, all his tiredness vanished, this is a different man walking these streets now, this is a different mind doing the thinking, seeing clearly what had been obscure before, amending conclusions that had seemed rock-solid and which now crumble between the fingers that touch them and decide, instead, that it is highly unlikely that providential ltd, insurance and reinsurance, since it is a secret base, would have been placed under surveillance, after all, posting police guards there could arouse suspicions as to its importance and significance, although that would not, on the other hand, be particularly grave, since they could simply take providential ltd somewhere else and the matter would be resolved. This new and negative conclusion cast stormy shadows over the superintendent's spirit, but his next conclusion, while not entirely reassuring, at least served to resolve the serious problem of accommodation or, in other words, not knowing where he would sleep that night. The matter can be explained in a few brief words. The fact that the ministry of the interior and the police commissioner's office viewed with more than justifiable displeasure the way that this public servant had unilaterally severed all contact with them did not mean that they had lost interest in where he was and where he could be found if needed urgently. If the superintendent had decided to lose himself in this city, if he had gone to ground in some gloomy backstreet, as outcasts and runaways usually do, they would have the devil's own job to find him, especially if he had established a network of contacts amongst other subversive elements, an operation which, on the other hand, given its complexity, is not something that can be set in motion in the space of six days or so, which is the time we have spent here. Therefore, far from guarding the two entrances to providential ltd, they would, on the contrary, leave the way free so that the homing instinct that is natural to all creatures would make the wolf return to its cave, the puffin to its hole in the cliffs. So the superintendent could still enjoy a familiar, welcoming bed, always assuming they don't come and wake him in the middle of the night, having opened the front door with delicate skeleton keys and forced him to surrender with the threat of three guns pointed straight at him. It is true, as we have said before, that there are times in life so grim that it's either raining on one side or blowing a gale on the other, and this is the situation in which the superintendent finds himself now, obliged to choose between spending an uncomfortable night under a tree in the park, like a tramp, within sight of the woman with the water jar, or comfortably ensconced between the stale blankets and crumpled sheets of providential ltd, insurance and reinsurance. This explanation did not prove to be quite as succinct as we promised, however, as we hope you will understand, we could not dismiss any of the possible variables without due consideration, detailing, impartially, the diverse and contradictory risk and safety factors, only to reach the conclusion we should have reached at the start, that there is no point running away to baghdad in order to avoid a meeting arranged for you in samarra. Having weighed and considered everything and decided to waste no further time on pondering the various weights down to the last milligram, the last possibility and the last hypothesis, the superintendent took a taxi to providential ltd, this was at the end of the evening, when the shadows cool the path ahead and the sound of water falling into pools grows bolder and, to the surprise of those who pass, becomes suddenly perceptible. There is not a single piece of paper left in the streets. Despite all this, it is clear that the superintendent feels slightly apprehensive and he has reason enough to do so. His own reasoning and the knowledge he has acquired over time regarding the wiles of the police have led him to conclude that no danger awaits him at providential ltd or will assail him later tonight, but this does not mean that samarra is not where it has to be. This thought caused the superintendent to place his hand on his gun and to think, Just in case, I'll use the time it takes to go up in the lift to leave the gun cocked. The taxi stopped, We're here, said the driver, and it was at that moment that the superintendent saw, stuck to the windscreen, a photocopy of the article. Despite his fear, all the anxiety and trepidation had been worthwhile. The lobby was deserted, the porter absent, the scene was set for the perfect crime, a stab wound in the heart, the dull thud of the body as it drops to the tiled floor, the door closing, the car with false number plates that draws up and leaves, bearing away the murderer, nothing simpler than killing and being killed. The lift was there, he did not need to summon it. Now it is going up in order to leave its cargo on the fourteenth floor, inside it a sequence of unmistakable clicks says that a gun has been made ready to fire. There isn't a soul to be seen in the corridor, the offices are all closed at this hour. The key slipped easily into the lock, almost noiselessly the door allowed itself to be opened. The superintendent leaned against it to close it, turned on the light and will now go into every room, open all the wardrobes where a person might hide, peer under the beds, draw back the curtains. No one. He felt vaguely ridiculous, a swash-buckling hero wielding a gun with nothing to point at, but, as the saying goes, slow but sure ensures a ripe old age, as providential ltd must well know, since it deals not only with insurance but with reinsurance. In the bedroom, the light on the answering machine is blinking, and the display indicates that there have been two calls, one might be from the inspector warning him to be careful, the other will be from one of albatross's under-secretaries, or they might both be from the police commissioner, in despair at the treachery of a man he had trusted and, at the same time, worried about his own future, even though he himself had not been responsible for appointing him. The superintendent took out the piece of paper with the names and addresses of the group, to which he had added the doctor's telephone number, which he dialled. No one answered. He dialled again. He dialled a third time, but this time, as if it were a signal, he let it ring three times and then hung up. He dialled a fourth time and, at last, someone answered, Yes, said the doctor's wife abruptly, It's me, the superintendent, Oh, hello, we've been expecting you to call, How have things been, Terrible, in a matter of twenty-four hours, they've managed to transform me into a kind of public enemy number one, Believe me, I'm really sorry for the part I've played in all this, You weren't the one who wrote what the newspapers published, No, I didn't go that far, Maybe the article that appeared in one of them today and the thousands of photocopies that were distributed will help to clear up this whole absurd situation, Maybe, You don't sound very hopeful, Oh, I have hopes, naturally, but it will take time, this business isn't going to resolve itself from one moment to the next, We can't go on living like this, shut up in this apartment, it's like being in prison, All I can say is that I did everything I could, You won't be visiting us again, then, The mission they gave me is over, and I've received orders to go back, Well, I hope we see each other again some day, in happier times than these, if there ever are any, They seem to have got lost en route, Who, Those happier times, You're going to leave me feeling more discouraged than I was, Some people manage to stay standing even when they've been knocked down, and you're one of them, Well, right now, I'd be very grateful for some help getting back on my feet, And I'm only sorry I can't give you that help, Oh, I think you've helped much more than you let on, That's just your impression, you're talking to a policeman, remember, Oh, I haven't forgotten, but the truth is that I no longer think of you as one, Thank you for that, now all that remains is to say goodbye, until the next time, Until the next time, Take care, And you, Good night, Good night. The superintendent put the phone down. He had a long night ahead of him and no way of getting through it except by sleeping, unless insomnia got into bed with him. They would probably come for him tomorrow. He had not arrived at post six-north as he had been ordered to, and that is why they will come for him. Perhaps one of the messages he erased had said just that, perhaps they had called to warn him that the people sent to arrest him will be here at seven o'clock in the morning and that any attempt at resistance will only make matters worse. They will not, of course, need skeleton keys to get in, because they will bring a key of their own. The superintendent is fantasising. He has an arsenal of weapons to hand, ready to be fired, he could fight to the last cartridge, or at least, let's say, to the first canister of tear-gas that they lob into the fortress. The superintendent is fantasising. He sat down on the bed, then allowed himself to fall backwards, he closed his eyes and pleaded for sleep to come soon, I know the night has barely begun, he was thinking, that there is still light in the sky, but I want to sleep the way a stone seems to sleep, without the traps set by dreams, but to be enclosed in a block of black stone, at least, please, at the very least, until morning, when they come to wake me at seven o'clock. Hearing his desolate cry, sleep came running and stayed there for a few moments, then withdrew while he undressed and got into bed, only to return at once, with hardly a second's delay, to remain by his side all night, chasing any dreams far away into the land of ghosts, the place where, mingling fire and water, they are born and multiply.

It was nine o'clock when the superintendent woke up. He wasn't crying, a sign that the invaders had not used tear-gas, he did not have handcuffs round his wrists or guns levelled at his head, how often fears come to sour our life and prove, in the end, to have no foundation, no reason to exist. He got up, shaved, washed and dressed as usual, then went out intending to go to the café where he had eaten breakfast the previous day. On the way, he bought the newspapers, I thought you weren't coming today, said the man at the kiosk with all the familiarity of an old acquaintance, There's one missing, commented the superintendent, It didn't appear today, and the distributor doesn't know when it will be published again, possibly next week, apparently they've had a massive fine slapped on them, But why, Because of that article, the one they made all those photocopies of, Oh, I see, Here's your bag, there are only five papers today, so you'll have less to read. The superintendent thanked him and went in search of the café. He could no longer remember where the street was and his appetite was growing with each step he took, the thought of toast made his mouth water, we must forgive this man for what may appear, at first sight, to be deplorable gluttony, inappropriate in a man of his age and standing, but we must remember that yesterday he went to bed on an empty stomach. He finally found the street and the café, now he is sitting at the table, and while he waits, he glances through the papers, here are the headlines, in black and red, so that we can get a rough idea of their respective contents, Another Subversive Act By The Enemies Of Our Country, Who Set the Photocopiers Working, The Dangers of Disinformation, Who Paid For Those Photocopies. The superintendent ate slowly, savouring every mouthful down to the last crumb, even the coffee tastes better than yesterday, and when he had finished his meal, his body now refreshed, his spirit which, ever since yesterday, had felt itself under an obligation to the park and the pond, to the green water and the woman with the water jar, reminded him, You so wanted to go there, but you didn't, Well, I'll go now, replied the superintendent. He paid, put all the papers back in the bag and set off. He could have caught a taxi, but he preferred to go on foot. He had nothing else to do and it was a way of passing the time. When he reached the park, he went and sat on the bench where he had talked to the doctor's wife and become properly acquainted with the dog of tears. From there he could see the pond and the woman with the water jar poised for pouring. Underneath the tree, it was still slightly cool. He drew his raincoat over his knees and, with a sigh of satisfaction, made himself comfortable. The man wearing the blue tie with white spots came up behind him and shot him in the head.

Two hours later, the interior minister was giving a press conference. He was wearing a white shirt and a black tie and, on his face, an expression of deep regret, of profound grief. The table was crowded with microphones and the only other ornament was a glass of water. As always, the national flag hung meditatively behind him. Good afternoon, ladies and gentlemen, said the minister, I have summoned you here today to give you the tragic news of the death of the superintendent who had been charged by me with investigating the conspiratorial web whose leader, as you know, has now been revealed. Unfortunately, his was not a natural death, but the result of a deliberate, premeditated murder, the work, no doubt, of a professional criminal of the worst kind if we bear in mind that a single bullet was enough to carry out the killing. Needless to say, all the indications are that this was a new criminal action by the subversive elements in our unhappy former capital, who continue to undermine the stability of the democratic system and its correct functioning, and to work cold-bloodedly against the political, social and moral integrity of our nation. I need hardly point out that the example of supreme dignity offered to us today by the murdered superintendent will, for ever after, be the object not just of our utter respect, but also of our most profound veneration, for his sacrifice has, from this day forth, and a most unhappy day it is, bestowed on him a place of honour in the pantheon of our nation's martyrs who, up there in the beyond, have their eyes always upon us. The national government, which I am here to represent, shares the mourning and grief of all those who knew the extraordinary human being we have just lost, and, at the same time, assures all the citizens of this land that it will not be discouraged in this war we are waging against the evil of the conspirators and the irresponsibility of those who support them. Just two further points, the first to tell you that the inspector and the sergeant who were assisting the murdered superintendent in the investigation had been withdrawn from the mission at the latter's request so as to protect their lives, the second to inform you that, as regards this fine man, this exemplary servant of the nation, who, alas, we have just lost, the government will examine by what legal means he may, exceptionally and posthumously, and as quickly as possible, be awarded the highest honour with which the nation distinguishes those of its sons and daughters who bring honour upon it. Today, ladies and gentlemen, is a sad day for decent people, but duty requires us all to cry sursum corda, lift up your hearts. A journalist raised his hand to ask a question, but the interior minister was already leaving, on the table only the untouched glass of water remained, the microphones recorded the respectful silence due to the dead, and, behind them, the flag tirelessly continued its meditation. The following two hours were spent by the minister and his closest advisors in drawing up an immediate plan of action that would consist, basically, in arranging a surreptitious return to the capital city of a large number of policemen, who, for now, would work in plain clothes, with no outward sign that might indicate to which organisation they belonged. This was an implicit admission that they had committed a very grave error indeed in leaving the former capital unsupervised. But it's not too late to correct that mistake, said the minister. At that precise moment, an under-secretary came in to tell the interior minister that the prime minister wished to speak to him immediately in his office. The minister made a muttered comment that the prime minister could have chosen a better time, but had no option but to obey the summons. He left his advisors to put the finishing logistical touches to the plan and set off. The car, with guards to front and rear, bore him to the building in which the cabinet offices had been installed, this took him ten minutes, and five minutes later, he was entering the prime minister's office, Good afternoon, prime minister, Good afternoon, do sit down, You phoned me just as I was working on a plan to rectify the decision we took to withdraw the police from the capital, I can probably bring it to you tomorrow, Don't bother, Why not, prime minister, Because you won't have time, The plan is almost finished, it just needs a few minor touches, You do not, I'm afraid, understand, when I say that you won't have time, I mean that by tomorrow you will no longer be interior minister, What, the question emerged just like that, explosive and somewhat disrespectful, You heard what I said, there's no need for me to repeat it, But, prime minister, Let's save ourselves a pointless conversation, your duties cease as of this moment, Such harshness is most unjust, prime minister, and is, if I may say so, a strange and arbitrary way of rewarding my services to the nation, there must be a reason, which I hope you will give me, for this brutal dismissal, yes, brutal, I won't withdraw the word, Your services during the crisis have been one long string of errors which I won't bother to enumerate, I can understand that necessity knows no law, that the ends justify the means, but always on condition that the ends are achieved and the law of necessity is obeyed, but you obeyed and achieved neither, and now there's the death of the superintendent, He was murdered by our enemies, Please, don't come to me with any operatic arias, I've been in this game too long to believe in fairy tales, the enemies of whom you speak had, on the contrary, every reason to make him their hero and no reason at all to kill him, There was no other way out, prime minister, the man had become a subversive influence, We would have settled our accounts with him later, not now, his death was an unforgivable blunder, and now, as if that weren't enough, we've got demonstrations in the streets, Insignificant, prime minister, my information, Your information is worthless, half the population is out on the street already and the other half will soon be joining them, The future, prime minister, will, I am sure, judge that I was right, And a fat lot of good it will do you if the present judges you to be wrong, and now, that's an end to it, please leave, this conversation is over, But I need to hand on any matters pending to my successor, Don't worry, I'll send someone over to deal with all that, But what about my successor, I'm your successor, after all, why shouldn't the prime-minister-cum-justice-minister also be the interior minister, that way we can keep it all in the family, so don't you worry, I'll take care of everything.

AT TEN O'CLOCK IN THE MORNING ON THIS SAME DAY, TWO PLAIN-CLOTHES policemen went up to the fourth floor and rang the bell. The doctor's wife answered and asked, Who are you, what do you want, We're policemen and we have orders to take your husband away to be questioned, and there's no point telling us he's gone out, the building is being watched, which is why we know he's here, You have absolutely no reason to question him, up until now, I've been the one accused of all the crimes, That's not our business, we've received strict orders to take the doctor and not the doctor's wife, so, unless you want us to force our way in, go and call him, and keep that dog under control too, we wouldn't want anything to happen to it. The woman closed the door. She opened it again shortly afterwards, and this time her husband was with her, What do you want, To take you in for questioning, we've told your wife already, we're not going to stand here all day repeating it, Do you have any credentials with you, a warrant, We don't need a warrant, the city's under a state of siege, and as for credentials, here's our identification, will that do, Can I change my clothes first, One of us will go with you, Are you afraid I'll run away or commit suicide, We're just following orders, that's all. One of the policemen went inside, they did not take long. Wherever my husband's going, I'm going with him, said the woman, Like I said, you're not going anywhere, you're staying here, don't make me have to get nasty with you, You couldn't be any nastier than you already are, Oh, believe me, I could, you can't imagine how nasty I can be, and then to the doctor, You've got to be handcuffed,

305

hold out your hands, Please, don't put those things on me, please, I give you my word of honour that I won't try to escape, Come on, put your hands out, and forget about words of honour, right, that's better, you're safer like that. The woman embraced her husband and kissed him, weeping, They won't let me come with you, Don't worry, I'll be back home tonight, you'll see, Come home soon, I will, my love, I will. The lift started to go down.

At eleven o'clock, the man in the blue tie with white spots went up onto the flat roof of the building almost opposite the back of the building where the doctor's wife and her husband live. He is carrying a box of varnished wood, rectangular in shape. Inside is a dismantled weapon, an automatic rifle with a telescopic sight, which he will not use because at such a short distance no good marksman could possibly miss his target. He will not use the silencer either, but, in this case, it is for reasons of an ethical order, the man in the blue tie with white spots feels that the use of such apparatus shows a gross disrespect for the victim. The weapon has been assembled now and loaded, with each piece in its place, a perfect instrument for the job it is intended to do. The man in the blue tie with white spots chooses the place from which he will fire and prepares himself to wait. He is a patient man, he has been doing this for years and always does his work well. Sooner or later, the doctor's wife will come out onto the balcony. Meanwhile, just in case the waiting should go on for too long, the man in the blue tie with white spots has brought with him another weapon, an ordinary catapult, the sort that is used for hurling stones, especially for the purpose of breaking windows. No one hears the glass breaking and no one comes running to see who the childish vandal was. An hour has passed, and the doctor's wife has still not appeared, she has been crying, poor thing, but now she will go and get some fresh air, she doesn't open one of the windows that give onto the street because there are always people watching, she prefers the back of the house, so much quieter since the advent of television. The woman goes over to the iron balustrade, places her hands on it and feels the coolness of the metal. We cannot ask her if she heard the two successive shots, she is lying dead on the ground and her blood is sliding and dripping onto the balcony below. The dog comes running out, he sniffs and licks his mistress's face, then he stretches out his neck and unleashes a terrifying howl which another shot silences. Then a blind man asked, Did you hear something, Three shots, replied another blind man, But there was a dog howling too, It's stopped now, that must have been the third shot, Good, I hate to hear dogs howl.